Beyond The Well

The Story of the Samaritan Woman Before and After the Well.

By
Lauree Brown

Cover artwork by Ryan Cass

Printed in the United States of America

Ebook :978-1-972344-11-8
Paperback: 978-1-972344-12-5
Hardback: 978-1-972344-13-2

Publisher: Parker Publishers

1st Edition

Foreword

Most readers know the brief, electric encounter at Jacob's well: a Samaritan woman meets a Jewish man who asks for water and, in doing so, sees her whole life. That scene has been read, preached, and argued over for centuries—part miracle, part scandal, part invitation.

Beyond the Well does not aim to teach theology or settle interpretations. Instead, it tries something simpler and, I hope, more intimate: to imagine the life behind that single, unforgettable afternoon.

This is a work of historical fiction. I have not tried to drag the Samaritan woman into our century or to make her a mirror of modern ideas. My aim was to place her in her own time and let her speak from the soil she walked and the language she might have known. I called her Photine — a name used in Eastern traditions that means "luminous one" — because it felt right for the woman whose courage and stubbornness would not be dimmed by rumor or fear. [In other sources such as The Book of Urantia she is called Nalda.]

I used research, anthropology, and a little psychology to build a world that feels lived-in: the markets and wells, the laws and debts, the daily barter of food and dignity. But make no mistake — this is imagination at work. Where the historical record is thin, I made choices guided by plausibility and compassion, not certainty.

Why tell this story? Because when I met her on the page, she would not leave me alone. She was fierce and fallible, practical and raw — someone who survived by wit and grit and who, I think, still has things to teach us about shame, agency, and forgiveness. Writing her felt like pulling a thread that led to every woman I have ever known who had to choose between survival and selfhood.

A few people deserve my thanks: Roelf, who first pointed me toward the woman at the well; Rachel, who reads everything and refuses to let me be lazy with a scene; and a couple of encouraging and helpful dance partners who are also friends — thank you.

If you come for a tidy moral, you will not find one. But if you are willing to sit with a woman as she navigates fear, bargaining, and the slow work of repair, then step in. Photine is luminous in ways I did not expect. I hope, by the end, she feels luminous to you too.

Table of Contents

CHAPTER 1
THE MEETING

Photine arrived deliberately late to the well.

Each morning, before the sun crested the hills and warmed the dust underfoot, the women of Sychar gathered here—just outside the city walls—filling their jars, trading news, and watching one another with the quiet intensity only women long held in roles of obligation can master. Photine had no patience for them. The sideways glances. The whispers that died on lips when she passed. The way they measured her like a garment sewn wrong—too bold, too strange, too marked by past husbands and unanswered questions.

She preferred the quiet. Midday meant heat, yes, but also solitude: no dodging questions, no obligation to smile, no performance of belonging she no longer owned. Better to sweat under the punishing sun than to endure the reminder of what she had lost—each look from them pressed like a finger into a bruise that never healed.

A dove startled from a nearby olive tree, wings skimming the sun-thick air before dropping into the shade. Photine felt the tug of that shade. It meant more than relief; it meant not being seen. Lately, she measured her days by how long she could move without drawing eyes—how few words she could spend and still get bread.

The strap rubbed the ridge on her collarbone where a hand had bruised her long ago. The mark was gone; the ache remained. She'd left behind a roof, a name spoken too hard, and the kind of help that costs more than hunger. She wasn't just hot—she was emptied. Tired of explaining herself, tired of being weighed like grain and found lacking.

A well, at least, was honest: you lower the jar, it gives what it has, and it doesn't ask where you've been.

The thought steadied her. Gravel bit. The jar tugged. Heat rose. A bead of sweat slipped between her shoulder blades, and with it came the old prickle of caution that never quite left when men were near.

As she neared a bend, two men came into view on the path ahead. They hadn't seen her—good. She slowed, lowered her gaze, and shifted the worn leather strap from her shoulder.

They wore linen tunics, sweat-darkened at the collar, cloaks flung back. Locals, perhaps shepherds or tradesmen. It was hard to say at a glance.

"…Josef said he was seen near Mount Gerizim," said the taller, voice low but urgent.

"If that's true, there will be trouble," the shorter replied, fanning himself. "He'll not be welcomed here. Not a Jew."

"Probably just rumors," he added, as if persuading himself.

"Maybe. But I've heard he seeks followers here in Sychar."

Photine kept her eyes on the strap joining her water jars, pretending to mend it as she passed, but her mind catalogued every word, tone, gesture. She lingered a breath too long behind the figs, listening.

A shift in their voices told her they had noticed her. Their words grew careless, sun-weary, soaked in bitterness.

She heard her name—half-whispered, half-laughed.

"The well is deep," one said, "but not as deep as her bed."

The other snorted, adding something low and sharp, a sound meant to cut through the words.

Their chuckles stretched thin in the late morning light, scraping at her spine.

Photine's grip tightened on the jar until her knuckles ached. She kept her gaze on the path, jaw set, feet hurried. Turning would only feed them—but she turned anyway, not to offer her face, but to claim her pace. Slow, deliberate, unbroken.

Let them laugh. Let them fill their mouths with dust and stories they did not earn. None of them had ever drawn water with her blistered hands and her raw heart. None had stood beside a grave too small for a dream. None had bargained a piece of her life just to keep the rest alive.

She passed them like a shadow crossing stone, their words still prickling under her skin. The heat pressed down, but the weight inside her pressed harder—and she carried it, as always, in silence.

She walked the worn path alone, dust fanning around her ankles, heat pressing against her skin. The market would be busy by now, women bartering, boys shouting, goats bleating like prophets. But out here, there was only wind, stone, and memory. A stray olive branch lay in the path ahead of her, its leaves curled and silvering in the sun. She paused, nudging it with her sandal. The clean snap of the brittle stem pulled something loose inside her — an echo she hadn't expected. That was when her father came back to her — Eleazar, kneeling beneath the olive trees, coaxing life from old wood.

You must wound the tree, he'd said. *Cut it open. Only then will it accept something new.*

He had been her first truth-teller, her first question-asker. While the town clung to purity laws and genealogies, he whispered stories of prophets who wrestled angels and lost—yet walked away blessed.

Some said he joined a rebel camp. Others claimed the Romans took him. There were even whispers he had been seen across the border, living as a Jew. No one asked her. No one looked her in the eye and said the word she carried like an unfilled jar: *abandoned.*

Eleazar came from a long line of builders—men who shaped stone for holy places. Their ancestors had helped raise the temple on Mount Gerizim. By Photine's birth, the family's standing had cooled to embers. Shepherding had replaced chisels. Zimri—her brother, stubborn and slow to learn—remained at home. He bristled at her quick tongue and quicker mind, resenting the way their father leaned toward her questions more than his answers.

Eleazar never sat her at a desk to teach, but Photine learned anyway, watching from corners as he instructed Zimri in letters and numbers and the study of men: the twitch of a mouth, the shift of a shoulder. Soon she outpaced her brother. Eventually, her father noticed.

Photine remembered the evenings most. When the sheep were penned and the last light clung to the hills, her father would take her down to the old shed where his tools lay in neat rows, still oiled though seldom used. He would sit on a block of limestone, broad hands steady, and pat the space beside him.

"Here," he'd say, handing her a chisel dulled by time. "Tell me what you see."

She would turn it in her hands, tracing the grooves where calloused fingers had held it before hers. "It's heavy," she answered once, squinting at the blade. "But the edge is worn—like it's tired."

Eleazar chuckled, the sound low and warm. "Not tired, little flame. Tested. That's how stone teaches you—by wearing down what is too sharp, leaving what is strong."

She leaned against his shoulder then, small enough that his arm could wrap her whole. "Will you build again?"

His gaze drifted to the horizon, where the mountain shadowed the land. For a moment, he was quiet, then he placed her hand against the seam of a half-built wall at their feet. "Strength hides here, in the places you cannot see. If you learn to feel for it, you can build anything—even if the world forgets your name."

To her, it felt like a secret pressed straight into her chest. She carried it as proof that she was not invisible, not wasted.

Photine carried her memories as proof that she was not invisible, not wasted. For a moment, the memory was balm—her father's voice, the steady rhythm of his breath, the promise that strength could be hidden but unbroken.

But memories never stayed kind for long. One thought led to another, and the wavering heat around her dissolved into darkness… He disappeared. That night would haunt her more than all the others, for it was the first fracture—the one that taught her how easily love could vanish.

"They came to the well asking about you," her mother Selah had said, her voice low, edged with worry. "Not Roman. Not Samaritan either. Outsiders—travel-worn cloaks, but their eyes knew too much."

Eleazar hadn't looked up. He was sharpening a small blade, slow, methodical, the scrape of stone against steel filling the silence. "Did you tell them anything?"

"I told them you were my husband," she answered, stepping closer, "and that if they had questions, they could return in daylight— when the neighbors could listen too."

His jaw tensed. The blade paused mid-stroke. "You shouldn't have confirmed I was here."

"I didn't confirm," she said, heat rising. "I warned. There's a difference." She moved to stand in front of him, forcing his gaze. "What have you done, Eleazar? What have you drawn to our door?"

He met her eyes—reluctantly, then fully. "There was a gathering," he said, each word deliberate.

"North of Tirzah. In the hills beyond the olives. Not soldiers. Teachers. Farmers. Sons of Levites.

They spoke—not of swords—but of justice. Of reclaiming the name stripped from our tongues.

Of worship without fear. Of law not written by foreign hands."

His voice dried and cracked. "I only went to listen, Selah. Just to listen."

"And someone saw you?" she asked.

He nodded, weight settling like ash across his shoulders. "They see everything. I didn't stand. I didn't speak. But one of the loud ones recognized me from the temple days. Now it doesn't matter what I did. Only that I was there."

The blade lay flat on the stone. His eyes darkened like storm-washed earth. "I'm marked. Not for violence. Not for heresy. For hope. For remembering who we are."

Selah's face softened, but her spine held. "And what does that make me? What does that make our children?"

He closed his eyes. "The reason I can't stay."

"They think you're stirring rebellion?" she asked, quieter.

"They think anyone who speaks too clearly is a threat."

She gripped his arm. "You have a son and a daughter who need you; I need you. We've already lost too much. Don't let the fire in you burn down what little we've built."

"I won't be silent," he whispered. "But I'll be careful. I'll go to Arumah. There are friends there—ones who still believe we can protect what's sacred without bloodshed."

"And then?" Selah asked.

He looked down at his hands. "Then I vanish for a while. Until they forget to look for me." Photine stepped from behind the curtain before Selah could answer—chin lifted, eyes hot. "Then take me," she said, planting herself between him and the door. "You said the road is safer in pairs. I can walk. I won't slow you."

He was startled—only a flicker—and set his hand on her shoulder to turn her aside. She didn't move. "I'm not a jar to leave in a corner," she pressed. "If you're hunted, I'm hunted by your shadow anyway. Better to keep together."

"Photine," Selah warned softly.

"No." Her voice didn't rise; it hardened. "You taught me letters so I could speak for myself. I am speaking: I won't stay here to count rumors while you vanish."

His grip gentled, then firmed. "The road south is no place for a twelve-year-old girl. Men are taken for less. Girls are taken for nothing. If they catch me, they bargain with you."

"Then teach me how not to be caught," she shot back. "You taught others."

He looked past her toward the lintel and the strip of sky, measuring a weight. At last: "I will send word from Arumah—hidden in the reed basket at Haggai's stall, where we buy salt. I'll write only your name. You'll know it's mine by the small nick at the edge." He pressed his seal—a carved shard of olive wood—into her palm. "Keep this. If anyone comes naming me, ask to see its twin."

She curled her fingers around the seal, fury sparking at the feel of it. "Bits of wood and promises," she said, voice shaking. "You fill other men with courage and leave me with tokens."

"I leave you with your mother and your brother. With a roof. With a name."

"My name is yours," she answered. "And you are walking away from it."

That landed. He closed his eyes. When he opened them, his voice was low. "If I take you, I endanger you. If I stay, I endanger all of you. There is no clean choice."

She shouldered past him to the chest, yanked out a shawl, tied it hard around a bundle with nothing in it but anger. At the threshold, he caught the knot, held it. The donkey stamped once; the oil lamp guttered.

At last, he loosened the cloth and, with a father's care that felt like an insult, retied it softer and set it back. "When I am gone," he said, "lock the back gate. Go to Hannah if soldiers come. Do not answer questions you are not asked."

"Coward," she said, barely above a whisper—hating him for making her say it, hating herself for meaning it.

He didn't defend himself. He cupped the side of her head with his rough palm, a blessing he had not used since she was small. "Live," he said. "That is the bravest thing I can ask of you."

He left before her knees could give way.

She stood in the doorway long after his steps faded, the seal cutting into her fist. Then she went to his table and slid a narrow sheet of papyrus from beneath the weights—a fragment he'd been annotating, his neat hand in the margins. She tucked it under her tunic as if it were armor. That night, she cried silently behind the woven curtain, fists clenched around the stolen parchment—the only thing of him that felt like a voice.

Twelve.

Alone.

Abandoned.

The day her father left, Photine stopped believing in safety. Her world cracked under the weight of his absence. No body. No witness. No justice. Only silence. Only the echo of his promise to vanish "until they forget to look for me."

She never told anyone what she knew. She carried the truth like an ember—hot, secret, consuming. Her father fled lest he be taken. Not by accident. Not by nature. By men and a system that deemed Samaritan minds dangerous. She blamed the Jews and the officials who served them. She blamed a world content to let it happen.

Her father had been gone nearly two years. The house still carried his absence like a shadow—tools untouched, ledgers missing his careful hand, their mother thinning a little day by day.

In his absence, Zimri tried to become the man of the house—tried to run the business, tried to keep their mother from fading into shadow. But Zimri was driven more by pride than wisdom. At sixteen, he had a man's frame but not yet a man's steadiness. Photine, precocious at fourteen, had already memorized the ledgers, tracked the weight of wool against the seasons, and mapped who cheated measures and who paid late but loyally. Eleazar once said she had the head of a banker and the hands of a weaver. Zimri, by contrast, struggled to read more than a line without sighing.

Still, he was the son. The man now. Each suggestion she offered registered as a challenge; each correction, a threat.

The trouble announced itself at the scales.

Zimri set the bronze pans on their frame, eager to appear competent, and nodded to a trader from Tirzah with sacks of raw fleece. The man laid down his "weights"—smooth river stones painted black to look official. Zimri didn't notice.

Photine did.

"Four measures," the trader said.

"Four," Zimri echoed, reaching for the reed pen.

"Three and a half," Photine said, stepping between them.

Zimri reddened. "Photine, move."

She lifted one "weight," tossed it lightly, then tapped it against the post. It clacked—wrong. She produced their true weight from the ledger box, set it on the pan, and the fleece rose like a liar caught in daylight.

"Three and a half," she repeated, calm and cutting. "And the half is charity."

Men snickered. The trader blustered about road-damp fleece and girls meddling in men's business. Photine's smile thinned. "Even the lamb knows when the scale is light," she said. She scratched an X into the fake stone with her knife and dropped it into the reject jar.

"Inside," Zimri hissed.

She didn't move. She counted out the coin, set it down, wrote the line in her neat hand, and slid the tablet toward him. "Sign."

On the walk home, he erupted. "You shamed me—again. In front of traders. In front of men."

"In front of thieves," she shot back. "If you could read a scale, you wouldn't need me."

His hand flashed, catching her wrist. She wrenched free, fury bright as noon. "Let go. Or I'll tell Mother, you let a stranger's stone stand for law."

They stared each other down, the street empty but for a sleeping dog.

"You think you're better than me," he said.

"At numbers? Yes."

Something settled in his face—hurt folding into pride, pride curdling into resolve. "This house needs peace," he said softly. "And a girl who knows her place."

That evening, she heard him with Abisha the broker, voices pitched low, names traded like coin. She held his gaze later, chin high, rage and disbelief warring. For once, she said nothing.

She didn't sleep. She lay rigid, counting breaths. Within a week, the matchmaker's token—twine knotted around a sliver of dyed leather—hung on their doorpost.

Zimri wouldn't meet her eyes. He didn't need to. If he couldn't master the ledgers, he would master the house. If he couldn't master her, he would be rid of her.

Selah sat most days by the window now, barely eating, hair loosed in long strands. No evening lamps. No humming. The house smelled of absence.

Photine cooked what she could. She cleaned. She kept the accounts in her head because Zimri refused to let her write them down. His temper sharpened. Customers grumbled that he shortchanged them and shouted. One day, he accused Photine of stealing figs he'd forgotten to count.

"You're poisoning this house," he growled. "You're just like him."

She answered with silence. She'd learned words can be weapons—and silence, armor. Still, that night, she cried into her bedroll, arms around the small bundle Eleazar had tied, the carved symbol of a water jar pressed to her cheek—his mark, a promise that she would carry life, not shame.

At fourteen, her days at home were numbered—though fortunately, weeks passed with no match sealed.

When Zimri stormed off mid-argument with a barley vendor—pride pricked and voice too loud—Photine waited until the dust settled. She then closed the deal herself: adjusted the weight, pointed out a flaw in the sack's seam, and saved nearly half a silver. The vendor handed her a fig with the change. "You're wasted behind that door, little flame," he said.

She walked home steadily, feeling briefly capable.

Zimri met her at the door, jaw clenched, arms folded. That night, she found her wax tablet—the one bearing her father's mark—snapped in two and tossed into the hearth.

The next morning, he went to market without her, refused her stew, and slammed doors. Two days later, as she weighed lentils in the courtyard, he swept the tray from her hands. Metal clattered.

Lentils scattered like seeds. That night, Selah sat beside her in the dark.

"You can't stay," Selah whispered. "You need a household of your own—a name, a protection." "This is my house," Photine said to the wall.

"It was," Selah breathed. "Your brother has decided."

The matchmaker returned with news. By Zimri's order, a husband had been chosen from several days' journey away—far enough that no neighbor could protest and no kin could intervene. A family with a growing grain business and a stone mill in Akrabbim. The patron's unwed son—quiet, broad-shouldered, nearly twice her age—managed the mill. He needed a wife who could keep books and not cause trouble.

All Zimri cared about was that they were willing—and able—to pay.

They didn't call it selling. Not aloud. They called it arranging—a bride price, a practical solution. Even at fourteen, Photine named it clearly: a transaction.

When the buyers came, she wore a clean tunic and brushed her hair. Matthias stood in the courtyard with his two sons: Mordecai, sharp-eyed, tight-mouthed, and Jotham, the one who would be her husband. Jotham's beard was patchy. His hands were pale with flour. He did not look at her—only at Zimri.

She stood beneath the almond tree, fists clenched in the folds of her tunic, tasting dust and betrayal. Selah watched from the threshold, saying nothing. Silence had kept her alive this long.

"She's quick," Zimri said, like describing livestock. "Keeps a house. Mends. Counts."

"She's small," Mordecai said.

"She's strong," Zimri snapped. "Stronger than she looks."

Matthias studied her, unreadable, then nodded. Silver changed hands in a linen pouch.

That morning, Photine packed what little she owned: two coarse blankets; her father's two parchments, and the shard of olive wood seal once pressed into her palm, tightly bound; a wax tablet and reed pen, wrapped in linen and buried at the bottom beneath needles, a worn spindle, and flax thread. She tied the satchel without trembling, though everything in her wanted to run.

The cart waited outside Shechem's eastern gate, wheels already caked in red dust. No one said goodbye. No one dared.

Jotham didn't speak as she climbed into the back. He didn't offer his hand. He sat rigid on the edge, gaze fixed on the horizon like a man who waited for grain to arrive. She didn't know which cut deeper—his silence or his indifference.

Matthias held the reins, posture relaxed but alert, eyes scanning the trail. Mordecai rode behind on a gray mule, muttering to himself.

The road south wound through olive groves and terraced hills, down the flanks of Mount Ebal. The sun rose high, then softened, painting limestone ridges with amber. It should have been beautiful. It might have been, had she not felt so hollow.

The first night, they stopped outside Shiloh, where shepherds still grazed flocks on hills once called holy. They slept beneath an open sky, air heavy with the smell of sheep and smoke. Photine lay with her cloak tight and her satchel under her head.

Days blurred: Lebonah's vineyards, Bethel's loud market and Roman patrols, Jericho's heat and palms and dates piled by the road. Each place was a pause, never a destination. She climbed in and out of the cart, body sore, amphora clinking faintly with every rut. Dust settled on her skin like memory.

South of Jericho, the land starved. Hills rose dry and stony, waterskins grew lighter, villages thinned, wells hid farther apart. They skirted the edge of the Wilderness of Judea, where caves pocked cliffs and the wind carried grit like ash.

Nearly two weeks of jolting wheels and shifting shadows, of strangers' stares and long empty stretches. No one asked if she was weary. No one looked into her eyes. She was cargo, bartered and carried south between sacks of grain and the hush of men who knew they had won something and would not be questioned for it.

What stung worst was not the distance but the reason. Word had traveled along trader routes, her name carried like a bargain whispered over scales. This was not merely an arrangement—it was banishment. To send her beyond Shechem, beyond childhood hills, cut her off from everything that remembered her. From olive trees where her father taught her. From stalls where she had bargained boldly. From corners where laughter once belonged.

She pressed her face to her knees and understood with cold clarity: this was exile. A way to lock her fire inside another household. She was now another man's keeping. The hollowness that followed had no bottom.

At last, the road bent toward Akrabbim—the Scorpion's Ascent—where the land dropped into barren ridges and the horizon stretched wide and merciless. There, clinging to the trade road, stood the mill: stone walls sun-bleached and solid, built to endure both wind and time. A wooden beam jutted from one side, affixed to the grinding stone within—a rotary quern powered by mule or donkey, circling endlessly. The air smelled of ground grain: earthy, warm, a promise of bread that did not reach the heart.

A modest home hugged the mill, flat-roofed and clay-packed, herbs drying in bundles from the eaves, a clay oven built into the wall. The main room held a large chest as a low table and woven mats; alcoves carved into thick walls housed lamps and jars. A small back room served as sleeping quarters—spare, cool, private enough to feel like a held breath.

Water jars lined the doorway. A fig tree shaded the courtyard where grinding stones rested at midday. Pour, turn, sift—the rhythm gave the place a quiet dignity. Not rich, but steady. Survival with a heartbeat.

That night, she lay awake in the quiet of the house that was now meant to be her home, though her heart had not yet caught up. The walls felt too close, the shadows too unfamiliar, and every sound reminded her that she no longer belonged to her mother's world. Jotham slept on the far side of the room, distant but present, a stranger whose breathing shaped the darkness. She held herself still, listening, waiting, hoping that time might soften whatever this was. But the quiet pressed in, and she felt the ache of stepping into a life she had not chosen.

Jotham had not spoken on the journey, not once. She had wondered whether this silence would stretch on forever, a wall between them. But the next morning, he surprised her. He set out figs and warm bread on the chest, the steam still rising.

She hesitated, searching his face. Why now? Why acknowledge her at all? His eyes skittered from hers, landing on the food, the wall, anywhere but the girl he had brought home. She felt the question pressing in her chest: was this hospitality, or apology?

For Jotham, the silence had been safer. Words at home were measured, weighed, and often found wanting in Mordecai's shadow.

He had learned to close his mouth before his father's scorn could pour in. Better to shrink, to be overlooked, than to invite wrath. With Photine, though, the silence was heavier, unbearable. She was his wife now—at least in name—and it seemed wrong to let her sit hungry when he had bread to share.

He cleared his throat. "It's fresh. From yesterday's bake."

She ate in silence, watching him from the corner of her eye. The bread was soft, the figs sweet, but her mind worked harder than her jaw. Perhaps this was not kindness but habit, an echo of what he had seen his mother do. Or perhaps—though she scarcely dared believe it—this was the beginning of something gentler.

The room held its breath with her. Awkward, tentative, but not without hope.

Jotham stood a head taller than Photine, a broad frame softened by years of steady labor. The black hair of his youth had begun to thin, gray seeding the temples, but his beard remained thick and neatly trimmed. Lines fanned his eyes from a lifetime of squinting into the sun. They were kind eyes—never sharp, always patient—as if he had all the time in the world to listen to the murmur of millstones or his own thoughts.

His hands were large and calloused, marked by work, yet gentle when he set a bowl of water before her or lifted a sack to spare her. His clothes were simple, nothing to attract attention. He was a man of routine, content within his small circle of life.

There was a warmth in him, an unassuming smile that might have charmed anyone who hadn't been carried there against her will. To Photine, Jotham's smile marked the life thrust upon her—the path she had not chosen but was required to walk.

He was not cruel. He was not unkind. He was a man whose world had no room for a fire that would not be quiet.

That gave her space—unexpectedly. Space to think, to read, to observe. She kept her father's parchments and seal hidden in a jar in a wall niche—worn and frayed from countless readings. Jotham permitted her ledgers and overlooked her long silences, her occasional sharpness, her questions no wife was expected to ask. He loved her in his way—quietly, awkwardly, without understanding her. In his eyes, her beauty was a marvel; in her mind, his affection was both shelter and cage.

She tried to be dutiful. She maintained the home, managed accounts, offered business advice—small at first, then bolder, until he followed her suggestions without noticing the shift. At market, she listened more than she spoke, collecting fragments, rumors, and truths. The more she understood the world, the more alone she felt inside it. No one spoke her language—the grammar of logic and longing, the pulse of questions beneath her calm exterior.

And yet, beneath all of it, another silence gnawed at her. Each night, she braced herself, waiting for the moment he would claim what the marriage contract had already named his. She told herself it was only a matter of time—wives were meant to be taken, to be used, to beget children.

But the moment never came. He touched her only in passing, if at all, and then with the same absent care he gave to bread or wool.

Is it disgust? Fear? Pity? The questions circled her mind, sharp as flint. She did not know whether to be relieved or insulted, safe or invisible. Some nights she thanked heaven for his restraint; other nights she lay awake with a heat in her chest that felt like shame, or hunger, or both.

And then there were Jotham's kin.

His father, Matthias, and his older brother, Mordecai, lived in the family home nearby. Their presence turned the air sour. Loud, coarse men with a practiced contempt, they treated their women like animals—less than animals. Matthias with his biting disapproval. Mordecai with his fists.

But within the house itself, there were gentler rhythms. Leah, Jotham's mother, moved like a shadow at first—quiet, dutiful, careful not to draw her husband's eye. Yet in the privacy of the kitchen, she let out small sighs, shared half-smiles, taught Photine how to stretch lentils into a meal or keep figs from souring too soon. She was worn, but her care was steady—a lifeline stitched into the fabric of the household.

Lois, Jotham's sister-in-law, carried a heavier burden. Two young daughters already clung to her skirts, and before long she was laboring again. Her cries muffled against the walls while the men drank in the courtyard. Photine knelt at her side that night, pressing cool cloths to her forehead, whispering words she did not know she knew. By dawn, a son was laid in Lois's arms. His wail pierced the rooms like a promise and a warning, tender and fragile against the backdrop of men who would break him before he was grown.

The children brought a fleeting warmth to the place, though they learned to play softly, to quiet their laughter when Matthias prowled or Mordecai's temper stirred. Photine gathered them when she could, telling stories in hushed tones, letting their small hands braid her hair like rope. In their eyes, she glimpsed what family might have been, if not for the shadows pressing in from every side.

Once, as the girls wove ribbons of her dark hair into a crown, Lois laughed softly—the sound quick and precious, like water spilled before it could be caught. Leah hushed them, but her eyes shone, a brief spark in the dimness of the house.

Then Mordecai entered, heavy-footed, his scowl already curdling the air. He paused in the doorway, taking in the scene: Photine seated with the children clustered around her, the women smiling despite themselves.

"Idle hands," he sneered. "No wonder this house eats through grain like mice." He slapped the doorframe for emphasis, the crack jolting the smallest child into tears.

The laughter fled. Lois bent quickly to gather the boy, Leah busied herself with the hearth, and the girls dropped Photine's half-braided hair as though it burned them. Photine sat very still, jaw tight, her fingers itching to strike back with words sharper than any tool in the mill. But she swallowed them, as she always did.

It was then that she began to watch in seething silence, cataloguing rhythms and triggers. Until the day she couldn't.

It started as a bruise—faint, unmistakable—blooming across Lois's cheek. Photine noticed it as they kneaded dough side by side, sleeves dusted with flour, hands working in an old rhythm. No one named it. Not even Lois. Lately, her shoulders rounded inward, laughter gone brittle and rare.

At supper, Mordecai barked for more wine and complained of the salt. Photine met Lois's eyes. Then turned to him.

"If she dies from your cruelty," she said evenly, "you'll have no one left to cook. And no one to care for a man so despised."

Silence dropped. Jotham's spoon scraped the bowl. Matthias leaned back, amused. Mordecai's face twisted—not with shame, but with a promise.

The blow came fast.

Photine didn't scream when she hit the ground. She looked up from the dirt, dazed, burning. Jotham reached for her too late, voice cracking as he mumbled that she should show more obedience before his family. That was all.

Later, behind a closed door, he sat beside her, wringing his hands, eyes clouded with confusion he mistook for sorrow. He said nothing that mattered.

That night, Photine didn't sleep. Stars wheeled beyond the window—distant, deliberate, untouched by any man's rage. She thought of Eleazar's voice, of how he taught her to question, to stand within herself. She thought of the papyrus hidden in the wall niche, the ghost of his ink murmuring, *You are more.*

Anger cooled to something colder, sharper. Not rage—resolve. A vow forged under the blue edge of pain and the iron of her stare.

She would learn. She would wait. And when the time came, she would not run.

She would rise.

The weight of memory loosened its hold. Heat lay its hand back upon her shoulders. The path brightened around her feet.

Photine gathered her scattered thoughts and pulled herself back into the present—to the sun-stunned road and the waiting well. A Samaritan woman on a Samaritan road, resilient and proud, carrying thirsts a jar could not measure.

The Samaritans were a people scorned—by Rome, by the Jews, sometimes by their own haunted memories. Old stories said the Jews had leveled the temple on Mount Gerizim, outlawed their worship, and called their women unclean. The rift had been torn open long ago, and it never stopped bleeding.

Photine had seen it. She had lived it.

So, when she overheard of a Jew coming to town—a teacher, some said, a miracle-worker—her heart tightened into suspicion. Another troublemaker. Another prophet with promises. She had heard men speak of magic and messiahs with the same lips that spat on women's names.

And still… something tugged at the edge of thought, like the dove angling toward shade.

It was midday—hot, dry, bright. The time when most women avoided the sun, when the well would be deserted. She preferred it that way. She was tired, irritable, worn thin by chores and memory. She wanted water and silence.

But as she neared the well, her steps slowed.

A man sat there.

He was alone. Dust clung to his robe with the hush of travel. His hair curled damp at the brow, silvered with heat. From a distance, nothing remarkable—just another road-worn figure resting in noon light.

As she stepped closer, the air shifted—subtly, like the moment before wind.

Her breath caught.

Jew, she thought, a flash like heat through dry grass. *What is he doing here—at our well?*

Her first instinct was to turn—vanish like a shadow down the path, leave the jar empty and her mouth drier than pride. She didn't need water that badly. But the sun pressed like a hand, and she had come so far through dust, memory, bruise, and vow.

Her feet hesitated.

He looked up.

The world went still.

His eyes met hers—not demanding, not startled—calm, as if he had been waiting. As if he had known she would come.

Her pulse quickened. Something old stirred in her chest—recognition without acquaintance. Her anger rose like a shield—serviceable, familiar. *What does he want?* she thought. *Why does he look at me as if I am already known?*

His gaze was unlike any she had known. It carried no hunger, no ridicule, no wariness. Not the stare of a stranger, a soldier, or a prophet. It was stillness. Depth. A knowing so clear it frightened her.

And it was gentle.

A thin, dizzying vertigo crept into her bones. She set her palm on the cool stone rim to steady herself. Heat shimmered; air thickened—not only with temperature, but with something unseen and vividly alive.

Everything she knew screamed caution. Turn. Walk away. Say nothing. But something older—stronger—than caution woke in her—older than fear and nearer than anger.

Not trust. Not yet.

The first stirrings of something more dangerous.

Curiosity.

Longing.

A thirst she could not name.

She swallowed—throat dry, tongue thick, mouth remembering water her jar had not yet tasted. Beneath the stone's coolness, another coolness seemed to rise—as though the well listened too.

She did not know what would happen next. But even before he spoke, before the water murmured in its depth, she knew:

Her life would not leave this well the way it had arrived.

CHAPTER 2
JOTHAM

Jotham had been a frail child, never measuring up to his brother Mordecai's brute certainty. He learned early that the house did not forgive weakness. Mordecai's laughter carried weight; his father's silence carried judgment sharper still. Jotham grew into the habit of shrinking, of choosing corners over tables, of listening longer than he spoke. If he could not be loud, he would be steady. If he could not be strong, he would be useful. His father, Matthias, praised strength in the only dialect he spoke—derision for anything softer. Chores that would have taught a son to stand were given to Mordecai. Chores that would have taught a daughter to endure were thrust at Jotham. Everyone learned their part; Jotham learned to make himself small inside of it.

His earliest memories were not of his father at all, but of the women. Leah's voice humming low while she pounded grain; his sisters' laughter spilling into the courtyard. They carried him on their hips when he was too small and weak to walk far, shielded him from Mordecai's sharp elbows, slipped him the choicest figs as if they could fatten him into strength. Their hands braided his hair, straightened his tunic, pressed cool cloths to his fevered brow. For a little boy who knew the language of scorn too well, their tenderness was a second tongue.

It only deepened Mordecai's contempt. To him, Jotham was coddled, made soft by women's touch. Every act of care became proof of failure, every kindness a mark against him. Mordecai learned to sneer where the sisters smiled, to shove where they steadied, to remind Jotham that softness was weakness, and weakness had no place in Matthias's house.

Anna—Matthias's second and ardently loved wife—died birthing a child she would never meet. Grief dented the house; blame found the softest surface. Jotham carried the absence, and with it a name that was not spoken. Matthias never said the words, but Jotham heard them: You survived the wrong grief.

Leah, Matthias's first wife, raised him with a quiet devotion that asked for nothing and taught him how to last. She combed his hair with slow hands, wrapped his coughs in thyme and steam. When Matthias's contempt grew loud, she touched Jotham's shoulder so lightly he barely felt it, as if to say, Not all hands are for striking.

Jotham did not ask for much. He did not argue when ignored. He learned the art of edges—how to be near enough to serve, far enough to avoid harm. When he began watching the village miller, no one objected. It was useful to have him elsewhere. He learned the rhythm men forget they live by: grain poured, stone turned, flour sifted, bread risen. A world that made sense and did not shout.

By sixteen, he apprenticed fully. In distant markets, he discovered places where he wasn't, yet had already decided and therefore could become something else—someone whose silence wasn't confusion but craft.

When the old miller died, Jotham took the work and moved into a narrow house near the beam and wheel. He mended what broke, oiled what groaned, strengthened thresholds and lintels with his own hands. He learned that a thing could be kept from collapse with the right attention and that attention did not require a tongue.

Years made him broad but not imposing; weather carved his face without hardening his eyes. He was awkward, quiet, easy to overlook, and—without knowing to name it—*safe*. Most didn't take the time to *learn* him; he took time with everything.

He never sought a wife. How could he? To seek meant to risk being seen, and Jotham had lived a safe, unremarkable life. He feared the shape of his father in himself—that if he ever raised children, they might inherit silence twisted into cruelty. Better to grind grain than gamble with love. The mill asked only for labor, and labor never wept when he failed.

He distrusted his own worth, having learned too early that his presence could be counted as a fault. He feared fatherhood like a cliff in the dark—not the child, but the repetition: Matthias's voice climbing out of his own mouth. He feared love because it demanded a language he did not possess. So, he told himself routine was enough. He told himself a house could stand upright on quiet alone.

He told himself many things.

Then, Photine arrived. Not as a choice—on either side—but as an event that rerouted a river without loudness, erosive and sure.

He did as he always did: made space. Before her, he cooked over an open flame with a flat stone and a clay pot. After, he built an earthen oven from sun-dried brick, shaped bowls and jars, asked what she needed, and went to fetch or make it. He raised a reed screen behind the mill for privacy, four walls of modest dignity where there had been only weather. She carved a corner for meals, set flat stones as stools, and wove sleeping mats that smelled faintly of thyme and smoke. Care gathered in the room like warmth that wasn't sure if it was welcome.

They spoke little at first. Silence between them had a different flavor than the silence he kept with men—not fear, not calculation— carefulness, like strangers sharing the same narrow bridge.

He listened when she corrected the barley tally. He let her reorder the ledger in her clean geometry. He didn't praise; he adopted. Praise felt like making noise. Adoption felt like the truth. It was not indifference that kept him apart, but restraint. She was too young, too newly torn from her mother's house, and he would not make her learn fear in his. He had no gift of words to explain this, so he let his silence carry it: *You are safe here, even if nothing else in your world has been.*

In winter, when fever took her, his hands shook as he held broth to her lips. He warmed cloths by the fire and touched them to her forehead with the reverence of a man who had known loss too nearly to take breath for granted. He did not pray aloud, but the way he stayed said what words could not: *Live. Please live.*

She did. And the silence between them changed shape again. Where once it had felt like absence, it now felt like a quiet shelter. She found herself watching as his shadow moved across the room, steady as the turn of a wheel, and drew strength from it.

He left a cup of tea by her corner before sunrise. She folded his tunics with attention that knew where the thread failed and mended before it did. When he carved a wooden dove through a storm and placed it on her sill, she kept it close not only for the calm but because it was the first gift she had received without a price.

Photine hadn't minded their living away from the rest of the family. In fact, she found comfort in the distance from Mordecai, who had struck her more than once. Jotham made a place for her, and in turn, she made a place for him. Inside their shared room, she carved out a corner for meals. Their storage chest doubled as a table, and she set flat stones as stools. She wove sleeping mats from dried grasses she gathered near the creek, placing them across from each other and covering them with the woolen wraps she brought from home.

Photine occupied herself with maintaining their home, helping with Jotham's trade, and continuing to read anything she could get her hands on. In those quiet hours, she connected to the memory of her father's voice still guiding her how to move through the world.

Her life was not what she had dreamed of, but she had vowed to make it her own. She would carry her father's wisdom, honor his memory, and survive—intelligent, determined, and unbroken. Maybe, one day, she would find the companionship she longed for. Until then, she would endure.

Her marriage had never followed tradition.

He never touched her possessively. But neither did he free her. Not because he liked the power of ownership—he did not—but because he did not know how to move in straight lines. The millstone had taught him one shape. He turned. What he could not say in words, he spoke in patterns. The cup of tea was placed where her hands would find it. The tunic folded with seams aligned just so. The dove whittled by firelight when storms rattled the shutters. His love was a slow language, written in acts so small they could almost be missed. But they were the only sentences he trusted himself to form.

He had not sought a wife because seeking required self-conviction he did not have. He believed himself a poor bargain: a quiet man with a good craft and an empty speech. He had made a life in which nothing asked him to risk being seen. A wife would see him. A child would mirror him. He had watched Matthias turn grief into gravity, and he vowed without words never to pull another human into his orbit unless he could guarantee they would not be crushed.

And a guarantee was not a thing the world offered.

When Photine came, he understood suddenly that he had been wrong in both directions: he could not keep a life untouched, and he could not keep from touching another life.

Jotham left at first light, mule's ears flicking at gnats, grain sacks shifting like sleeping bodies. The air still violet at the edges. He preferred the early hours: the world before men's voices took up all the room.

He had not slept well. Letters moved through his thoughts like fish beneath water—a thing passed hand to hand that was not his to own but had chosen his quiet as a path. He had come, lately, to carry more than flour. A weaver in Bethel had pressed a folded sheet into his palm with a look that said more than the ink ever would. A teacher north of Tirzah had received such sheets and sent others, and Jotham's name was spoken among men who preferred to stay unnamed. He did not agree to be brave. He agreed to be useful.

On his path, past the figs clinging to the slope, three men stood near a broken wheel. Too still. Too watchful. Not peasants but predators—faces lean, sandals worn from miles, eyes that measured what a man carried more than who he was. Hired blades, most likely, the kind who traded loyalty for coin and fear.

He almost passed. He almost didn't.

"Peace to you," he said. Habit and hope.

"Brother," said the one with the good smile that never reached his eyes. "The wheel snapped."

And he knew. Not in words, but in the tightening of his gut, the sharpness of their stance, the absence of the broken wheel they named.

The first blow was a horizon that wouldn't hold still. The second cut the light into pieces. He reached for Photine's name with his mouth and found blood. The third unstitched the world.

They stripped what could be sold and left what could not. Grain sacks scattered, mule reins dragging in the dust. The men disappeared down the slope as if they had never been, except for the ruin left behind.

By noon, the vultures made their slow journey in the sky. A water-carrier learned, then the elders, then Matthias. Some griefs travel fast. Others never move at all.

At night, while Jotham was away, Photine slept with his cloak draped across her like a shield. It smelled of ash, cedar, and flour. Some nights that steadied her. Some nights, it felt like a reminder of quiet that was not hers.

Tonight, she woke to a wrongness in the air. A shift at the threshold. Breath that was not the house's.

Mordecai filled the doorway: wine, sweat, the ugly assurance of a man who enters believing every room already belongs to him.

Where was Jotham?

He had been gone longer than usual—three days. An urgent delivery, he'd said, farther along the Roman road. He'd kissed her brow without meeting her eyes—a gesture that felt like a door closing. Lately, his errands had carried more than flour. A folded scrap here, a whispered name there. Men who spoke carefully, as though the air itself might betray them, trusted him because he was forgettable. Jotham told himself he was only a miller, only a path. But each time he passed a message into another's hand, he wondered if this was the one that would cost him.

She feigned sleep, heartbeat thrumming against her ribs, fingers curled around the wooden dove beneath her mat.

"Wake up," he said. A boot or a voice; she could not tell which moved her.

"Jotham—he'll be back—" she began.

"Your husband is dead."

The words struck and then kept striking. She folded down on herself as if the earth wouldn't hold. He held out Jotham's satchel—frayed strap, familiar wear—and she cradled it like a child that wasn't there.

She could not ask *how*. She had to know.

"Get up," Mordecai said now. "You belong to me. You know the law."

Levirate—the custom that could keep a name from dying out, meant to bind a widow into a protection she did not choose. In a just man's mouth, it was a duty of care. In Mordecai's, it was a leash.

Photine's gaze moved quickly, cataloguing: the alcove where a small jar hid within larger jars; the reed screen; the door; the distance to night.

"Let me gather my things," she said, voice turned submissive so it would pass. "Let me mourn."

"Take your clothes," he answered. "Nothing else."

Pain lifted her to her feet by the hair. She kept her eyes on the floor so he would not see the calculation in them.

She reached for a folded tunic. With her body turned just so, her fingers slipped along the wall niche and found the small jar behind the larger ones. Parchment, thin as a held breath, and a small wooden seal. She could not take the jar. She slid a single strip and a shard of wood into the hem of her garment with the speed of a woman who has trained her hands to do two truths at once.

Photine's fingers lingered at the hem of her garment, pressing the hidden strip of parchment flat against her skin. The words she had many times read burned there like coal. It steadied her—reminded her that her father's voice, and Jotham's quiet trust, were not wholly erased.

But steadiness was a fragile thing. Already, the old ache of abandonment gnawed at her ribs. First, Eleazar, vanishing into shadows. Now Jotham, gentle Jotham, cut down for carrying what others feared to touch. She was left again, always left, as if men dissolved the moment she began to lean toward them.

Her heart beat hard, not only with fear, but with a kind of fierce clarity. *They cannot take all of me.* The thought came sharp as a blade, and with it, a sudden pulse of anger—hot, fleeting, real. Anger at being made to survive every leaving, anger at Mordecai's smirk, at Matthias's silence, at the weight of loss laid at women's feet. Always at women's feet.

Even as Mordecai's shadow loomed, she straightened her shoulders by a hair's breadth. Her chin lifted. Her eyes, storm-dark, flashed toward the alcove once more, memorizing its hollow like a map for return.

It was the smallest of gestures—too small for most to notice—but Mordecai did. He had lived his whole life sniffing out resistance, and he knew the look of a woman who still carried secrets. "You dare," he muttered, eyes narrowing. "Even now, you carry yourself like you have something left that is yours."

Photine did not answer. Silence had always been her armor. But her stillness, her refusal to cower, was enough. He saw it as rebellion, and he could not permit rebellion.

The darkness in his eyes hardened into something brutal. With a rough hand, he seized her arm and pulled her toward the door. She stumbled, her sandals scraping against the packed earth floor, but he didn't slow. Her heart pounded—not just with fear, but with a rising heat that burned in her chest. Not passion. Fury. Defiance. Something in her refused to break, even as he dragged her across the threshold.

The shadows of the mill thickened, and the scent of crushed grain clung to the air like dust on her tongue. The familiar space, once tolerable, even quiet, now turned hostile—every beam, every stone, every crack in the wall watching and silent.

Jotham had never touched her that way. Never claimed what law and contract had said was his to claim. In his restraint, he had preserved her youth, her innocence, her sense that she still belonged to herself. Whatever else he could not give, he had given her that.

Mordecai, in his fury, meant to take everything.

He threw her forward. She fell hard against the chest-table, the edge biting into her ribs. Pain flared. Before she could rise, he twisted her arm behind her back and, with his free hand, ripped her garments aside. Her breath caught. She gasped, but no sound came loud enough to matter.

Above her, Mordecai's voice was a low snarl. The words were lost, drowned beneath the roar of her heartbeat. She could hear him— angry, slurred, thick with the stench of wine. But the words came like echoes down a long hallway. Warped. Muffled. As if she were underwater and drowning.

The floor was spinning. No, it wasn't the floor—it was her. Her body was untethered, shaking beneath the weight bearing down on her back. His breath was hot and sour against her neck, reeking of fermented dates and bile.

She tried to scream. Nothing came.

Pain, sudden and sharp, ripped through her belly, shot up her spine, and burst behind her eyes like lightning. Her one arm that held her up gave out. Her hands scrabbled for purchase against the wooden chest he threw her over. Splinters tore at her palms.

Her hips slammed against the edge with each violent motion. The breath was knocked from her lungs. Again. Again. Her skin scraped raw, her muscles clenching uselessly.

The straw broom lay nearby—abandoned, limp, useless. Just this morning, she had used it to sweep the dust from the corners of the house, to make it feel clean, safe. Hers.

Now even the dust betrayed her.

Mordecai grunted, his hand digging into the back of her neck, grinding her down like an animal. "You think you're better than me?" he spat. "Too clever, too proud. Your mouth always running—see how far that gets you now."

She tried to pull away, but there was nowhere to go. The chest was cold against her thighs. Her face smashed against the table's rough surface. Her fingers clawed at the grainy wood. One nail cracked. She didn't feel it.

Another stab of pain—raw, ragged—tore through her insides. She bit her lip until it split, blood trickling into her mouth. She would not cry. She would not scream. She would not give him that.

Her mind fled.

She saw Lois—tired, folding laundry with dead eyes. Always quiet. Always enduring. Her back bent, her spirit hollow. Was that what came next? A life of silence and hands that never stopped aching?

Then her father's face flashed behind her eyes. His laugh. The way he had held her chin and called her *wise beyond your years*. The way he *believed her mind mattered*. And now, he would be ashamed.

"I'm sorry," she gasped, voice torn by memory more than pain.

"That's more like it," Mordecai growled into her ear. "You understand now."

A final thrust slammed her forward—her temple cracked against the chest's edge. White exploded behind her eyelids. Her body went still. Her soul went elsewhere.

He collapsed against her with a grunt, his sweat soaking through her tunic.

Then silence.

Only her breathing—shallow, ragged, more animal than human.

When he withdrew, she collapsed to the floor, a discarded object.

She did not cry.

She lay still, cheek pressed to the dust-caked floor, the grit clinging to her torn lips.

Later, she would not recall how long she stayed there. Hours. Maybe days.

When at last she blinked, her gaze drifted upward. In the dim light, she saw it—the small wooden dove Jotham had carved, still perched in the window where she had kept it. Its shape was simple, but in it, she felt his steadiness, his quiet presence.

A thought flickered through her: *They cannot take this from me. Not his kindness. Not what he gave me.*

Just like that, she returned to herself.

The pain didn't stop. Her limbs ached. Her cloak hung in shreds, her knees dust-streaked, her face smeared with tears, blood, and soil. Something in her had snapped and gone quiet—something soft and tender. Finished, Mordecai yanked her up by her arm. She stood, dazed, her legs trembling.

The mill, which had been a place of labor and mercy, narrowed. Grain-scent turned to dust in her throat. They cannot take this, she thought—Jotham's quiet, Jotham's steadiness, what had been decent in him. Some violences are designed to unname; she would not let this one.

Her gaze snagged on the sill as he dragged her forward. The wooden dove sat there, small and waiting, carved on a storm night when Jotham could not sleep. With a sudden, desperate surge, she tore her arm free just long enough to snatch it, pressing the little bird hard into her palm. Its wings bit her skin, but she clung to it as if to breath itself.

Then his grip closed again, iron and merciless. He hauled her through streets that felt like someone else's dream toward a life she couldn't fathom.

Her feet stumbled over stones she had walked a hundred times, yet each step felt strange, like treading another woman's path. Faces blurred at the edges—neighbors pausing at their doors, merchants leaning from stalls. She thought she heard her name once, hushed and bitter, but it drifted away like smoke. The world had collapsed to the heat of his hand on her arm, the wooden dove pressed hard into her palm, and the jagged silence inside her where words should have been.

Her thoughts splintered: her father leaving, Jotham's last quiet gift, the feel of the mill's chest biting into her ribs. Abandonment stalked her with every step. *It happens again. It always happens again.* The refrain circled like a hawk overhead, relentless, waiting for her to fall.

Matthias's courtyard opened before her, pitiless under the sky. On a board inside, wrapped in linen, the still form that used to answer to Jotham's name. Leah's grief poured not like a wave but like a river that had lost its banks. Lois, steady as bread, washed Photine's face and dressed her in a clean garment with hands trembling only at the edges. No one asked what had happened on the way there. The house was full of men who only asked questions if the answers could pay them.

Jotham was buried by sundown beneath a cairn beyond the mill. The grave was shallow and honest.

Seven days she mourned. People came and filled the air with the sound of themselves. Strangers tried on memories of Jotham like garments that didn't fit, and then left them in a heap for someone else to pick through. Photine sat in the near-dark and did not add to the noise.

Lois sat beside her; the children's laughter fretted the edges of sorrow; Leah moved, saying his name as if speech alone could build him back. Matthias looked relieved. Some losses please the wrong hearts.

Mordecai ran the house like a conqueror who mistook a table for a throne. The mill—now in the hands of a field hand too old for it— began to fail. Ledgers tell stories to anyone who can read.

Photine read.

She said nothing. Listen long enough, and a house will tell you where it splits.

At night, she lay on a thin mat and missed Jotham, not for romance but for the peculiar safety of his steady orbit—the way his presence kept cruelty from finding a straight path to her. That safety had been a thread. Now it was ash.

The fire in her did not go out. It moved lower, hotter, where air cannot easily reach. The veil tied at her brow was for mourning. Beneath it, something else sharpened.

She waited, not as surrender, but as a strategy.

Jotham had not loved with practiced words. He had loved as he knew how: by building, by bearing, by never raising a hand. He had not sought a wife because he could not trust the power he might have over another, and because love seemed to ask for a tongue he did not possess. Photine taught him that presence could be a dialect all its own. He had begun, quietly, to learn another: a risk that served something larger than himself.

He left one morning with a kiss pressed to a brow he didn't feel permitted to claim. He meant to return to the little stove and the ledger written in her finer hand and the wooden dove watching the window. He meant to say something like *thank you* and something like *stay*. He meant too many things for a man who thought he had more road.

A part of him believed—without naming it—that he didn't deserve a wife because he hadn't sought one. And he did not deserve a child because he feared what he might become. He thought abstention was a virtue. He did not yet know that goodness sometimes requires a yes.

He did not die a hero. He died as he lived: trying to help, trying to believe what people tell you about their need, trying to be of use. It does not make the end less cruel. It does make life true.

On the eighth day, the silence changed shape. Men stopped arriving with stories about themselves. The house thinned to those who actually lived there: a bitter father, a brutal brother, two women who had learned to survive a weather that did not change, and a widow who refused to be renamed.

Photine moved through rooms like a person pacing the fence of a field she intends to leave. She watched who spoke to whom, when grain disappeared, which hired hand looked away when Mordecai lifted his arm. She traced small maps in her mind of alleys and doors and hours when vigilance slept.

At dusk, she stood by the door and placed her palm against the wood the way she once placed it against the well: listening. Not for voices—she had heard enough—but for the sense a thing gives when it is ready to open.

Behind her, the wooden dove—carried from the mill in her hand and quietly placed on the sill—caught the last of the light, its small carved wing holding steady.

And beneath the veil, beneath the bruises, beneath the carefully lowered eyes, a vow shaped itself with the economy of a miller's measure:

I will live. I will remember. I will not turn in circles to make bread for the mouths that broke me.

I will choose my road.

The vow burned quietly inside her, but the world around her did not bend to meet it. Life went on in the house as if Jotham had never lived, as if her grief and rage were just another vessel to be set in the corner. The courtyard became her cage and her stage—every glance watched, every silence measured.

The family home was built around a central courtyard, open to the sky like an ever-watching eye. This was where they prepared meals, gathered around a fire when the evenings grew cold, and performed the mundane rituals of daily life. Rooms circled this open space—simple structures with low thatched roofs and woven cloths draped from wooden beams for walls.

Matthias and Mordecai each kept a room for themselves, while the women and children were grouped and tucked into shared spaces that offered little privacy and less comfort.

Matthias still lived, but age and bitterness had hollowed him. His strength had soured into suspicion, his authority into muttered judgments from the shadows of the courtyard. He had spent so many years breaking his sons into roles that when the quieter one was buried, the louder one simply stepped forward. No ceremony. No blessing. Just the natural order of a man who shouted loudest, taking the seat.

Mordecai had always been quick to fill silence, and Matthias—half-blind, weary, and content to sneer rather than command—did nothing to stop him. In truth, Matthias seemed almost satisfied to watch his surviving son thunder where he himself had grown tired. The father ruled in name; the son ruled in practice.

And Mordecai led his home with all the subtlety of a conqueror. He barked orders at the hired hands, spat in the dirt when Lois passed too close, and occupied the head of the table as if it had always belonged to him. He barely acknowledged Photine, except to scowl when she touched the ledger or spoke out of turn.

"Women have their place," he muttered once, loud enough for her to hear.

But the bluster had roots. Mordecai had grown up watching Matthias favor strength over sense, praise the fist over the mind. His earliest memory was of pushing a smaller boy into the mud while his father looked on, lips curled in something like approval. From then on, he equated cruelty with power. Kindness, in his eyes, was weakness—proof a man could not rule his own house.

What he never admitted, even to himself, was how quickly shame turned his stomach. He struggled with numbers, stumbled through contracts, and hated the way Jotham's sisters once shielded their frail brother as if he deserved more tenderness than Mordecai himself ever received. He saw in Jotham's quiet endurance not weakness but a kind of mirror—one that reflected his own inadequacy. The more others pitied Jotham, the more Mordecai seethed.

Fear drove him, though he clothed it in swagger. Fear of being seen as stupid, fear of being overlooked, fear that without his shouting, no one would listen at all. He mistook obedience for respect, possession for love, and volume for authority. Women, to him, were either servants or threats—servants when they complied, threats when they dared to know too much.

In private moments—few as they were—Mordecai remembered the sting of being ignored by Matthias once, twice, a hundred times, except when he managed to dominate. That memory hardened into creed: better to be feared than invisible.

So, he thundered. He ridiculed. He filled the silence with himself. Because silence left room for doubt, and doubt was the one enemy he could not conquer.

Photine said nothing, but the muscles in her jaw ached from holding back words. The numbers in the ledger told their own story— profits slipping, workers leaving. Mordecai was too proud to admit it, too stubborn to ask for help.

She stayed out of his way when she could, but the house was too small for silence to hide.

Sometimes, she caught him staring. Not with lust, not exactly. With ownership.

It made her skin crawl.

Lois remained her only ally. Even she, usually mild and submissive, had grown quieter, more guarded. Her bruises took longer to fade. The tension in her face never did. She spoke less of the children, less of hope.

At night, Photine lay on her thin mat, listening to the restless shuffle of feet in the hallway, the clatter of pots as Leah tried to feel useful, the occasional grunt or slam from Mordecai's quarters.

She missed the quiet—for the fragile balance it had offered. The rhythm of her own keeping. The safety of a corner that belonged to her alone. In that stillness, she could breathe, could think, could almost believe herself untouched. Now, even that space had been devoured.

And in its place, another rhythm grew: Mordecai's voice, Mordecai's steps, Mordecai's rule. The house no longer held the distant memories of the quiet, the caution, and the attention of the boy who once lived there under his sister's protection and admiration.

Photine closed her eyes, but sleep would not come. She felt it pressing in from every side: the weight of another man she had not chosen, the shadow of a future that would demand her body, her silence, her children.

The walls seemed to lean closer, listening, as though the house itself knew whose name would soon be written over it.

CHAPTER 3
MORDECAI

Matthias's heart pounded as he waited, nerves fraying with each passing second. Behind closed doors, the midwife attended to both his beloved Anna and his first wife, Leah—each in labor at the same time. He yearned for a son, a boy to inherit his wheat fields, his tools, and his legacy. Leah had borne him three daughters but no sons. Marrying Anna was supposed to fulfill the one thing Leah had not—give him heirs.

He never intended to fall in love with Anna. But her soft hair, radiant smile, and angelic voice had disarmed him. She sang as she worked—melodies her mother had taught her as a child—and when she laughed, it cracked the hard edges of his pride. At first, he had admired her from a distance. Then he needed her near. Now, he felt doubly blessed—love and lineage, both within reach.

Anna brought out the man he wanted to be. Gentle. Hopeful. Responsible. She had dreams of a large family, of a garden filled with herbs and pomegranates, of children who would grow up learning music and mercy. She calmed his anger. He thought, perhaps, she was his redemption.

And Leah—dutiful Leah—was a bridge between them. She should have hated Anna, but she did not. Anna's presence lightened her burdens, softened Matthias's temper, and gave the daughters another lap to run to. Leah found in her a companion more than a rival. When Matthias shouted, Anna sang, and Leah felt her shoulders unclench.

Once, in the courtyard at dusk, Leah found Anna humming while weaving a basket. The younger woman paused, cheeks flushed, as if caught in a secret.

"You needn't stop," Leah said, lowering herself onto the step beside her. "The girls sleep better when they hear you."

Anna's eyes brimmed with relief. "I was afraid it would wound you—my being here."

Leah shook her head. "It eases me. Matthias smiles more. He looks at you the way he never looked at me. But I do not begrudge you. I am grateful."

Anna reached for her hand, and they sat that way a long while, the dusk filling with song and silence.

Together, the two women shaped a home that might have endured. Anna's laughter softened Matthias's pride, and Leah's steadiness gave Anna's dreams something solid to lean on. For a short season, the house knew something like peace.

But deep down, Matthias feared it would not last. He feared love could not protect what lineage demanded. He feared fate, or God, or some unseen debt waiting to be paid.

Then came the cry of an infant. Matthias's breath caught. He busied himself sharpening his sheathing tools, trying to appear composed. He ached to run inside.

The midwife emerged first. "Leah has given you a son," she said with relief. "She's resting now."

Matthias exhaled, a flicker of joy lighting his face. Then the midwife's voice tightened. "Anna is… struggling. Her child—"

"Go do your job, woman," he cut in sharply. "Anna is strong. She'll be fine." He turned away, unwilling to entertain any alternative.

Matthias stood outside the birthing chamber, the heavy curtain drawn tight, muffling the groans and cries within. The moon had risen higher, casting its cold light over the courtyard's stone floor. He paced, his sandals scraping grit with every pass, every heartbeat like a hammer behind his ribs.

The joy of Leah's son had barely begun to take root before it was choked by the midwife's tone. *Anna is struggling.*

No, that wasn't possible. Anna was healthy. Young. She had woven a tunic for the baby just days ago, humming while she stitched. She had kissed his forehead that morning with the confidence of a woman whose future had already begun.

"She's strong," he whispered to himself again. "She'll be fine."

But his fingers trembled as he rubbed them over the carved handle of the knife at his belt—a gift from Anna's father. His stomach churned. The smell of smoke from the hearth mixed with something metallic in the air, something sharp.

He remembered the first time he saw her: standing in the shade of the olive trees, laughing at something Leah had said. Her laughter had caught him off guard. *That* was what had undone him. Not her beauty, not even her kindness—though both were evident. It was her laughter. Bold. Free.

And now she might be—

No. He couldn't finish the thought.

He sat on the bench, elbows on his knees, head in his hands. He tried to pray, but the words tangled in his throat. All he could do was breathe and wait and listen.

Anna's cries rose again, fierce and raw. He flinched. It was not the sound of strength—it was the sound of pain without progress. Of something going wrong.

He stood abruptly, straining to listen.

Then, the piercing wail of a newborn.

For a heartbeat, relief flooded him.

But it was followed by silence.

Not the silence of peace.

The silence of something *missing*.

He turned toward the door again, waiting for someone—anyone—to emerge and tell him what had happened. The seconds stretched. His heart pounded against his chest like a caged bird. "Please," he whispered. Not to the gods. Not even to the stars. Just to *anyone* who might still be listening.

The midwife returned, cradling a second infant. Her face was pale. "You have another son, Matthias," her voice shook. "Anna… she didn't survive the birth. The child was too—"

Matthias erupted, grief boiling into rage. "Take him away! He is not my son. He is a curse and has murdered my beloved!"

The midwife flinched but held her ground. "He is strong. He will be a good son to you, in time—"

"I said take him away," Matthias growled, vanishing into the night. His footsteps faded, leaving the women in silence.

The midwife bent close to Leah, laying the newborn in her arms. "Listen to me. If he grows up marked as Anna's son, Matthias may never let him live in peace. Let no one know which child came from which womb. Raise them together as brothers. Swear it, for their lives may depend on it."

Leah gazed down at the boy, his fists clenched tight against his chest. He was not hers by blood, but in that moment, she felt something fiercer than blood—an oath of protection. She nodded solemnly. "Then both are mine. Both will be sons of this house."

In time, she came to name them Jotham and Mordecai.

Anna was buried before sundown.

Women keened in the courtyard while the men carried her on a simple board to the family plot beyond the fig trees. Oil lamps burned low in the doorways; the smell of crushed thyme and hot dust clung to the air. Leah walked behind the body with the midwife at her elbow, both infants swaddled and bound to her chest—one on the left, one on the right—so close they breathed in the same rhythm. Matthias did not look back. He kept his eyes on the ground and spoke to no one, not even when the last stones were set to keep the night dogs away.

After the burial, the house filled and emptied the way houses do when grief moves through them—neighbors bringing round loaves and lentil stew, a jar of olives pressed into someone's hands, murmured blessings that never knew quite where to land. Leah, learning the new weight of two at once, fed them in turns. The smaller boy rooted lazily and often fell asleep before he'd taken much. The larger latched with a will that made Leah wince, eyes open, fists kneading at the fold of her tunic as though he were already making claims on the world.

Matthias kept to the edge of the rooms. He ate standing, when he ate at all. At night, he lay on the roof where the evening wind could not soften him, and at dawn, he went out before anyone had the chance to speak his name. When the midwife tried to hand him one of the boys, he stepped back as if from flame. Leah felt his gaze sometimes—hard, undeciding—fall on the smaller child, and she drew him closer without making a show of it, shifting her shoulder so he slept with his ear against her heartbeat. Then she offered the larger infant the other breast with a steady, resigned patience. Two sons, one pair of arms.

Matthias had not been born cruel, though few remembered otherwise. His earliest memory was of his own father's hand on the back of his neck, pushing him down into the dust when he reached too slowly for a tool. "A man must learn quick, or be crushed," the old man had said. He grew up knowing that softness invited blows, and hunger was answered with silence. His mother's face blurred in memory—she died too young, leaving him in a house of men where laughter was weakness and mercy a word never spoken.

By the time Matthias had sons of his own, he no longer knew how to hold a child. To him, babies were fragile, treacherous things—reminders that life could slip away as easily as Anna had slipped away in childbirth. His grief sharpened into suspicion: if you did not clutch too tightly, perhaps you would not feel the tearing when the world took what you loved. So, he refused to clutch at all.

It was easier to call one son cursed than to risk calling either beloved. Easier to sneer than to soften. He told himself it was strength, that he was teaching them survival, but Leah saw the truth: he was teaching them his own fear, the old wound passed down like an inheritance.

On the eighth day after the boy's birth, as the Law requires, they gathered in the small front room for the circumcision. The floor had been swept at first light; a low stool was set near the threshold with a basin beside it and clean strips of linen folded on a board. The oil lamp on the shelf sent a thin blue flame toward the ceiling, and the smell of heated olive oil mingled with the sour edge of men's sandals.

A kinsman—older, careful with his hands—stood ready. Matthias came at the last possible moment and took his place under the lintel, arms locked, jaw set. He did not greet the neighbors or the elder, and he did not look toward Leah's lap where the infants lay bundled, faces soft with that slack, newborn dreaming.

The kinsman lifted the first boy. "Blessed are You… who sanctifies Your people," he murmured, voice low enough to be prayer and public enough for the room to hear. The midwife steadied the lamp; Leah set her palm on the baby's feet. A breath held, a practiced cut, a quick wash, linen tied. The wail rose and fell like a shofar in miniature, then dwindled to hiccups.

"Mordecai," the elder announced, wrapping the child again and laying him in Leah's waiting arms. A murmur of approval moved along the wall—good strong lungs, someone said, as if merit could already be measured in volume. Leah's heart clenched at the name. *Servant of Marduk*—a foreign shadow clinging to her son. Yet strength would be demanded of him, she knew. If this world valued force above tenderness, then perhaps the name itself might shield him.

The second boy was slower to stir. He blinked once, twice, as if deciding whether this world was worth the work. The elder's hands were just as steady; the blessing just as true. The cry that followed was thin, more question than protest. Leah bent close, her cheek brushing the softness of his crown.

"Jotham," the elder said gently, and there was a kindness in the way the name left his mouth, as if he were already making room for the boy to be exactly what he was and no more. *The LORD is upright*, Leah thought, clinging to the word as prayer and defiance alike. If Matthias would never call him son, then God Himself would.

No one asked which child was Leah's by blood and which was Anna's. The midwife's eyes met Leah's for the length of a heartbeat, then fell to her own hands. Leah knew the truth must never be spoken—not to Matthias, not to the neighbors, not even to the boys themselves. They would be brothers, bound by her silence, raised as sons of the same house.

The room exhaled. Bread was broken. A small bowl of wine was passed and sipped. Blessings were spoken over both sons, equal in their swaddling.

Matthias stepped backward into the threshold shadow and then into the street, as if the naming had been a task for other men. By nightfall, he was gone—no explanation, no instructions—just the absence of a husband who would not be consoled. He left the house to Leah, to the midwife's counsel, to the older daughters who moved like small, steady birds between the hearth and the sleeping mats.

Leah learned the measure of the days by the boys' different hungers. Mordecai's mouth was a fist; he wore himself loudly in the world, always reaching, always ready. Jotham, light and easily wearied, needed coaxing and quiet. She would rub his tiny back in slow circles to wake him enough to feed, sing under her breath until the latch held, then shift him to the cooler breast and count heartbeats while he swallowed. When he slipped away from the work of it, she tried again, lifting his heel to startle a cry, trading sides, offering milk warmed in a small cup. The worry sat in her chest like a stone: not enough, not enough.

At times, when the room was empty and the older girls were fetching water, Leah would lay both boys on a folded cloak and look from one face to the other. The small differences that already seemed to speak of a future: Mordecai's furrow, Jotham's uncertain mouth. And she would make herself stop. Names are not destinies, she told herself, only doors; they do not have to open where men expect.

She loved them both, and she told herself she would love them as fiercely as if both had come from her own womb. One had not, but he had come from Anna, and Leah had loved Anna. To love her son was to honor her memory, to keep some remnant of her gentleness alive in a house that had too little of it left.

When the sun sank and the work thinned, she lit the oil lamp and thanked the dark for the mercy of a cool wind. The midwife came and went, bringing fennel for the babies' bellies and a quiet reminder to drink more broth. At night, Leah lay on her side with both boys tucked in the curve of her body, and if Matthias's shadow crossed the threshold of her thoughts, she turned her face toward the wall and listened for two different kinds of breathing until sleep took her.

The house adapted around the fact of two sons and one woman's resolve. The older girls learned to grind a finer flour; a neighbor's wife showed them how to fold the swaddles to ease the strain on Leah's back. Life narrowed to what could be carried in two hands and widened to include all the mercies that could be gathered without asking leave.

Weeks bled into months. News of Matthias came in pieces—seen on the road to Shechem with packmen, sleeping under a goat-hair awning near the presses at Sebaste, doing accounts in a wine courtyard with men whose clothes spoke of coin. He did not send word. He did not come home.

Leah did not speak his name to the boys. She said only "Papa" when the older sisters asked, with a tone that made questions feel like bad manners. She learned to live inside the in-between—the place where two sons could be her sons because no one else had the courage or kindness to claim them. When Mordecai cried loud enough to wake the neighbors, she rocked him until his anger softened into sleep. When Jotham went too quiet for too long, she pressed him against her skin and counted his breaths to keep him tethered.

Sometimes, when the house was finally still and the lamp guttered, Leah lifted both boys at once and carried them to the doorway. She stood in the threshold, where a person belongs neither to inside nor out, and let the night air lay its cool hand on their brows. "You will both live," she whispered into the dark, as if saying the words would teach the world the trick of them. "You will both live."

And the house, with its chalked lintel and its tired, faithful stones, held the promise she made until morning.

Eventually, Matthias returned and spoke not a word about his absence. His anger never fully resolved but tempered to be tolerable. In time he began to favor one child—the one he believed Leah had birthed. Anna, in his mind, could not have produced something so weak and sickly.

Mordecai, full of vigor and brute energy, became the son he invested in, assuming he was Leah's. Matthias poured his effort into shaping Mordecai into his heir.

Leah never corrected him. She wanted to—oh, how she wanted to—but the midwife's warning had sunk deep: *If he grows up marked as Anna's, Matthias may never let him live in peace.* So, she bore the secret in silence, letting Matthias believe his own story. Each time he set Mordecai at his side and waved Jotham away, Leah's throat burned with words she dared not speak. To defend Jotham was to expose them both, and to expose them was to endanger them.

She dealt with it as mothers often do—with the quiet work of love. She doubled her tenderness toward the boy Matthias despised, teaching him to read the ledgers, tracing letters into his small palm with her finger. She praised his patience when Matthias mocked it, gave him her stories when his father gave him nothing but silence. With Mordecai she was steady as well, though his temper strained her. She could not undo Matthias's favoritism, but she could soften its edges.

At night, when both boys slept, Leah sat in the dim glow of the oil lamp and prayed—not for Matthias to see rightly, for she had stopped expecting that—but for both her sons to endure. For one to remember he was not weak, and for the other to learn that strength was not cruelty. It was the only way she knew to keep Anna's memory alive and her household from shattering.

Jotham was not hated, just overlooked. His sisters adored him, though their fondness for him only deepened their resentment toward Mordecai. By nine, Mordecai towered over them, demanding obedience. Mealtimes became battlegrounds until Matthias declared Mordecai would eat with the men.

Encouraged by Matthias's rare and conditional praise, Mordecai cultivated dominance like a second skin. He strutted through the household with his chin high and voice raised, mimicking his father's tone with every word. He barked orders before he understood the tasks they belonged to. He pushed others down, not out of cruelty alone—but because it was the only way he knew to feel taller.

By eleven, he'd already learned what "strong" meant in Matthias's house: don't cry, speak loudly, move first, never flinch. He copied his father's hard voice and kept his shoulders squared like armor, hoping it would earn a nod. But beneath the show he was still a boy with a soft place he didn't understand, and he was sure that if he ever stopped acting tough, someone would see it—and laugh.

The fieldworkers saw it immediately.

Men with sun-darkened faces and stories in their calluses, they watched him warily, saying little. They'd known boys like him before—untested sons playing at command. And they'd seen what happened when such boys grew up unchecked.

The quarrel came late in harvest, the kind of day when the sun sits straight over your skull and even the flies move slow. Matthias had gone to Tamar to settle accounts. Twelve-year-old Mordecai watched him vanish in a shimmer of heat and felt something rise in his chest. Something that wasn't quite courage.

He strode to the barley strip where men worked in a rota—one crew binding sheaves, one gleaning the edges, one resting in the fig shade to keep heads from splitting in the noon glare. A goatskin hung from a branch, clay cups tucked in its shadow. Sickles lay on the ground teeth-up, a warning to clumsy feet.

"Clear this field by nightfall or go hungry," Mordecai shouted from the bank, planting his fists on his hips the way he'd seen Matthias do. A few heads lifted. Most did not. The binders kept their rhythm. In the shade, men rolled their shoulders and drank.

He marched to the fig tree, heat pushing sweat down his spine. "Up," he snapped, toeing a heel.

"No one told you to stop."

An older man—broad through the back, the kind whose hands remember every season's nerve—lifted his cup and took a slow sip. His name was Shimon, a tenant who'd saved a harvest once by reading the wind before a storm.

"We're on the turn," Shimon said, setting the cup down. "One crew works, one binds, one cools its blood. You don't reap men as if they were stalks."

Mordecai's face tightened. With a quick slap he knocked the cup into the dust, water darkening the ground between them. "You answer to me," he said. "Not the sun, not your bones."

He reached to grab the front of Shimon's tunic. The older man moved the way a millstone turns—without hurry, all weight. He caught the boy's wrist, rolled his shoulder, and set Mordecai on his knees before the boy understood how he'd left his feet. The grip wasn't cruel, just unbreakable.

"You'll stand when we stand," Shimon said, level as a plumb line. "The rota keeps men from dropping in the field. That's the custom here. Your father knows it."

Mordecai twisted and felt heat climb his neck, shame and fury pairing like twins. "I'll have your plot," he spat. "I'll see your sons begging bread."

A murmur ran along the shade line—not laughter, just a kind of tired warning. Another worker drew a whetstone along a sickle's teeth: skrr—skrr—skrr, the sound of patient work.

Shimon lifted Mordecai by the back of his tunic and set him on his feet. When he spoke again, the iron came into his voice.

"Listen, boy. We've cut on this land since before your mother bled her last. Don't make grown men choose between custom and a child's pride. You swing your words like a blade, but out here blades are real. Keep your hands down. Keep your mouth from writing debts your body can't pay."

The words landed harder than the grip had. Your mother bled her last. Not Leah's name. Not Anna's. Just *your mother*, as if the whole field knew a story Mordecai did not. Something cold opened under his ribs.

He looked past Shimon to the others—their sun-browned faces unreadable, their eyes not mocking, only sure. They were not afraid of him. Worse, they were measuring him and finding little to measure.

His mouth worked and found nothing. *I am the heir* would sound thin in the heat. *You don't know anything* felt like a child's cry.

He jerked his wrist free and stumbled back. Dust clung to his knees where they'd touched the ground—not in reverence, but in a lesson. The men didn't taunt him. They simply returned to their work: one crew rose, another took the fig shade, the whetstone sang its small, steady song.

That, somehow, burned most of all.

Mordecai turned and walked fast up the bank, then faster, until he was running. The field kept its rota without him. He did not go back that season, or the next.

At home, the women prepared the evening meal. With Matthias gone, their chatter was loose and light—flour on fingers, laughter on lips, the kind of sound Mordecai had never learned to trust.

He followed it through the house like a ghost trailing warmth, arriving at the garden where Jotham and the girls were gathering herbs and onions. He stood in the doorway, watching them.

Jotham—soft-voiced, delicate in his movements—laughing alongside Leila and Miriam. They never had to prove their worth. They had never been crushed beneath the weight of expectation. They had never looked into Matthias's eyes and seen disappointment masked as scorn.

Mordecai watched them, and what he felt wasn't just anger.

It was rage at being outside of something—something tender, something safe. They had each other. He had nothing but his own shadow. The memory of the fields still burned: the older men's laughter at his mistakes, the muttered curses when he tripped a yoke, the way they looked past him as if he were still a boy. He wanted them to bow their heads when he spoke, to stop questioning, to stop smirking. He wanted to matter.

And here were his siblings, laughing, weaving threads of closeness in a way he could never touch. Their safety felt like mockery. Their love, an insult. He stormed into the garden, fists clenched.

"Watch your step, Mordecai! You'll ruin dinner!" Leila called, not afraid yet, just irritated.

He didn't answer. He crossed the garden and yanked Jotham up by the tunic, lifting him off the ground with ease. The boy's thin frame only fed the fire in his chest.

"You worthless… thing," Mordecai hissed. "Not man, not woman. What are you even doing? Stop playing with the girls. You'll earn your keep, or you'll regret breathing."

Jotham gasped, feet dangling, eyes wide with panic. He wasn't even fighting back—that was the worst of it. No fire, no defiance, just silence. That silence mocked him louder than words ever could.

Leila darted forward, slapping Mordecai's arm. "Let him go!"

He flung the arm still holding Jotham, knocking the boy into Leila. They fell to the ground together, dazed.

Mordecai stood over them, voice sharp as flint. "Anyone else? No? Good. Jotham goes to the fields. He can fetch water if nothing else."

He never told the workers. Just sent the boy. Let him stumble. Let him taste humiliation too. Maybe then the world would stop laughing at Mordecai alone.

Jotham went, because he was too afraid not to. He trembled through the morning, skin pink with sun, fingers raw from lifting pails. But the men saw. They gave him shade. Water. Eventually, they passed him off to the miller, who needed a gentler hand for the stones anyway.

Jotham thrived where Mordecai had been broken.

That only made the hate worse.

Mordecai stayed home after that—ruling over the sisters with a mix of disdain and silence. He learned that his hands could control, and his voice could silence. It was enough. Until it wasn't.

By seventeen, Mordecai had found something new: strong wine from the presses outside Tamar and the sweet burn of date-wine sold in skins at the edge of the market. It numbed the emptiness. It warmed the ache where his mother's name should have been. With a cup in his fist he could laugh at his own stories, feel larger than the man he couldn't become.

The house had thinned around him. His older sisters had married—as was the custom—into their husbands' family courtyards, taking their dowries and their laughter with them. They visited on market days, arms full of bread or swaddles, then left at dusk to return to other hearths and mothers-in-law. The rooms felt longer after they were gone, the mortar quieter, Leah's steps slower. Jotham spent most days at the mill, his clothes ghosted white with flour. Mordecai told himself that the stillness suited him.

He returned to the fields only to drink. Work didn't suit him, so he told himself. He leaned on tools he didn't use, one heel dug in, giving orders no one followed. In the heat haze the men moved by their rota anyway—one crew binding, one gleaning, one resting in the fig shade. His barked words dried quicker than spilled water in the scorching heat. When a wineskin passed, he took it first. When a task was named, he named another and did neither.

Nights were worse. When the voices stopped and the wine wore off, he lay flat on the roof under a plain of stars and stared into the dark rafters of himself. Wind tugged at the edge of his cloak; the clay cooled beneath his back. He could hear Leah turn once, twice, on the mat below. He could hear Jotham come in late from the mill, careful with the latch. Mordecai swallowed, and in that space between swallow and sleep, he whispered things no one ever heard. Unfinished sentences, bargains with no partner.

He wanted to be respected.

He wanted men to pause when he spoke, to set down their cups and listen.

So, he kept drinking, because it was the only thing that made the room tilt his way, the only time his shadow looked long enough to step into. And when morning came, he washed his face at the jar, spat wine from his mouth, and told himself that today he would act the man Matthias expected—loud voice, hard spine, no flinch. By noon, he had a skin on his shoulder and a story in his teeth, and the field kept its rhythm without him.

He wanted to be feared.

But most of all, he wanted to be someone his father could love— if only for a moment.

And because he couldn't be, he made sure no one else could be either.

Matthias, blind to everything but the boy's potential, saw only strength in his son. "It's time he had a wife," he said. "A strong one. Someone who'll bring us a good alliance."

Mordecai married Lois in the spring of his nineteenth year. She was sixteen—wide-eyed, quiet, with hair the color of clay after rain. The match was Matthias's idea. "She's strong," he said, slapping Mordecai's back. "Good blood. Sturdy hips. Her father owes me."

Leah said nothing, but her fingers trembled as she helped braid Lois's wedding hair. That night, after the ceremony—barefoot dancers, figs, and bread passed hand to hand under a moon that watched too much. Leah pulled the girl aside.

"Take these," she whispered, pressing a cloth bundle into Lois's palm. Inside: acacia leaves, soaked in honey, and a ball of soft wool. "Use them. Quietly. Every time." She didn't explain, didn't need to. Lois nodded, fear and something like relief flickering across her face.

Two years passed. No children came. The whispers began—soft at first, then sharper, like stones underfoot. "Defective," some said.

"Barren," others muttered. Matthias grew restless. Mordecai said little, but his silence was heavy.

Only Leah knew the truth. And each month that passed with Lois' blood and without swelling, she lit a quiet oil lamp and thanked the dark.

When Leah could no longer protect her without risking Mordecai's wrath, she stopped.

Mordecai berated Lois constantly—defective, useless, weak. He grabbed, shoved, and struck. She lived in fear, tense as a pulled bowstring. Leah offered comfort, but even she had limits.

Lois coped in silence. She worked diligently, hoping to avoid his ire. Mordecai's cruelty wasn't just physical—it was total. He controlled the air she breathed.

Still, Lois endured.

Lois learned to endure Mordecai's anger in quiet, measured ways. Survival, for her, became an art—threaded with fear, but stitched through with stubbornness. The bruises didn't always show on the skin. More often, they hid in the tightness of her shoulders, the long silences she swallowed.

Leah became her lifeline. She brought herbs to ease the swelling, warm compresses for the aches. But more than that, she brought her presence—steady, watchful, tender. She never asked for details. She didn't need to. In the hush of twilight, when the house held its breath, Leah would brush Lois's hair or sit beside her, humming an old melody that remembered peace even when they didn't.

In stolen pockets of time—just before dawn—Lois reclaimed herself in slivers. She knelt by her garden patch, fingers working the soil with quiet reverence. She stitched and unstitched fabric until her hands remembered beauty, even if her heart couldn't feel it yet. These simple tasks grounded her. They gave her a rhythm that was hers alone, untouched by rage or demand.

And always, she prayed. Not loudly. Not for show. Just small whispers offered up into the night.

She didn't ask for deliverance, only endurance. A God who saw in secret became her refuge. In that hidden space, she gathered strength—not loud or triumphant, but rooted, like a plant clinging to life between stones.

It wasn't ease that sustained her. It was grit. It was Leah's quiet love. It was the fierce hope that maybe—someday—something might grow from the hollow places.

When Lois finally became pregnant, a strange hush fell over her spirit—half prayer, half dread. She had waited so long for this moment, yet it came wrapped in uncertainty. The tiny life growing inside her stirred a fragile sense of purpose, a flicker of light in the dim corners of her days. But always behind it, like a shadow, loomed Mordecai's expectations.

She carried the child carefully, moving through each day with measured breaths and cautious steps, trying not to draw his ire. Leah brought her herbs for strength, warm soup for the nausea, and whispered blessings for peace. But tension coiled through the household like smoke. Lois kept one hand protectively over her belly, often without realizing it.

When labor came, it was long and brutal. The midwife arrived just before dawn, her hands steady even as Lois cried out into a pillow to muffle the sound. And then—at last—a child. Small, wet, wailing. A daughter.

The moment the baby was placed in her arms, Lois wept—not from pain, but from the sudden, consuming love flooding her chest. The world narrowed to that tiny face—red, squalling, and perfect. In that instant, Lois knew she would burn the world to the ground to keep her safe.

But the air shifted when Mordecai entered the room.

He stood in the doorway, eyes narrowing as the midwife murmured the words he didn't want to hear. *A girl.*

His jaw tightened. "Another mouth," he muttered. "What use is a daughter?" He turned and walked out.

The air inside the house still reeked of blood and boiled herbs. Lois lay in the corner room, silent, too exhausted to weep. The child—a girl—slept at her side, unaware that her first breath had been met with clenched teeth and averted eyes.

But Mordecai was already gone by first light.

From that day on, he barely acknowledged the child. He refused to speak her name, referring to her only as *it* or *the whelp*. His disappointment twisted into bitterness, and he took it out on Lois— through coldness, through blame, through the back of his hand when no one else was looking.

Still, Lois loved fiercely. She wrapped her daughter in soft cloth and softer songs. She whispered old stories into her tiny ears and prayed for protection over her sleeping form. Each smile, each grasp of a small hand around her finger, became fuel for her endurance.

Her daughter Miriam was not a burden. She was a reason. A reason to resist despair. A reason to live. A reason to hope.

But hope was not evenly divided in the household. While Miriam gave Lois cause to endure, Mordecai chased his own cause—respect, numbers, and the weight of being taken seriously.

Mordecai rode into Tamar on a borrowed mule, the cracked leather reins biting his palm as he ran the figures again in his head. A trader from the hill towns had taken thirty sacks and paid for twenty-two—the shortfall neat as a cut in the ledger. Matthias's numbers crawled in the margin on a shard of pottery, an ostracon tucked in Mordecai's sleeve: simple, precise, and enough.

The storehouse stank of chaff and old oil. A balance scale sat near the doorway; a row of stone weights—polished, stamped with a city seal—waited on the shelf. The apprentice came first, all grin and swagger. "My master's out," he lied, glancing at the road.

Mordecai set the ostracon on the table and, without looking at the boy, nudged the two-shekel weight with a knuckle, feeling its true heft. "Tell him he can meet me here or at the archon's bench with this shard in my hand."

The boy's grin slipped. Moments later, the merchant came from the back, palms up, smile oiled.

"A misunderstanding," he began.

"No," Mordecai said, voice flat. "A subtraction."

He moved with the kind of stillness that crowds a room. He did not raise his voice. He did not bargain first. He put the trader at the scale and chose the city-stamped weights himself. When the apprentice tried to slip a lighter stone into the pan, Mordecai tapped it once with a fingernail and shook his head. "This one," he said, and set the proper weight down so gently it felt like a judgment.

"Thirty taken," he went on, sliding grains from one bowl to another in a measured fall. "Twenty-two paid. Eight owed—in silver, or in cloth and oil at fair measure." He held the merchant's eyes. "And one for the insult."

"Your father holds the contract," the merchant said, but the protest was breathless now.

"My father holds the mill," Mordecai replied. "I hold the account."

Silence stretched. Outside, a donkey stamped at flies. Inside, the scale settled, and the hiss of grain in the bowl stopped. At last, the merchant counted out silver—real weight, not promise—and added a bolt of dyed wool and a skin of oil. Mordecai did not smile. He pressed the ostracon's edge into soft wax, took a sealed receipt, and stepped back into the heat.

On the road out of Tamar, the hills opened, bleached and quiet. The mule's ears flicked. Mordecai let the reins go slack and let himself feel it: not joy, exactly. Visibility. At home, he was dismissed; in the field, he was measured and found lacking. But here—numbers, weights, the pause of another man's breath while a scale decided—the room had tilted toward him.

He did not go home.

A crooked sign swung above a low doorway—the Olive's Shadow. Inside smelled of sweat, vinegar, and spiced meat. Strong wine bled into clay cups. A lyre in the corner fumbled a melody. He tossed a coin, took a seat where he could see the door, and kept his back to the wall.

A girl with kohl on her eyes drifted near. "Company?" she asked. He waved her off without malice. "Just the drink." His eyes followed her anyway.

At the far table, men grumbled in low, sour voices—Roman taxes, unfair scales, caravans that shaved weight with clever sacks. Mordecai listened, letting the wine loosen the knot in his jaw without taking his hand from it.

"Fools," he said finally, just sharp enough to turn a head. "You sell to men who choose the weights. Make them use city-stamped stones. Weigh the silver yourself. Ask about their fodder—if they lie about feed, they lie about the bags."

A scar-browed man eyed him. "And you know this because?"

Mordecai took a slow sip and set the cup down where the table's wobble would not rattle it. "Because I made one pay today," he said. "In silver and wool. With a receipt sealed for the archon's shelf if he thinks to forget."

A few snorted; one nodded, reluctant. The girl with kohl laughed at a joke that wasn't his. The lyre missed another note.

He finished the cup and did not ask for another. He sat with the noise running over him and measured the room. Counting calmed him—fingers, breaths, the steady rasp of a man's knife on a skewer. In for four, out for six. He had taught himself that this year, when sleep hid behind roofs and stars: slow the exhale; let the body obey.

One day, he would count to stay conscious under a Roman vine staff. One day, he would measure the seconds between a question and an answer when a soldier's face told the truth, his mouth did not. He did not know that yet. But some piece of him was already practicing—holding still, choosing which words to spend, letting another man's anger burn out against his silence.

The talk at the far table turned to roads—where the milestones were newly set, which patrols drank at which springs. Mordecai cataloged details without intending to, tucking them away like coins. Power, he was learning, was not loud. It was the right weight, at the right moment, set down without tremor.

When he rose, he left two coppers and the emptiness of a chair that had almost learned to hold him. Outside, the heat had softened; dust lifted from the road in little breaths and settled again. He stood a moment in the doorway and looked toward the hills where the path broke in two. One ribbon curling toward home, the other running along the ridge toward other accounts that might want settling.

For a heartbeat, he pictured the courtyard as it would be now: Leah's lamp a small, patient flame; the rooms quieter for the sisters who had married into other houses. Jotham no longer slept there—he had taken over the mill, living among the stones and grain, steady in a way that only deepened Mordecai's resentment. The family house, once crowded, felt longer in the silences between Leah's steps. And still, the wail of an infant daughter filled the air—a child who, in her father's eyes, would never count as an heir. Mordecai pressed his thumb into the wax seal until it cracked.

Then he swung into the saddle.

The mule flicked an ear. The road took him. He did not look back. He did not hurry. The light leaned. His shadow walked beside him, finally long enough to measure. Mordecai kept pace with it, counting his breaths—four in, six out—like a man learning how to live inside a body that might yet obey.

CHAPTER 4
THE HIDDEN PATH TO FREEDOM

Years passed, measured less by seasons than by children's cries and the steady grind of grain. Mordecai was nearing thirty now, heavy with the certainty of his own authority. Lois, twenty-seven, had already borne three children—Miriam with her sharp eyes at eight, Ruth with her quick laughter at six, and little Caleb, still unsteady at three. Photine, not yet eighteen, had long since crossed the threshold from girl to woman, though in this house her youth still clung to her like a garment others would not let her shed.

As the weeks bled into months and then years, Photine learned the uneasy rhythm of life as Mordecai's second wife. The house itself taught her—its courtyard opening to the sky like a held breath, the soot-smudged tabun oven whispering heat into dawn, the two worn quern stones sleeping against the wall until hands woke them. The rooms were narrow; footsteps carried. Nothing stayed secret for long except what women kept together.

Lois moved through the space as if she'd been born to its turns and thresholds—oil lamp nested in the crook of her hand, shawl gathered tight when strangers passed the gate. Photine watched the pattern: when Lois paused before speaking, when she pressed her lips thin and called the children close, when she smoothed the air with a lullaby even as her shoulders ached. There was sorrow in Lois, yes, but an iron filament, too—thin, unbreakable, running the length of her spine.

Mordecai's moods set the weather. Some mornings he rose with forced cheer, tossing a date into his mouth, jabbing at Jotham's absence as if the mill's steady hum were an insult. Other days, he returned from Tamar with wine on his breath and grand plans in his tongue, only to fall asleep in the corner before he finished the sentence. By evening, he might wake hungry for power more than food, looking for a face to blame for the emptiness he could not name.

Photine learned the house's unspoken rules quickly. Speak softly when the amphorae are low and the noon heat is cruel. Keep the tabun fed with thorn and chaff; bake early; store flatbreads in a linen wrap near the cool jar. Avoid the courtyard when a neighbor man lingers at the gate. Be in motion when Mordecai steps over the threshold: hands busy, gaze level, voice even. Above all, read the air the way a miller reads wind.

Lois taught her the rest. "Never meet rage head-on," she said once, shelling chickpeas into a wide bowl. The shells chimed softly against clay. "Step aside and let it spend itself." Then, after a silence, "Still, there are times to plant your feet."

From the start, the women found a phrase for the surface of things: *as custom*, the polite fiction that everyone agreed to, so the day could go on. Under that fiction, they built another truth: a quiet conspiracy of care.

When Photine's first bleeding returned after the weeks of mourning, Lois caught her wrist gently and led her to the small inner room. The shutter was pinned half-open; light entered like water. Lois set a small jar on the reed mat and loosened the stopper.

"From Leah," she said. "Passed to me when I married, and to you now. Acacia and honey, and a fold of soft wool. Use it." She held Photine's gaze. "You do not owe this man your womb."

The mixture smelled faintly of sap and sweetness. The gesture smelled of mercy. Photine swallowed. There were so few spaces in this world where a woman could call any part of herself her own. Here was one. She nodded and closed her hand around the jar.

In return, Photine shared what she had salvaged from her father's teaching—a kind of inner weather sense. "When a man roars," she told Lois, "he's often trying to drown the smaller noise in his chest. If you listen for that smaller sound—the fear—you'll know which way he'll turn." She taught Lois the habit her father had loved: three breaths longer on the exhale than on the inhale. It slows the heart; it steals the edge from terror.

They found each other in the ordinary work—kneading dough, hauling water from the public trough, trading a bundle of dried mint for a scoop of salt, matching steps with other women under baskets on the path. At the communal oven, they learned who among the neighbors could be trusted and who greeted with a sweet word and a bitter mouth. At the well, women turned their faces toward each other to hide tears under laughter; hands brushed along the jar handles in greeting and promise.

As Lois's belly swelled with her fourth child, the house shifted to meet her pace. Photine carried the heavier jars, stoked the tabun, and went to market in her place. The pregnancy reached for Lois as if tugging her from the inside—an ache in her hips, a fatigue gathering behind her eyes. Photine watched the way she held her back; she warmed water with thyme and poured it over Lois's hands at day's end as if pouring a blessing.

"This one is different," Lois admitted once, voice thin as the edge of a clay cup. "The others swam. This one… drags."

"Then we go slowly," Photine said. "We move like women who intend to live."

The night labor began, even the wind seemed to hold its breath. The courtyard stones, warmed by the afternoon, exhaled their heat in slow waves. The midwife came in before full dark, her sandals dusted, her hands scrubbed with ash and oil. She set down her basket: clean linen strips, a small knife, sprigs of hyssop, a clay lamp, a narrow-necked bottle of oil.

Lois's pains came like the beat of a distant drum—far, then near, pulling her under and letting her surface. Photine cooled cloths and counted in her head, marking the time between waves. She rubbed Lois's lower back when the pain climbed. She dabbed her lips with water when her mouth went dry. The midwife's face betrayed little, but her movements spoke—less talk, more hands, an extra strip of linen set within reach.

"It's too soon," Lois whispered once, fingers clenching Photine's shawl.

"I know," Photine said. "But you are not alone."

When the child came, she came quiet and blue-gray. The midwife rubbed her chest, puffed her breath into the baby's lungs, tapped the soles of tiny feet. Silence held. At last, the midwife wrapped the infant in cloth because that is what you do for the living and the dead, and set her in Lois's arms.

"A girl," she said, and the word was not a judgment but a naming.

Lois traced a tiny eyebrow with a shaking finger and pressed her lips to a cool forehead. "I had dreamed of your laughter," she murmured. "Go with God."

Photine did not look away. There is a tenderness reserved for the moments when love arrives and cannot stay; she let that tenderness fill the room without reaching for any words to tame it.

Before dawn, the midwife, Leah, and Photine prepared the little body. No wailing procession, no long prayers—just a strip of linen, a soft wrap, a small hollow in the family plot where wild thyme grows. The earth received what it is always ready to receive. Lois stayed inside, a low moan working through her like a thread knotting and unknotting itself.

In the days that followed, they walked carefully through the house as if it were a sleeping animal. The children learned to set their voices down gently. Lois moved like a woman who had given blood to the ground and was waiting for it to grow into something she could carry. Photine kept watch the way hill shepherds do—without rest, eyes tuned to the edges.

Grief can harden a person or make space inside her for other lives to fit. In Lois, grief made room. She leaned into Photine's shoulder without apology. She accepted the cup of broth; she allowed herself to be guided to the mat when she swayed. In that brokenness, the women's pact held. But survival, once learned, is not the only curriculum. The women began to plan.

Photine could not settle. Not truly. The rooms grew familiar, the rhythms tolerable, but she never let her roots sink too deep. At night, with the children pressed to sleep in their corners, she would take out the shard of olive wood her father had given her. *One day you'll be given its twin,* he had whispered before he vanished. She still believed it, or forced herself to. That promise, more than Mordecai's house, was her home.

Her usefulness was her shield—keeping accounts, measuring grain, bartering with vendors. But usefulness was not belonging. She wanted more than survival. She wanted her father, her freedom, and the other half of that olive wood.

Perhaps it was inevitable, then, that she began slipping coins. A clipped drachma here, a clipped denarius there—small enough to escape Mordecai's anger, but noticeable to grow his suspicion. He watched her more closely, questioned her errands, and scowled when she lingered too long at the market.

Leah and Lois saw it too. They read the tightening of his jaw, the way his hand hovered at his belt when Photine passed too near. They understood that suspicion left unchecked would bloom into something worse. So, they devised a plan—not for rebellion, but for survival.

They did not call it escape. They called it sending Photine to safety. Language matters in a house where names can bless or bruise.

The plan was simple because simple plans live longer: sell what could be sold without notice—a skein of dyed wool here, a pinch of saffron wrapped in waxed linen there, a small jar of almond oil traded for coins. Hide the coins not under a loose tile, but in a thumb-sized jar set into a wall niche in the cellar, tucked behind a wax-sealed amphora—the cellar wall itself keeping the secret.

On market days, Photine practiced walking like a woman who belonged to no one—back straight, gaze respectful but not deferent, hands steady. She learned which vendors would pass a folded cloth with a coin stitched into the edge and which would talk too loudly about bargains. She mapped the secondary paths—the goat tracks running behind stone walls, the gap between two compounds where a woman could slip if a man were shouting in the street.

They allowed time to do its work. Plans that ripen slowly are harder to see.

The night that forced the choice came like a storm with no wind. Mordecai lurched in with wine in his throat and insult on his tongue. He raked a jar from the shelf; it burst, oil bleeding across the floor as if the clay itself had cut an artery. Then—eyes on Photine—he hooked his heel under the wreckage and kicked. A fan of shards skittered through the slick. One caught her ankle and opened it clean, a bright line of blood threading the oil.

She did not cry out. You can teach your mouth to save your skin.

"She's not yours to break," Lois said. Not loud. Not defiant. Just iron laid on velvet. Mordecai's lip curled. He spat on the floor and lurched into the night.

They did not sleep. Before the first swallows stitched light into the sky, Lois watched him stagger toward the fields, shoulders tilted, mouth moving. She turned and found Photine already binding the small bundle—bread, a cloth of dates, a second shawl, the little jar of acacia and honey wrapped like a relic.

"It's time," Lois said.

They did not weep or clutch hands or rehearse what was already known. Photine kissed the top of the littlest one's head where curls made a crown. Caleb had been born just 3 years ago, Lois's only son. She touched the doorway lintel with her fingers and then her lips, a habit she had brought from childhood. Lois opened the back gate.

"Go by the animal pens," she said. "Hadassah waits. From there, the long path."

It had been arranged in whispers days before—Lois sending word through a borrowed spindle, Leah nodding toward the lamps at dusk. Hadassah knew when Mordecai left and what the signal meant.

Photine went.

She kept low along the courtyard's blind side, moving when roosters crowed so feet shuffling would sound like wing beats. The village smelled of damp straw and ashes doused. Her shawl pressed rain-cool against her neck, though the rain was days past. She passed a sleeping donkey that blinked once and let her be. At the alley's bend, a scrawny cat threaded her ankles, pausing to sniff the blood-soaked gauze on the injured ankle, as if it knew a woman on the threshold of a decision when it saw one.

Hadassah's door opened the width of a hand and then enough for a body. Inside the animal room, the warmth was thick and musky; goats shifted, hooves clicking quietly. Photine folded herself behind a sack of barley stacked high as a woman's shoulder. Hadassah pressed a fig into her palm and kissed her forehead the way old women do when blessing costs less than bread.

"Wait," Hadassah whispered. "Listen. Leave only when the sound you fear is farther away than the sound you hope for."

Photine waited. The day unrolled itself: a bucket rattling at the well, a child's sudden cry, the swish of brooms, a quarrel swallowed by birdsong. When the alley quieted to the soft collusion of women's work, she stood, wrapped her shawl higher, and went out the back way.

The world outside the village was not safer; it was merely wider. Roman patrols liked the main road and the springs. *Avoid water in daylight*, the women had warned; *thirst draws soldiers the way light draws moths.* Photine walked the high goat paths where the stone breaks into thorn and wild thyme, where men do not bother because haste and horses cannot live there. She kept her sandals tight. She scanned for whelps of jackal and left them their peace.

By the second night, she knew which olive trees carried a hollow, where a body can curl unseen. On the third morning, she learned where snakes like to lie and how to thump her walking stick along the rock to send them elsewhere. She learned the generosity of the land: a fig split and perfect; a handful of capers near a wall; a spring that only reveals itself by the dark line it draws through stone.

Messages moved the way water does in a city that has learned drought: quietly, relentlessly, downhill to where they are needed. At a shared oven, a woman told another woman to tell a cousin that a shawled stranger should avoid the crossroads near the stone with the carved bird. At the well, a girl handed a jar to a man who was not her kin, and the man carried the jar to a place beyond the threshing floor where a second jar waited with water under a cloth. No one spoke Photine's name. Names are nets; she needed air.

One night, as Photine tucked herself into the lee of a limestone outcrop, footsteps stitched the gravel. Her hand found a smooth stone. Then a whisper: "Photine."

She knew the voice: Sarah, Hadassah's niece, a runner of messages who could carry three loaves on her head and a rumor in her sleeve without dropping either.

"We must go," Sarah said. "Now. A merchant waits near the wadi. He will take you under his protection."

Photine's body shuddered with the hunger that comes after fear yawns and closes: she needed sleep more than food. She did not need to be taken anywhere by any man. Sarah put a hand to her forearm.

"He is Ezra," she said. "Widower. Not greedy. He gave his sister a plot in his courtyard when her husband left, and no man does that without kindness. If you refuse, he will still give you a loaf and show you a safe mile. He made me promise I would say this exactly." Photine nodded once and rose.

They walked the olive groves like shadows, counting the between-spaces—walls, cistern mouths, sheepfolds. Near the streambed, where the water carved a shallow S, and tamarisk leaned in to listen, a man stood beside a laden donkey. He straightened when he saw them and did not take a step closer.

"Peace to you," he said. No reach of hand. No possessive gaze. "I am Ezra. If you come, I will give you my protection as far as you choose to take it. If you will not, I will still give you bread, water, and a blanket for the cold part of the night."

Photine searched his face. It was the kind of face life makes when it is finished with arrogance—a weathered kindness, an alertness without hunger. She wanted to say no because saying no is sometimes the only way to hear your own voice. She wanted to say yes because her feet were bleeding and her mind had counted threats until numbers lost meaning.

"If I come," she said, "you will not call me wife until I call myself that."

Ezra bowed his head once. "I will call you a guest. And I will keep that vow even if men ask questions."

The donkey blew softly, grass-scented breath in the night. Photine thought of Lois—of the lamp set in the window each dawn like a small promise. She thought of the women's coin jar hidden in the wall and the slow braid of courage it had taken to fill it. She thought of the threshold she had crossed with her fingertips against the lintel and found herself whispering a prayer. Not for safety. For steadiness.

"For now," she said, and stepped to the donkey's flank.

Ezra did not move to help. He only adjusted the pack so the load balanced better and gestured toward the upstream path where patrols rarely bothered. They walked until the moon slid down the sky on its own feet and the first bird cleared its throat. When they made a small nest of cloaks behind a fall of rock, Ezra slept turned away, a forearm folded under his head, his knife out but sheathed. Photine stared at the slow rise and fall of his back until her eyes shut without her permission.

Back at the house, Lois felt the hour when the fear eased. People who live in the same rooms for long years can feel each other at a distance like wind on skin. She lit a lamp in the window alcove before dawn—something she did after Photine left—and watched its small flame tremble once, then stand.

When Mordecai returned three days later and banged the gate wide with his palm, Lois had words ready. Words are tools; she had honed these to a bright edge.

"She's gone," she said, holding out a pouch whose weight he could feel. "There was a rift in the house. You know how it's been— tempers short, children unsettled. She said she would not stay where she was not wanted. A merchant passed through yesterday. I bargained with him high. The coin eases the loss."

It was a lie told cleanly, but not carelessly. She kept her jaw loose, her gaze level. She did not over-explain. Men who want reason will supply their own.

Mordecai stared at the coins, his lips curling as if silver itself had insulted him. "She took from me. I knew it. Little things gone missing, too small for anyone else to notice. You think she slipped out clean, but she was a thief from the start."

His voice was low, but the promise in it was sharp: if she lived, he would find her.

The room swallowed him as a boulder swallows a thrown fruit—leaves a stain, keeps its shape.

He did not speak Photine's name again. He began to prowl the edges of market talk, throwing questions like ropes to see what might catch—any rumor of a shameless woman, any mention of a stranger in a gray shawl. The sisterhood—Hadassah, Sarah, the oven-keeper Miryam, the midwife with her eyes like evening—and they turned his questions the other way. A shelf in the oven was always full when Mordecai arrived; jars were swapped; the woman at the well whose tongue loved malice found herself busy elsewhere whenever his shadow crossed.

Lois lived like a woman who had shoved a stone under a door to keep it open just enough for air to move. She did not relax. She kept the children in her sight. She hid the little lamp Photine had made her, the one with vines scratched around the base, then brought it out at dawn to feed its wick a thimble of oil and set it in the window. A light. A prayer. A rebellion that the women and the children understood.

Leah said little. She moved through the rooms with the same measured steps as always, but her silence carried a new hollowness. Jotham's death had already carved her in half. Photine had been the one thread left to that softer part of her—the girl who had loved

Jotham, the woman who had kept his steadiness alive. Now that thread was gone too. At night, when the house settled, and even Mordecai's mutterings fell quiet, Leah would sit by the doorway, her hands idle for once, eyes fixed on nothing, as if listening for two voices she would never hear again.

"Where Auntie go?" Caleb asked, curling into her lap each night with his curls damp from sleep.

"To a better place," Lois said, and for once the phrase felt like truth, not a lullaby.

Sometimes, after the children's breathing settled and Mordecai's footsteps took to the roof to walk off his wine, Lois allowed herself a quiet pride. Not the pride that puffs up and demands notice, but the one settling in the bones and says, *I did what love required.* She had chosen a lie that gave another woman a life. Let the men choke on honor. She would take freedom.

News of Ezra and Photine traveled the way the best news does— arriving not as a trumpet but as a handful of certainty placed into a palm, heavy enough to matter. A trader's wife in a town to the west told a cousin who sent word by a boy who carried pigeons. "She is safe," the message said. "She eats bread at a table and sleeps under a roof. The man calls her a guest."

Lois read the words with the greed of the starving and then folded them very small and tucked them in the hem of her shawl where cloth thickens. She did not let herself picture Photine's face too clearly; the ache would have doubled. Instead, she pictured hands—Photine's hands lifting a bowl, tying a cord, smoothing a child's hair—and let that be enough.

Around Lois, the old house shifted again—not because daughters married out, but because little lives grew louder inside its walls. Miriam was quick-eyed and solemn when guests were near. Ruth was forever spinning stories at the hearth. Caleb trailed after Lois with sticky hands and questions that came out like songs. They learned what children always do: which floorboards give, what silence means danger, and what silence means safety; how to read their mother's hand as she reaches without looking for a falling cup. Miriam stopped asking questions she knew no one would answer. Ruth told tales of queens and clever foxes and women who turned into birds when men tried to cage them. Caleb kept a place in his small heart shaped like Photine and did not know it.

It was not only Jotham's absence hanging over them, but something older, heavier—a shadow passed from father to son, husband to wife, house to house. A curse that taught men to roar and women to endure.

Matthias—once flint, then weathered oak—began to forget the names of tools and the path from his mat to the door. His hands trembled; his anger, when roused, burned without aim and then guttered. Some days, he sat under the olive tree with crumbs on his tunic, watching the lane as if it might hand him back a missing word. Other days, he wandered to the gate and stood there, muttering accounts only he could see.

And Leah—who had held a house together with bread and song—would not let grief make her a liar. She had stopped pretending that cruelty was strength. When Mordecai swaggered, she did not praise him. When he snapped, she did not soothe him. "Not in my hearing," she said once, low but edged, when his hand twitched toward a child. She kept her dissent small and steady—turning her back, setting a bowl down harder than needed, refusing a false blessing—the kind of resistance that teaches a room which way the truth faces.

She tended Matthias because love required it, and she guarded the children with her presence. But she knew, as all women in that house knew, that the curse was not gone. It still breathed in the walls, waiting to speak through another man's mouth.

Mordecai carried himself like a man who thinks a posture is a self. He kept ledgers by lamplight and spoke with traders as if the grain moved at his word. He counted breaths when rage climbed—a habit learned by accident and sharpened by practice. If anyone asked where the second wife had gone, he grunted something about a sale and turned the talk to weights and measures.

In the morning, the quiet news of Photine's safety—carried along the roads from Akrabbim to the northern reaches near En-Dor— finally reached them. Lois went to the olive tree in the courtyard and pressed her forehead to its trunk. The bark patterned her skin. Leah stood a pace behind her, palm flat to the same tree—two women anchoring a house that had endured too much weather.

Lois whispered thanks to the God who hears in secret, and to the women whose courage does not wear a sword. Then she returned to the kitchen, lit the oil lamp with the vine-scratched base, and set the dough to rise.

Work waited. Bread must be baked, garments washed, little bodies scrubbed of dust, old hands held steady while a cup meets a lip. Matthias needed guiding to shade in the heat; Leah needed her shawl settled when the evening wind stole her warmth. Lois did it all with the steadiness of someone who knows salvation is not a single event but a stitching—a thousand small threads pulled through the same cloth until the tear holds.

The physician called it a wasting of the mind, a rot beginning in the blood and moving inward, like mold on bread. Whatever pride Matthias still clung to shriveled. He stopped going to the mill altogether, and when Mordecai questioned him, the old man flew into a fury, only to collapse into vacant silence moments later.

By the end of that year, Matthias was a ghost tethered to a broken body. He stared at the walls for hours, eyes clouded, hands trembling. His anger would be the last part of him to leave.

And Leah—who had once carried fire in her voice and in the rhythm of her cooking—withered beside him.

She had once ruled the kitchen with music in her hands, the scent of lentils and cumin dancing through the courtyard like a promise. Her laughter, once sharp as pomegranate wine, had held the household together when silence threatened to split it apart. There were times when Lois swore Leah could stir peace into a pot simply by the way she moved her spoon.

But that Leah was gone.

The warmth Lois and Leah had once shared—the sisterhood, the secrets, the tears over late-night cups of wine—seemed now like a dream Lois had dreamt alone.

Even the fire, the defiance Leah once wore like a second skin, had gone quiet. She no longer defended herself against Mordecai's mutterings. No longer shielded her grandchildren. She simply folded into herself, shrinking from the world like a shadow at dusk.

Ever since Jotham's death, she had unraveled slowly, almost invisibly—as a garment left too long in the sun, losing color thread by thread until only shape remained.

Sometimes, when dusk laid its blue hand on the courtyard, and lamps winked one by one along the lane, Leah hummed a tune she had not let herself sing since Jotham's last morning. It was not loud. It did not ask permission. It ran under the ground of the day like a thin river, moving whether men noticed or not. And in that sound, Lois felt something answer—a quiet joy that did not cancel sorrow, only kept it company.

Somewhere beyond the ridge, a woman walked under a sky she could claim with her own eyes, beside a man who did not take what was not offered, counting her breaths—until the dark loosened and morning put its hand on her shoulder. Back at the house, the lamp in the window burned small and sure—Leah's dissent, Lois's prayer, the children's future—one shared flame holding against the night.

As for Mordecai, he paced and questioned, and then, when questions failed to gather more than dust, he turned his attention back to accounting. He found that numbers obeyed him in ways people did not. He began to practice a different kind of control: stillness. He learned to set a coin on a table without tremor, to choose the stamped city weight over the trader's personal stones, to measure out grain with a flat of the hand and not the hunger of the gut. He filed away routes and patrols, which archon listens to and which watches, which spring a cohort favors and which they spoil. The habit would save him later. He did not know that yet.

The house did not turn gentle. There were still nights when wine drove Mordecai's feet to kick at the threshold and his tongue to look for targets. There were still mornings when Leah stared at a wall long enough for the light to change twice upon it. But there was also this: a lamp in the window, vines etched around its belly, flame no bigger than a fig seed, burning because women decided it would. A sign. A secret. A prayer the house could keep without speaking.

And that, in a world where men wrote contracts and soldiers wrote fear, was a kind of power.

CHAPTER 5
MORE THAN SHELTER

The road was quiet beneath the stars, the hush of wind in the olive trees the only sound between them. Photine sat beside Ezra on the low cart, a head scarf drawn close around her face, a veil that kept her from the eyes of strangers. A rough cloak that smelled of cedar wrapped her shoulders, its weight both foreign and reassuring.

Her hands, still marked by the life she'd escaped, were folded tightly in her lap. She kept her eyes on the horizon, where the track from the northern skirts of Akrabbim stretched toward the hill country of Ephraim—the long road carrying them on to En-Dor. Ezra did not press her with questions.

The road itself became her answer. For nine days, they had been traveling north since Sarah first brought her to him. They traveled past the edge of Akrabbim, climbing out of the Arabah by Tamar (the oasis some old traders still called Thamara), sleeping once beneath the walls at Moa, skirting the Arad heights, then following the ridge road through the hill country until the outlines of Moreh and Tabor began to rise ahead, blue shoulders lifting against the sky.

The road wound northward through the hill country, carved between olive groves and dry ravines. It was spring, but the earth still carried winter's fatigue—dusty, cracked in places, generous in others. Wild thyme perfumed the breeze. A pair of vultures circled lazily overhead.

Ezra spoke softly, when he spoke at all—about the way the stars shifted from east to west, or how the donkeys walked straighter uphill than on flat ground. He commented on which fig trees were likely to bear early, and once told a story about a boy who tried to plant barley upside-down. He never looked at her when he spoke. He seemed to speak to the trail, to the trees, to the space between their footsteps, letting the words drift like seeds across still water.

She didn't answer most of the time. She didn't know how. Every other man she'd known had used silence as a weapon. With Ezra, silence felt like permission. Like a blanket wrapped around tired limbs. Like air, finally, without tension.

They camped the first night on a slope just beyond a cluster of thornbushes. He built the fire small, low to the ground, shielded from view. She watched him move—quiet, competent, never hurried. He gave her a blanket without comment and placed his pack several paces away before lying down with his back to her, leaving space between them like it was something sacred.

In the dark, she listened to the night insects and the occasional cough of the donkeys. Ezra breathed slow and steady, like someone long used to traveling with only himself for company.

Photine could not match his calm. Her thoughts kept circling back to Akrabbim. Had Mordecai discovered her absence yet? Had Lois managed to keep her story clean, her face steady? Were the children safe under his suspicion? The fear that she had dragged them into danger knotted her stomach tighter than hunger.

She had never been able to settle into the life Mordecai demanded. She had stolen coin, told half-truths, and courted his anger with her restless questions. She had set the fuse that might now be burning back toward Lois and the little ones. Her freedom came at their risk, and the weight of it made her chest ache.

Still, beneath the guilt there was something else—something sharper, harder to name. She had refused to be erased. She had chosen not to vanish inside a life that was not her own. That choice was dangerous. It was also the only thing that still felt true.

She lay with her eyes open to the stars until sleep crept up on her like an unwelcome hand, shallow and restless.

By the second day, her body had begun to adjust to the rhythm of the road. The ache in her feet dulled to a throb, and the sun on her shoulders no longer felt like punishment. Ezra showed her a shortcut through a grove of almond trees, and she startled when he reached up, snapped off a branch, and handed her a few tender buds.

"They taste bitter," he said, "but they clean the mouth after too much dust."

She took them. Ate them. Said nothing.

That evening, they camped beneath a cluster of cedars, high enough for a view of the road behind. As the fire crackled low, he offered her the last of the dried figs without asking anything in return. Then he sat quietly, carving something into a bit of wood with a small, curved blade—hands busy, eyes down.

She watched the firelight play across the lines of his face and wondered—not what kind of man he was, but how long it would take before she believed he wasn't pretending.

He had not asked about her past. He had not asked for anything.

And still, something inside her had begun—just barely—to unclench.

"I once saw a market in Petra," he said on their second night, as they camped near a dry wadi. "The stone walls shine rose red at sunset. A woman there traded dyed cloths from Babylon. Fierce woman—sharper than the traders who tried to cheat her. She taught me how to spot a false weight in a scale."

Photine watched him quietly, skeptical. "And you learned from a woman?"

Ezra gave a small shrug. "Of course. She knew what I didn't. I listen to anyone with wisdom—doesn't matter the shape it wears."

That caught her off guard. Mordecai would've laughed at the idea, or worse.

They traveled on, and the silence between them softened. Photine began to ask questions about trade routes, bartering tricks, the best times to cross certain roads. Ezra answered freely, with a teacher's patience and a traveler's wit.

"You have a mind for this," he told her after she negotiated a good price for a bundle of spices in a small village. "Sharper than mine in some ways. You should handle the bargaining from now on."

She blinked at him. "You'd trust me with that?"

Ezra nodded. "It's your life too. Why shouldn't you have a hand in building it?"

That night, as they sat by the fire, Photine held a clay cup of warm fig-wine and let herself believe that she was not only surviving, but becoming someone new. She studied Ezra across the firelight: the way his shoulders eased when he spoke, the steadiness of his gaze when he listened. The thought pressed in on her unbidden—*what would it mean to call him husband? To be called wife, but by choice, not by contract or command?*

The idea unsettled her. Jotham had given her gentleness, but not desire. Mordecai had taken everything by force. What lived between those two poles, she did not yet know. She only knew that Ezra's patience left her room to imagine.

Still, shadows of her past clung close. There were nights when a raised voice in a tavern made her flinch, or when she woke suddenly, unsure where she was. But Ezra never questioned her silences. When she couldn't speak, he filled the space with stories of cities he'd loved or foods he missed. He never pressed her, never demanded. She began to laugh again—quietly at first, then freely. Her own voice sounded strange and bright in her ears.

They did not hurry. Ezra kept his pace for the donkeys, not for pride. "If a day gives you a few safe miles," he once said, "take the miles—and the safety." They started before first light, when the stars were still close, and the desert smelled like stone and cold iron. At dawn, the wind lifted, pushing the last coolness off the Arabah floor. By midday, Photine's steps had found the caravan rhythm—walk, breathe, count seven, sip; walk, breathe, count seven, sip.

On the third evening, they reached the Arad heights, the old ridge way-station by the fortress cistern. A toll-keeper in a sun-bleached tunic sat at a rough table beneath a tamarisk, recording names and weights and making a show of his seal. Ezra greeted him with the patient courtesy of a man who had learned that smiles travel faster than horses. They paid a small toll in salt and kept their goods unprodded. Near the fort wall, a water-seller hawked skins that tasted faintly of goat and resin. Photine traded a pinch of cumin for a cleaner strap, and the woman winked without words. The oasis had that sound caravans make when they stop: leather settling, animals sighing, the clack of a loose pot lid, someone laughing too loud because they are where the knives aren't.

That night, by a shared fire, a Nabataean boy showed Photine how to knot a lead rope around a donkey's jaw so an opportunist couldn't lift the animal and vanish by moonlight. Ezra said nothing, watched her hands mirror the knot on the second try, and passed her the figs first.

On the fourth day, they pushed north along the incense road and slept outside Moa, the caravanserai whose stones still held heat after dark. A spice factor was present, as they tried to buy the smaller of their two donkeys at a price that seemed fair to anyone who had not taken into account the cost of fodder or winter. Photine did the sums out loud, deducted shoeing, added the price of barley after harvest, and smiled the way women smile when men expect them not to. The factor folded. Ezra's mouth curved, not at the win, but at the way she had made the arithmetic sing.

On the fifth, the land turned rough and then rougher, the road climbing out of the long spine of the Arabah toward the Negev skirts. The wind rose and the dust with it, stinging their faces until they looked like they'd been sanded. Photine wrapped her scarf higher. When her steps grew short and hard, Ezra did not tell her to rest. He pointed to the shadow line on the slope. "Walk in the shade of that boulder, and you'll steal three breaths for free." She did. It helped. By noon, they were higher than hawks, or so it felt.

They camped within sight of the Arad heights. Below the ridge lay the ghost of an ancient city—the kind whose walls still remember the hands that laid them. A shepherd from the foothills stopped at their fire and traded a story for bread: how, in the last rains, lightning had struck the old fortress and made glass out of sand along one edge. Photine listened, chin in her palms, and told him a story back—of a miller who could tell wheat from barley with his eyes closed and both hands tied. When he laughed, it startled her; she had not thought stories could be traded like any other good.

On the sixth day, they angled into the hill country proper. The air cooled, the light changed, and the way the wind moved through groves of terebinth and olive made a sound like someone reading scripture too softly to scold you. Ezra's talk turned from distances to springs—which ones were clean after a rain, which ones tasted of sulfur, which ones were worth the detour when you were carrying pottery you didn't want to break. Photine put the knowledge in order in her head the way she would have organized a ledger: left bank, right bank, brackish, sweet.

At a way-station north of Hebron, a man with a chest like a bread oven and hands like paddles laid a set of weights on a table that would have cheated a bishop's mother. Ezra's face stayed pleasant. Photine leaned in so the light caught the bronze—saw the shave at the base where someone had filed a breath off each stone. "Your mina is thin," she said, and touched the tiniest one with her nail. "And this half is a hungry little liar." The man blinked, feigned offense, and then—catching Ezra's stillness and the sensible weight of the small knife at his belt—offered to fetch a different set. "Of course," Photine said. "Fetch the ones you use for your sister." Ezra coughed a laugh into his sleeve that sounded like a man refusing to be proud.

They took the ridge road north instead of drifting to the coast. It was slower, safer, and threaded the villages where someone always knew someone who knew Ezra. They slept two nights in upper rooms where children stared from behind doorways and grandmothers brought water with mint, and said things like, "You are too thin," whether it was true or not.

On the road, Photine learned the market accents—how Galilean vowels fell soft, how Samaritan traders clipped them short, how a Roman's Aramaic was a sandal on the wrong foot. Ezra let her make the small purchases and most of the trades. When someone tried to wave her off with, "We'll speak to the man," Ezra tilted his head toward the ledger in her hands and said, "You already are."

Something shifted in her then. The words landed not as a courtesy but as recognition. For so long, "wife" had meant property, silence, erasure. But here, in the dust of the ridge road, she saw another meaning of wife—partnership, voice, belonging. That night, as they ate bread dipped in oil beneath a fading sky, she set her cup down and spoke before she could lose her nerve.

"If they ask," she said softly, not looking up at first, "I am your wife."

Ezra's hand stilled, then lowered in quiet acknowledgment. He did not press her with questions or oaths. He only bowed his head and said, "Then so it is."

The words startled her even as she spoke them, but they did not taste bitter. For the first time, "wife" did not feel like a chain. It felt like something she had chosen, and that choice made all the difference.

On the eighth night, they shared a fire with two stonecutters headed south for a job near the wilderness. The men spoke of tax tallies and toll gates and the ways to pass without being remembered. Ezra listened with that angle to his jaw. Photine had begun to read: he cared for useful knowledge, not for quarrels. Later, when the stonecutters snored, Ezra took out a small bundle from his pack and unwrapped a wooden flute. He did not blow it. He turned it in his hands, oiling the grain with a rag the way a man keeps a promise he has not yet spoken. Photine watched in the dark, eyes half closed, and understood without being told that the flute had a story of its own.

On the ninth day, Moreh and then Tabor climbed out of the haze, blue against the valley. Ezra took the lower path to spare the donkeys' knees. En-Dor sat where the slope softens—stone houses like teeth, a stream that remembered winter, and a communal oven breathing out the day's last warmth. They came into the square at twilight, and nobody cared, the way villages don't care until they decide to. Ezra lifted a hand to two men at the well; one lifted a chin, which meant more than if he had offered wine. Photine's shoulders lowered without her telling them to.

Ezra's house stood a little aside, as he had said, with a fig tree pressing its elbow into the roofline as if it owned the place. The entry was a curtain, not a locked door. Inside was neat without boasting: jars along a wall; a hearth, a stool smoothed by sitting; a stack of wax tablets tied with string. Photine ran her fingers over the jars as if reading, found the water skin without asking, and filled the shallow lamp without spilling. Ezra set his pack down, struck fire, and made the room glow as if it had been waiting.

Ezra's home stood a little apart from the others—close enough to hear the village murmur, but removed enough to be its own world. It was simple: a single-story dwelling built from pale stone and clay, with a flat roof shaded by an overhang of woven reeds. The walls bore the soft, irregular lines of something shaped by hand, not measured by perfection. A fig tree leaned over one corner, its limbs gnarled and generous.

Photine stood at the threshold and took it in. There was no gate. No door that locked with a heavy latch. Just a cloth draped across the entry and the sound of wind moving through olive branches nearby. It felt… open. Not careless, but welcoming—as if it had nothing to hide.

Inside, the space was spare but thoughtfully arranged. A woven mat lay in the center of the floor. Clay jars lined one wall beside low wooden shelves, filled with dried lentils, grains, and herbs. A small hearth held the memory of a not-so-recent fire. In the corner, a folded blanket and a neatly stacked set of writing tablets sat beside a smooth, worn stool.

Ezra placed their few belongings near the back wall and lit a shallow dish of oil. The glow warmed the room in soft flickers.

Photine ran her hand across the surface of a jar, feeling the ridges, the cool clay under her fingertips. The silence gave her space to remember. Her father's small dwelling, where the hearth was never quite enough to chase the draft; the narrow room with Jotham, where kindness existed but no true belonging; the crowded house with Lois, where the cellar no one entered kept its secrets, and where grief and fear soaked into the walls. She breathed in the air of this simple, unadorned room, and found it warm in a way none of the others had been.

"It's not much," Ezra said behind her, setting down a basket of dried apricots, "but it's quiet.

Safe."

She nodded slowly. Then, to her own surprise, she said, "It's more than I've ever had."

Ezra didn't answer at once. His eyes moved across the room with a careful reverence. He had lived here before, with another woman whose name he still carried in his chest. The memory brushed him like the scent of her weaving, the sound of her voice at evening prayers. She was gone, and the house had been an empty shell since. Now, watching Photine touch the fig tree in the doorway, he felt the space shift—not erasing what had been, but adding something different, fragile, and alive.

That night, Photine swept the floor before they lay out their mats. She refilled the jar with water from the stream. She touched the fig tree outside the door and whispered something no one heard.

Ezra lay awake longer than she did, listening to her breathing settle into even rhythm. The house felt less hollow. Less haunted.

For the first time in years, she slept without waking. And for the first time in years, so did he.

And when the morning came, she opened her eyes not in fear, but in stillness.

The days that followed unfolded with an unfamiliar rhythm. Gentle. Predictable. Healing. Photine rose early, swept the floors, tended the hearth, and sometimes walked to the stream alone. Ezra gave no orders, asked no expectations—only left space, and filled it with trust.

One evening, when the lamp burned low and the fig tree's branches swayed in the doorway, Ezra spoke. His voice was quiet, almost careful.

"I don't know all you've carried," he said. "But I can see it was heavy. I won't ask you to lay it down before you're ready. And I will

never press myself on you. You are not a duty or a debt. You are—"
he hesitated, searching for the word, "—a woman of beauty, of
strength. Desired, yes. But not owned."

Photine stared at the flame. Desired. The word struck her like
water against parched lips. Jotham had been kind, but never reached
for her. Mordecai had taken everything and called it right. Between
the two, she had learned to believe she was either invisible or
property, nothing in between.

But Ezra's words opened a space she had not imagined—life with
no assumptions, no bargains, no demands. She did not know what to
do with that freedom. Part of her longed to step into it; part of her
feared it was only a dream, fragile as blown glass.

She touched the olive-wood shard she kept hidden in her garment
and breathed deep. *Not owned.* The words felt strange, but also true.

It was during their second week in En-Dor that he brought her
into the market with him. At first, she simply observed. The stalls
bustled with woven goods, dried fish, fragrant herbs, and baskets of
spring produce. Ezra moved through them easily, exchanging a sack
of ground flour for a spool of dyed thread and a pouch of copper nails.
He greeted vendors by name, always polite, never hurried.

But when one merchant—an aging salt dealer with sharp eyes
and a habit of muttering—tried to undercut Ezra by inflating the rate
of trade. It was Photine who stepped forward.

"That's not the rate you gave the leather worker two days ago,"
she said, calm and certain. "I saw the exchange. Two measures of salt
for one of ground wheat. You're raising the price because I'm new."

The man blinked. Then frowned.

"You must have sharp ears."

"Sharp eyes," she corrected.

He studied her a moment longer. Then, with a begrudging nod, they agreed to the original terms.

Ezra said nothing until they had passed three stalls down the road.

"That was well done," he murmured, just above the market noise.

"I'm tired of people pretending I don't see," she said, surprising herself.

He smiled. "Then they'll have to stop pretending."

From that day forward, Ezra let her lead at the stalls. She calculated weights and ratios faster than some could count their change. She remembered which merchant preferred dates over coin, who had children ill at home, who would bend on price if spoken to kindly. And she smiled a little—when people began to greet her first.

In one town, a widow with a crooked smile handed her a basket of dates and said, "I've heard of you—Ezra's wife, the smart one who out-traded the salt dealer. You've got a good head. He's lucky."

Photine blinked, the basket warm in her hands. The woman's words settled over her—kindly meant, and strangely steadying. She had never thought of herself as someone people would hear of, much less as Ezra's wife. Yet instead of bristling, she felt a quiet pride rise in her chest, a comfort she had not known before. She didn't revolt. Instead, she accepted the gift with a murmured thanks, a blush rising unbidden to her cheeks.

Somewhere along the way, without realizing it, she had stopped looking over her shoulder. And here, in this life made of quiet markets and soft laughter, she was becoming something more than what she had escaped.

For a moment, she couldn't find her voice. Then, slowly, she looked up and said, "We're lucky to have found one another."

It was the first time she'd spoken the words aloud. And the first time, they felt entirely true.

Their bond grew not from passion, but from something steadier: trust forged slowly, respect given freely, and space to be wholly human.

But under the comfort of her new life, questions remained. Could she really leave the past behind? What if Mordecai found her? What if Ezra's kindness was only a mask that time would peel away?

She didn't know yet. But she did know this: she had her name, her voice, and her place at the table.

And for the first time since girlhood, she believed she might have a future worth claiming. That hope followed her into the ordinary— into markets, into the rhythm of days that added up to seasons.

The market buzzed, but Photine kept to the edges, eyes sharp, hands quick. Ezra had taught her how to move through crowds without drawing attention, how to read body language like a merchant reads weights. She soon understood everything had a balance, a center of gravity, even people.

They'd been together more than a year now.

They had not joined their bodies, not yet. Both had wounds that needed time, and both had spoken of it once, quietly, beneath the fig tree. He told her that grief does not loosen its grip quickly. She told him that scars take longer to fade than bruises. They agreed to build trust first, to let laughter and work stitch what violence had torn.

And in everything that mattered, they were partners. She helped rebuild the olive press and kept the ledgers. He negotiated trade routes and repairs. They shared meals, laughter, and long walks at dusk. He had taught her how to spot a spy. She had taught him how to stretch a single coin over three transactions.

And together, they were becoming known. Not feared. Not pitied. Known. Trusted.

They lived on the edge of a hillside village that overlooked the valley. The house was modest, stone with a clay roof, ivy winding through the cracks. But it was theirs. Ezra patched every corner himself, and Photine insisted on carving vines into the front door frame—an echo of the ones she'd etched on Lois's oil lamps long ago.

"Vines root," she told him once, tracing the curls with her finger. "Even in dry places." Ezra smiled, touched her cheek, and said, "Then we'll grow wherever we're planted."

She had never known affection to feel like safety.

That evening, he returned from the fields with dust on his cloak and a grin in his beard.

"Barley's early," he said, setting down a woven basket. "Enough to sell and still keep half."

"Should we bake to celebrate?" she asked, brushing a lock of hair from her face with the back of her flour-dusted hand.

"Only if you let me help knead the dough again."

"You ruined the last batch."

"I made it memorable."

She laughed. The sound surprised even her.

They made bread that night by lamplight, elbow-deep in dough and stolen smiles. Flour dusted his nose. She smeared more there just to hear him groan and chase her around the table. Their laughter echoed through the stone house, full and round and alive.

Later, they sat on the roof under a sky bursting with stars, their legs dangling over the edge.

He looked at her—truly looked—and said, "Whatever comes, I would choose this. Even the hard days. Especially the hard days."

She didn't answer aloud. But she leaned her head against his shoulder.

And for a moment, Photine forgot she had ever been anything other than home.

The next morning, the market would change everything.

But tonight, there was only Ezra.

Only peace.

They had been in the small market in a nearby town for no more than an hour, Ezra bargaining with a wool merchant for a new set of cloaks, when Photine felt a strange prickling at the back of her neck. She brushed it off, but the sensation remained—a warning her body had learned to heed over years of surviving under Mordecai's reign.

The town square bustled with trade, the air thick with the scent of fresh bread and the cries of children playing. Ezra's easy voice mixed with the merchant's deep baritone as they negotiated prices. Photine wandered, pretending to examine a basket of dyed linens, but her eyes were sharp, scanning the crowd. She could feel the tension crawling up her spine, a quiet voice in her mind whispering that something was wrong.

Then she saw him.

A man in his middle years, dressed in the rough clothing of a laborer but with eyes that betrayed something sharper. He was standing by the bread stall, talking with a vendor, but when his gaze landed on her, everything stopped. For the briefest moment, his eyes locked onto hers, and then his mouth tightened into a thin line. He shifted his stance as though deciding whether to move forward or retreat.

Photine's heart hammered in her chest. *No, it can't be.* She forced herself to look away, pretending to browse, but her mind was already racing. The man wasn't one she recognized immediately, but his familiarity gnawed at her.

She felt a coldness in her stomach. The way his eyes moved over her—too knowing, too direct—was a telltale sign. This man was from her old life.

"Photine," the voice came from behind her, low and soft but unmistakable.

Her breath caught in her throat. She didn't need to turn around to know who it was. It was him—the man who had been part of Mordecai's network. His name was Rafa, a scoundrel who helped track down women who escaped forced marriages and returned them or sold them to another.

Her pulse quickened, and without thinking, she stepped away from the linen baskets, closer to Ezra's side.

Ezra's hand brushed against hers, a silent question in his touch. He must have sensed something was wrong, the tension in her posture too sharp, too unnatural.

She forced herself to meet Rafa's gaze, though a cold lump settled in her throat. "I'm sorry, I don't believe we've met," she said, her voice even but her heart hammering beneath her ribs.

Rafa's lips curled into something between a sneer and a smile, but there was no warmth in his eyes. "Oh, I'd recognize you anywhere," he said, stepping forward, his voice too loud in the crowded space. "You were with Mordecai. How's the old man treating you? I'd heard you'd gone missing, and now here you are, in a merchant's company."

Ezra stepped forward, his voice even, but his eyes sharp as flint. One hand moved subtly toward the fold of his cloak—slow, deliberate.

Rafa noticed. His gaze flicked downward, narrowing. The shape of a hilt, barely visible.

Ezra didn't draw it. He didn't need to. The threat lived in the silence between them, in the quiet tension of that gesture, in the way his body shifted—not to threaten, but to protect.

"My wife was once bound to a cruel man who sold her like livestock," he said, voice steady. "She was rescued, and she has made a new life. I suggest you forget whatever name you think you remember."

Photine's breath caught. Ezra's words were true enough to ring clear, and firm enough to silence Rafa's curiosity. The man looked between them, uncertain, then shrugged. "Must've been mistaken," he muttered and walked away.

That night, by the fire, Photine sat quietly, her hands trembling slightly as she passed Ezra a bowl of stew.

"I never told you how I got away," she said.

Ezra looked up, gentle as ever. "Only when you're ready."

"I think I need you to know."

The night wind lifted the doorway curtain, brushing the edge of a woven cloth so it swayed like a lullaby. The coals on the hearth had burned to embers, casting a faint, golden glow flickering against the walls. Ezra returned from tending the animals, his movements quiet, his presence unhurried as always. He lowered himself to the mat across from her, not speaking, waiting as though he already knew words were gathering in her chest.

Photine's fingers toyed with the olive-wood shard, smoothing its edge against her palm. Her voice, when it came, was thin at first. "I've never told anyone. Not all of it. Not my father. Not Jotham. Not Lois—not even her." She drew in a breath that shuddered. "But you should know who I am before we go any further."

Ezra inclined his head, the firelight catching in his eyes. "I'll hear whatever you wish to give.

And if it grows too heavy, I'll hold it with you."

So she let the knot loosen. She spoke of Eleazar—how he had taught her grafting by the olive trees, how he left with promises of a twin shard she still kept, and how his absence hollowed the family until everything fractured. She spoke of Jotham's gentle steadiness, of his cough-wrapped silences and the kindness that never touched her body, of the small space they carved together before death carried him away. Her voice hardened when she spoke of Mordecai—how he broke her body in the mill, how he dragged her through the streets, how every breath after was marked by his contempt.

The words spilled into guilt. "I brought danger to them," she whispered, eyes lowered. "To Lois, to the children, to Leah. I couldn't fit the life they gave me. I stole a coin more than once. I drew

Mordecai's suspicion, I forced their hands. If he hurt them because of me…" She broke off, pressing her fist to her mouth.

Ezra leaned forward, his voice steady. "Photine. You did not endanger them. Mordecai's cruelty was already a fire in that house—you did not light it. You only refused to burn in it. That is not guilt. That is survival." His jaw tightened. "And I will find out about Lois. You deserve to know she is safe."

Her tears blurred the firelight. She had not expected such a vow, spoken so simply, as if it were already certain.

After a long pause, Ezra exhaled and leaned back against the wall. His voice dropped low, rough with memory. "I had a wife once. Tirzah. She made this place a home—her songs still linger in the beams if I listen hard enough. Fever took her. It burned so fast the healers could not name it, only shake their heads. One day, she was kneading bread, the next she was gone. I buried her in the fig grove behind the press. I thought the house would never breathe again."

Photine raised her eyes, startled. "You've carried this alone all this time?"

"I thought that was what men did," he said, his mouth twisting wryly. "Work. Survive. Keep moving. But the silence eats at you. Tonight, maybe we both put some of it down."

She studied him, the way his grief sat beside hers without competing. For the first time, she felt what it meant to be heard—not endured, not pitied, but known.

The embers on the hearth dimmed to ash, and still they sat together, two voices trading truth in the dark until dawn edged the horizon.

The next night she waited up, her mind turning, her heart steadying. When he stepped inside, she looked up.

For a long moment, neither spoke.

"You're home," she said softly.

He crossed the room and cupped her face in his hands—not claiming, not conquering—then rested his forehead against hers. Their breath found the same rhythm.

"I'm always home when I'm with you," he whispered.

For a long time, she hadn't let anyone touch her. Especially, not in that way. He never asked. Never pressed. He simply waited, letting love live in the pauses—between shared bread, quiet laughter, the brush of fingers over ledgers and tools. Now, something had shifted. She wasn't afraid.

She was ready.

She stood in the glow of the fire, slowly unfastening the tie at her neck. The shawl slipped from her shoulders. The linen tunic beneath it clung to her like breath.

Ezra didn't move.

"Photine…" he said, voice rough with reverence. "You don't have to—"

"I know," she said, her voice steady. "But I want to."

Her hands trembled slightly as she reached for him, but he steadied them with his own, brushing his thumbs over her knuckles. Then he leaned in, his lips grazing hers—not devouring, not claiming—just *asking*.

She kissed him back.

It was nothing like before. No violence. No shame. Just heat. Just *presence*.

Ezra's hands were slow, reverent, as if she were something sacred—something he didn't want to unravel, but uncover. He paused at every inch of skin, as though he were memorizing her, not with hunger, but gratitude.

When they reached the bed, he lay beside her, not over her.

Ezra brushed her hair back from her face, his fingertips barely grazing her cheek. His eyes searched hers, asking a thousand silent questions—and finding the answer in the way she leaned into his touch, the way her breath quickened, not from fear but from *wanting*.

He kissed her again, deeper this time. Slow, anchoring. She parted her lips, inviting him in, and felt the heat rise beneath her skin like the first embers of a long-awaited fire.

His hands explored her like scripture—delicate, deliberate, full of reverence. He traced the line of her collarbone, then lower, brushing the edge of the tunic with trembling fingers. She arched slightly beneath his touch, a quiet gasp escaping her lips. The sound stirred something low in his chest.

Still, he paused.

His mouth hovered near her ear. "If you change your mind…"

"I won't," she whispered, already breathless. "I want this. I want *you*."

At that, something inside him unraveled.

His lips trailed down her neck, her shoulder, the edge of her breast. She drew in a sharp breath, her body awakening beneath his mouth. Her hands moved now—freely—running through his hair, over his shoulders, down his back. She marveled at the way he responded to her, how even the smallest touch made him tremble.

Ezra kissed every scar she carried, not to erase them, but to bless them.

When he slid her tunic down, he did it as if unveiling something holy.

She pulled his shirt over his head, fingers lingering on his chest, tracing the faint mark from an old wound. He caught her hand, brought her fingers to his lips, and kissed each knuckle.

They tangled together slowly, limbs wrapped, breath mingling. He moved against her, beside her, not rushing. His hand skimmed the length of her thigh, her hip, the small of her back, coaxing her body open with care, with patience, with awe.

And when he finally entered her, it was not conquest—it was communion. A joining that felt less like flesh and more like *home.* Their bodies moved in sync, a rhythm born of longing and trust. A prayer spoken not in words, but in skin.

She gasped again, but this time it was freedom.

She clutched him tighter, her breath catching, her whole being trembling with the overwhelming truth of being fully known, fully wanted.

When it was over, they lay tangled together, her head on his chest, their bodies slick with warmth, the silence between them thick with peace.

Ezra kissed the crown of her head.

Photine closed her eyes, and for the first time since her father left, she let herself believe she was worthy of joy.

Their bond deepened over time, rooted in the shared work and the small mercies that make a life. Photine's strength and resilience complemented Ezra's wisdom and kindness. His steadiness gave her voice room. Her clarity sharpened his dealings. They faced lean weeks and better ones, a cracked axle, a sick kid goat, a tax collector with a new appetite—each trouble met shoulder to shoulder.

She never forgot the women who helped her escape. When trade took them near, she and Ezra sought those villages, carrying oil or flour, slipping coins where coins could not be seen, leaving help without names. Her life had been rebuilt from the hands of others; now her hands became part of that hidden scaffold.

Ezra had kept his word. On one of their earliest journeys south, he sought word of Lois and the children. The news came back quiet but steady: they were safe. Mordecai still thundered in the markets, but his questions about Photine faded. Some said he had stopped asking altogether, as if speaking her name only fed a ghost he could not master. The relief was sharp enough to bring tears to her eyes. Lois was safe. The children were safe. The weight she had carried in secret for so long eased, if only a little.

Some evenings under the fig, Ezra lifted the little flute and let a line of music run like water under stone. Photine leaned against the wall and listened with her whole body. They did not speak of safety as if it were guaranteed. They learned it as a practice—paths rehearsed, neighbors noticed, ledgers honest, lamp trimmed, love tended.

In the end, what began as cautious companionship became something unshakable—two souls, tempered by loss and shadow, learning how to hold light again. And on market days, when people waved from stalls and called her by name, Photine could feel it: not the old reflex to shrink, but a new root taking hold.

A house. A fig. A partner who did not make her smaller to feel large.

A village beginning to expect to see her tomorrow.

More than shelter. A life.

CHAPTER 6
THREADS OF A NEW LIFE

The rhythm of the marketplace had become the cadence of their days.

By late morning, En-Dor's bustling streets pulsed with sound—hooves clattering, pots clanging, and the endless haggling and laughing. Photine once wove through such noise like a ghost, head down, movements small and silent. Now, she strode beside Ezra with her chin lifted and her basket swinging, the linen of her mantle catching the breeze.

Their stall, nestled near the southern road, was modest but well-kept. Ezra's woodcraft shared space with folded cloth, herbs, and the occasional amphora of dried figs that Photine bartered for herself. She had become sharp-eyed, quick-tongued—a match for any merchant. More than once, Ezra leaned over to whisper with pride, "You're better at this than I ever was."

They spent the afternoon amid bustle and trade, fingers brushing as they passed tools or bread, their small smiles exchanged like sacred things. By the time the sun cast long shadows, they were headed home—past terraced fields of wheat and olive, their feet worn but hearts light.

That year, En-Dor's communal oven was the village's heartbeat. Women queued at dawn with bowls tucked under shawls. By mid-morning, steam and gossip braided above the domed clay like incense. Photine learned the cadence of the place—the flour-dusted jokes, the murmured prayers brushed onto dough with fingertips, the way an older widow would press her cheek to the oven wall to judge heat with a kind of listening that made talk fall quiet.

She started leaving loaves for those who had none. Not publicly. A round placed at the edge of a door, a heel tucked under a sleeping mat for a boy who ran errands for spice-sellers. Ezra said nothing the first few times, only found her eyes and smiled as if the world had just done something right of its own accord.

On the seventh day, when trade gentled and the lanes thinned, he played his reed flute by their threshold. The tune was simple, a three-note rising that always felt like a gate opening. Children gathered, then scattered when a hawker called; an old man stopped and wept without warning, saying the melody had belonged to his wife. Ezra listened more than he played. Photine watched him and thought, 'I have never met a man who could be so still without going away.'

She copied prices and weights with a scribe's neatness in their ledger, adding marks for things that didn't fit on lines. Which stall lies about salt? Who overpours oil when no one is watching? Which girl needs sandals before the winter rains? It wasn't charity she kept; it was a map of care. When a widow with a cough traded her last skein of wool for lentils, Photine lied about the rate and slipped the difference back as if she had miscounted. Ezra let the lie stand. That night, he carved a small olive-wood spoon and set it at her place. "For taking less than life owes you," he said. "And for taking more joy than you're told you can."

News traveled on donkeys and in the hem of garments. A mason from Shunem said a Roman clerk had begun counting heads at the crossroads near Megiddo. A tanner swore two zealots were hiding in caves above the Jezreel. An old Samaritan farmer muttered that soldiers had asked questions about Mount Gerizim again. Photine marked none of it on the ledger. She folded it into her breath instead, longer on the in-draw when the road bent west, softer on the out-breath when Ezra's hand found her wrist and stayed there.

The midwife in En-Dor kept her house shaded with hanging gourds. She taught Photine what to brew when sleep wouldn't come. "You carry yourself as one who has been emptied by grief," the woman said, unafraid of truth. "But the body remembers how to make room for joy." Photine cried then—quietly, as though the tears belonged to someone who wasn't used to being allowed to feel them, and when she finished, the midwife set a sprig of hyssop in her hand. "For cleansing what won't," she said, "and blessing what will."

By dusk, the olive leaves turned their pale undersides to the wind. Ezra came home dusted white from the mill road, the sharp at his jaw softened by flour. He kissed the tops of her fingers rather than her mouth, as if to say he loved the work she'd done that day as much as he loved the woman who'd done it. In the far field, a boy practiced with a sling; the stone sang, then fell. Somewhere, a lamb found its mother. Somewhere, the world didn't. They ate lentils with thyme and a single fig split between them down the delicate spine.

That night, the flute stayed inside. The stars were loud enough.

Their home lay on the edge of a small grove, just beyond the city's stone walls. It still wasn't grand, but it had grown, just as they had.

What had once been a simple one-room dwelling now stretched modestly at the sides, expanded by patient effort and quiet seasons of building. A low awning of woven reeds shaded the entrance, supported by beams Ezra had hewn himself. Beneath it, two clay jars sat ready to catch rainwater, and a small bench—her addition—waited for tired feet and conversations that didn't need words.

The clay oven by the door still held warmth from the morning's bread, its surface blackened and well-used. A pair of sandals rested beside it, dusted with flour.

Inside, Ezra's tools still hung in neat rows along the wall, sharing space with scrolls Photine had collected from traders and scribes— half-charred, dog-eared, and precious. Dried bundles of rosemary, hyssop, and thyme hung from the ceiling beams alongside strings of garlic and crimson peppers. A carved wooden rack near the hearth held shallow bowls, oil lamps, and a polished pestle they had bartered for after a successful market season.

Near the back wall, a second mat had been added—wider, softer, handwoven by a woman in the village who owed Ezra a favor. A basket of mended linens and spare thread sat beside it, along with a spindle Photine reached for more often these days.

Their lives had settled into the walls. Not in the sense of stillness—but in roots. The kind that holds firm through both storm and drought.

And though the house was simple, it was unmistakably theirs. Not just a shelter, but a story—built day by day, woven with shared laughter, silent grief, and hands that hold without harm.

One evening, Photine rinsed lentils in a basin while Ezra mended a cracked chair by the doorway. The breeze drifted in, bringing with it the scent of dust and thyme. He hummed as he worked, and she found herself smiling for no reason other than the sound of it.

After supper, they sat outside on woven mats. Ezra leaned against the wall, flute in hand. The notes he played were simple and familiar, but tonight they seemed to carry further. Photine lay back, arms behind her head, eyes tracing the blinking stars.

"They say a prophet is crying out by the Jordan," Ezra said after a while, lowering the flute.

"John, son of Zechariah. Some call him mad. Some say he's Elijah returned."

Photine turned her head. "And Rome?"

Ezra's mouth curved in a wry half-smile. "Rome calls everyone mad who will not bow. They watch him, of course. They always watch. But the people still go. They leave their plows and flocks and walk for days to hear him."

She considered that the hush of the night pressed close. "What would make a man do such a thing? Leave everything for a voice in the desert?"

Ezra glanced at her, his eyes soft in the starlight. "The same thing that makes a woman walk away from fear. Hope."

The night deepened. Inside the house, the fire flickered low. But outside, beneath the stars, laughter still lived—and two hearts beat in a quiet, grateful rhythm.

Their business thrived. Ezra's knowledge of trade routes and long-standing relationships blended seamlessly with Photine's uncanny instinct for reading people. She could tell when a seller was bluffing, when a buyer was hesitating, or when a village was on edge.

Together, they traveled the northern roads through the fertile valleys of Jezreel, the shaded paths near Shunem and Megiddo, and sometimes as far east as the markets of Scythopolis. When the season allowed, they wound their way south through the borderlands of Samaria, stopping in smaller towns like Tirzah or Arumah, where Ezra had once bartered for tools, and Photine had learned to trade stories for information.

From time to time, they circled back—quietly, carefully—toward Akrabbim. Not only for trade, though the olives and pressed oil fetched a good price, but to check in on the women who risked everything to help Photine flee.

She never allowed herself to be seen. She knew too well the danger of recognition. But she also knew how to move unnoticed— when to blend, when to vanish. She'd become a shadow of her former self, in the most literal sense. Watchful, measured, unseen.

And yet, no matter how far they traveled or how long they stayed away, one name lingered most in her thoughts.

Lois.

Her image never faded. Her worn hands. Her fierce and defiant gaze.

Photine did not know if she was still alive. But sometimes, when she passed a woman with fire in her voice or kindness in her stance, she would imagine it was because Lois had lived, had endured, had taught someone else how.

Back in Akrabbim, the afternoon heat pressed against the mud-brick walls. Lois crouched in the courtyard, grinding barley for the evening meal. The rhythmic scrape of stone against grain offered her something steady to hold onto. Her hands were raw and cracked from labor, but her mind wandered far from the dust and silence.

Photine.

Three years had passed since Photine vanished into the night. Three years of silence, of pretending, of endurance.

Lois no longer flinched at Mordecai's footsteps. Not because she wasn't afraid—but because she had learned to wear fear like a second skin. It did not slow her movements, nor did it soften her resolve.

The house had not changed much. Mordecai had brought in new furniture—heavier, darker pieces that filled the rooms like threats. But the bones of the place were still the same, and so were the ghosts. Leah's laughter still echoed faintly in the corners. Matthias's quiet warnings lingered like the scent of oil and stone.

Lois did what she had always done.

She mothered. She worked. She remembered.

Miriam, now twelve, had begun asking questions that Lois struggled to answer. "Why do we stay?" "Why does Father always glare at us like we've failed him?" "What did Aunt Photine do that was so wrong?"

Ruth, ten, had taken to drawing in the dust with a stick—images of vines and flames and birds taking flight. Sometimes she stared at Lois as if trying to see through her skin to what lay beneath.

And little Caleb, six now, still asked if Photine would ever come back. Lois only smiled. "When the time is right," she said. "When the world can hold her again."

Mordecai had grown more controlling, more calculating. He didn't strike Lois or the children, but his words were sharp, and his silences sharper. He came and went on odd business that had nothing to do with selling grain.

He did not speak of Photine. He never once asked if Lois knew where she had gone.

But she caught him once—months after the escape—standing at the carved mantel above the hearth. His fingers traced the faint mark Photine left there as a girl when she had just arrived: a symbol like a cup, a flame rising from its center. He had stared for a long time before scraping it away with a knife.

Lois said nothing.

She had learned long ago that power lived in restraint.

Each night, when the children slept, she sat by the hearth and mended clothes by firelight. She stitched prayers into the seams. Hope into the hems. Names into the collars—names of those she had lost, names of those she prayed would return.

She did not dare light the old lamp anymore. Not with Mordecai always watching.

But she still set it by the window. Empty. Waiting.

She had no illusions. She was not strong like Leah once was, or fiery like Photine. She was made of quieter stuff—woven from thread and tenderness, from routines and lullabies.

But she had survived. And so had her children.

And that, she told herself, was enough.

For now.

Lately, she'd heard murmurs from traders. A woman matching Photine's description was seen on the northern roads, traveling with a merchant. Lois never asked aloud, but she listened with the hunger of a mother awaiting word of a lost child.

The lie she and Photine had spun to protect them both still held. Mordecai still spat bitterness about the merchant who "stole his property," but the fury had faded into muttering and drink. He spent most days away, chasing rumors of trade, or ghosts of pride long buried.

The sun dipped low, casting long shadows across the courtyard as Lois moved about the kitchen.

It wasn't peace, not really, but in Mordecai's absence, the quiet no longer choked.

Old Matthias sat nearby in the shade, his milky eyes drifting over things no one else could see. His hearing faded, but not his judgment. From time to time, he mumbled half-prayers, half-regrets. Leah, his wife, sat beside him, slowly working a piece of linen that hadn't needed mending in years—just something to keep her hands busy.

Lois had not been close to them for years, just taking care of their shadows of the lives they once held. In the early years of her marriage to Mordecai, Leah had quietly helped her avoid pregnancy, and for that, Lois would always be grateful. It hadn't freed her from the life she'd been given, but it allowed her to carve out a few more years of her own. But after Jotham's tragic death, something in Leah dimmed. She withdrew from everyone, retreating into a grief so deep it seemed to hollow her out from the inside. Jotham had been her son—her heart—and she would mourn him until her dying day.

They belonged to another generation, one that understood men like Mordecai and had long since stopped questioning them. Matthias rarely spoke unless spoken to. Leah avoided eye contact whenever Mordecai's name was mentioned.

Still, they were always watching.

Lois had grown used to silence, but tonight something stirred uneasily in her chest. Mordecai had been gone longer than usual—weeks now. She didn't miss him.

What she missed was freedom.

A knock at the door startled her. She wiped her hands on her sash and opened it a crack.

Standing there was an older woman, her head veiled and her eyes sharp with memory.

"Sarah?" Lois whispered.

The woman smiled. "She is well. She carries joy where sorrow once lived."

Lois swallowed the sob rising in her throat. "Then it was worth it."

Sarah nodded. "But the world is shifting. Roman patrols are thickening along the roads. There's word of uprisings—men called zealots stirring trouble. Akrabbim may not stay quiet much longer."

Lois stepped aside to let her in, heart thudding with fear—and something fiercer. "Come in," she said. "We have much to speak of."

Far from Akrabbim's dusty courtyards and stifled silences, Photine's days were shaped by a different rhythm now. Ezra was never possessive, never wary of her voice or vision. When she out-negotiated an elder or secured a rare herb for half its price, he didn't bristle. He beamed. In his eyes, she saw not the tight leash of control, but the open hand of trust.

Their home had long since settled into a kind of living warmth. Inside, familiar textures told their story—woven rugs from distant traders, sun-faded cushions, and hand-thrown clay cups bearing the marks of daily use. Photine had filled the space with quiet signs of their journey: a row of pressed herbs drying above the hearth, scrolls and scraps of parchment tucked into shelves, and a well-worn ledger where her looping script captured not just names and goods—but memories, questions, observations. A life being lived.

Ezra often returned from the market with something unexpected: a carved figurine, a fruit she'd never seen before, or a curious phrase spoken in a trader's tongue. These gifts were not just tokens; they were reminders. They were building something. Not just shelter—but meaning.

It was in this new rhythm of peace that her body changed.

At first, she thought the long travel days and shifting diets had thrown her off. But when the second moon cycle passed, and her skin grew more sensitive, her breath tighter, Photine began to suspect. A quiet joy bloomed within her, shy but persistent.

For days, she carried the secret in silence, pressing her palm to her middle when no one watched, testing the word in her own mouth but never saying it aloud. Finally, one evening as Ezra stacked kindling by the hearth, she found her voice.

"Ezra." Her tone was so different, he turned at once.

She swallowed, her hands clasped tight. "There is life in me," she whispered. "Our life."

For a heartbeat, he only stared, as though he had to make sure he had heard rightly. Then he crossed the room in three strides, dropped to his knees before her, and pressed his cheek to her belly. His breath caught; his shoulders shook. He whispered words she could not make out, words she would later ask him to write in her ledger so she'd never forget.

When he looked up again, his face was wet with tears, but his eyes were steady. "I prayed," he said, voice breaking. "Not for a child—but that if ever one came, it would be with a woman who would raise them in courage."

Photine trembled. "But what if all I give them is fear? What if that is all that's left in me?"

Ezra shook his head slowly, his palm still resting against her. "Fear did not bring you here, Photine. Courage did. Courage walks through fear, but it walks. And our child will learn that from you."

Her lips parted, but no words came. Instead, she covered his hand with hers, pressing it firmly against her belly. For the first time since girlhood, she let herself believe in a future she had chosen.

Tears welled in her eyes—from a love that no longer had to hide or earn its place.

They began preparing. Ezra fashioned a cradle from olivewood scraps, smoothing every edge. Photine visited a midwife known for her gentleness and wisdom, learning which teas to drink and what signs to watch for. The women of the market smiled knowingly when she placed a hand on her belly. She no longer had to pretend. She belonged.

Photine had never used the herbs Lois once taught her to brew—not with Ezra. She hadn't wanted to prevent anything that might root their love more deeply. And yet, months had turned to years, and no child came. By the time she turned twenty, she had begun to believe her womb was empty soil, that the brokenness of her past had sealed her against the hope of new life.

Just as she had accepted that she would never know the love of a child, it happened.

And she wept—from awe.

It felt impossible. Unworthy. Sacred.

She had never thought herself deserving of this much joy, and yet here it was, growing within her like a promise.

A blessing. Unlooked for. Undeniable.

But just as the spring winds began to shift, so too did the atmosphere of the town.

Rumors came first—whispers from travelers that Roman patrols were doubling, that another rebel cell had been found near the cliffs outside Perea. A caravan arriving from the north spoke of harsh interrogations at checkpoints. Taxes were rising again. One man, dragged off for suspicion of hiding zealots, was later found beaten near the wellspring.

Ezra grew quiet in the evenings, listening more than speaking. He had lived long enough to sense when peace frayed at the edges.

Photine watched the way his fingers tapped the edge of his cup, how he paused longer before each journey. And though she still rubbed her swelling belly with oils and hummed lullabies to the child within, the songs carried a different tone. Still hopeful, but edged with the awareness that the world outside their home was shifting once more.

Even so, she pressed herself to hope.

"This child will be born into love," she told Ezra one night, as they lay with the stars stretching wide above them. "Whatever comes, that will be our beginning." And Ezra, ever the steady flame, answered, "Then that will be enough."

But not all beginnings were born in peace.

While Ezra and Photine built their life in the northern reaches, the winds in Akrabbim shifted.

News trickled in slowly at first—whispers in the markets, murmurs among caravans. A Zealot uprising in a village near Mount Gerizim had left several soldiers dead, and in retaliation, a nearby Roman cohort descended on Samaria with ruthless efficiency. They didn't discriminate between rebels and civilians. Entire households were questioned, beaten, or dragged away.

Lois heard the shouting long before the soldiers reached the house. It started as a distant roar. Men's voices in a mix of Latin and harsh, provincial Aramaic, cutting through the stillness of dawn. She stepped into the courtyard, sash still dusted with flour from the morning's bread. A flock of birds burst from the trees beyond the gate. Something was coming.

She knew before she saw them.

Mordecai returned just three nights earlier from his self-proclaimed "journey south," where he claimed to have met men with vision—men who would soon rise against Rome. He'd come back louder, meaner, swollen with drink and self-importance. At the table, he spoke of burning fields and ransacking grain stores as if he'd been a hero. But Leah saw his trembling hands.

Lois noticed the gauntness beneath the bluster.

The others thought it was empty boasting. Just Mordecai being Mordecai.

But someone must have been listening.

The soldiers came at first light—four on horseback and at least eight on foot, armor clinking like the rattle of a viper. They didn't knock. They slammed through the outer gate with the flat ends of their shields, splintering the wood and scattering chickens into the alley.

Lois stepped back, shielding little Caleb with one arm. Leah screamed. Matthias, already pale with age and grief, struggled to rise from his mat and collapsed with a harsh gasp, with one hand clutching his chest.

Mordecai staggered from the rear of the house, bare-chested, reeking of wine and sweat. He blinked blearily at the soldiers and laughed.

"You're late," he slurred, arms outstretched as if greeting old friends. "I was beginning to think Rome had gone soft."

A soldier barked something in Latin. Another stepped forward, lifting his staff. Mordecai spat at them, the glob landing squarely on the man's boot.

"What are you going to do?" Mordecai taunted. "Bind me? Beat me? Go ahead. I've survived worse."

The staff struck without warning. A sickening crack rang out as wood met jaw. Mordecai dropped to one knee, blood pouring from his mouth.

Still, he grinned.

Lois moved instinctively, pulling Caleb behind her, eyes wide with fury and fear. "He's no threat to you," she said, her voice shaking. "He's just a drunk fool."

One of the Roman men glanced her way, amused. "Then he should've held his tongue."

Two soldiers seized Mordecai under the arms and dragged him toward the gate, his feet trailing furrows through the dirt. He turned his head just enough to see Lois standing there, motionless.

"You always knew," he hissed, blood staining his teeth. "You were always on her side." She didn't answer. There was nothing left to say.

Behind her, Leah knelt beside Matthias, whispering prayers through tears. The old man's chest rose in shallow bursts.

And just like that, Mordecai was gone—swallowed by the dust and iron of Rome's unyielding justice.

Later, neighbors would say they saw the soldiers stop at other homes. That Mordecai hadn't been alone. That someone must have reported them. A name whispered. A bribe taken. A grudge fulfilled.

But by then, the gate was broken. The house was silent.

For the first time in years, Lois did not look over her shoulder. She simply sat in the courtyard as the sun climbed higher, her hands resting in her lap, eyes fixed on nothing at all.

A small hand slipped into hers.

Caleb stood beside her, barefoot, the hem of his tunic dust-stained and torn. He said nothing. Neither did she. Not at first.

Inside, Ruth was already packing dried dates and hard bread into a cloth satchel. Miriam sat near the hearth, braiding lengths of twine and watching the door like she expected it to explode again.

They were children—old enough to understand that when the Romans came once, they often came again.

Lois looked at them and knew they were not safe here. Not with the gate broken and rumors already circling. Not with their family name still sharp in the mouths of neighbors. Not with Rome uncertain, who else in Mordecai's house might have heard the talk of rebellion?

She squeezed Caleb's hand and finally stood.

"We won't wait to see if they return," she said, voice clear and tight. "We're leaving by dusk." "Where will we go?" Ruth asked, eyes wide but steady.

"Somewhere small. Away from the roads. A cousin of your grandmother lives near Tamar. She's old, but kind. I'll trade what we have left for bread and safe passage."

She sent Miriam to the neighbor woman, who sometimes sold wool and heard every rumor before it spread. Lois didn't ask for shelter. She asked for news: were the Romans still in the area?

Were names being taken? Miriam returned with a whisper that more arrests were expected before the Sabbath.

That settled it.

By sundown, they'd hidden what they could not carry. Lois wrapped Caleb in her shawl and handed Ruth a water skin. She left a single lamp lit in the window—not as a signal, but a farewell to a life now extinguished.

They left under the cover of night, skirts brushing the dry path, their steps quiet but sure.

She did not know if they'd be hunted. She did not know what waited in Tamar.

The road leveled as they reached the plateau, the rising sun casting long shadows across the terraces of Tamar. From afar, it looked like a promise—low stone homes scattered among almond groves, sheep bells echoing faintly in the cool morning air. A spring trickled from a rocky bluff near the town's edge, feeding a cluster of date palms. After days of hiding and half-sleep, the sight made Miriam gasp aloud.

"We made it," Ruth whispered, her voice cracking with relief.

Lois felt no such relief.

Her legs ached from holding Caleb on the rough path, and her shawl clung to her back with sweat. But it wasn't exhaustion twisting in her gut—it was the silence. No laughter. No greetings. Only wary eyes peering from doorways as they passed.

A man with a gnarled staff stepped into their path near the edge of the village. His tunic was dusted in flour, and his beard braided close to his chin.

"You're not from here," he said flatly.

Lois straightened. "I seek Mara, daughter of Selah. She used to trade wool here."

The man tilted his head. "Mara died at New Moon. Her hut is empty now. Wolves took two goats before anyone noticed she was gone." A cold weight settled in Lois's chest.

Still, she asked, "Is there work? I can weave. My daughters can cook, fetch water—"

"We're full," he cut in. "Too many mouths already. Roman taxmen are tightening the neck of every farm between here and Nebo. No one wants strangers. Especially not from the south."

He looked her over—eyes lingering on her worn shoes, the tremble in her hands, and the boy at her hip.

"I'll not turn away hungry children," he added, almost reluctantly. "The temple women keep a dormitory. Girls may stay. But you—" he pointed with the end of his staff, "you'll bring trouble. You've got that look. Like someone running from something." Lois didn't answer.

They stayed the night near the courtyard of the elders' house, were given bread and a blanket, but no welcome.

As dusk fell, Lois sat by the fireless hearth and watched her daughters sleep curled together under a goat-hair blanket. Miriam's arm was slung protectively over Ruth's shoulder, their breath rising and falling in tandem. Caleb slept beside her, fingers clutching the edge of her tunic.

She brushed his hair back, her heart a storm.

He needed her. He needed space to run, to ask questions, to cry when the memories returned. And the girls—growing fast, learning to move through the world with sharp eyes and quiet resolve—they needed a place free from her enemies.

They needed more than she could give if she stayed.

At first light, she kissed her daughters' brows and pressed a silver button into Miriam's palm.

"Trade this if you need to," she whispered. "And remember what I told you—listen twice before speaking once. Watch for kindness, but don't mistake it for safety."

Tears filled Ruth's eyes. "Mama… please. Stay."

"I can't," she said softly. "Not now. But I'll come again, if I can. And you—you be good for your sister. Promise me."

Ruth nodded, jaw trembling.

By the time the village stirred to life, Lois and Caleb were already gone—walking through the narrow paths carved in stone, the rising heat already pressing at their backs.

She didn't know what waited in Akrabbim. But she knew this: she could not give her daughters peace if she stayed in fear. And perhaps in saving them, she was finally learning to save herself.

Upon their return, having been gone two nights, they found Akrabbim had grown silent. The house, once loud with conflict and decay, was now stifled by a different kind of heaviness. Leah rarely left her room. Matthias barely ate. And Lois, though outwardly unchanged, began moving with purpose—asking questions, bartering for news, watching the roads.

That's when word came.

A caravan from Decapolis brought herbs, cloth, and whispers. Mordecai, it was said, had not simply vanished into his own rage; he had entangled himself in Roman dealings, carrying messages and favors too dangerous for a man of his temper. When the Romans tired of him—or when he failed them—he was taken.

But men like Mordecai never fell alone.

Now the rumors spread: a woman named Photine, traveling with a merchant husband called Ezra, had been seen near En-Dor. Some swore she had spoken with a Roman envoy about safe trade routes and loyalty oaths. Lois knew it wasn't true. Photine had run from such snares, not toward them. But truth mattered less than the shape of a story. And in uncertain times, a rumor could be as sharp as a sword.

Lois's heart clenched. If the Romans believed Photine was linked to Mordecai, or if Mordecai's old enemies sought to tie up loose ends, she would be hunted. She needed to be warned before someone else came looking.

So she wrote a message on the back of a linen scrap, sealed it inside a packet of dried hyssop, and gave it to a trusted trader heading north.

"They've taken him. The girls are safe but sent away. Others are watching, and they know where to look for you. You and Ezra are not safe. Be ready to move. –L"

She reread it three times, then folded the scrap carefully, pressing it to her chest.

Ezra looked up from his ledger. "Is it your past?"

Photine nodded. "No… It's my right now. And I must go to her."

He didn't argue. "Then we go together."

The stars were still bright when Photine rose, long before dawn broke the horizon. The world around her slept in silence—Ezra beside her, the household animals tucked away, the fire reduced to a low amber glow. She moved through the house quietly, her hands brushing over the familiar: a bowl of dried olives, the reed baskets they used for trade, Ezra's cloak still damp from the previous day's rain. All of it, ordinary. All of it, loved.

She had not expected to feel so rooted.

She wrapped her shawl tight around her shoulders, the air sharp against her skin despite the warm season. As she stepped outside, the chill of the earth underfoot grounded her more than she expected. The same ground that had once held her captive now held her fast in freedom. And still, she was about to leave it behind.

A Roman torch, a name spoken in suspicion, a warning from a woman who once risked everything for her. These were not things she could ignore. But she was not the girl who had fled Akrabbim in the middle of the night, ribs bruised and spirit frayed. She was not hiding anymore.

She was going back with eyes open.

She placed a hand gently on her belly.

"This child will be born into love. Whatever comes, that will be our beginning," she had told Ezra just days before. But now she wondered—could love protect what blood, empire, and men could not?

She exhaled slowly. She hadn't told Ezra the whole of what she felt: that something in her spirit stirred with unease even before Lois's note arrived. A tension in the air, in the way certain traders avoided eye contact, in the increasing presence of Roman boots on Samaritan soil. She was not afraid for herself. But for the life she was growing, for the peace they'd nurtured from so many ashes. Yes, she was afraid.

Tomorrow, they would begin the journey. Tonight, she let herself mourn the peace she was leaving, and hope it would not be for the last time.

The night air was cool against her face, carrying the faint salt of the Dead Sea to the north. Photine sat by the low wall of the courtyard, her shawl pulled close, staring into the shadows of the fig tree. The branches shifted, their leaves whispering like old women in secret conversation. She traced the scar on her wrist absently, not out of pain, but memory.

A gentle rustling came from the doorway behind her. Ezra stood there, rubbing the sleep from his eyes, already wrapping his cloak around his shoulders. His hair was uncombed, his voice rough with tenderness.

"Couldn't sleep either?"

Photine shook her head. "Too many memories in Akrabbim. Too many roots."

"Too many debts?" His smile was tired but warm.

"No," she said softly. "Too much unfinished."

Ezra crossed the courtyard and came to her side, sliding his arm around her waist. He pressed his forehead gently against hers. "We'll go, and we'll return. And whatever happens, we go together."

She leaned into him, grateful, though the unease in her chest did not dissolve.

The next morning, before the sky had fully broken open, Ezra was already at work. He moved with the precision of a man who knew eyes could be everywhere. He loaded jars of oil and sacks of grain onto the cart, their bulk arranged to suggest ordinary commerce.

"This must look like trade," he murmured as Photine approached, her scarf pulled low across her cheek. "Not flight."

She nodded, carrying a bundle of figs to tuck near the front. Her fingers brushed the olive-wood shard hidden in her sash, and she wondered if her father had once left under a dawn like this, carrying more secrets than goods.

For years, she had fed her anger at him, replaying the silence he left behind, the weight it pressed on Selah and Zimri, on her own unsteady girlhood. But now, with her own child hidden beneath her ribs and danger pressing close, the anger bent toward something else. If leaving had been the only way to keep them safe, perhaps Eleazar had not abandoned her at all. Perhaps he had chosen exile over watching them burn.

The shard warmed beneath her palm. For the first time, she did not think of it as a reminder of loss but as proof that he had carried love with him, even into absence. And she thought: *I would do the same. I would leave everything, carry nothing but this child and Ezra, if it meant they could live.*

Her thumb traced the grain, remembering his promise of a twin piece carved from the same branch. Did it still exist, hidden in some distant pouch or pressed into another hand? Did he still carry it? The thought lit something in her chest—a thread unbroken. Somewhere, perhaps, her father still walked beneath a dawn like this one.

Ezra tightened the mule's bridle himself, then stopped at the blacksmith's for a brief word. The man's shoulders tensed as Ezra leaned in, his lips moving low and quick. Later, in the marketplace, Ezra clasped hands with an older merchant. The man's eyes darted to the side before his words came. *Safe roads. Eyes behind you. Rome is restless.*

These were the ones Ezra trusted, men who murmur warnings like prayers. Men who knew when silence was loyalty.

Photine followed half a step behind, her gait measured, her chin neither too low nor too high.

Ezra had taught her this walk, the posture of a woman who belonged but did not invite questions.

She carried a basket of lentils, her hands steady, her breath even, though inside her thoughts roiled.

Mordecai was gone. Taken. But the Romans who had swallowed him whole were not finished. And if whispers tied her to him—if anyone believed she had inherited his dealings—then every step on this road was lined with unseen knives.

By midday, they cleared the gates of Akrabbim. The ridge path rose before them, dust and stone winding toward the north. Photine drew the scarf tighter around her head and glanced back. The walls of the town looked smaller already, but their weight pressed against her chest like a millstone.

The road was long, and she was with child. She had not told anyone but Ezra yet, but her body reminded her with every small wave of nausea, every new tightness in her chest. She touched her belly as they climbed and wondered if this child would inherit fear or freedom—whether the world she carried them into would let them breathe without looking over their shoulder.

Ezra noticed the gesture but said nothing. He kept his eyes on the track ahead, scanning the ridges. His hand never strayed far from the short staff at his side.

By nightfall, they reached a narrow shelf of land between two limestone outcrops. Ezra kept the fire low, shielded by rocks. He spoke briefly with two herdsmen camped nearby, men who knew him by name. One nodded toward the valley. "Patrols passed there yesterday. Not local.

Strangers in Roman leather."

Ezra returned to Photine, his face set. "They'll spread word of a caravan behind us," he said quietly, "so if anyone follows, they'll chase shadows instead."

Photine lay awake on her mat long after, the stars wheeling overhead. Every sound carried a question: the cough of a donkey, the crack of a twig, the hush of wind through the thorns. Past, present, and future pressed against her all at once—her father's voice low and insistent, telling stories of prophets who wrestled angels and limped away blessed; Jotham's steady hands smoothing rough wood into something useful, his silence carrying more care than words ever could; Mordecai's shadow across every silence; Ezra's vow steady beside her; the faint flutter of life within. It was too much to hold, and yet it was hers to carry.

The second day, they skirted the edge of the Arabah, the land bruised with stone and scrub. Traders passed in twos and threes, their cloaks dust-stained, their eyes quick to measure. Ezra spoke little, but when he did, it was to men he trusted—men who knew which roads were watched, which villages had seen soldiers.

"Word travels faster than coin," one murmured, slipping Ezra a flat cake of pressed dates. "Lists are being drawn up. Names of those who speak too loudly. Names of those who trade too freely."

Ezra tucked the warning away without reply.

Photine felt the eyes of every passerby on her. Did they see her face beneath the scarf? Did they know her name? Once, Mordecai had dragged her through the streets, and she had thought the humiliation would never leave her skin. Now she feared anonymity just as much as exposure.

Both could kill, and both could be true in the same breath.

That night, when they stopped near a small spring, Ezra brought her water cupped in his hands. "Drink," he said gently. "And rest. The child will need your strength."

She drank, the coolness sliding down her throat, and stared at him in the starlight. "Do you ever wonder if we will live to see peace?" she asked.

Ezra's jaw worked. "Peace?" He looked toward the horizon. "I wonder if anyone alive has ever seen it. But I will settle for safety, even for a little while. And I will fight for that, for you."

Her heart clenched. She wanted to believe him. She wanted to trust that safety was not always borrowed time.

On the fifth day, the hills thickened with scrub oak and terebinth. From a ridge above, they saw a Roman patrol in the valley, six men on horseback, armor glinting in the sun. Ezra pulled the mule to a stop and motioned her into the shadow of a boulder. They waited there, breath held, until the soldiers vanished into the haze.

Only when the sound of hooves faded did Ezra speak. "They're sweeping wider. Looking for something—or someone."

Photine's stomach tightened. "Us?"

"Perhaps. Or anyone Rome decides to fear today." His eyes flicked toward her. "But they know your name now. Lois's letter was right. We must assume they'll come."

She pressed her palm against her belly, willing the child to be still, willing her own heart to stop pounding so loudly.

Days blurred into weeks. Villages passed: Tamar, where old women sold salt blocks; Moa, where they slept against a crumbling wall; the ridge road above Arad, safer than the coast though longer. At each stop, Ezra sought men he trusted, trading news like coin. At each stop, Photine kept to the shadows, her scarf pulled low, her silence her best shield.

Yet even in the fear, life pressed forward. She rinsed lentils in a basin, listened to Ezra's low humming as he mended straps, and watched him tilt his head toward her in the market when men tried to wave her off. *You already are speaking to the one in charge,* his eyes always seemed to say.

And she thought: *This is different. This is not survival alone. This is a partnership.*

Still, the unbalance never left her. In her heart, her father's absence still echoed. In her bones, Mordecai's cruelty still lingered. In her womb, a child grew who would need a world better than the one she knew.

On the fourteenth day, as the path bent toward the highlands near Ephraim, Ezra let the mule rest. He glanced at her, his hand brushing hers briefly.

"Another day or two. We'll be beyond their reach."

Photine searched his face. "Are you sure?"

"No," he said simply. "But I will make it true."

He drew in a breath, eyes on the ridges ahead. "The pass of Akrabbim is harsh, but it is safe. The Romans do not patrol there—too narrow, too broken for their horses. Only the shepherd clans know the trails. Sarah spoke with them before we left. They agreed to shelter us, just as they did once before when others fled south."

Photine felt a flicker of warmth at the name. "Sarah."

Ezra nodded. "She has arranged food, water, even a place to rest until the search fades. Without her, we would have had no clear path. She trusts them, and they trust her."

Photine pressed her hand to her belly, remembering Sarah's steady eyes, the way her voice had carried certainty when everything else was falling apart. "She has been our shield from the beginning."

"Yes," Ezra said, a quiet conviction in his voice. "She saw what I could not. She saw you, and she saw this path. Akrabbim will hold us long enough for me to keep my vow."

She leaned into him, exhaustion softening into trust. Tomorrow, they would press onward.

Tonight, by a small fire, Photine let herself rest in the fragile hope Sarah had made possible.

CHAPTER 7
THREADS UNRAVELING

The road to Akrabbim pressed them onward, mile by mile, but what weighed most heavily was the air itself. Everywhere they turned, the land seemed taut with expectation. Villages spoke in whispers, markets thinned, and soldiers' shadows stretched longer across the lanes.

Roman banners marked crossroads where once there had been open trade. Mothers drew children closer when riders passed. Doors closed too quickly. Even the dogs barked less.

At a broken cart along the ridge, Photine saw a centurion's fist twisted in the tunic of a Samaritan boy, his mother on her knees in the dust. No one else interfered. The merchant who owned the cart stared at the horizon, feigning blindness. Photine turned her face away, though the image burned itself into her memory.

Later, at a bend in the Jordan, voices carried on the wind. A wiry man stood in the river, thunder rolling from his mouth:

"Repent—for the kingdom of heaven draws near!"

The people answered with their bodies, crying out as if the water itself might wash the fear away.

"John," Ezra said. "A prophet—or a madman. Perhaps both. But the crowds grow, and the priests grow uneasy. And the Romans…" His jaw hardened. "They fear any gathering not their own." Photine carried the echo of that voice long after they passed. By night, she lay awake, the fire's light paling before the vast dark, turning his words over like stones in her hand.

This was the world tightening around them. Zealot raids whispered of resistance in the ravines. Retaliation flared in the markets. A burned village spoke its silence more clearly than any survivor's tongue. And always the rumors of Mordecai. His name slid through conversations like a blade hidden in cloth.

Yet even in this tightening, life stirred. At the edge of a fig grove, Photine paused beneath the shade, pressing a hand against the flutter within her. She remembered the boy's frightened eyes, the prophet's voice rising like a storm, the silence clinging to every village door.

"This is the world we're bringing this child into," she said.

Ezra did not answer with promises he could not keep. He only took her hand, steady, grounding her to the earth.

Ahead lay Akrabbim—thorned ridges, sharp winds, shelter only in the hidden places. Yet it was more than survival that pulled them forward. It was the sense that they were walking into a turning of the age itself, into the space where rumor, prophecy, and empire collided.

They met Sarah on the outskirts of a grove where olive and date mingled in a thin ribbon of shade. She had been waiting, and when she saw them, her hands opened as if to gather both into her keeping.

Photine let herself be guided to a low stone, Sarah pressing cool water into her palms, laying herbs across her lap. "You look like you've walked the backbone of the land itself," Sarah murmured.

So Photine told her. She spoke of the Roman soldier's hand twisted in a child's tunic, of the crowd at the Jordan where John thundered prophecy, of villages too quiet, their silence loud with fear. She described the burned houses, the mothers clutching children, the way even the dogs barked less.

Sarah listened without flinching, her eyes steady, her hands busy tearing bread and pressing it into Photine's fingers. "This is the land now," she said softly. "Rumor in one ear, soldiers in the other. But still, children are born. Prophets rise. And the God of our fathers does not sleep."

Ezra sat across from them, shoulders uncoiling for the first time in days. "You've made the way open?"

"I have," Sarah answered. "The shepherd clans near the ascent are watching for you. I sent word through them. Safe paths, safe food. And Lois has prepared a place. You will not be turned aside at her door."

She took Photine's hand and laid it against her own chest, the beat of her heart solid beneath. "You carry life into a land that feels like death. Hold fast. That is your defiance."

When they rose to go, Sarah wrapped Photine in a woven shawl, smelling faintly of rosemary and smoke. "For the nights," she said. "And for the dreams." Then she leaned close, her voice low enough for only Photine to hear: *When you doubt the road, remember this— God has hidden lamp oil in you. Do not be afraid when others cannot see it.*

On the sixth evening, as they crested the final hill above the Akrabbim ascent, Photine felt her chest tighten. Below, the hamlet clustered at the foot of the scarp—palm fronds rattling in a dry wind, roofs holding the day's heat. The stillness wasn't peace. It was a pause. Holding breath.

They entered from the eastern slope, where travelers once found welcome at the well and the roadside bread stall. Now, the lane seemed deserted. Two men hurried past without greeting. A boy playing with a stick was yanked into a doorway by his mother. A merchant tied his sacks without looking up.

Photine met Ezra's eyes.

"They're afraid," she murmured.

Ezra nodded. "They have reason to be."

Lois's home sat just off the path, tucked behind date palms and prickly fig. Photine's heartbeat thundered in her ears as they approached. The stone threshold looked the same. So did the cracked basin where she'd once helped draw water.

Years had passed, but the dust still remembered her name.

From the shaded doorway, a figure stepped forward, wrapped in a faded shawl.

Lois.

Older. Thinner. Her hair was more streaked with gray. But her eyes, fierce and glinting with recognition, were the same. For a moment, neither woman moved.

Then Lois stepped forward, her arms open, and Photine was home.

For a breath, she faltered. Every memory rushed back: shame and survival, the weight of eyes that had once measured her worth too cheaply. Then Sarah's whisper rose within her: *God has hidden lamp oil in you. Do not be afraid when others cannot see it.*

Photine straightened, her hand tightening around Ezra's. She turned to him, searching his face—the steady jaw, the watchful eyes, the man who had walked beside her through fire and silence both. Pride welled up in her chest, fierce and undeniable.

When Lois opened the door, Photine stepped forward first. "Lois," she said, her voice carrying not just memory, but strength. She gestured to the man at her side. "This is Ezra. My husband. The one who has kept me alive, and the one I love." Only then did she fall into Lois's arms.

They embraced, wordlessly, the kind of hug that carried years of stories. Behind them, Ezra waited, watching with respectful distance.

Lois pulled back at last, her eyes shining. She turned to Ezra, offering both hands. "Welcome," she said. "Any man who guards her as you have is kin to me." For a moment, relief softened her face. But as she drew them both inside, the lines of fear returned, tightening at the corners of her mouth. Her gaze flicked toward the empty doorframes, the unlit corners.

"My daughters…" she whispered, almost to herself. "I pray every hour for their safety and their return. Until they are home, my joy carries a shadow."

Inside, the house felt heavy with unsaid things. Leah sat on a stool in the corner, her fingers still working a worn piece of cloth. She did not look up at first, the dim light catching only her bent shoulders and the slow rhythm of her hands. Matthias dozed beside the hearth, muttering under his breath.

When Leah finally raised her eyes, they landed on Photine. For a heartbeat, her hands stilled, the cloth slack between her fingers. Confusion flickered there, then something softer—recognition that had no words.

"Jotham," she breathed, almost soundless, as if a memory had stepped into the room. Her gaze searched Photine's face, not quite understanding, but drawn all the same. It was as though some ember long buried in ash had caught at the sight of her.

Photine's throat tightened. She wanted to speak Jotham's name, to honor him, but no words rose. Only the quiet truth of Leah's eyes meeting hers, saying, *a piece of what I lost stands here again.*

Then Leah blinked, the spell breaking. Her fingers returned to the cloth, moving faster now to hide what had flared in her. But the air between them carried it still, faint as a lamp newly lit.

Lois wasted no time. Once Photine sat and Ezra secured the animals, she shut the door and lowered her voice. "He's gone," she said. "Mordecai. The Romans took him."

Photine froze. "And you're worried…?"

"There's been unrest. Some say he was jailed. Others…" Lois hesitated, then lowered her voice even further. "Others say he joined them. The Zealots."

Photine exchanged a glance with Ezra. "Willingly?"

"He's bitter, proud, desperate to reclaim something. I don't know. But if it's true…"

Ezra stepped forward. "The Romans will use any excuse. If he's involved, you could all be targets."

Lois nodded grimly.

"That's why I sent for you. There's more. Someone's been asking questions about you."

Her voice dropped lower, trembling not with fear—but with fury. "A Roman. Not a soldier—worse. One of those scribes who move like shadows between the law and the sword. He came with papers, not chains, but the weight was the same. And he knows about Shechem. About you."

Photine's breath caught.

Her hand moved instinctively to her stomach, where new life stirred—slow and soft, a gentle reminder of everything she'd built since fleeing.

She turned toward the small window beside Lois, gazing out at the quiet road, the stillness of the hamlet that no longer felt still at all.

"What does he know?" she asked. The words came out tight.

Lois hesitated.

"He asked about a girl who vanished from Shechem," Lois said quietly. "Asked about a man named Eleazar. About Mordecai. About a young woman once seen at a millhouse in the north.

Too many questions—too exact to be idle curiosity. He wasn't just guessing."

Photine's lips parted, but no words came.

"They know you are from Shechem," Lois went on. "Or at least, someone suspects you are. And if this scribe is digging, it means someone with reach wants the truth—whether to harm, or perhaps…" Her voice faltered, eyes narrowing as if unwilling to finish the thought. "…perhaps to claim what was lost."

Ezra stepped closer, his jaw tight.

"Could it be Mordecai?"

Lois shook her head. "What I do know is this man wasn't here for trade. He was looking for leverage."

Photine turned fully to Lois now, her expression shifting from fear to clarity.

"Then he's not just here for the past," she said. "He's here for something that's still moving."

Lois reached out, pressing her hands over Photine's. "Then we move faster."

Ezra's hand found the small of Photine's back. His voice was calm, but beneath it ran the same current that hummed through the land outside—the pull of something dangerous drawing near.

"We'll leave tonight if we have to."

Photine looked once more out the window.

She remembered the stone streets of Shechem, the smell of bread from Selah's oven, her father's scrolls, and the night she was taken.

Now it was all surfacing again as a threat.

She exhaled slowly.

"He knows about Shechem," she said softly. "But he doesn't know who I've become since then. I was fourteen when I left my home, two years after my father…"

The threads of peace were unraveling.

And she wasn't sure they could be sewn back together again.

Outside, the world kept moving—rumors carried on wind and water, whispers traded in markets and courts. Somewhere far from Lois's hearth, another story was being written in stone and iron.

The prison at Caesarea Maritima was little more than a pit with iron teeth. Salt wind from the sea slid through the cracks in the stone, carrying damp that gnawed the skin raw. Chains clinked whenever Mordecai shifted, iron biting into bone where flesh had thinned. Rats traced the edges of the floor, bold in the dark.

He woke to the groan of waves battering the harbor wall, a sound that never ceased, night or day. Time slipped. He counted shifts of light through the grate, then lost count again when clouds swallowed the sun. Hunger pressed harder than the manacles.

In the first days, they came in groups of three. Torches smearing the walls with red light, boots grinding in the sand that always blew in from the shoreline. They didn't ask questions, didn't want confessions. Their fists and clubs fell for the sheer memory of it—for the pleasure of watching a man bend.

One Roman—a broad one with a scar like a hook across his cheek—spat between blows. "This is for nothing," he growled in crude Aramaic. "And nothing is all you are."

Mordecai staggered, his body folding under the weight, but he set his jaw. He would not cry out. Not yet. To break was to let them win, and he would not gift them that.

So he swallowed his rage like blood, tasting iron on his tongue, pressing the fire of it deep where they could not reach.

They beat him at first.

Not for information.

Not even for defiance.

For sport. For memory.

To remind him that he was nothing.

But Mordecai refused to break.

At least not at first.

When the interrogator came—a man in fine linen robes—he carried no whip. Just questions. Precise. Measured. Too familiar.

"You traded across Judea," the man said. "You know the roads. Who takes them? When? Why?"

Mordecai said nothing.

"You've seen how zealots slip through, hidden among caravans. You've watched the way grain moves one way, and weapons another."

Still silence.

"You were born Akrabbim," the man continued, studying Mordecai's face. "But your coin crossed borders. You bartered in Galilee. You dealt with Jews, Nabataeans, and even Romans. You speak the tongues. You know the customs. You are… adaptable. You are useful." A pause. Then, quieter, "We don't need loyalists. We need leverage."

Mordecai looked away. But the flicker in his eye betrayed what he would not say.

That word *useful* rang louder than any chain.

In the weeks that followed, Mordecai was moved. Not freed but repositioned. His cell shifted from the damp stink of the lower hold to a smaller room with light. He was given better food. The beatings stopped. A thin scroll was placed before him, along with ink and a reed.

"Names," the scribe had said. "Traders. Towns. Contacts. Anyone who trades on the fringes, near ravines, in desert markets, along the Jordan where patrols go blind."

At first, Mordecai offered lies. Places that no longer existed. Men already dead. Routes swallowed by flood or war.

Then, half-truths—just enough to keep their interest.

Old names from villages he'd passed through, merchants long gone, zealots already dead.

Then, names. Real ones.

At first, he offered them calculation, telling himself each syllable was a shield, a diversion. That to give them something was to keep them from digging deeper. Survival.

But one night, after the lash had split him open again and the torches flickered low, spite rose in him like bile. He let her name slip between his teeth—Photine. Not in confession, not as weakness, but as venom. A way of saying *you cannot take me, so take her instead.*

The guard leaned closer, savoring the syllables, rolling them like coins across his tongue. "Phō-tēnē," he repeated, slow, deliberate. "We will remember."

Mordecai told himself it meant nothing. That a single name in a sea of names was only smoke.

That he still held the true fire of himself hidden.

He told himself it was survival.

But when the chains settled against his ribs that night, heavier than before, he could not silence the echo of her name ringing in the dark.

When they returned him to the road weeks later, it was without ceremony. No chains. No escort. Just a silent glance from a soldier who knew better than to speak of what had passed. But the mark on his shoulder—burned flesh in the shape of a Roman numeral—spoke volumes.

He was branded.

Informant.

Not Roman. Not rebel.

Something in between.

Despised by both.

He wandered after that, never sleeping in the same place twice. He avoided crowds. Avoided the old trade routes unless the price was high or the silence worth breaking.

Outside Nazareth, it nearly ended. A small Zealot band—young, rash, and burning with purpose—recognized the mark beneath his cloak. They dragged him into the olive grove at dusk, strung him up with a coarse rope from the pack mule.

"You fed Rome our names," one snarled, tightening the knot. "Tell us one lie, and your neck snaps like a dry twig."

Mordecai didn't beg.

He spoke plainly. Deliberately.

"If I fed Rome your names, I wouldn't be here. I'd be rich. I'd be dead. But I'm here—on your road, with your enemies behind me and nothing in my hands." They hesitated — sensing some truth in his words.

"I know the soldier rotations near the gorge," he added. "The patrol that breaks for bread just past the third hour. You want weapons past the checkpoint? You'll need someone who's walked that road blindfolded."

The youngest one—barely more than a boy—loosened the rope.

The others followed.

They didn't trust him. Not fully. But they didn't hang him either.

He stayed a few days, passed messages between camps, traded silence for protection. Then he vanished again—slipping between camps, smuggling, informing, always calculating.

Mordecai became a man without a nation.

No home.

No family.

Only leverage.

He heard, months later, that Lois's house had been searched again.

That Matthias was nothing more than a shell of a man.

That Leah had gone quiet the way lamps go quiet when oil runs out.

That Photine had returned.

He stayed away. Not out of guilt, but out of instinct. He'd become what the Romans wanted: a shadow.

What he didn't tell anyone—what he couldn't say aloud—was that somewhere in the middle of all the bargaining and betrayal, he started to believe someone had to control the chaos. If it weren't Rome, it would be bloodthirsty zealots. If it weren't zealots, it would be mad prophets stirring peasant mobs.

He had seen too much of the world to trust idealism.

He only trusted leverage.

And secrets.

And staying alive.

Until the rumors started.

A man in the wilderness. A voice crying out by the Jordan.

Not armed. Not political. Too loud to be ignored.

John, they called him. The Baptizer. He preached repentance like it was a weapon. Waded waist-deep in water, calling the righteous to confess their filth.

Some said he was Elijah returned. Others said madman. But they all listened. Even the Romans were watching.

Mordecai leaned in from the shadows of the tavern, cloaked and still, the hum of danger threading through his chest.

John didn't name names. Not yet.

But he spoke of one who would come. Greater.

A messiah, he claimed. A fire-bringer.

Not a zealot.

Not a king.

Something else.

And Mordecai didn't know whether to laugh or to start running.

He had not always been a man of control—anger and wine once controlled him. Captivity stripped even that.

In the Roman cells, there were no deals to be made, no favors to collect; he only had spare time. Time and silence and the scraping rhythm of chains. He fasted, not by choice, but his body hardened in its hunger. His mind sharpened.

At first, he raged. Then, he listened. And then, he watched.

He watched a zealot beaten for refusing to kiss a Roman's foot.

He watched a tax collector weep after his fingers were broken, whispering names for leniency.

He watched a boy die, crying for his mother.

And he felt something crack—not in grief, but in clarity.

There was no justice here. Only power.

And if power were a game, Mordecai would learn every rule.

He took up humble work, sweeping alleys behind a wine shop in Scythopolis. He bowed when he spoke. He quoted John the Baptizer, "Make straight the way." He offered bread to beggars and prayed at twilight.

Those who knew him once watched with suspicion. But even they began to wonder.

"Maybe prison changed him."

"He speaks like one who has seen the abyss."

"He's not the same."

And for a time, even Mordecai entertained the thought. That he could start over.

He washed the blood from his past and let the world write hope across his name.

But the shadows never really left.

They waited. They coiled.

He began visiting sympathizers in the hills, smiling when they spoke of revolution. Offering a name here, a warning there. Never enough to betray his mask.

And always, always listening.

It was in a market square, under the hush of an olive-seller's awning, that he first heard her name again.

"Photine," said the man, unaware of what he stirred. "She's back. With a husband now—Ezra, I think. Quiet folk, but smart. Kept their heads down during the worst of it."

The air left Mordecai's lungs like smoke. He turned, thanked the man, and walked away, face unreadable. But inside, a fire lit. A cold, searing hatred that had only smoldered until now.

But chains in Caesarea were not the only iron tightening. Rumors carried, sharp as glass, from coastal courts to hill-country doors. What began in a pit with salt and mildew found its echo even in Lois's threshold.

The house had fallen into a tense stillness after the initial reunion. Lois had prepared a modest meal—lentils, figs, and warm bread—but barely touched her plate. Ezra ate in silence, his eyes flicking toward the door more than once. Photine noticed how the neighborhood, once lively and loud with children's laughter and hawker calls, now whispered around them. A thick and uneasy hush had settled.

Lois finally broke it, her voice low and edged. "They searched the house two weeks ago.

Romans, with a scribe in tow. Turned over baskets, pried at the walls as if bread ovens hid rebels.

They asked about travelers—about me taking in those who don't belong."

Her hands tightened around her cup. "I told them nothing. But they will be back. A house once searched is never left alone."

Photine glanced at Ezra, and in his clenched jaw she saw the same truth: whatever chains bound Mordecai in Caesarea, suspicion had stretched its hand all the way here.

Lois pushed back her chair. The scrape of wood on stone made them both flinch. "Come," she said, her voice low but firm. "There is more I must show you."

She crossed the room with purpose, lamp in hand, and moved toward the narrow frame behind the hearth. Photine rose, heart tightening, and followed. Ezra came behind, shoulders stiff, eyes sharp as though expecting soldiers even within these walls.

Lois ducked through first, the lamp throwing a thin arc of gold onto the steps beyond. Ezra stooped to keep from scraping the low ceiling. Photine hesitated at the threshold, brushing her hand against the cool stone, before stepping after them.

The cellar opened into a chamber barely taller than a man, its air cool and damp, carrying the scent of earth that had been sealed away too long. Shelves lined the walls—jars of lentils and barley, pressed figs wrapped in waxed leaves, bundles of herbs hung from the beams to dry. In one corner sat a small water jar, another filled with oil. A pallet lay rolled against the wall, with folded blankets atop it.

"This was never used when I was young," Photine whispered, her voice low, reverent. "It was shut up… forgotten."

"I remembered it," Lois said, setting the lamp on a stone ledge. "After the first Roman raids. After hearing how neighbors vanished because they were too slow to flee. I couldn't keep the world from turning cruel, but I could make sure my house had a place for hiding. For waiting.

For surviving."

Ezra ran his hand along the nearest beam, solid and carefully set. "It's built to last."

Lois gave a short nod. "I couldn't do it alone. Caleb carried stones and held the lamp when my hands were full. Leah brought water and sand, steady as ever. It was quiet work—done at night, when no one noticed. If questions came, I said it was a root cellar. That much was true." She looked between them, her eyes burning. "But I meant it for more. For times like these."

Photine let her palm rest on one of the jars. The thought of Lois, year after year, quietly preparing this place—it pierced her with both gratitude and grief. "You thought of us," she said softly.

"I thought of all of you," Lois replied. "Of every child, every sister, every husband the world would try to take. And I decided my house would have a corner it could not reach."

Ezra crouched, inspecting the supplies, the careful order. "This could hold a family for weeks."

"Long enough," Lois said. "Long enough to outlast soldiers on patrol, or zealots scouring for food. Long enough for a mother to shield her children until the noise passes."

Photine lowered herself to the cool stone bench against the wall. For a moment, she closed her eyes, letting the cellar's damp quiet hold her. "It feels like a tomb," she murmured.

Lois laid a hand on her shoulder. "No. A tomb is where things end. This is where they wait to begin again."

The silence between them thickened, like the cellar itself was listening. Above, the faint creak of the house reminded them how thin the walls of safety really were.

Ezra broke it first. "Then if danger comes, we go here."

Lois met his gaze and nodded once. "If danger comes, you go here. And you stay alive." A pile of scrolls drew Ezra's eye—bundled carefully, wax seals unbroken.

"These aren't trade records," he said.

"No," Lois replied. "They're letters. Messages. Some from Judean families. Some from Galileans trying to find each other after raids. Some are warnings—coded, passed through hands I trust."

"And you kept them?" Photine asked.

"I'm not just an old woman selling fruit," Lois said quietly. "I've been watching. For years.

Because I knew this day would come."

"What day?" Ezra asked.

"The day you two would need to disappear."

The lamplight wavered, brushing the walls as though the stones themselves were listening.

Lois's eyes grew distant, as if she were remembering the years between. "When you escaped," she said, looking at Photine, "I thought it would break me. The soldiers questioning, the neighbors whispering. But it did the opposite. It woke me. I saw how many others were trapped—how many daughters had no way out. And I began to notice who still had courage left."

She lifted a small bundle of folded scraps from a shelf, bound with twine. "We found each other. A widow near Shiloh who smuggles oil past tax collectors. A mother in Tirzah who hides zealot sons beneath her floor. A girl in En-Gedi who memorizes names because she cannot write. They call it gossip, this thread between us, but it is more. It is survival."

Photine's throat tightened. She remembered Lois as a weary mother, bent under Mordecai's shadow, carrying silence like a second skin. Now, in the glow of the lamp, she seemed different—harder in some ways, sharper in others, yet also fuller, as though she had grown into a role she had not asked for but could not refuse.

"You're at the center," Photine whispered.

Lois shook her head. "No. I am only one hearth in a chain of them. But women trust me. Maybe because I lost as much as they did, maybe because I listen. The letters come, and I pass them. Sometimes bread with a mark in the crust. Sometimes a jar sealed with wax pressed twice. No man thinks twice about a woman with baskets."

Ezra studied her with new respect, his voice low. "You've built something Rome cannot see." "Not yet," Lois murmured. "But eyes are everywhere now. That is why you must know—the moment you set foot here, you became part of it."

She untied the twine around the packet of scraps and spread them across the low table. Most were written in a hand cramped and hurried, some in charcoal, some in faint ink. Others carried no words at all.

"This one," she said, holding up a strip of cloth dyed unevenly, "came from Galilee. It looks like a scrap from a market stall, but the pattern means the Romans are pressing conscriptions there. Families must scatter before the lists are made."

She set it aside and opened a small pouch. She drew a shard of pottery, its edges worn smooth. On its surface was a faint mark, two lines crossing with a third curved stroke. "A child carried this to me. It means zealots are gathering near Jericho. The mark is a sling, see? We pass it along, so others know to avoid the road."

Ezra leaned closer, studying it with careful eyes. "Simple. Nothing to trace."

"Exactly." Lois placed the shard back in the pouch. She lifted a piece of linen with a clumsy stitch in red thread. "This is from a woman in En-Dor. One stitch means safety. Two means danger. She sends it knotted into the hem of a basket cloth. No soldier asks a woman about her mending."

Photine touched the cloth with trembling fingers, her heart tight. "You've built a net," she whispered. "And all of us are inside it."

Lois nodded, her face shadowed but resolute. "It is women who hold the threads now. Men fight, men vanish, men betray. But we carry the baskets. We bake the bread. We pass the word. And we will not stop—not until our children have a world worth living in."

Outside, the night seemed too quiet, as if every sound had been swallowed. Photine's hand curled protectively around her stomach. Every rumor, every letter, every mark on cloth seemed to close around them, pointing to one truth: there was danger everywhere. In the markets. On the roads.

Even in their neighbors' whispers.

"We can't run. Not again," she said.

Ezra looked at her, then at Lois. "What do you want us to do?"

Lois walked to the far side of the cellar, pulled back a woolen blanket draped over a clay cistern. Inside floated a small, sealed vessel made of dark glass, and lifted it carefully.

"This came from someone inside Scythopolis," she said. "He said there's a man there—hidden in plain sight. The questions in Samaria, the merchant probes, the sudden uptick in road patrols—they trace back to him."

She unsealed the jar and tipped it, letting its contents spill into her palm. A shard of olive wood slid out, its surface worn smooth with age. The lines carved upon it were unmistakable—the same sling-mark Photine had carried in secret since her girlhood. Only this one was doubled—two strokes crossing, twin marks where there should have been one.

Photine's breath caught. Her hand went to her sash, fingers brushing the hidden shard her father had pressed into her palm when she was twelve. The last gift before he vanished. She drew it out with shaking fingers, holding the two side by side. They matched, as though born of the same hand.

Ezra's brow furrowed. "This came from Scythopolis? Then…" He looked at Photine. "You think it's him, don't you?"

"I don't think," she said, her voice low and trembling. "I know."

Lois exhaled sharply, clutching the lamp tighter. "It could be a trick. Someone who's seen your shard, someone trying to draw you out."

"Or," Photine whispered, unable to pull her eyes from the wood, "it's him. After all these years. This—this is the closest I've come to him since he left."

They were only guessing, but the weight of it pressed on them like certainty. Whether it was warning or invitation, the message had found her.

Ezra leaned against the cold stone wall, arms crossed. The lantern's flickering light cast long shadows behind him. Lois was quiet, watching him, her gaze shifting to the shard as though it still burned in Photine's hand.

"Mordecai, if he lives, won't stop," Lois said. "Not now. Not with Rome behind him. He's become something else. Not just bitter. Capable. Trained."

Ezra's jaw tightened. "Then what do we do? Wait until he knocks on the door?"

Three paths lay before them, each edged with danger. "We could go back," Ezra said, though the words sounded hollow even as he spoke them. "Back to the vines, the nets, the life we built."

"And wait for Mordecai or Romans to come?" Photine shook her head. "That would be walking into his hands."

"Scythopolis, then," Lois said quietly, her gaze fixed on the olive shard. "Follow the trail, see if this message truly comes from your father. But that's a road with no guide, no allies. You would be walking blind."

Photine felt the weight of both choices pressing into her chest. Home was a trap. Scythopolis was a void. Only beside Lois, within the shelter she had carved into the earth was something steady to hold to.

She curled her hand around the shard, its grain warm from her palm. "We stay," she said at last.

"Here. With you. At least until we know more."

Ezra searched her face, then gave a slow nod. "We stay."

Lois's shoulders eased, but only slightly. Her eyes darkened. "Then you must know this: staying will not keep him away. If it is truly Mordecai behind the questions and the patrols, his shadow will find its way even here."

The fire in the lamp guttered once, and for a breath, it seemed as though Mordecai himself stood among them. Unseen. Watching.

"You'll never outrun what we haven't outsmarted," Lois said, crouching near the sealed letters. Her fingers brushed the twine as though weighing the words inside. "And if you flee, he'll continue looking. The Romans will follow his lead."

Photine's gaze lingered on the cellar door, her thoughts tangled with the weight of the shard in her palm. "He wouldn't expect us to stay."

"No," Lois agreed. She hesitated, then added, "Especially not here. Especially not beneath this roof."

Lois glanced between them. "You could make it look like you've moved on. That you're just a family, running a quiet press. If he sees no threat, he may not strike."

Ezra frowned. "Or he might strike harder."

Photine stepped closer to him, her hand resting on her stomach. "Then we'll be ready."

The silence that followed was not the silence of fear, but of agreement—taut, deliberate, sealing itself like wax on a letter.

Ezra looked at her—really looked. Saw the set of her jaw, the steel in her spine, the life stirring beneath her hand. "If we do this," he said slowly, "we do it with open eyes. We give ourselves new names, new faces. We make the house a press, nothing more. When danger comes, we retreat here—" he gestured to the cellar walls, "—and we wait it out. And above all, we never let him see our fear."

Photine nodded, her gaze steady. "No more running. If he comes, let him find us standing."

Lois's lips curved faintly, the ghost of a smile. "Then it's decided. From tomorrow, you're no longer Ezra and Photine. You're my cousin, Nathan and Mara—an olive-worker and his wife. You run the press, you sell jars, you mind your own trade. Nothing more."

She moved to the shelves, pulling aside a bundle of plain garments. "Nathan wears the worker's tunic. Mara carries the baskets to market. The neighbors will learn these names quickly, and they will repeat them as if they always belonged."

Ezra—Nathan, now—exhaled slowly, as though shouldering a new skin. "The beams upstairs need shoring. The press needs to look busier than it is. We'll stack wood by the door, hang nets where they can be seen. If anyone watches, they'll see a home worth ignoring."

Mara ran her hand over the folded cloth, the name settling heavy but solid. "And if danger comes?"

"Then you come here," Lois said, touching the cellar wall. "You wait. The house above becomes the mask. The cellar remains the truth."

Nathan nodded once, firm. "Then we'll need more wine. If Romans come, let them drink and move on."

The plan hung in the air like a thread pulled tight. Their cover was chosen, their story rewritten. Aboveground, Nathan and Mara would run a quiet press. Belowground, in stone and silence, Ezra and Photine would endure.

That night, when the house finally hushed, Photine lay awake on the woven mat Lois had given her. Ezra's breathing settled beside her, steady, already carrying the weight of tomorrow's labor. But her chest rose too quickly, heart fluttering against the dark.

The shard pressed into her palm, warmer than it should have been. Her father's mark. The only proof of him she had carried since she was twelve—now doubled, answered, as if the past had reached across years and found her.

Was he alive?

The question gnawed like hunger. Had he somehow endured, wandering the ridges, leaving messages through hidden hands? Or had someone else picked up his sign and twisted it for their own?

Did he know she had been married into Akrabbim? Did he know what had become of her—her shame, her chains, her escape? Did he know she had survived? That she was still carrying his mark, hidden in her sash all these years?

Tears welled, sharp and sudden. She turned her face toward the wall. If he had lived, why had he not come back? Why leave his daughter to face men like Mordecai alone? And yet—if he was gone, if he had perished long ago—who had sent this shard now, echoing his hand, answering her silence?

Her chest ached with longing and suspicion. Hope, reckless and fragile, beat against her ribs even as dread whispered that it was a trap.

Beside her, Ezra stirred in his sleep. She pressed the shard to her lips, closing her eyes. "Father," she breathed silently, "is it you?"

The only answer was the weight of the olive wood and the sound of the sea wind groaning faintly through the shutters.

Sleep came late, tangled with memory and fear. In her dreams, she stood again at the millhouse, twelve years old, her father's hand warm around hers. Only this time, when he let go, she did not know if he was walking toward light or into shadow.

CHAPTER 8
BENEATH THE OLIVE TREE

The sun rose over Akrabbim like it always had, casting golden light across familiar hills and waking the sound of market carts and crowing roosters. But everything felt changed.

Nathan stepped into the courtyard with a bucket in hand, his steps easy, his face open. The fig tree stretched overhead, leaves rustling in the soft breeze. A neighbor passed by on the road, pulling a creaky cart filled with sacks of barley.

"Morning to you," the man called.

Nathan lifted the bucket slightly in greeting. "And to you."

The press stood behind him—quiet for now, its beams oiled and polished, the basin scrubbed clean. A show of peaceful industry. Anyone passing by would see a man rebuilding what had been lost—nothing more. But Nathan had spent the last two weeks reinforcing every hinge and latch, sharpening not only tools, but instinct.

Below, in the cool dark of the cellar, Photine sat at the stone table with her ledger open and a wax tablet beside it. Morning light didn't reach this far, but the lantern's glow was steady. She dipped her stylus and made another mark. Just a name. A dialect. A shift in tone.

Photine drew in a breath. The cellar was cold, but she no longer shivered. She'd grown used to the stillness. What had once felt like hiding now felt like watching. Listening. Recording.

Her herbs still grew in clay pots on the upper windowsill—fennel, thyme, rue. They weren't just for medicine now. They served as markers: one pot turned meant danger, two knocked together meant Ezra should vanish. A system born from shadows.

Upstairs, Lois sat beneath the olive tree, a spindle resting in her lap. She worked flax into thread with practiced ease—slower than she once had, but steady. At thirty-three, she had already lived lifetimes of loss and endurance. Those who passed by saw only a quiet woman with calloused fingers and a faraway look. Some thought her meek. Others thought her fading.

But her gaze missed nothing.

She kept time with the rhythm of the street. Who passed when. Who looked twice. Who stopped to ask about figs that weren't for sale.

Photine—Mara now—joined her by midday, offering a clay mug of water. Lois took it, sipping quietly.

Leah sat a few paces away, her fingers worrying the edge of a worn cloth. Her eyes tracked the spindle, then drifted, as if caught between past and present. When she looked up, her lips curved faintly. "Photine," she murmured. "Jotham will be glad you're home."

The name landed like a stone in the quiet yard. Mara froze, pulse racing. Lois's hand stilled on the spindle, her eyes flicking to the street, then back to Leah. "Shh, em," she said softly. "It's too hot for stories today."

Leah blinked, confused, then dropped her gaze back to the cloth, her fingers resuming their restless work.

Mara exhaled slowly, forcing her shoulders to relax. To Leah, she was still Photine—still tied to a marriage long dissolved in grief and stone. A slip of the tongue here, a careless word to the wrong ears, and everything could unravel.

Inside, Matthias muttered from his place near the hearth, his words slurred and trailing like smoke. No one answered. He spoke to ghosts more often than the living now.

Lois set the spindle down, her eyes sharp despite her calm face. "She knows you as Mara," she whispered, low enough for only Photine to hear. "But memories are tricky things. You must never answer when she calls you otherwise. Do you understand?"

Mara nodded, though her throat felt tight. "I understand."

"They've added another patrol near the south well," Mara murmured, her gaze on a passing group of boys chasing a goat. "Didn't stop, but they looked around more than usual." Lois nodded faintly. "They're mapping the town with their eyes. Measuring the ordinary." "They're watching for us," Mara said.

"No," Lois replied, her voice low and certain. "They're watching for a mistake. So we won't give them one."

Inside, Nathan restacked crates of oil jars, counting aloud just loud enough for those outside to hear him. The jars were real. The business was real. But beneath the last row, under a plank sealed with tar and wax, sat scrolls and messages.

The mill had gone silent nearly two years ago. After Jotham died, no one stepped up to run it properly. Mordecai had tried, but lacked the patience and trust of the workers. His temper drove away the last of the hands, and eventually, even he stopped pretending to care. By the time the Romans took him, the grinding stones sat still, vines creeping through the outer wall.

Matthias, once a formidable figure, now barely rose from his bed. His presence alone shielded the household—his name still carried weight among old allies—but it was a brittle kind of protection, fading with each season.

Left with three children and a hollowed household, Lois had adapted. The courtyard became a drying yard for herbs and threads. She bartered flax and olives, stitched garments for caravaners who needed quick repairs, and quietly rented out one of the old storage rooms to a spice trader passing through.

She did what had to be done.

By evening, the household shared bread and lentils under the fig tree. Caleb lingered close, his eyes always darting toward the lane. When a boy from the neighborhood came by with a basket of olives, Caleb brightened, slipping him a grin. The two darted off a few paces, laughing over some secret only boys their age could keep. Lois pressed a heel of bread into the boy's hand before he left, asking after his mother's cough.

Nathan ruffled Caleb's hair as he returned, sending him back to the table. Mara poured wine with steady hands and laughed when Nathan said something only she could understand.

For a moment, they looked like any family: ordinary, small, touched by hardship, but mending.

But the glances they exchanged weren't ordinary. They were deliberate.

Every moment was layered. Every gesture rehearsed.

They were no longer running. But they weren't safe.

Mara learned that sometimes, danger didn't arrive with shouting and spears. Sometimes it arrived smiling, asking the price of olives, already knowing the answer.

The days passed with unsettling rhythm—quiet mornings, cautious afternoons, and fire-lit evenings, and nights of strategizing behind closed doors.

By the second week, Mara's belly had begun to swell enough to be visible. It changed things—how she moved through the streets, how others looked at her. People smiled more readily now, offered her figs and well-wishes and hands to steady her step. The town softened in their presence.

She had helped it along. Lois had cut her hair blunt at the shoulders, and Mara darkened it with walnut stain until the sun struck it differently. A scarf draped low across her brow, hiding the line of her cheekbones, and a faint smudge of ash blurred the familiar curve of her jaw. Small changes, but enough that those who might have known Photine would pass her in the lane without pause.

It was her belly, though, that did the rest. A woman with a child was seen differently: less suspect, more rooted, folded into the rhythm of village life. No longer a wanderer. Just Mara—Nathan's wife, expecting, tending the press.

But the danger hadn't softened.

In the evenings, she and Nathan sat at the hearth, husking barley or binding scrolls with waxed thread. Nathan's fingers had grown rough again—calloused from the press, from carving messages in olive wood slats disguised as ledger covers. Mara noticed how he now walked the perimeter of their courtyard twice before sunset, how he kept a satchel near the back door with just enough silver, water, and dried meat for two days' travel.

"You still think we'll need to flee," she said once, as she watched him testing the knots on the satchel's drawstring.

"I don't plan on it," he answered. "But I remember what it feels like to wish I had."

They began developing contingency routes—one north through the hills, disguised as shepherds; another south through a dry ravine, hidden by a network of cave paths that only Lois knew well.

A third involved passage down the old Roman road disguised as laborers for a vineyard. Nathan had a friend near Taanach who owed him more than one favor.

Mara's role in these plans was more subtle. She rewrote trade ledgers with hidden patterns—rows that looked like inventory but read like dates and places when spoken aloud. She trained her eyes to recognize military gait, the way an officer's footfall carried authority even when dressed in homespun. She taught the neighborhood children a song about "the olive who ran from the sun," embedding the instructions to hide or alert Lois if soldiers came to the press.

Lois herself grew sharper with each passing day. She had stopped selling figs altogether. Now she offered tea and stories to anyone who lingered, making her more valuable. The men spoke freely to her, assuming she was too old to matter, too soft to threaten. She became their ears and warning bell.

One morning, Mara sat in the shaded alcove of their home, grinding fennel and coriander while pressing gently against the life moving beneath her ribs.

Nathan appeared in the doorway, holding a folded cloth. "For you."

She raised a brow. "It's not my name day."

"No. But I had it made."

She unfolded the cloth. A dark blue tunic, soft linen with intricate embroidery around the collar—swirls with the patterns she doodled in her ledger. Inside the hem was stitched a phrase in Greek:

Mētēr kai phylax — Mother and guardian.

Her throat caught. "It's beautiful."

"It's true," he said. "You carry life. And you guard it. Not just the one inside you—but ours, too."

She ran her fingers along the stitched words, then rose slowly and wrapped her arms around his waist. Her belly pressed between them. "I'll never stop."

Neither of them spoke for a long while. The fire crackled low, the night outside cloaked in wind and rustling palms.

Nathan gently pressed a hand to her back, steady and silent. In moments like this, when the world narrowed to breath and heartbeat, Mara often wondered how a man like him had come to be—so careful, so constant.

The truth was, Ezra ben Haggai had been shaped long before they met.

He was born in a Galilean hill town not far from Sepphoris, the son of a stoneworker and a healer. His father, Haggai, worked on Herodian projects, shaping stones for opulent bathhouses he'd never be allowed to enter. His mother, Naomi, passed quietly through the villages with her herb pouch and unshakable dignity, healing fevers and midwifing babies from one side of the region to the other.

From his father, Ezra learned patience—the way one must chisel slowly, that haste could crack the whole foundation. From his mother, he learned to listen. To human voices, to pain, to plants.

But by the time he was twenty, Sepphoris had burned twice— once under Roman retaliation, and once by zealots trying to provoke that retaliation.

Ezra watched the cost of both.

He lost a brother, Malachi, to a conscription sweep—arrested by Roman scouts who never gave a reason. Just a name. He was never seen again.

The grief sharpened Ezra. While others around him picked sides—join the rebels or report to the authorities—Ezra learned to move between them. He became a smuggler of letters, carrying hidden messages in hollowed-out tools and layered parchment. He never joined a sect, never shouted in the streets. But his hands were always in the dust where others wouldn't look. He brokered safety. Not rebellion—survival.

Eventually, it became too dangerous. A name surfaced on a Roman list. His name.

So he disappeared.

He left behind a betrothal he didn't ask for and a family he couldn't endanger. With forged trader's papers and the help of an old friend from Taanach, he re-emerged in En-Dor years later, rebuilding himself as a merchant—olive oil, grain, figs. The kind of honest labor no one questioned too closely.

In those early years, he had not been alone. Tirzah had come into his life like spring rain—gentle, steady, unexpected. They married quietly, and for a season he let himself believe the world might grant him peace. Their home smelled of pressed oil and baked bread, their laughter weaving easily into the rhythm of market days. But the fever came swift and merciless, burning through her within a week. Ezra buried her beneath a grove of olives, the soil still soft with blossoms.

After that, something in him closed. He worked. He traded. He kept his face toward the ledgers and his heart turned to stone. Love was a door he locked tight, unwilling to open it to grief again.

Until Hadassah and Sarah interfered. They saw what he would not: the way Photine's resilience mirrored his own, the way her sharpness could soften him, the way his steadiness might anchor her. They arranged their meeting with the kind of boldness only women possess—the certainty that two broken halves might find wholeness in each other.

Sarah, niece to Hadassah, brought her to him—broken, fevered, half-starved after slipping away from Mordecai's house under the cover of night. Ezra had been in the region on trade, gathering dried herbs and mineral salts from southern merchants, a route he only took twice a year. He had crossed paths with Hadassah once before, years earlier, when he helped settle a debt for her cousin in the Decapolis. She remembered him—not just for his fairness, but for the way he listened without judgment.

Ezra offered what he could. A name. A marriage contract. A home carved from silence and cedar. A place no one would think to look for a woman like Photine.

At first, Ezra and Photine were strangers in every sense. She distrusted him—men in general, and Galilean men most of all. He gave her space. Let her speak when she wished. Gave her tools for the press and left her alone in the garden. Slowly, something unspoken softened between them. They worked side by side in silence that wasn't hostile but healing. Trust came in glances. In shared bread. In the way, he never asked what she didn't offer.

Then came laughter—rare at first, then more frequent, like a well thawing in spring. She brought new life into the press. He brought calm.

Without either of them realizing when, their quiet survival became love—became life—became family.

Now, as Nathan sat with his back to the plastered wall of Lois's house, the lamp-light warm across the room, he let the memory sink back into the marrow of the past and opened his eyes to the present. The years between seemed both long and short. He could still see

Tirzah's grave beneath the olive blossoms. He could still picture Sarah's determined face, arranging, insisting, nudging him toward a woman whose eyes burned with fire and grief all at once.

And here they were.

Mara sat across the room, speaking softly with Lois. Their voices mingled—low, thoughtful, tinged with affection. Mara's hands rested on her lap, one curved lightly over her belly, the other turning a clay cup as she spoke. Lois leaned closer, her face lined with weariness but softened with love. They were speaking of the girls again. Lois missed them fiercely—her daughters gone to a women's shelter in the hill country, a monastery of sorts, where vows and community kept them safe from raids and prying soldiers. She spoke of them with a blend of pride and ache: how strong they were, how they had learned to keep silence when needed, how they laughed too loudly when they were safe.

"They are safe," Lois said, though her eyes shimmered with tears she did not wipe away. "Safer there than here, where patrols pass every week now."

"They'll return," Mara murmured. "And when they do, they'll find you waiting. That will steady them more than you know."

Lois smiled faintly. "Leah believes them to be betrothed."

At the mention of her name, Leah glanced up from the stool by the hearth. She held a small cup of tea in both hands, sipping carefully as if savoring each drop. Mara had brewed it for her earlier—mint and a touch of wild thyme. Leah's eyes were distant, but at the sound of her sisters' names, something flickered there.

"They're married by now," she said, almost dreamlike, though a note of certainty threaded her words. "Married and happy. I can feel it."

Mara and Lois exchanged a glance over her head. Neither corrected her. Some truths were better left gentle, not sharpened. Mara only smiled and reached to refill Leah's cup, brushing her hand with tender care.

On the other side of the room, Caleb sat cross-legged on the floor, a flat board balanced across his knees. Nathan leaned over him, guiding his hand as he scratched marks into the board with a bit of charcoal. The boy's tongue stuck out in concentration, his brow furrowed.

"Like this," Nathan said softly, steadying Caleb's wrist. "Strong, straight line. Then cross it here.

See? It holds together, like beams in a roof."

Caleb grinned when the shape appeared under his hand. "It looks like a gate."

"It is a gate," Nathan said. "Every letter is a kind of gate. It opens into meaning."

The boy nodded solemnly, his grin still tugging at his lips. He tried another mark, then another, smudging his fingers with charcoal dust. Nathan let him, correcting gently, never impatient. Teaching Caleb felt like tending vines—you guided, but you didn't force. Growth came in its own time.

Across the room, Lois's spindle rested unused in her lap. She had set it aside to listen more fully to Mara. Nathan could hear fragments of their conversation—bits about water jars and pressing olives, about the marketplace and who had asked after figs that day. But beneath it all was the steady undertone: they were making a life here, weaving threads of ordinary days to mask the danger pressing in at the edges.

For the first time in many weeks, the house sounded like a home. The crackle of the hearth. The murmur of women's voices. The scratch of charcoal. The soft clink of Leah's cup against the table. Even Matthias's low, half-coherent muttering from his corner felt less like a burden tonight, more like part of the familiar hum of family.

Nathan's chest tightened unexpectedly. He had lived so long in fear, in loss, in the restless drive to survive. To sit in a room filled with warmth, laughter, and quiet care. It felt almost dangerous to hope. Yet hope was there, fragile but real.

Mara laughed suddenly at something Lois said, her head tipping back, her hand brushing her belly as if steadying herself. The sound caught Nathan off guard. He hadn't heard that kind of laughter from her since… maybe ever. Not sharp, not bitter, not wry—pure laughter, the kind that belonged to a woman who felt safe for a heartbeat of time.

He met her eyes when she glanced his way. For a moment, the world narrowed to that look, the firelight catching in her gaze, the corners of her mouth still curved. Nathan felt the same rush he had when he first realized he loved her. Not out of pity, not out of duty, but with the fierce certainty that she was his life's companion. The past had been lost, yes. But the present was this: a woman who had chosen him, who had built trust from the ashes of betrayal, who carried his child.

He wanted to hold onto that moment forever.

Caleb tugged his sleeve. "Did I do it right?" the boy asked, pointing to the crooked line on the board.

Nathan smiled and bent again, steadying Caleb's hand. "Almost. But even crooked lines have meaning. Try again."

The boy beamed and set to work, eager to please.

Mara rose after a while, moving to Leah's side with a gentle grace. She refilled her tea, smoothing her hair back from her face.

Leah leaned into her touch, sighing softly. "They'll come home," she said again, almost like a child. "The girls will come home."

Mara's eyes flickered. She kissed Leah's temple and whispered, "Yes. They will."

Memory tugged at her—of Leah, when Mara had first come into the household as a frightened fourteen-year-old bride. Leah had been steady then, her voice soft but firm, her hands capable and always busy. Mara remembered how Leah used to set figs and honey before Jotham, smoothing the table with the same tenderness she now used to fold cloth or sip tea. She had hushed the household's quarrels with a single look, drawn water with her sleeves rolled back, and prayed over the hearth with a quiet faith that seemed to steady the whole house.

Now, older and worn, Leah's fingers trembled slightly as she clutched her cup, her hair threaded with silver. Yet Mara still saw the same tenderness that had once soothed her terror as a young bride. The same care that had once wrapped around Jotham, and by extension, around her.

Nathan watched them, his heart heavy and light at once. He thought of the first days with Mara—her mistrust, his silence, the long hours at the press when words were few but glances were plenty. And how slowly, unavoidably, love had come.

Now, here in Lois's house, with the press humming quietly in the yard, with Caleb learning letters at his side, with Leah sipping tea and Mara laughing again—he knew he had not merely survived. He had lived.

Danger still prowled at the edges. Mordecai's shadow stretched long. Rome's boots still echoed in the streets. But tonight, for this one evening, Nathan allowed himself to believe in more than survival.

He believed in family.

He believed in hope.

He believed that love, however fragile, was stronger than fear.

When the lamp burned low and Lois finally ushered Leah to her bed, the household began to soften into night. Caleb curled onto his mat, clutching the board with his crooked letters as if he'd written something holy. Mara smoothed the blanket over him, her touch gentle, her eyes tender.

Her breath caught as she looked at him—no longer the small, wide-eyed three-year-old she had left behind, but a boy of seven, though wise for his years. His limbs were long now, his shoulders already showing strength. He carried himself with a quiet pride, steady and observant, nothing at all like his father. Thank God for that.

The memory of leaving him rose sharply in her chest. She had kissed his curls once more, pressed her palm to his cheek, and walked away with her heart breaking. For years, guilt had clung to her—guilt for not staying, for not shielding him, for not knowing if she would ever see him again.

And now, here he was, warm under her hand, growing strong, learning letters at Nathan's side. She let herself smile, but the guilt did not vanish. Instead, it twisted into a deeper fear: would she be forced to leave him again? Would the fragile safety, the laughter, the small semblance of family be torn away once more?

She leaned down, kissed his temple, and whispered a prayer into his sleep. "Not again. Please, not again."

Nathan stepped quietly outside. The night air wrapped cool around his shoulders, a sharp contrast to the warmth of the hearth. Above him, the stars spilled across the sky in their ancient, familiar scatter. He stood still, listening. The distant hush of wind through fig leaves. The muted lap of water in the jars. Somewhere far off, the faint clatter of hooves—Roman patrols, always circling.

He tilted his head back, breathing deep. How many nights had he stood like this—alone, guarded, waiting for danger? Too many to count. But tonight was different. Tonight, behind him, there was a home full of life. Mara's laughter still lingered in his ears. Caleb's questions still tugged at his heart. Lois's steady wisdom still anchored him. Even Leah's fragile murmurs carried weight—threads of memory binding them together.

For a fleeting moment, he imagined Tirzah standing beside him under these same stars. Her absence no longer stabbed, but pulsed gently. He closed his eyes, let her memory settle, and then opened them again to the present. Mara.

The child she carried. The fragile web of family that, against all odds, had become his.

He whispered into the night, not sure if it was prayer or promise: "We will endure. We will live."

The stars gave no answer but their quiet, ancient glow.

When he turned back inside, the air grew warmer with each step, scented with bread, oil, and the faint sweetness of Mara's herb tea. He paused at the threshold, watching for a moment. Lois had settled back at her spindle. Leah was curled on her side, still clutching her cup, though she slept. Mara caught his eye from across the room, her hand resting on her belly, her face lit by the last of the lamplight.

Nathan's heart steadied. Whatever storms gathered beyond these walls, tonight there was shelter. Tonight, there was love.

And for the first time in many years, he allowed himself to believe that might be enough to carry them through.

CHAPTER 9
A ROMAN RETURN

Months had passed since they returned, and still no one had come knocking. No messengers, no questions. Only silence. Nathan knew this was not peace—it was a coil drawn tight, waiting to snap.

Nathan and Mara. The names no longer felt like costumes but like garments worn into shape. In the market, neighbors knew them as the olive-worker and his expectant wife, quiet people who minded their trade and their household. Nathan had learned to nod in greeting, to ask about the weather and the harvest, to lean on the press as though it had always been his. Mara carried baskets to the stalls, spoke softly with the women. Even Caleb had settled into the role of their boy, running errands, carrying jars, practicing his letters by lamplight.

Mara moved more slowly now. Her belly had grown heavy with life, but she refused to be idle. She still helped with the press when she could, though Nathan watched her closely. Lois, ever watchful, had taken over most of the housework and kept a quiet vigil at the window each evening. Leah drifted in and out of clarity, sipping the tea Mara brewed for her, sometimes calling her by the wrong name, sometimes speaking of Jotham as though he might walk in the door.

The town, too, had changed. Roman boots scuffed the cobbled lanes more frequently. Market whispers died quickly when patrols passed. Trade had slowed, and travelers kept to themselves.

There was a thickness to the atmosphere. Nathan had learned to read these signs in other towns, other lives. This was what came before an incursion.

And yet, for all their readiness—for all the hidden scrolls, the escape route behind the hearth, the signals they'd practiced—nothing prepared them for how Mordecai returned.

Not through the gate.

Not with soldiers or fanfare.

But quietly. On a market morning.

Wearing new robes. A limp he hadn't had before. And a Roman seal pinned to his chest.

At first, it was only talk.

A merchant passing through mentioned a new official seen near Scythopolis—a local, some said, but dressed like a Roman. Wore the seal, walked with their posture, but didn't speak like one of them. Not quite. He had the air of a man who'd studied his enemies too well and become like them.

Then came the baker's son, delivering bread to the outpost south of the town. He spoke of a man with a crooked step and eyes like cold metal who asked too many questions about olive yields, water access, and the "old families" of Akrabbim.

Mara heard the story in fragments. First from Lois, then from a traveler passing through the press, and finally from Nathan, who brought it home with the same look he'd worn the day they descended into the cellar for the first time. That look that said: *Something is coming. Get ready.*

Mordecai had always known how to disappear. What was more unsettling was how well he'd learned to return.

They didn't know what the seal meant exactly—whether it was ceremonial, or symbolic, or worse: earned. But Lois believed it was tied to Rome's new obsession with local control. Why conquer outright when you could recruit? Why use force when you could twist loyalty into something sharper?

"He's not a soldier," she said one night over figs and wine. "He's worse. He's a convert. The kind Rome uses to gut its enemies from the inside."

Nathan didn't answer. He just stared into the flickering lamplight. Mara sat beside him, her hand resting on the curve of her stomach.

It was one thing to prepare for an attack. Another thing entirely to prepare for someone who still knew where the trapdoor was hidden, and how to make you question whether he might've changed.

The first time Mara saw him again, it was not in a dream, though it felt like one.

It was just before dusk, that strange golden hour when the town softened and even the shadows looked weary. Nathan had gone to speak with a buyer from Damascus, and Lois was in the garden pulling fennel. Mara had climbed to the roof, where rows of clay jars lined the parapet and bundles of figs, onions, and thyme lay spread to dry in the waning heat.

She moved slowly between them, settling low beside a half-sealed jar of olives. The air was heavy with dust and sweetness, the faint hum of bees still circling the fig bundles. She bent to knot a muslin sachet of herbs, but a sudden glint of metal caught her eye through the narrow gap between jars.

She stilled.

From her vantage, she could see the street below. A man moved through it with a gait she remembered in her bones—slight drag of the left foot, the same rhythm she had once heard in the night outside her chamber. Mordecai.

Mara's breath caught. She ducked instinctively lower, though she knew he wasn't looking up.

Her hands pressed against the rough clay rim of the jar, grounding herself as her pulse raced.

He wore new robes, ochre-dyed and edged in crimson, and a Roman seal pinned to his chest. But it was not the seal alone that chilled her—it was the way the people shifted aside, out of unease, leaving a pocket of emptiness around him as he passed.

From her hiding place among the jars, Mara watched him pause at a market stall, lift an orange, turn it slowly in his hand, then return it without a word. The vendor forced a smile.

Mara pressed herself deeper into the shadow of the jars. The muslin sachet slipped from her lap, spilling thyme sprigs across the roof tiles. She didn't stoop to gather them. Her gaze stayed locked on the man below.

When Mordecai turned slightly, his face caught the dusk light. No smile. No hate. Only calculation.

Mara's hand curled over her swelling belly. Life stirred beneath her palm, a flutter against the silence. She stayed crouched, unseen, watching the man who had once broken her world move as if he now owned the ground he walked on.

Only when he vanished into the crowd did she sink fully to the tiles, breath trembling out of her chest. The jars around her suddenly seemed too fragile, too breakable—like everything she had built since.

She stilled.

Then he was gone, swallowed by the crowd, as if he'd only stepped into view to remind the earth he was still upon it.

Mara sank back against the low parapet, heart hammering, a tremor running through her legs. She wasn't afraid of him. Not exactly. What she feared was the knowing—that no matter how far she'd come, no matter how much she'd built or how strong she'd grown—he still haunted the very soil of her story. And now, he had come back to claim it.

The roof should have felt safe. Up here, she was hidden among the jars and drying bundles, a woman at work in the ordinary rhythms of the household. The clay beneath her palms still held the heat of the day, anchoring her. From this height, she could see without being seen—or so she told herself. Yet the higher she sat, the more exposed she felt, as though the whole street could feel her eyes pressing down. The rooftops of Akrabbim were open places, not fortresses. They gave sight, yes, but not shelter.

She curled against the line of jars and kept her gaze fixed on the street corner where Mordecai had disappeared. The sounds of the town rose around her—the thump of a closing shutter, the bray of a tethered goat, the hiss of fish charring on a brazier. Every note seemed sharpened, edged with threat. Even the scent of thyme, drying in neat bundles at her side, felt laced with bitterness.

The sun had dipped low by the time Nathan climbed the narrow steps to the roof. His shadow stretched long across the tiles before he reached her. He found her still crouched among the jars, hands motionless though the bundles around her brimmed with figs and herbs. She hadn't moved in several minutes, and Nathan knew her well enough by now to recognize when silence meant danger.

He touched her shoulder gently. "You saw him, too."

Mara didn't answer at first. Her eyes stayed locked on the place where Mordecai had been, as if staring could keep him from returning. Finally, she turned, her voice low. "That was him." Nathan furrowed his brow. "The man in the crimson trim? With the Roman seal?"

She nodded once. "Mordecai."

Nathan's mouth parted slightly, but no sound came. He looked toward the street again, as though he might catch the shadow lingering. "He walked like someone who expects the earth to make way."

Mara wrapped her shawl tighter around her shoulders, though the evening air was still warm. "Because he's wearing Rome now. And Rome doesn't kneel."

They rose slowly, leaving the scattered herbs where they had fallen, sprigs of thyme spread across the roof like spilled prayers. Nathan kept close as they descended the steps together, his hand brushing hers without fully gripping it. From below, the roof looked ordinary again—jars, bundles, sun-warmed clay. But Mara knew better. From now on, every rooftop in Akrabbim would feel like both a watchtower and a target.

Nathan, steadying himself, then said, "We've been preparing. We thought he might come back."

"Not like this. Not with a badge on his chest and guards shadowing him like he's become…" Her voice trailed off, then firmed again. "He's not a man anymore. He's a symbol now. And those are harder to kill."

Nathan exhaled, a long breath of disbelief and rising anger. "You knew it was him the moment you saw him?"

She nodded. "His eyes haven't changed. He looked through people then, and he still does."

Inside the home, Leah sat on a low stool, weaving cord beside Matthias's cot. The old man's breath came slow and ragged, his skin pale as linen. A bowl of broth sat untouched beside him. Lois emerged from the back room, wiping her hands on her sash, her gaze lifting instantly to meet theirs.

"You've both gone pale," she said. "What did you see?"

Mara didn't answer. Nathan spoke first. "A man in Roman colors. Seal on his chest. Looked like a command."

Lois's eyes narrowed. "Did he speak?"

"No," Mara said. "He didn't have to."

Leah rose from her stool, brow furrowed. "Who was it?"

Mara stepped forward, voice steady but cold. "Mordecai."

The room fell quiet except for the low hiss of the fire. Lois's face went unreadable. Leah looked from one to the other, confused. "I thought he was—"

"Gone," Lois finished. "We all thought that. Until today."

Mara crossed to the window, her hand again resting on the curve of her stomach. "We need to prepare."

Nathan moved beside her. "For what?"

Mara stared out into the fading light. "For the part of the story he thinks still belongs to him."

Lois nodded grimly. "Then tonight, we make the house ready."

Behind them, Matthias stirred in his sleep and murmured a word no one understood. The sound lingered in the room like an omen, then faded back into silence.

Mordecai stood in a tented pavilion pitched near the old watchtower above the ascent, where the ridge fell sharply into the valley. Torchlight rippled over the polished bronze basin before him, the reflection showing a man both familiar and not. His beard, once unruly and stained with dust from the road, was now trimmed to precision. His hair was slicked back with oil. But it was the seal on his chest—red and black and stamped in wax above his heart—that marked the true transformation.

The desert wind carried the smell of dust and scorched brush. From this height, the lamps of Akrabbim glowed faintly below, scattered like fireflies across the stone. He could have entered the gates. He could have claimed a house, sat in the square, let the people kneel or spit. But why take the town by force when he could take it by waiting?

Staying outside was no hesitation. It was a strategy. He knew the people would feel his nearness more keenly if he lingered just beyond reach, letting rumor stretch its legs before him. Every shutter closed too quickly, every whisper cut short in the market, every child pulled closer by a nervous hand—those were his heralds.

He didn't need to walk their streets to command them. All he needed was to let them imagine his footsteps. To let the thought of his return scrape against their minds until the fear became louder than his presence.

From the ridge, he watched the town flicker below and smiled thinly. *Let them wait. Let them wonder. The dread will do half my work before I even descend.*

Mordecai of Akrabbim was dead. He had buried that long ago, deep beneath blood and strategy and the hard choices only survivors were willing to make.

The tunic he wore had been tailored in Caesarea. The ring on his right hand was cast with the insignia of a Roman courier, though his authority stretched beyond mere message-bearing now. He was the liaison between Rome's garrisons and the smaller Jewish provinces, a man fluent in the tongues of both rebellion and empire. A useful man. A dangerous man.

He flexed his hand slowly, the skin pulling tight where an old scar ran from wrist to elbow—a wound carved in the heat of his own rage. He told himself it had been buried, like the night Photine vanished: the jar, the shards, the look in her eyes. Yet standing here, back in the ridges of his youth, the memory rose again like a thorn under the skin.

That night, he stepped into the khan on the edge of the square, the place where traders stopped before heading north. The air was thick with smoke and goat stew, laughter cut with suspicion. Conversation dipped when he entered. Men noticed the seal before they noticed his limp.

He didn't call for wine. He didn't need to. The barkeep slid him a cup without asking, because of the crimson trim on his robe, because of the Roman seal on his chest.

At first, he said little. Let them watch him, let them measure the sash, the ring, the limp that had not slowed him. Then he leaned on the counter, voice low but carrying.

"Town like this," he said, not to anyone in particular. "Too many old names. Too many people hiding behind them."

A murmur spread. One man at the corner asked carefully, "And who decides who's hiding?" Mordecai smiled thinly. "The one with the seal." He tapped his chest once, deliberately.

He drank the wine, set the cup down without finishing it, and turned to leave. At the door, he paused, just long enough for his words to sink in.

"Tell your neighbors," he said. "Rome is listening."

By the time he stepped back into the night air, the message was already working. Windows shuttered early. A woman pulled her child inside, though the street was quiet. Men glanced at one another with unease, wondering who he meant, who Rome suspected.

And below him, the town of Akrabbim lay hushed, its narrow lanes bathed in the faint glow of oil lamps. From his perch above the ridge, Mordecai could see the scatter of rooftops, the press yards, the garden plots pressed against stone. One house, shaded by a fig tree, held its light longer than the rest.

He did not stare at it. He didn't need to. His shadow stretched across the ridge and seemed to pour down into the valley, long and dark, as if the town itself already lay beneath his hand.

Inside, Mara shivered though no wind had entered. Nathan drew her close. Lois stood by the window, gaze fixed outward, eyes sharp as flint.

They all knew what the town would soon whisper:

Mordecai had returned.

Not as a man.

As Rome's shadow.

The night held its breath, and then it passed.

Dawn rinsed the streets of Akrabbim with thin light and a breath of cooler air. Market women lifted their awnings with broom handles, boys ran errands with heel-bread in their fists, and the first jars clinked against one another as traders set out their wares. The square always woke before the sun had fully cleared the ridge.

Caleb was there early, as Nathan had taught him. "First feet, first sales," Nathan liked to say, and Caleb had taken it to heart. He carried a small tray with two stoppered vials of oil and a wedge of olive wood for tally marks, proud of how he could keep count like a man. He set the tray beside the fig seller's stall, then darted to the well to draw water for Lois before the women formed their line.

He was halfway back, sloshing a little and grinning at his own speed, when he heard the men near the brazier. They weren't speaking loudly, but Caleb had learned to hear the kind of quiet that mattered— the kind people used when the words had edges.

"Came in last night, seal bright as blood," one said, turning fish on the grill. "Didn't order stew, just ordered silence."

"Local." The other sniffed, half disdain, half fear. "Not born to Roman bone. Wears their trim like a borrowed cloak."

"Borrowed or not, it fits him," the brazier-man replied. "He says Rome is listening."

"He didn't need to say it," a third voice cut in. "He looked like Rome."

Caleb eased closer until the heat of the brazier kissed his shins. He pretended to watch the fish, eyes on the spit, ears drinking in the words. He knew he should move on. Nathan always said:

Don't let your feet root where men bury secrets. But the names tugged at him like a fishline.

"Who's he after?" the second man asked.

"Snakes," the brazier-man said. His laugh was small and mean. "Whatever that means today."

"Old families first," someone muttered. "He asked the baker's boy about water rights, olive yields, names that still open doors."

"Names like…?" The word trailed off suggestively, as if the man wanted to say it and swallow it in the same breath.

Caleb swallowed for him. He didn't speak, but inside his head the names lined up in a row, neat as jars: Lois. Leah. Nathan. Mara.

He took one step back, then another, tray wobbling. The brazier popped, sending a fleck of hot fat against his ankle. He didn't yelp, though he did flinch; still, he listened.

"He's camped up by the old watchtower on the ridge," the third man said. "Not a soldier, exactly.

A listener."

"Worse," the brazier-man said. "A rememberer."

Caleb's fingers tightened on the wooden handle until his knuckles paled. *A rememberer.* He knew what that meant. Men who remembered could string small things into ropes. They could pull on those ropes until the houses moved.

A boy he knew from the olive grove—Asher—sidled up, breathless, too pleased to be the bearer of what he knew. "Did you hear?" he whispered, eyes bright. "He tapped his chest and said Rome listens through him."

Caleb forced his shoulders to lift like he didn't care, like he was only there for the smell of fish. "Who cares what he says?" he muttered, trying on Nathan's steady tone, the one that made grown men stop talking.

But Asher's grin only widened. "You should care. My father says it's *your father*—the one with the limp. He's the man with the seal."

Caleb's breath snagged. He hadn't seen his father in more than a year. He remembered broad shoulders darkened by the press, a voice that barked more than it sang, a presence that filled a room like fire fills a lamp. And now that same man was a shadow on the ridge, carrying Rome's mark.

His stomach lurched. The tray wobbled in his hands, jars clinking. He tightened his grip until the wood bit into his palms.

"My father's gone," he said too sharply, almost to himself. "He's gone."

But Asher only shrugged, careless of truth. "Not gone. Changed. Rome keeps what it wants."

Caleb turned away before the boy could see the wet gathering at his eyes. He walked fast, almost spilling the water he carried, and told himself it was only dust stinging his throat.

"Move along, boys," the brazier-man called without looking, as if kindness was something that must be concealed. "You'll smell like fish all day."

Caleb bobbed his head and turned, tray steady again. He kept his pace even until he cleared the square and the talk bent away from him. Only then he quickened, slipping into the side lane where the stone held the night's cool, cutting across the little yard where the goat chewed the same patch of fence, back toward the house that smelled of oil and bread and mint.

Mara was by the doorway, tying a clean cloth around a basket handle. Leah sat beneath the window, cup cradled, eyes soft and far. Lois stood a little back from the threshold, watching the street like she could weave it into obedience with her gaze.

Caleb stopped just short of them, the tray braced against his hip. His throat felt tight, his words fighting to come out and stay hidden at the same time. He tried to make his voice sound casual, the way Nathan's could when speaking of heavy things.

"They're saying a man with a seal went to the Inn," he told Lois, because she was the one you told first. "They said he told people Rome is listening."

Mara's hand froze on the knot. "Did they say his name?"

Caleb shook his head quickly, too quickly. "They didn't have to." He hesitated, then dug his fingers into the wood of the tray. "They said… they said it was my father." The word trembled out of him like a loose stone rolling down a hill.

Leah blinked, her eyes stirring at the sound of it, but Lois's gaze didn't waver. She only pressed her lips thin, and for a moment, that steadiness made Caleb want to both collapse against her and run.

"It can't be," he blurted. "He's gone. He's been gone. He doesn't—he wouldn't—" His voice broke, and he bit down on it hard, as though silence could shove the words back where they belonged.

Mara came toward him, her belly heavy, her face soft with worry. But Caleb stiffened, shoulders squared in a way too old for seven years. He had been the one to fetch water, to split figs, to carry jars before Nathan came. He had been the one to keep the household steady when the air was thick with loss. He didn't want to be held now like a child who didn't understand. He understood too much.

"They said he has Rome's seal," he whispered. His voice was small now, almost ashamed. "If it's him… then he's not my father anymore."

Lois stepped forward, laying a hand on his shoulder. Her touch was firm, anchoring, not coddling. "Listen to me, Caleb. Blood doesn't decide who you are, or who we belong to. What matters is who we choose to stand with. Do you hear me?"

Caleb nodded, though his jaw clenched. He wanted to believe her. He wanted to believe Nathan's steady hands and Mara's quiet laughter were enough to hold the house. But in the back of his mind, a voice whispered: *What if it really is him? What if he comes here?*

Just then, Nathan stepped around the corner with a coil of rope over his shoulder and a smile meant for the neighbors. "Caleb," he said easily, "help me hang the nets where the road can see."

Caleb exhaled in relief. A job. Something solid, something that didn't twist in his chest. He hurried to Nathan's side, balancing the tray with one hand and the rope with the other.

As they walked toward the press yard, Nathan bent slightly, his voice pitched for Caleb alone. "You did right to listen," he said, "and better to walk away when the words get sharp. But next time, tell me first. You don't have to carry it alone."

Caleb nodded, though his eyes burned. "Yes, Nathan." The name tasted heavy but safe, like bread that filled the stomach even when it was hard to chew.

They set the nets where passersby would see the day's work: a household busy, a trade alive, nothing more. Nathan pegged the rope, his hands quick and sure. Caleb mirrored him, learning by motion, the way boys do when the world is watching. He focused on the knots, on the roughness of the rope, anything but the words still echoing in his head: *They said it was my father.*

Inside, Mara leaned closer to Lois, her hand resting on the swell of her belly. "If it's true…" she whispered.

Lois's jaw tightened. "Then we give him nothing to claim."

"Then we flood him with ordinary," Lois said. "We drown his memory in sameness. The same baskets. The same jars. The same smiles. We make the days so dull he forgets what he came for."

Leah looked up, the tilt of her head like a bird's. "What did he come for?" she asked, her voice mild and far.

Mara touched Leah's shoulder. "To test our faith," she said gently, and Leah accepted this as if it were a proverb and returned her gaze to the window's square of light.

But when Leah's eyes drifted away, Mara and Lois shared a glance. Did he already know Photine was here? Or was he probing, waiting for the cracks to show? Was his presence above the ridge meant for her specifically, or for the town at large?

Lois folded her hands together, knuckles white. "If he suspects," she murmured, "we'll see it soon enough. If he doesn't… then we must give him nothing that tells him otherwise."

Mara nodded, though her heart pressed hard against her ribs. The not-knowing was its own kind of torment.

By midday, the story had already moved ahead of its teller. Children repeated it with mismatched details—some said the man had gold at his throat, some said he carried a whip, some said his eyes were two coins stacked on their edges. Men tested the words for weakness. Women tucked them away and sorted them by usefulness. The town did what towns do: it made the rumor into a garment everybody would have to wear for a while.

Nathan kept his hands busy and his face easy. Mara sold two jars and traded for fresh bread and salt, her scarf drawn carefully so the light caught her differently. She spoke softly, never lingering in conversation, her laughter practiced and quiet. Every movement was measured to make her look like any expectant wife at market, not a woman with a history worth noticing.

Lois asked about a neighbor's cough and recommended thyme steeped in honey. Leah drank her tea in sips and folded a cloth and laid it flat, like smoothing a troubled brow.

Across the square, a shutter moved when no wind lifted it. A figure stood for a heartbeat and was gone. The town's surface kept its rhythm—jars, bread, goats, voices—but a new current ran beneath it now, like water finding a crack in stone.

Near evening, Caleb came back to Nathan with a small triumph. "I made four tallies," he said, tapping the olive wood with charcoal-blackened fingers. "Two vials and two jars. I did not forget."

Nathan ruffled his hair, a real smile this time. "You remembered what mattered."

Caleb glanced at the road, then at the fig tree, then back at Nathan. "Not everything that is remembered is good," he said, repeating the brazier-man without knowing he was quoting him. "No," Nathan agreed, tying the last knot. "So we give the town better things to remember."

They stepped back to see their work: nets hung, rope tight, jars stacked, the press smelling of clean fruit and labor. It was an ordinary picture, and it was beautiful.

Above them, the sky deepened toward violet. Lanterns blinked on one by one, small stars caught in clay. The market thinned to a hum. A patrol passed and did not pause.

In the last of the light, a shadow lengthened across the lane. Boots scuffed the stones, armor catching the dusk. A Roman patrol passed the fig tree, their formation neat, their silence deliberate. Mordecai was not among them, but the way the men carried themselves—watching doorways, slowing near Lois's garden wall— left his mark all the same.

Inside the house, Leah looked up and frowned as though she had heard a name spoken softly in another room. Mara's hand went to her belly, not in fear but in promise. Lois stood, wiped her palms on her apron, and stepped to the door to place her palm flat against the wood, as if feeling the heat of a fire on the other side.

Below, the cellar waited—lamps trimmed, blankets folded, jars sealed, the stair cleared of every trace that it had ever been opened. It was ready, as ready as they could make it. One call, one knock too sharp on the door, and they would vanish below like water slipping through stone.

Caleb felt it too, though he didn't see the shadow. He felt it in the way Nathan's breath shortened once and then steadied again. He felt it in the way the nets stopped moving, though there was still a breeze.

"Come eat," Lois called, voice even. "Come eat and be a family. The work will wait for the morning."

Nathan lifted the tray from Caleb's hands. "You heard her."

Caleb nodded and followed him in, ducking under the rope. He took one last look at the lane as he crossed the threshold, as boys do who are measuring themselves against the size of the world.

It looked like any evening in Akrabbim—stone, dust, olives, lamps.

But the rumor had found its legs. And the shadow had found its mark.

Night gathered. The fig leaves whispered. Somewhere beyond the market, a man in a crimson-trimmed robe turned away from the square, satisfied that he had not needed to knock.

Inside, they broke bread. They passed the bowl. They spoke of small things on purpose. And over them, like a roof stronger than beams, hope settled—stubborn, deliberate, made of repeated acts: the teaching of letters, the brewing of tea, the smoothing of a cloth, the choice to stay.

In the morning, there would be more whispers. In the days after, more watching. But for this night, the house held. And in the narrow space between fear and faith, a family stood their ground.

CHAPTER 10
THE SHADOW AT THE GATE

The next morning did not begin with trumpets or alarms, only the small sounds of a house pulling itself awake.

Mara stirred the embers, coaxing them back to flame. Caleb fetched water from the jar and steadied Leah's hands as she tried to sip her tea. Nathan bent over Matthias, whispering encouragement as he pressed broth to his lips. Lois worked at the kneading trough, her palms steady, her mind half on the dough, half on the silence beyond the walls.

It was then she heard it.

Not the scrape of sandals, not the patter of children running, not the shuffle of neighbors greeting the day. This was different.

Boots. Heavy, measured, deliberate.

Lois froze, flour clinging to her fingers. The sound lodged in her chest, pulling her breath shallow. Her stomach tightened, her shoulders tensed, as though her body had recognized the rhythm before her mind could name it.

She knew that sound. It carried more than weight; it carried authority. It was the sound of order imposed, of presence announced.

Her throat went dry. Her palms pressed harder into the dough, but the motion no longer steadied her. The cadence grew louder, closer, until it throbbed in her ears like the pounding of her own heart.

She wiped her hands on her sash, though the flour still clung, and stepped toward the door. Each step was heavy, as if the ground itself wanted to hold her back. Her breath came shallow, her chest tight.

Her mind whispered what her body already knew: this was no passing patrol. This was a man leading, riding, claiming.

Lois squinted into the rising light.

And there he was.

Mordecai.

Not the boy she once married. Not the reckless young merchant whose temper had danced dangerously close to madness. Not the man who stumbled through grief and failure like a wounded dog. No, this was someone else entirely.

He rode slowly, not as a centurion in full command, but at the head of a Roman envoy. He was mounted, though not armored for battle. A courier's sash crossed his chest, but the polished gleam of the armor beneath it betrayed more than the role of a simple messenger. Two guards flanked him, their spears upright, their faces unreadable.

The villagers parted for them without being asked. Some nodded stiffly. Others simply stepped aside, eyes lowered. The clatter of shutters being closed sounded like teeth snapping shut.

Mordecai drew the animal to a halt before the old well at the village square—the one Lois had drawn from since girlhood. With deliberate slowness, he swung down from the saddle. His boots struck the stones with a weight to claim the ground. He touched the lip of the well, almost reverently, before turning to face the people.

"I bring no decree today," he announced, his voice calm but edged as a knife dulled from long use. "Only provisions. And presence."

In the back of the house, Mara froze mid-step, her hand braced against the cool wall. She had heard the shift in sound too—that unnatural silence, the kind that follows the scent of danger.

Nathan stood at the threshold of their cellar, eyes dark, jaw locked tight.

"It's him," Mara whispered, her voice barely audible over the rustle of dry palm fronds.

Nathan didn't ask who. He knew. "Downstairs. Now."

Mara's belly strained beneath her tunic; the child inside twisted, unsettled by her pulse. She moved slowly but with purpose, her feet steady despite the thunder in her chest. Nathan helped her descend into the cool, earthen shelter they'd long prepared but hoped never to use in this way.

Once she was settled on the pallet, he crouched beside the trapdoor and looked at her.

Mara reached for Nathan's hand. "You stay invisible. I'll be safe here."

Nathan held her gaze for a long moment, his brow furrowed. Then, with a quiet nod, he helped lower her onto the bed of woven mats and wrapped her in a wool blanket. He touched her cheek with his thumb, then turned and ascended the ladder. The trapdoor creaked closed, followed by the soft click of the latch sealing them apart.

Above, Nathan bent and pulled a straw mat into place, smoothing it flat with his palm until the seams disappeared into the floor. To anyone glancing across the room, it was nothing more than woven reeds on stone. No sign of the hollow space beneath, no hint of the lives hidden there.

She lay back in the dim cellar, her palms pressed to the curve of her belly. Above, the muffled world continued—boots on packed earth, voices filtered through wood and stone. And then, unmistakably, *his* voice—Mordecai. Still deep. Still controlled. Still laced with something venomous beneath the velvet.

But Mara did not tremble. Not this time.

Above, in the courtyard, Mordecai stood before the villagers, a courier's sash across his chest and Roman provisions behind him. He gestured, and one of the soldiers stepped forward, setting a crate at the edge of the courtyard—oil, cloth, and grain stacked neatly inside. Another followed with an amphora of wine, marked with a Roman seal. A peace offering. Or a bribe.

Lois stood in the doorway, her hands still faintly dusted with flour from the morning's bread. She stepped forward slowly until she was no longer shaded by the threshold.

He saw her.

Their eyes locked.

A flicker passed between them—recognition, memory, old wounds reopening with a glance. It was there, then gone.

Mordecai walked toward her with the slow, deliberate pace of a man long practiced in appearing composed. His gait was confident, his features harder, older, honed by something far colder than time. But his eyes, those hadn't changed. Still sharp, still searching for control.

She did not bow.

"Lois," he said.

Her lips pressed into a thin line. "Mordecai."

He paused at the edge of her shadow, the smooth rhythm of his breath hitching—just once. The name from her lips, sharpened by the steel of memory, struck something old and brittle inside him. A flicker crossed his face—not quite pain, not quite guilt. Then it vanished, buried beneath the familiar armor of poise.

"It's been a long time," he said, voice quieter now.

"Has it?" She responded as if it had not been nearly enough time.

The words landed with the force of truth. For a beat, the mask wavered. His gaze dropped. When it rose again, it was unreadable.

From behind the trapdoor, Mara strained to hear, her hand protectively curled over her belly. Nathan stood in the storeroom, pressed against the far wall, eyes locked on the door, every muscle tensed.

The soldiers busied themselves with the crates, villagers murmured, but Lois and Mordecai stood like statues carved in tension.

He stopped a few paces from her, hands behind his back. "You've aged well."

"I've aged," she replied, voice dry. "It's what time does."

A smirk tugged at the corner of his mouth. "Still sharp."

She tilted her head. "Still married, technically."

A pause. "Technically."

She crossed her arms, watching him with eyes that knew too much. "Rome's leash must be longer than I thought."

"Rome doesn't leash useful men," he said evenly. "It trains them."

Her gaze dropped—just for a second—to the ring on his hand. The insignia of a courier, but the cut of his tunic and the weight of his cloak told a different story.

"You're not here for tribute," she said.

"No."

"And not just for diplomacy."

Another pause. "No."

She watched him closely. He gave nothing away, but she felt it. That low hum of unrest beneath the surface.

"You're not the only one who's changed, Mordecai."

"I expect nothing less."

Still, neither of them mentioned Photine. It sat between them like smoke, curling around every word. Her absence from the conversation was more present than her name.

"I've kept the old house," she said, as if idly.

"Does it still leak in the back corner?"

"Yes."

"Still a cellar beneath the kitchen?"

She paused, then nodded once. "It stays cool."

He gave the faintest smile. "Some things hold their shape."

She took a step back. "Some do. Some rot from the inside."

Mordecai's smile faded. "Do let me know if you need anything. The governor has extended Rome's generosity to this region."

"I'm sure he has."

He turned, cloak catching the wind. "Lois."

"Mordecai."

And then he walked away.

Lois stood in the doorway, watching the dust settle behind him. Only then did she notice the small figure tucked behind the olive press—Caleb. Barefoot, a date half-eaten in one hand, the other clenched at his side.

"Is that…" he whispered, eyes wide. "Was that my father?"

Lois knelt beside him, brushing a curl from his forehead. "Yes, love. That was him."

Caleb stared at the road, brow furrowed—not with recognition, but something quieter. A question he didn't know how to ask. "He didn't even look at me."

Lois pulled him close. "He doesn't see what matters anymore. But you… you are more than what he left behind."

She held him a moment longer, then gently guided him inside.

Down below, beneath the kitchen floor, the cellar held its breath.

The trapdoor creaked softly as Lois descended, Caleb clinging to her hand.

Mara sat on a folded blanket, hands pressed over the firm rise of her belly. Nathan stood tense by the wall, eyes flicking to Lois, then to the boy.

"Well?" Nathan asked.

"It was him," Lois said, her voice low. "He came with soldiers. With gifts. Said it was goodwill.

But it's a warning."

"And Caleb?" Mara asked softly, watching the boy shrink into the corner.

"He saw him. Heard him. But Mordecai never even looked."

Nathan's jaw tightened. "Typical."

Mara reached a hand toward Caleb. He hesitated, then leaned into her side, his hand resting just above the baby within. "He won't find you," he said suddenly. "I'll help hide you."

Mara blinked. "Thank you, little lion."

Nathan exhaled slowly, crouching beside them. "We're not running yet. But if we must, I'll lead us."

Lois nodded. "He's patient. He'll wait for the exact moment. But so will we."

Above, the olive tree whispered in the wind, its leaves sighing like a warning. The ground beneath them remained cool.

But the storm was near.

Outside, Akrabbim stirred to life in fits and starts. Roman soldiers moved with the careful choreography of men told to *watch*, not *strike*. They set up a small post near the village square—just a single tent, a marked crate of supplies, and a brazier already warming despite the rising sun.

Children crept closer to peer at the shiny armor, until their mothers hissed them back behind doorways. A goat bleated near the well, unattended. Dust swirled in lazy patterns.

A young man—Eli, son of the baker—mustered courage and approached one of the guards with an offering of bread. The soldier took it, nodded once, and said nothing. Eli returned home with no wound, no warning. Just the hollow look of someone who expected violence and received silence instead.

By midday, the commander read aloud from a scroll, declaring nothing more than "an increased Roman presence to ensure regional peace." No threats. No accusations. No arrests.

Some of the elders gathered near the well, murmuring that perhaps this wasn't an occupation—just an inspection. A gesture. A precaution. One even said, "Maybe they're here to keep the zealots out." But no one said it too loud.

And yet, there were signs. Too many questions were asked by men who claimed to be merchants. Too many glances that lingered too long. Too many cloaks with no dust on them.

Even so, the market reopened. Bread changed hands. Olives were sorted. Children laughed again, briefly, before being hushed.

And somewhere in the lull between shadow and sun, Akrabbim dared—for a breath—to believe that maybe, just maybe, they were safe.

But safety was a story told in daylight.

As the afternoon sun dipped westward, casting long shadows over Akrabbim's stone lanes, the village settled into a tense rhythm.

Familiar tasks resumed, but every gesture held a hitch, every glance a second thought.

Near the edge of the square, old Hamutal stitched figs into bundles beneath her canopy, eyes narrowed at each passerby. She'd lived through three governors and too many purges to count.

"They're watching for something," she muttered to no one in particular. "Not someone. Something."

Across from her, Abner the weaver welcomed two strangers into his stall—Romans in civilian robes, claiming to be buyers. He smiled, showed them linen, and even offered them tea. But as soon as they left, he turned to his daughter and whispered, "Do not speak to anyone new without me."

At the well, children tossed pebbles into the water to watch the ripples spread. One boy, perhaps seven, asked his sister, "Will they take someone?" She shrugged, chewing her lip. "Maybe only if someone's bad."

Down the lane, a quiet altercation flared. A zealot sympathizer— young and loud—accused a neighbor of collaboration. Voices rose, then fell. Someone slammed a door. Dust rose in the silence. Still, the Romans did nothing.

By early evening, a small fire had been lit near the square. One of the soldiers sharpened his blade, like a man preparing for something he already knew would come.

Some villagers prayed. Others packed small satchels and tucked them beneath their beds. Just in case.

Akrabbim was breathing—but not freely. The kind of breath you take before diving under.

And beneath it all, one truth echoed through shared glances and half-whispered words:

Peace never came with polished armor.

It came with absence.

And this was not an absence.

At Lois's house, the lamps were lit early. The light caught the edges of the woven mats, the stacked jars, the fig branches shading the window. Outside, the street had emptied faster than usual. Inside, the air was thick with the weight of too many questions.

Nathan set the last bolt across the door and turned to the others. Mara sat cross-legged near the hearth, rubbing her belly absently. Lois stood at the window, eyes narrowed at the darkening lane. Leah dozed in her chair, the cup still in her hand, and Caleb sat near her feet, staring into the fire like he was old enough to read its meaning.

"They're not here for trade," Nathan said. His voice was low, controlled. "Envoys don't sharpen blades for leisure."

"No," Lois agreed. "They're here for presence. To remind us who rules the air we breathe."

Mara lifted her eyes. "How long?"

Lois hesitated. "As long as they wish. As long as it takes for someone to stumble, or for someone to resist."

Caleb shifted, restless. "So, they're waiting for us to do something wrong?"

Nathan crouched beside him, hand resting on the boy's shoulder. "Not wrong, Caleb. Just visible."

The boy frowned. "But why? If we stay quiet, if we work, if we don't fight, why would they still come?"

Lois answered this time, her voice like stone. "Because Rome doesn't come for justice. Rome comes for order. And order doesn't ask who deserves it. Order asks who obeys." Mara closed her eyes at that, her hand tightening over her belly.

Later, after the evening meal was cleared, they gathered in the back room where the hearth wall concealed the trapdoor. Nathan rolled back the straw mat just far enough to reveal the faint seams of the wood. Caleb leaned close, staring at it like a promise and a curse.

"If they come," Nathan said, "this is where you go. You, Mara, Lois, Leah, and Caleb. I'll hold them as long as I can."

"No," Lois cut in. "We all go. You don't martyr yourself in the doorway."

"They'll search," Nathan countered. "If they see an empty house, they'll search harder. They need someone upstairs to convince them it's just an old widow's place, not worth the trouble." The fire cracked. No one spoke for a moment.

Finally, Mara said, softly but with steel, "Then we plan both ways. If we hide, we hide completely. If we stay, we stay with eyes open."

Leah stirred then, muttering half-formed words. "Jotham… figs… wedding cloth." Caleb reached to steady her cup and set it aside, his movements careful, practiced. He had learned to be her hands when hers shook.

"She thinks I'm still his wife," Mara whispered, her throat tight. "Sometimes she calls me Photine out loud."

Lois touched her arm. "Then we teach Caleb to guide her. To keep her quiet when it matters. He knows how to listen."

Caleb flushed at the weight of their eyes but nodded quickly. "I can," he said. "I will." The night deepened. They spoke in fragments, never raising voices above the fire's hiss.

"Do we run?" Mara asked at last.

Nathan rubbed his temples. "Where? The roads are worse than the town. Patrols on every route.

To flee would mark us guilty before we'd even crossed the ridge."

"Then we stay," Lois said. "And we act as though nothing has changed."

"But everything has changed," Mara whispered.

Silence again. Caleb pressed his knees to his chest and leaned against the hearth, listening.

Nathan finally broke it. "Occupation never announces itself. It just settles. One soldier here, two there. A patrol at the well. A question at the press. And then—" he spread his hands—"life shrinks. People forget what free breath feels like. That's how they win." His words hung in the room like smoke.

Lois drew her shawl tighter around her shoulders. "Then we must remember for them. Even if we can't fight, we can remember. And remembering is a kind of resistance."

When the lamps were lowered, and the household lay in uneasy rest, Mara lay awake beside Nathan, listening to Caleb's steady breathing across the room. The boy's shoulders rose and fell, small but squared like a man's.

She whispered into the dark, "How long before he sees them take someone?"

Nathan didn't answer right away. When he did, his voice was a whisper edged with grief. "Not long. They don't bring blades to polish them."

Mara shut her eyes. In the stillness, she thought of how quickly a house could become a trap, how suddenly peace could turn to running again. She thought of the child within her, turning, waiting, about to be born into a world where men with seals could appear at any door.

She pressed her lips against the back of Nathan's hand. "If they come, promise me one thing," she whispered.

"What?"

"That you don't let him grow up thinking obedience is the same as safety."

Nathan's breath caught. He pulled her closer, but he did not answer.

The ridge outside the town was quiet, but it was not absent. Torches burned in the Roman camp like stars scattered low against the earth. The people of Akrabbim slept lightly, their dreams tethered to the sound of armor shifting, of horses stamping the ground, of silence stretched too far.

And in Lois's house, beneath the fig tree, the trapdoor was hidden, the cellar waiting, the family above lying in the dark with the knowledge that peace would not come with polished armor.

Not tomorrow.

Not for a long time.

Caleb lay on his mat near the hearth, eyes open to the flicker of lamplight painting the rafters. He knew he should sleep, but sleep never came quickly anymore. Not since the Romans had arrived.

Not since whispers in the street had turned to stares and stares had turned to silence.

The grown-ups thought he didn't understand. They lowered their voices, spoke in half-sentences, used words like *rememberer* and *envoy* as if such words could keep him from hearing what mattered. But he understood. He had understood for a long time.

He remembered the years before Nathan came—when he had been the one to carry jars, to haul water, to sweep ash from the hearth because Leah's hands trembled and Lois's back ached and Mara's grief was too heavy. He had been seven going on seventy, the only one with enough strength to keep the house standing.

Now Nathan was here, strong and steady, and Caleb was grateful enough to bite his tongue when Nathan corrected his knots or told him to fetch water more carefully. But part of him still burned with the need to prove he could do it alone. Because what if Nathan left, like the others? What if the Romans came and dragged him away? Then it would be Caleb again, carrying more than his size allowed.

He thought of the words Asher whispered that afternoon: *It's your father. The one with the seal. The one on the ridge.*

Caleb's chest tightened. He didn't want it to be true. The father he remembered smelled of sweat and pressed olives, and of wine, his voice rough but certain. He remembered broad shoulders bending over the press, the way his shadow filled the doorway. He remembered the fear too—the sharp words, the slammed fist—but even fear had been present. Now there was only absence, stretched across more than a year.

And now Asher said he had come back. Changed. Wearing Rome.

Caleb pressed his hands to his ears, as though he could shut the thought out, but the silence only made it louder. If it was true—if the man with the seal was really his father—then what did that make Caleb? The son of Rome's shadow? The son of betrayal?

He turned onto his side and stared at the wall, where the seam of the trapdoor hid beneath straw. He knew how to open it. Nathan had shown him. One tug on the latch, one push, and he could vanish into the earth. He wondered if he'd have to. He wondered if, when the footsteps came, he would be quick enough to get everyone down there. He wondered if Leah would cry out the wrong name, if Lois's knees would carry her fast enough, if Mara—heavy with child—could descend the steps before the soldiers broke the door.

Caleb swallowed hard. He hated the thought of hiding. He hated the thought of his father. He wanted to stand, to fight, to shout that they were not snakes in the grass, not names to be written on a list. But he was only seven, and the weight of the rope and nets still ached in his shoulders.

His eyes drifted to Nathan, who slept lightly, one hand curled near the door as if he could rise at any sound. Caleb studied the shape of him in the shadows. This man had chosen them, chosen *him*. He wasn't blood, but he was something better. He was present.

And still Caleb's heart whispered: *But what if your father really is the one with the seal? What does that make you?*

Tears pricked his eyes, hot and unbidden. He pressed his face into the blanket, not wanting anyone to hear. In the muffled dark, he whispered words no one else would: "If it's him… I'll never call him father again. Never." As if not confirming what he knew could leave room for it to change.

He stayed that way until his breathing evened and sleep crept in, listening even in his dreams for boots on stone.

Outside, the torches still burned on the ridge. Akrabbim lay beneath them, restless in its beds, waiting for the morning to bring answers. Or more silence. And in one small house by the fig tree, a boy lay awake carrying the weight of fathers and futures alike.

CHAPTER 11
ASHES AND EMBERS

A storm had passed in the night, scouring the hills with wind and washing the stone alleys clean with rain. Now the village lay in that rare hush that followed thunder—the kind of silence that made the birds wait, the dogs stay curled in doorways, and the air itself hold its breath.

Lois rose before the others. She moved through the house with the quiet grace of someone used to carrying too much without complaint. The hearth took coaxing, the embers reluctant after the damp, but she fed them slowly with kindling and breath until they sparked again. The smell of smoke drifted low, mingling with the cool, damp air.

Matthias and Leah still lay in the small room off the main room. Lois pushed the doorway cover open gently, balancing a clay lamp in her hand. Leah stirred, muttering something about figs, but Matthias did not move. His face was turned toward the wall, his chest still. Lois waited for the thin, rasping breath she had grown used to hearing through the night. But it did not come.

She stepped closer. Her heart gave a dull, familiar ache as she set the lamp down and touched his shoulder. Cool. Not the cool of a man shifting in sleep, but the cool of stone that would not warm again.

Lois drew in a slow breath, steadying herself. This was no surprise—not after so many weeks of decline. The moment of truth always struck like a stone dropped into still water. She bowed her head, whispered a prayer too quiet for Leah to catch, and smoothed Matthias's blanket as though he might still feel the gesture.

Behind her, Leah blinked awake. "Matthias?" she asked, her voice thick with sleep. "Is he—?"

Lois turned, sat on the edge of her pallet, and took her trembling hand. "Rest now, Leah. He's at peace."

Leah's eyes widened, confusion and grief tangling together. She clutched at Lois's wrist, her lips quivering like a child's. Lois pulled her into her arms, rocking her gently as the truth sank in.

From the courtyard came the sound of small feet. Caleb, rubbing his eyes with the back of his fist, stood in the doorway. One look at Lois's face, and he knew. His throat tightened, but he did not cry. He only whispered, "What will we do?"

Lois reached her free hand toward him, beckoning him close. "We will carry him as we carried him in life—with dignity. And we will decide together what must be done."

Beneath their feet, in the cool dark of the cellar, Mara stirred. She and Nathan slept there now, wrapped in blankets on the hard floor, because nights were the most dangerous. Soldiers sometimes came in the dark or at the break of dawn, pounding on doors before households could rouse. Better to be hidden already than to scramble down the ladder half-asleep.

Mara had not heard words, only the shift in Lois's steps above, the faint wail of Leah muffled through stone. She pushed herself upright slowly, one hand pressed to her belly, wincing at the stiffness in her back. The stairs felt longer every night now; each climb or descent left her winded, her balance fragile.

Nathan lifted his head beside her, listening, his jaw tight in the lamplight's glow. The baby pressed against Mara's ribs, restless, as if the child, too, could feel the balance of their fragile refuge tipping.

Lois lingered a moment longer with Leah, stroking her hair until her sobs softened to hiccups. Then she lifted her head. "I'll wake them," she said, meaning Mara and Nathan. Her voice was steady, but her hands trembled as she rose.

Lois lifted the lamp and made her way to the back wall, pressing against the floor while lifting the latch until it gave way with its familiar groan. She descended the narrow stairs into the cellar, the flame casting long shadows on the stone.

Mara stirred first, blinking at Lois's face before she sat up quickly, hand to her belly. "What is it?"

Nathan was already half awake, pushing to his feet. "Patrol?"

Lois shook her head. "Matthias." The word fell heavy, final. "He's gone."

For a heartbeat, the cellar was still. The lamplight wavered against stone walls, catching their faces in half-shadow. Then Mara covered her mouth with her hand, eyes filling until the tears blurred the edges of the room. Nathan exhaled hard through his nose, his hand instinctively touching her back.

Mara's thoughts tumbled faster than her breath. Matthias was gone. That meant burial before sundown—custom demanded it, and the neighbors would expect it. There would be no excuse, no hiding. Seven days of mourning would follow, people coming and going, offering condolences, sharing bread. *Seven days of open doors and footsteps in the courtyard.* Seven days when Mordecai's men could slip among the mourners without question, when watchful eyes could study every face in Lois's house.

Her hand pressed harder against her lips. How could they do this? How could they honor the dead and still guard the living? How could they bury Matthias with dignity while knowing every shovel of earth might draw Rome's notice?

And behind it all loomed Mordecai. His name had already returned to the square like a shadow. If he suspected Photine—no, *Mara*—was here, a funeral would be the perfect snare. Grief made people visible. Grief loosened tongues. Grief pulled a household into the center of the town's gaze.

Her tears slipped past her fingers as she whispered, almost to herself, "How will we bear this? How will we bury him without losing ourselves?"

Nathan's jaw tightened. He did not answer yet, because there was no simple answer.

They came up the steps, joining Caleb by the door of the small room. The boy stood stiffly, as though rooted there, his chin high but his lip trembling. Mara reached for him, but he shook his head, not ready for comfort.

"What do we do?" Caleb asked, voice sharp with the urgency of someone much older.

Nathan looked at Lois, waiting.

"Burial," she said, her jaw tightening. "Before the sun is high. Quietly. Without notice." She glanced toward the shuttered window. "But we must be careful. Romans ask questions about gatherings. About graves. Even about grief."

Caleb's brow furrowed. "But he was family. We can't just... hide him."

Mara knelt beside him, cupping his cheek. "We will not hide him. We will honor him. But we must also protect the living."

Caleb swallowed hard. He wanted to argue, to shout that a man's burial should not be something to fear. But he looked at Leah—lost in

her grief, murmuring Jotham's name as though calling a ghost back—
and he knew they had no choice.

Nathan stepped into the room and pulled the blanket over
Matthias's face. His hand lingered on the cloth, head bowed. "He
should be carried to the olive grove," he said. "The soil there is soft.

Roots will hold him."

Lois nodded. "Before the soldiers notice he has passed."

Together, Nathan and Lois lifted Matthias's frail body, wrapping
him in a clean cloth. Mara prepared herbs, their sharp scent filling the
air, while Caleb fetched the spade from the corner of the press yard.
His small hands gripped the handle so tightly his knuckles whitened.

When the time came, they slipped from the house one by one, as
though leaving for ordinary work. Nathan led, the bundle cradled in
his arms, Lois close behind. Mara walked with Caleb, her hand firm
on his shoulder, guiding him through the silence of streets already
watched by unseen eyes.

The olive grove lay just beyond the ridge, where the wind always
seemed to whisper through the branches. They dug in silence, the
scrape of the spade loud in the dawn. Caleb worked beside Nathan,
his breath coming hard, sweat mixing with tears he refused to wipe
away. Mara and Lois prepared the herbs, tucking them into the folds
of cloth around Matthias's body.

When the grave was ready, they lowered him in. Lois whispered
a prayer of release, her voice low, steady, like a river smoothing
stone. Mara added words of blessing for rest, while Caleb whispered
nothing at all. He just stared until Nathan's hand settled heavily on his
shoulder, pulling him back.

They covered the grave quickly, tamping the earth flat, scattering leaves and fallen olives so no fresh digging showed. It was not the burial Matthias deserved, but it was the only one they could give.

On the walk back, Caleb finally spoke, his voice small but sharp. "The Romans took even this from us. Even how we say goodbye."

Lois squeezed his hand, her eyes dark. "Then we remember, Caleb. That's how we keep him. We remember."

When they reached the house, Leah was waiting in the courtyard. Her face was lined with confusion.

She looked at Mara and whispered, "Where is he?"

Mara swallowed hard, then knelt before her. "At rest," she said gently. "Safe now."

Leah nodded slowly, though her eyes drifted, as if searching for a figure that had already gone.

Inside, Nathan brushed soil from his hands and glanced at Lois. "What happens when the soldiers notice he's gone?"

"They will notice everything," Lois replied. "They always do. The question is whether we act afraid before they ask. Fear draws eyes. We must carry on as though nothing has changed."

But everything had changed. Matthias was gone. His absence left a gap in the household—one more hollow for grief to fill, and one more risk if the Romans chose to ask questions about the missing man.

In the cellar that night, Mara lay awake, her hand on her belly, thinking of how quickly life and death brushed against one another in this place. A child about to be born. A life just ended.

As the household settled into uneasy rest, the wind through the
fig leaves carried the sound of boots again—a reminder that grief was
only one of the burdens they would carry.

Dawn came pale and thin, creeping into the courtyard with the
smell of damp earth and olive leaves still heavy from the storm. The
house moved more slowly than usual, its rhythm dulled by the weight
of absence. Caleb fed the fire with too much wood at once. Leah sat
staring into her cup as though it might tell her where Matthias had
gone. Mara lingered longer than usual before rising from the cellar,
every step a negotiation with her body.

Lois moved among them quietly, steady in the way of women
who could not afford to collapse. She set bread to warm, gathered
herbs for tea, and ladled water into the basin, her sleeves pushed up
past her elbows. It was there, bent over the stone lip, that she heard it.

A knock—soft, but deliberate.

Three taps. A pause. Then one more.

Her body went still.

It was not the sound itself that startled her, but the rhythm. She
hadn't heard it in years.

She wiped her hands on her sash and walked to the door, and
opened it halfway.

A man stood just beyond the threshold, hood drawn low, wool
cloak damp from travel. His beard was streaked with gray now, his
frame leaner, but the eyes—sharp, steady, knowing—were the same.

"Benaiah," she said softly.

He inclined his head. "Lois."

For a long breath, they said nothing more. Then she stepped aside, and he entered.

He walked the room slowly, the way someone might pass through a memory. His hand brushed the doorframe where a gouge from an old argument still marred the wood. He glanced toward the hearth, where the fire now crackled back to life.

"Didn't know if you'd still be here," he said.

"Still standing," Lois replied.

He dropped his satchel near the bench but didn't sit. His eyes swept the room—just aware, like a man used to danger.

"Came to see if anything's still burning here," he added, his voice quieter now.

Lois studied him. "How long's it been since the last time you said that?"

"Since before Jotham died."

A long pause stretched between them.

Benaiah had been one of the few men Jotham ever called a friend. Not in the loud way of the marketplace or the boisterous way of the tavern, but in the rare and quiet way of men who understood one another without needing much talk. Jotham had been a different man in public—calm, reserved, often tired. But away from home, in small gatherings under the trees or during long walks along the ravine, he had spoken more. Thought more. Even laughed.

It was in those spaces that Benaiah had come to know him—and by extension, Lois.

He hadn't returned for Jotham's burial. No one knew why, though rumors swirled. Some said he'd joined the Zealots. Others that he'd traded too close to Roman lines and vanished into exile.

Lois had stopped wondering. Life moved on. Bread still had to rise. Children still had to eat.

Now here he was—older, scarred, silent.

"Why now?" she asked.

Benaiah's hand tightened slightly on the strap of his cloak. "There's movement in the south. Tensions rising, yes—but not just that. Whispers. Names are being spoken again. Places remembered."

Lois's eyes narrowed. "What names?"

He hesitated.

"Ezra. Yours. Photine. Even Jotham's."

She turned fully toward him, face tight. "What do they want with the dead?"

"Not the dead," he said. "The stories that live on. There are those who still believe Jotham knew things. That he may have written them down."

Lois shook her head. "He didn't."

"Doesn't matter," Benaiah said. "All it takes is a whisper. The kind Mordecai listens for." His name dropped like a stone between them.

Lois's mouth went dry. "He's here."

Benaiah didn't flinch. "I figured."

Finally, he lowered himself onto the bench, setting his satchel beside him. "I didn't come to stir ghosts. I came to offer help. If you need it."

She didn't answer immediately. Her eyes flicked, almost against her will, toward the far wall—the place where a straw mat covered what lay hidden below. Mara. Nathan. The child waiting to be born. A family trying to hold together in the shadow of a man remade by Rome.

Lois forced her gaze back to him, steady but cool. She wasn't entirely sure she could trust him—not anymore, not when trust itself had become a kind of currency too easily spent.

"I might," she said at last.

He nodded once, as though that answer was enough.

Lois poured him water, waiting to see if his silence would reveal more than his words.

"I've been in Perea," he said. "East of the Jordan. Near the salt hills. There's a man there... wild, prophetic. Says the time has come. Says the kingdom is at hand."

"John," Lois murmured.

Benaiah's eyes sharpened. "You've heard of him?"

"Only whispers. The kind that travel fast and vanish when questioned."

Benaiah drank. "He's not like the others. He doesn't carry a sword, but his words cut deeper. He speaks of repentance, of judgment, of one who is coming greater than him. Says we must prepare."

Lois leaned back. "And what of the Zealots?"

"They're divided," he said. "Some think he's a distraction. Others think he's the sign we've been waiting for. But Rome…"

His voice dropped. "Rome is paying attention. More crucifixions. More patrols. They've begun recruiting locals to spy. To infiltrate."

"Mordecai," Lois said flatly.

Benaiah nodded grimly. "I passed through Caesarea. His name carries weight there. He has power, and not just on paper. He speaks their tongue better than most of them do. And he remembers what we used to be." He paused.

"I came for another reason," he added.

Lois met his eyes.

"I met a man outside Jericho. He carried Jotham's ring."

His words hit her like a wave. Her brother-in-law, Photine's first husband. Long gone—nearly six years now—yet never absent.

"Where did he get it?" she asked, her voice barely above a whisper.

Benaiah's eyes flicked to the satchel beside him, then back to her. "From a boy. Maybe seventeen. Said he knew Jotham. Carried this for years, waiting for someone to give it to."

Lois reached for the object—wrapped in cloth, the weight of it familiar even before she unwrapped it. A blade hilt. Cracked. Burnished smooth by time and weather. The last thing Jotham would have touched.

"Said he was with him," Benaiah continued, his tone gentler now. "Near En-gedi. Said they stayed behind to buy time for a group of villagers escaping a Roman sweep. Not soldiers—families. Refugees. Zealots had passed through the area and left chaos in their wake. Rome came after everyone.”

Lois's hand trembled as she traced the worn handle. “And Jotham?”

“Held them off with a broken blade. Took down two. Maybe three. Gave the rest time to flee into the hills.”

Benaiah shifted, his gaze lowering as though the next part was heavier to speak. “The boy said Jotham gave him something before it happened. Pressed it into his palm—his ring. Told him, ‘If anything happens to me, take this back to Lois. She'll know what to do.’ He was twelve then. Just a child.”

Lois's throat tightened. She remembered the ring well—simple bronze, engraved with the faint pattern of an olive branch. Jotham had never taken it off, not even when the press cracked his knuckles, and the oil stained his skin.

Benaiah went on, softer now. “The boy wasn't meant to be there. He'd followed Jotham without his knowing—said he wanted to see what real courage looked like. When Jotham stopped to help travelers on the road, he hid behind the rocks and saw it all. Jotham struck down before he could even see what was happening. Three men who dressed like travelers but looked like Romans delivered the final blow.”

Lois's eyes stung. “He watched?”

“He watched. And when he couldn't anymore, he ran. Afraid. He thought they'd seen him. Thought he'd be next. But later, when the men moved on, he came back to find Jotham dead. He took his blade and walked into the camp pretending to be a messenger. Said he'd been sent to tell of Jotham's death.”

Lois pressed the hilt to her chest, closing her eyes. She could almost see Jotham's hand, rough and calloused, closing over that boy's small one. Passing on the ring. Passing on trust. Passing on a piece of himself.

Benaiah's voice broke the silence. "He said he never forgot your name, given to him by Jotham.

He carried it like a weight until he could bring the ring back."

Lois drew in a shuddering breath. "And now this is what's left."

Her thumb brushed the hilt's edge, and with it came a rush of memory—not the image of Jotham, but of him as he truly was. Gentle where others were sharp. Sweet where others mocked. She remembered how he laughed like water spilling from a jar, how he carried figs in his pocket to give to children on the road. How he had once brought her a loaf of bread still warm, apologizing that it was misshapen from his clumsy hands.

She had loved him in a way that was not romantic but no less fierce: a bond between kin, between two souls who understood that kindness was its own form of strength.

When he took a bride so young, a girl with eyes too wide and a future too heavy, Lois had honored Jotham by honoring her. By softening the edges of a house that was often too hard. By slipping Photine the choicest fruits, by pressing a kiss to her temple when no one else thought to, by shielding her from harsh words when she could.

It had been her way of loving Jotham even after he was gone— through the kindness she gave the girl he had once cherished.

Now, holding the relic of him, Lois felt the weight of that vow again. She had kept it then. She would keep it still.

Lois looked down at the knife and the ring in her hands, her palms heavy with memory.

Now this was all that remained.

She narrowed her eyes. "And yet that was years ago. Why come now?"

Benaiah looked down, rubbing his thumb over a scar on his knuckle. "I'd fought beside him once before. We got a family clear that night—sent them into the hills with nothing but hope. The Romans closed in fast, and Jotham stood his ground longer than any man had the right to. I caught a blade myself, bad enough that I nearly bled out where I fell. Shepherds dragged me into the lowlands and kept me breathing until the fever passed.

After that, our paths split. I moved east, always hiding, always watching the roads for patrols. Thought I'd never hear his name again. But here it is, back on the air—like the dust itself remembers him, like Rome never could bury him clean."

She nodded slowly. "So much lost."

She closed her eyes.

They sat in silence for a long while.

Then Benaiah leaned in, his voice low beneath the hum of midday flies. "They say things are shifting. That something, or someone, is coming. Not just another rebellion. A reckoning. A voice strong enough to gather both the broken and the bold."

Lois folded her arms. "Reckonings cost blood. Usually from the innocent."

He nodded, eyes shadowed. "But this is different. There's talk of visionaries. Men and women who aren't calling for war, but for awakening. Rome doesn't know what to do with that. Mordecai isn't just watching this town. He's seeding it. Setting eyes in every window. Listening at the doors. If he finds what he's looking for…"

Lois's jaw tightened. "He won't."

Benaiah's gaze searched hers. "You've always been brave, Lois. But courage and time don't always walk together. You've got children under your roof. You know he won't hesitate."

"I can't protect them forever," she admitted, voice tight, "but I can make it cost him."

His expression shifted—respect tempered by worry. "Then you'll need more than flour and hiding places. You'll need people who still remember what justice smells like. North of here—near Hebron's edge—some haven't bowed to fear. Who still remembers Mordecai's brother. Who owes him."

Lois studied him for a long moment, then lowered her voice. "There's something else." Benaiah tilted his head.

"She's here." The words left her mouth like a confession.

He blinked. "She…?"

Lois gave a subtle nod. "Photine. Due any day."

His brow furrowed, and for a moment, no words came.

"I don't want to know more than I need to," he said quietly. "But that changes things."

"Yes," Lois said. "It does."

"She can't be seen. Not even by friends. Not now."

"She won't be. I've kept her buried deeper than the grain. Also, her husband, who is fairly unknown here other than Nathan, who is my cousin helping since Mordecai left."

He nodded, the lines around his mouth deepening. "Then listen closely. When you need to move—because that time is coming—I'll have places ready. Routes no Roman watches. But you'll need to signal. The olive branch and the flat stone beside the well."

Lois exhaled, the weight of the moment thick on her chest. "Thank you."

As he stepped toward the door, he paused. "One more thing. When this child comes, he'll carry more than a name. He'll carry history—blood that Rome tried to crush, and spirit that refused."

Lois nodded. "And what he won't carry is fear."

They exchanged a final look, and Benaiah turned toward the rising light of the street.

Only when the door clicked shut behind him did Lois let herself release the breath she'd been holding. She turned back toward the trapdoor, her steps slow, steady.

Below, in the quiet dark, life stirred.

And above, in a world not yet ready for truth, danger held its breath.

CHAPTER 12
WHAT THE CHILD CARRIES

In the cellar, Mara sat curled on a wool blanket, her back against the cool stone wall, her hands on her swelling belly. The lantern cast a small flickering circle of light. Nathan paced a few feet away, stopping occasionally to adjust the hanging cloth masking the trapdoor.

Mara hadn't spoken much since Lois came down from her conversation with Benaiah. She had heard every word. The knife. Jotham's name. The ring. The way he fought and bought time for others to flee.

Nearly six years.

And only now did the story come.

She had been fourteen when they married. Still a child, really. Jotham had treated her kindly—never as property, never roughly as some girls feared, as most experienced. He had allowed her to read her father's parchments. Had listened when she spoke, even if he didn't always understand. But they had not truly been husband and wife. Not in the way the law understood. There had been no wedding night. Just friendship. Respect. A kind of patient mentorship that made his absence all the more bitter.

She had been allowed just seven days to grieve. One day he was there, the next he was smoke—vanished into silence that was replaced with violence. Others spoke of him only in half-truths or not at all. Her own story had been swept forward too quickly for mourning, into another man's house, another name.

Now, pieces began to fit. The quiet conversations Jotham shared with travelers who lingered longer than they should. The scraps of parchment folded into his cloak, the maps she'd once glimpsed when she was meant to be grinding grain. The way he spoke of freedom— not the loud, reckless words of zealots, but something gentler. Freedom from Rome, yes, but also from fear. From cycles that turned sons into slaves of bitterness.

She remembered how his eyes would soften when Leah sang. How he smiled when Lois pressed figs into his hands, even when the table was lean. He had carried secrets then, but not in the way of betrayal. He had carried them like seeds, waiting for the season when they might take root.

Now, holding the fragments of his story at last, Mara realized what she had never allowed herself to think. Jotham had not abandoned her. He had chosen a different kind of battle. And the cost of it had been silence, absence, and death on a nameless road.

Her hand drifted to her belly to the child within. She whispered so low only the stone could hear: "You would have been kind to him, Jotham. You would have taught him how to live without fear."

"Nathan," she said softly.

He turned, eyes weary.

"Did you know Jotham was helping the Zealots?"

Nathan hesitated, his thumb worrying the edge of the table. "I suspected. But it was never spoken aloud."

Mara frowned. "What made you suspect?"

He leaned back, pulling the memory up from where he had long buried it. "Once, years ago, I saw him in the market at Shiloh. Not trading—at least not like a man selling his wares. He was passing something off to a traveler. A bundle wrapped too neatly, too heavy for figs or bread. He caught sight of me before I could pretend not to notice. And the way he looked at me…" Nathan shook his head slowly. "Not guilty. Not afraid. Just—measured. Like he was weighing whether I was the kind of man who would ask questions."

Mara's brow furrowed. "And you didn't?"

"No. Because I knew it wasn't a common trade. At the time, I told myself it could've been taxes, maybe a debt paid in goods. But now, after meeting Benaiah, he was with Jotham that day. After hearing how Jotham died, it fits. The bundle, the look, the silence. He was already helping the Zealots. Already carrying things that weren't supposed to be seen."

"And you didn't?" Mara asked.

"No. Because I already knew the answer. The Zealots were moving through those hills, and men like Jotham, men who knew the roads and the families who lived along them, were worth more than a sword. He wasn't a fighter," Nathan admitted, "but he believed something was coming. Something that would change everything."

Mara's hand went to her lap, fingers tracing the fabric there. "And now we know what it cost him."

Nathan's jaw tightened. "And what it still might cost us."

She looked down. "I don't know. But something's happening. Bigger than us."

Above, the trapdoor shifted. Nathan stood instantly, hand on the hilt of the blade Benaiah had left behind. But it wasn't soldiers.

A soft voice called, "It's me. Caleb."

Nathan lifted the door.

The boy looked breathless. "Roman men are asking questions. They came to my friend's house. I wanted to warn you. They're coming this way. Nathan, you should go to the edge of the grove now. Benaiah is waiting."

Nathan handed him a pouch of figs and water. "Thank you. Go now, quickly."

Benaiah stood at the edge of the grove behind Lois's house, his back to the rising sun. The trees whispered in the wind, branches trembling with anticipation—or warning. Nathan approached with cautious steps, arms folded beneath his cloak. His eyes were shadowed with sleeplessness and resolve.

"I thought you'd gone south," Nathan said, voice low.

Benaiah didn't turn. "Not yet, I feel I am of more use here."

Nathan nodded once. "You saw the men Mordecai brought?"

"Bribery and silence wrapped in Roman red. Standard tactic." Benaiah finally faced him. "They won't strike yet. He's softening the ground. Making people unsure."

Nathan studied him. "You knew Jotham well."

"Better than most." Benaiah's jaw tightened. "He believed in timing. In fire that waits until the wind shifts."

Nathan's eyes flicked back toward the house. "Pho…Mara is soon to be in labor."

"Then the timing may be now." Benaiah stepped closer. "You can't wait for peace to arrive. You have to carve a path to it. Are you ready for that?"

"I didn't ask for war."

"Neither did she," Benaiah snapped. "But it's here."

They stared at each other in a taut silence, the morning light creeping between them.

Nathan broke first. "What would you have me do?"

"Establish allies. Quiet ones. I'll place two men near the crossroads, one at the well. If soldiers come, you'll have a warning. We build routes. Safe passage. If she needs to flee, we don't hesitate."

Nathan nodded slowly. "And if Mordecai comes for her?"

Benaiah's voice was steel. "Then we remind him that not all ghosts stay buried."

The breeze kicked up, rustling the fig leaves overhead, and for a moment, Nathan let the sound wash over him like surf against a broken hull. He lifted his gaze toward the house, where lamplight glowed behind the shutters, fragile and warm.

"She's naming him Elior, if it's to be a boy."

Benaiah blinked. "Jotham spoke that name once. Said it meant something. 'God is my light.'"

Nathan's mouth curved faintly, but the smile did not reach his eyes. "Then maybe the child was always meant for this moment."

Benaiah laid a hand on his shoulder. "Then guard him well. Light makes men bold. But it also draws shadows."

Nathan didn't answer. He turned back toward the house, his steps slowed. His mind carried him back to another house, another life. Tirzah's laughter, the way she had warmed a room just by being in it. How quickly fever had stolen her, how helpless he had been, watching as the woman he loved slipped from his arms. He had promised himself never again. Never to risk that hollowing ache.

And yet here he was—standing in the same story, only sharper, heavier. Mara was not Tirzah. She carried scars, silences, secrets he could never fully untangle. Her past was not some quiet life lost to illness, but a labyrinth of betrayals, escapes, and a brother who had sold her soul as if it were his to spend. And still he had fallen in love with her. Perhaps because of those scars. Perhaps despite them. He no longer knew.

What would it mean to raise a child now, with Rome breathing down their neck, with Mordecai's shadow stretching across the lanes of Akrabbim? What kind of father could he be if tomorrow soldiers dragged him away—or worse, dragged Mara into the streets while he stood powerless?

He thought of the cellar—dark, close, ready. Of Lois, who had already lost too much. Of Caleb, the boy who carried a man's weariness in a child's shoulders.

And he thought of Elior. The name itself was like a flame in his chest. *God is my light.* A prayer, a plea, a burden.

Was he enough to bear it? To guard not just a woman who had survived too much already, but the child she carried, and the stories clinging to her name like thorns?

Nathan's hand brushed the wall as he reached the threshold, grounding himself against the stone.

Inside, a cry rose—raw, new, insistent. The sound of life splitting the silence in two.

His breath caught. Fear and wonder braided so tightly he could not tell one from the other. He pushed the door open and stepped inside.

Mara shifted, trying to stand. A sharp pain arced through her abdomen. Her breath hitched. She cried out.

Nathan ran to her. "Is it time?"

She grabbed the stone wall, her face pale.

"It's time."

Lois descended the steps moments later, lips pressed in a tight line. "We can't move her now. We make do here."

Nathan helped arrange the bedding while Lois retrieved clean cloths, herbs, and a flask of boiled water she'd prepared—just in case. The cellar filled with urgency, the kind that holds only focus.

Time passed in a blur. Pain. Breath. Whispered prayers.

Nathan never left her side.

And then—a cry.

Small. Wet. Alive.

Lois wrapped the child quickly, her hands steady. She handed the bundle to Mara, who wept from the ache of everything she'd survived to reach this moment.

"A boy," Lois said softly.

Nathan touched Mara's forehead.

Mara looked down at the child in her arms.

"He was not born into peace," she whispered, "but he will carry its promise."

She looked up at Lois and Ezra.

"His name will be Elior."

The words left Mara's lips with a steadiness that surprised even her. They rang soft but sure in the dim room, as though naming itself was an act of defiance.

Lois's eyes shone, though her hands stayed busy swaddling the child. "Elior," she repeated, the syllables tender on her tongue. "*God is my light.*"

Lois bent over the child, tucking the linen close beneath his chin. Her voice was soft but steady.

"If he lives to the eighth day, he'll need a blade and a blessing, a name spoken before witnesses."

She paused, then shook her head sharply, correcting herself. "No—when he lives. When he does.

And when that day comes, whether in a courtyard or in this cellar, he will be counted among the living. Born into secrecy, carried in silence, but no less a son of promise."

She met Mara's eyes, fierce and tender all at once. "Some children begin with more weight than others. That does not make them weaker. It makes them needed."

Nathan knelt at Mara's side, his hand hovering over the swaddled bundle as if afraid to touch. The thought of the naming ceremony— the day when fathers lifted their sons before God and community— twisted in him. Would they make it that far? Would Elior's first cry of belonging echo in a courtyard, or would it be whispered underground, hidden beneath figs and stone?

Mara looked at him then, tired but fierce, her hair damp with sweat, her gaze unwavering. "If we reach the eighth day," she whispered, "he will be named before heaven even if no men hear it."

Nathan bowed his head. He had feared this birth, feared the loss of another wife, feared the weight of fatherhood in a world like this. Yet hearing her claim the child's future in the very teeth of secrecy, he felt resolve rise in him.

Elior stirred, a small fist pressing against the linen. Lois brushed her thumb across his brow, and for the briefest moment, the house felt less like a hiding place and more like a sanctuary.

And around them, the cellar held its breath.

Above, the world waited.

The baby lay wrapped in soft linens dyed with crushed walnut, his breath shallow and steady against Mara's chest. Morning light filtered through the shutters in thin, golden stripes. Lois moved like breath itself—silent, steady—tending to the hearth and steeping herbs that would strengthen Mara's body and quiet the infant's restlessness.

Outside, the village was already awake. Vendors lifted awnings, children chased one another down the lane, and the iron ring of a soldier's laugh carried too easily through the still air. Life pressed forward as though nothing had changed.

Nathan shifted against the rough wall, the ache in his back a reminder of another night spent on stone. The cellar was cool, its air damp with the scent of earth and pressed figs, but Lois had made it gentler for Mara—pallets layered with wool and linen, cushions stuffed with straw, a clay lamp burning low through the night.

Mara lay there still with the infant swaddled against her chest. She had dozed in snatches, waking at each stir of the child, her face pale but softened by the steady rhythm of his breathing.

Nathan pushed himself upright slowly, joints protesting, and stood just watching them—the woman who had carried him into a life he never expected, and the boy who bound him to it now with a cord invisible yet unbreakable. Something tightened in his chest, equal parts awe and dread. This was morning. A new day. But not one without shadow.

He crossed to the hearth, speaking low. "We'll need more wood before evening." His eyes flicked toward the shutters. "And word of the patrols. If they're still here, better we know."

Lois poured steaming water over the bundle of herbs, the scent of thyme and fennel filling the room. "Then we keep to the rhythm. Bread in the oven, jars on the press. No more and no less.

Let the world see what it expects."

The child stirred, letting out a soft cry. Mara kissed his brow, whispering, "My son."

It was the first morning of his life. The first day of their new uncertainty.

At the back of the home, the mood was not so still.

Nathan crouched beside a cedar crate, checking the bindings of a small cache: dried meat, rolled maps, two sealed jars of oil, and a narrow pouch with silver coins, a spare sling, and a hidden blade. Benaiah stood nearby, shoulder pressed against the doorframe, his arms crossed, eyes scanning every angle of the inner room as if it could betray them at any moment.

"Three more days," Nathan muttered. "That's all we need. The mule can be ready by then, and the rain will have softened the lower paths enough to hide the trail. Mara will be strong enough to travel in the back of the cart."

Benaiah nodded. "I've secured a place near Tamar. Remote farmstead. Belongs to an old friend of mine who owes me twice over. We can get her and the baby there quietly. From there we travel on to

En-gedi and then on to Qumran, where you all will be safe for a time being."

Nathan's brow furrowed. "And if Mordecai shows up before then?"

"Then I stall," Benaiah said, deadpan. "Or bleed. Whichever comes first." Nathan didn't smile.

A creak from inside—the faint shuffle of Lois's footsteps—and the muffled cry of the newborn broke. The tension eased only slightly, like a bowstring slackened but never unstrung. Nathan rose, spine aching, rubbing a hand over his beard.

"He looks like you," Benaiah said.

Nathan's eyes softened, just for a breath. "He looks like something new."

They had meant to leave within three days, to keep moving before eyes or rumors turned their way. But Mara had not regained her strength quickly. The bleeding lingered longer than Lois liked, and the newborn's cries were thin, his breath shallow in the first nights. Travel with a donkey cart over rock and ridge was impossible in such a state. So they stayed, one day folding into the next, each morning a choice between risking the road and risking the child, Mara or both.

And so the days inched forward, until at last the eighth arrived.

There were no trumpets, no witnesses from the village. No crowd gathered, no elders presided. Only Lois, Caleb, Leah, and the small circle bound together by secrecy. At dawn, Lois boiled water, steeped rosemary in the pot to cleanse the air, and laid out the cleanest cloth she had left.

The act itself was quick, carried out by Nathan's steady hand with Lois guiding his movements.

Mara, pale but resolute, held the infant close and whispered his name aloud for the first time.

"Elior," she said, her voice trembling and sure at once. *"God is my light."*

The name echoed softly against the stone, as if even the cellar walls bore witness. Caleb leaned forward, eyes wide, as though he understood the weight of this moment better than his years. Leah murmured something half-coherent, but there was recognition, a thread of memory tethering the child to the family she still grasped in fragments.

For a few hours afterward, it almost felt like peace. They ate flatbread with honey. Nathan even managed a smile when Elior's tiny hand wrapped around his finger. For one fragile morning, life seemed to push back the shadow.

But by nightfall, Mara's skin burned with fever.

At first, it was brushed aside—exhaustion, the heat of summer, the toll of childbirth. Lois pressed cool cloths to her brow, brewed teas of thyme and sage, and whispered prayers over her while Nathan sat sleepless at her side. Yet the fever did not break. Days stretched into a week, her strength rising and falling like a tide. Some mornings, she could hold Elior, her eyes bright with the stubborn fire Nathan had fallen in love with. Other nights she drifted in and out of delirium, murmuring names from a past that made Lois's heart clench and Nathan's jaw harden.

The planned departure—the careful gathering of supplies, the whispered routes north—was quietly abandoned. They could not risk the road with Mara so frail and the infant still needing constant care. Each day they lingered in Akrabbim felt like pressing their backs against a door they could not lock, knowing someone was testing the latch from the other side.

Weeks passed. The Romans did not leave, but neither did they act. Their presence hung over the village like a storm cloud refusing to break. Patrols circled the square. Mordecai's name surfaced in whispers, carried on the breath of merchants and travelers. Still, he did not appear at their door.

In the town, life bent and twisted around the occupation. The market still opened each morning, but voices that once rang with barter now dropped to murmurs. Women selling olives tucked their baskets closer to their bodies, wary of the soldiers who lingered too long. At the well, children still threw stones to make ripples, but they stopped when a centurion came near, the splash of water suddenly sounding like defiance. Even prayers at the synagogue grew quieter— men bowing their heads not only in reverence but in fear of who might be listening outside the door.

A tavern near the edge of the square stayed busier than before, not because of joy but because wine dulled men's tongues and made their silence easier. Merchants from the hill country passed through more quickly, anxious to move their goods and leave before questions came. Some villagers kept shutters closed even at midday, as if hiding would make Rome forget them. Others tried too hard to appear loyal, offering fruit to passing guards or bending their heads in false respect.

Caleb felt it too, though a little differently. He carried water jugs and fetched bread, but his eyes were always searching—for a limp, for the crimson trim he'd heard whispered about. Sometimes he slipped away under the excuse of errands, circling the square, scanning the tavern door, lingering by the well. He wanted to see his father for himself, to measure the stories against the man. But Mordecai was never there. Just patrols, merchants, and villagers pretending the air wasn't thick with fear.

Each time Caleb returned home empty-handed, Lois caught the flicker in his eyes and pressed a hand to his shoulder, firm enough to remind him of the danger without scolding outright. "Some shadows," she told him once, "grow larger the more you chase them."

And so the house bent itself around the rhythm of waiting. Nathan tended the press by day, Caleb at his side, both of them careful to keep up the guise of ordinary labor. Lois watched the street and prayed with her hands as much as with her voice, weaving cloth, boiling herbs, grinding grain.

When Mara's fever left her too weak to rise, Lois took the infant into her arms, pacing the courtyard with him against her shoulder. She hummed old songs she barely remembered, songs she had once sung to Miriam, Ruth, and Caleb. Elior's tiny breath warmed her collarbone, and for those moments, she felt that not all things had been stolen by Rome. Sometimes she sat near the window with him swaddled close, rocking gently as she scanned the lane for movement.

Even Leah, lost so often in the fog of half-remembered days, found herself pulled back by the infant's cries. She would reach for him with trembling hands, and Lois, cautious at first, let her hold him. Leah rocked him in a rhythm older than her confusion, whispering nonsense words, sometimes calling him by Jotham's name, sometimes only smiling faintly when his fist curled around her finger. In those moments, the child seemed to give her back a spark of herself, a piece of tenderness that had not yet withered.

In those weeks, Caleb turned eight. There was no feast, no village laughter, no gifts save what the household could spare—a small carving knife Nathan had sharpened and wrapped in cloth, and a cord Lois braided from wool scraps to wear it by. Still, the day was marked. Nathan took him out to the press yard and taught him how to knot ropes properly, how to stack jars so they would not topple even in a tremor, how to judge the weight of a full skin by the tug on his arm. They worked until Caleb's hands blistered, but Nathan's patience never frayed. At dusk, he ruffled the boy's hair and said, "You're not a child anymore, not if you can carry your own knots."

Caleb tried to hide his pride, but it glowed in his chest like coals. That night, as he lay on his mat, he thought of the father he remembered only in fragments—bitter words, hands that were never gentle, a presence that filled a room with unease. He thought of how Nathan's silence felt different: not heavy, not waiting to strike, but steady, like a wall that kept the wind out. For the first time, Caleb realized how little a father meant if he never taught you anything worth holding.

And how much a man could become a father without ever claiming the word.

In the cellar, Elior grew stronger, even as his mother fought to do the same. His cries were steady, his fists small but fierce, his very existence a defiance against the shadow looming outside.

By the time the fever broke and Mara's strength returned, the household had changed. They had not left. They had endured. And in enduring, they had carved out something more dangerous than flight: a family rooted in defiance, too bound to one another to scatter.

CHAPTER 13
THE DAY THE WIND TURNED

Weeks had passed since Elior's birth, and the rhythm of hidden life had begun to settle into the walls of the old house. Lois kept her voice low, her steps softer. Nathan came and went by shadowed paths, meeting Benaiah's scattered network at odd hours. Mara moved little, still recovering, but her strength returned faster than Lois had expected. Faster than Lois had dared to hope.

But the wind shifted.

It came first in the silence. No birdsong. No market calls. No clatter of water jars at the well. Only the rustle of leaves, whispering: *Too late.*

A boy came running from the hills—one of Benaiah's lookouts. "They're here," he said between breaths. "Romans. A full unit. And Mordecai."

Ezra was already tightening the straps on his satchel. "We'll go now."

"No," Benaiah said, emerging from the shadows of the alley. "They've come too close. We try to flee now, we'll lead them straight to her. We hold the line."

Lois stood in the doorway, arms folded. "He'll want to see me. And Matthias. He still believes him to be alive."

Nathan turned to her, pleading. "Let me take Mara. The child—"

Lois shook her head. "We protect the child by not leading them into the open. You stay. You guard the house. I'll let him in."

Benaiah nodded grimly. "I've placed men behind the olive press. And at the well. We'll hold as long as we can."

The heavy crunch of boots echoed closer. Red banners appeared through the trees like blood blooming in water.

Mordecai rode at the front, cloaked in imperial formality. His eyes scanned the village with the cool detachment of a man who expected fear.

"Lois," he said.

Lois opened the door, her expression unreadable.

He stepped across the threshold and looked around slowly. "Strange. Everything feels smaller."

"Memory does that."

"I wanted to see the place again," Mordecai said. "Before… decisions must be made."

Lois offered no response, only watched as he moved through the house like a ghost returning to the bones of his old life. He touched the edge of the table where they had once eaten in silence.

His fingers brushed the chair backs, paused at the hearth.

"Father's not here?" he asked.

Lois's hands stilled over the dough she had been kneading. "He's gone," she said quietly.

"Buried at sundown. You weren't here to see it."

Something flickered in Mordecai's eyes, but it quickly smoothed into indifference. "Then there's nothing more to say."

"No," Lois said, her voice low but steady. "There's more than ever. You weren't here when he slipped away. You weren't here when his breath rattled, when Leah wept herself empty, when we laid him in the earth. You left that to others—again."

His jaw tightened, the mask slipping for just a breath. "You think I don't carry it? That I've forgotten?"

"I think you've buried it," she said. "Deep. Under Rome. Under orders. Under a name that's no longer yours."

"I had no choice."

"There is always a choice."

For a moment, he said nothing, staring at the shadows trembling along the wall. Then his gaze shifted toward the back room, where Leah's murmur carried faintly through the door left ajar.

A creak of floorboard.

A small figure stood there, barefoot, thin, holding a wooden toy he'd carved himself. Caleb.

Mordecai's gaze locked with the boy's. The faintest crack split the air between them.

The boy blinked, stepped forward uncertainly. "Are you...my father?" he asked. His voice wasn't afraid, just curious.

Mordecai didn't answer. He looked at the boy like he was staring into a mirror made of years and dust and choices he couldn't undo.

"I—I'm Caleb," the boy said, trying to sound stronger than he felt.

Lois stepped behind him, gently placing a hand on his shoulder. "Caleb," she said softly, "go wait in the courtyard."

But Caleb didn't move right away. He looked up at Mordecai again—studying him like he would a carved puzzle. "Why did you come back?"

Mordecai opened his mouth, but no answer came. The words jammed behind the armor of who he had become. He looked down, then back at Lois. His jaw tightened.

"Go on now," she said again.

This time, Caleb obeyed, his steps soft as dust on stone.

When the door swung shut behind him, Mordecai exhaled as if he'd been holding his breath for eight years.

"That's him," he said.

Lois nodded. "You missed more than a name."

Silence again—heavier now.

"He has your eyes," Lois added.

Mordecai didn't speak. But his hand twitched once at his side—whether toward the door or away from it, even he didn't seem to know.

The gate clicked shut behind the boy, but the echo rang long in Mordecai's ears.

Caleb.

A name he'd never spoken aloud except perhaps on his naming day.

A face shaped by years he hadn't earned.

Mordecai stared at the closed door, his expression unreadable. But inside, something broke and rearranged. He didn't know what he'd expected. A hollow feeling, maybe. A vague curiosity. But the boy had his eyes. His eyes. The same sharp brown that had once looked up at Matthias from under a mop of black curls, asking too many questions with too much defiance.

He hadn't felt eight in a long time. But the boy had pulled the memory from him like a splinter from the skin.

At eight, he had sat beside Jotham at the edge of the olive grove, their legs swinging in the heat, arguing about which fig tree bore the sweetest fruit. Jotham had been precise, patient, always trying to teach. Mordecai had wanted the loudest voice, the final word, the power to be heard. Even then.

And their father?

Matthias had been different then—stern, but capable. His hands calloused with labor, his voice heavy with expectation. He had wanted sons who would build, not question. Jotham had tried to meet those expectations. Mordecai had learned to bend them.

He took a step toward the hearth and leaned one hand on the mantle. The wood was the same. The stone was worn smooth where he used to tap it nervously while Matthias scolded him for squandering coin. That night came back sharply—the one where he'd stormed out, clay pitcher still broken on the floor, Photine's gaze like fire chasing him into the dark.

He'd thought he was done with this house. That he could bury the man he used to be.

But then the boy said, "Why did you come back?"

The question echoed still.

He didn't have the answer.

He just knew that seeing his son shifted something. A tremor deep beneath the layers of armor he'd forged from Roman steel and broken loyalties.

He turned to Lois.

"The girls," he said, quieter now. "Where are they?"

Lois's brows lifted, just slightly. "Safe."

"Are they…" He cleared his throat. "Are they well?"

She didn't answer right away.

"They're strong," she said at last. "More their mother than you."

He nodded, jaw clenched. "I never meant…" He stopped himself. The words felt foreign on his tongue.

No one had taught him how to be a father. He had learned how to command men, infiltrate camps, use silence as a blade—but fatherhood? That was Jotham's realm. Jotham, who died being robbed, couldn't even defend himself. Jotham, who still haunted every corner of this place like the echo of a better man.

And now here was his son he hadn't seen in half a decade. No word, no letter, no coin passed.

Just the clean cut of abandonment.

He didn't know what to do with that.

So he turned away, the questions piling up inside, unanswered. Unvoiced. But not uncarried.

Mordecai stood a moment longer, his hand grazing the edge of the doorframe. The house smelled of bread and oil, but beneath that—something else. Life. Secrets.

He looked away then, toward the olive grove swaying in the wind.

"I was eight when father taught us to butcher a goat with a dull blade. Jotham cried after. I stayed quiet. Thought that made me stronger."

"Silence doesn't make you strong," Lois said. "It just keeps the wounds from healing."

He turned back toward her, voice low now. "You think I don't carry it? All of it? I've been bleeding under armor for years."

She said nothing. Just watched him.

Finally, he adjusted his cloak, the fabric snapping faintly in the wind. "Tell the boy…" He paused. "No. Don't tell him anything."

Then he nodded once to Lois—no more sarcasm, no veiled jabs. Just a quiet, almost reverent:

And he began to walk away.

"I'll go to the grove. I'll only stay a moment," Mordecai said, stepping back toward the door.

Then it happened.

From the back room behind the door cover, muffled but unmistakable, came a baby's cry.

Mordecai froze mid-step. The sound hung in the air—small, fragile, but impossible to ignore. His eyes flicked toward Lois;

something unreadable moved behind them. Surprise, yes. But something else. Calculation.

Lois met his gaze evenly. "A neighbor's child," she said quietly. "Leah's been watching her during the harvest."

Mordecai's jaw flexed, but he said nothing. He stepped out into the courtyard slowly, like a man weighing scales no one else could see. His fingers drummed once on the horn at his side—but he didn't lift it.

Instead, he turned and looked back at the house.

"I'll be in the square at dusk," he said. "Tell the villagers there will be a gathering. A meal. Rome offers peace, but it requires clarity. I expect everyone to be present."

Lois gave no reply. She simply watched.

Mordecai mounted his horse without urgency. The soldiers followed his lead. Not a retreat. Not an attack. A coil tightening.

When they were gone, the silence returned.

Lois closed the door. Beneath her, the trapdoor seemed to pulse with breath.

Nathan and Benaiah stepped out from the shadows. "He knows."

"He suspects," Lois corrected. "But he won't strike until he's certain."

Nathan turned to the cellar hatch. "We need to move them. Soon."

Lois nodded. "Tonight."

And outside, under the fig tree, a boy named Caleb stood with his hands clenched at his sides, watching the dust trail left by the father he'd never known.

Something inside him twisted—part ache, part anger, part curiosity too strong to resist. Before he could think better of it, he slipped from the courtyard, feet quick and quiet on the stone. He kept to the shadows of the lane, darting behind baskets, shutters, and walls, trailing the figure who walked with Rome's bearing but carried a gait that felt like his own.

Mordecai didn't look back. He moved steadily toward the edge of the square, where the Romans lingered near the well. Caleb followed at a distance, heart hammering. He watched the way people stepped aside for him—how men dropped their eyes, how women pulled their children close. He had never seen anyone part a street like that, not even Nathan.

For a moment, Caleb imagined stepping into the open, calling out "Father!" and watching the man turn, recognition breaking across his face. But the word stuck in his throat. He remembered Nathan's hand steady on his shoulder, the way Lois's eyes grew sharp when she spoke of shadows.

So he stayed hidden, following until Mordecai paused, speaking low to the vendor. Caleb could not hear the words, but he saw the tension in the merchant's jaw, the way the man nodded too quickly.

When Mordecai turned down a side path toward the governor's quarters, Caleb froze. He could go no further without being seen. His throat felt dry, his hands damp. Quietly, he backed away, retracing his steps until the fig tree came into view again.

By mid-afternoon, the sun hovered low, casting a golden glare over Akrabbim. Word had spread quickly—Rome would dine tonight. No decree was issued, but the message was clear: clean your fronts, prepare your best, and smile.

The villagers moved like sleepwalkers, faces tight with something between dread and resolve.

Bread was kneaded with trembling hands. Clay vessels were polished until knuckles cracked. Chickens were plucked, stew was stirred. All while eyes kept flicking toward the well where Mordecai had first arrived.

"They say it's a peace gesture," an old man muttered while sweeping his stoop.

"They say a lot of things before the spears come out," his wife replied, hanging figs to dry with more force than needed.

Children were scrubbed. Tunics mended. Oil lamps filled.

But it wasn't a feast. It was a performance. A test.

Everyone knew it.

Behind one home, a young boy paused while gathering herbs and watched Roman soldiers set up a shaded table in the square. Fine linens. Imported wine. A goat roasting over an open fire, manned by a villager whose eyes never lifted from the flames. Mordecai passed nearby, nodding at him with practiced ease, but the boy only swallowed hard and went back to his basket.

Back at Lois's home, a second performance was unfolding—one far less ceremonial.

Lois boiled clothes and packed jars of honey and vinegar into a satchel. Nathan sharpened his blade behind closed shutters, and Benaiah mapped out the night in whispered tones by oil lamplight.

"She'll go at dusk," Benaiah said. "One cart, covered. A path through the date grove and onto the northern ridge. Everyone will be in the Square, including Rome."

"Too exposed," Nathan said. "They've stationed sentries at the well and near the market road."

"Then we move early," Lois added. "Before the sun rises. After the wine numbs their vigilance." Mara sat silently, the baby at her chest. She didn't speak, but her eyes followed every movement, memorizing the exit path with fierce clarity.

In the corner, Caleb helped gather dried figs and tucked them into pouches. He didn't ask questions, but his brow was drawn.

Later, as the torches were lit in the square and villagers laid out platters of dates and flatbread, no one laughed. No one sang. They just waited.

For the meal.

For the signal.

For the end of something.

Or the beginning of something else.

And in the hills beyond, the winds began to shift.

The baby slept with his head tucked beneath her chin, warm and heavy, a living question mark against her chest.

The room felt close. Nathan moved as though to speak, but Lois touched his arm, holding him back. This wasn't a wound words could cauterize too quickly. Mara needed the ache to be heard before it could be healed.

Mara leaned forward, face buried in her hands. "I should never have come back. Every time I try to build something, it shatters. Every time I let myself hope, it costs someone their life. Maybe I should have stayed gone. Maybe I should have vanished for good."

Nathan rose then, slow but steady, crossing the room until he knelt before her. He didn't touch her at first. He just looked at her, eyes steady, voice low. "You think you're a curse because the world has broken you more times than it should have. But listen to me—" His hand reached for hers, prying gently until her fist opened. He pressed her palm flat against his chest. "I'm still here. Because of you. Not despite you."

Her breath shook, but she didn't pull away.

"You talk of graves," Nathan went on, voice taut with feeling. "But what of the lives you've carried forward? Lois, who still breathes because you gave her courage once. Caleb, who looks to you like the world hasn't ended. This child—" he glanced toward the cradle, where Elior stirred faintly, "—this child exists because you refused to stay silent. You refused to bow. Curses destroy. But you— Mara, Photine—you endure. That is not a curse. That is defiance. That is strength."

Mara's lips trembled, tears welling though she tried to swallow them back. "And what if it costs you too? What if you're next?"

"Then I die knowing I stood beside you, not behind you, not against you." His thumb brushed across her knuckles, grounding her. "And I'd rather that a thousand times than live safe while you believe you're poison."

Her eyes met his then, wet but searching. For the first time in hours, her breath came steady. The baby let out a small cry, breaking the silence, and Lois moved to lift him, rocking gently. Even Leah stirred from her seat, humming a faint tune from some distant memory.

Nathan finally stood, helping Mara to her feet. His hand lingered on her back. "You're not a storm that leaves ruin," he said softly. "You're the soil that grows again, no matter how many times fire passes over it. That's what Rome fears. That's what Mordecai fears. And that's why we keep going."

Mara closed her eyes, letting the words settle—not fully believing, not yet, but holding onto them like a rope stretched across deep water.

"We don't know what he plans tonight. This could just be a gesture. A performance. A Roman dinner with Roman wine and nothing more. You're preparing for escape like there's already blood in the streets." She looked directly at Lois. "He didn't raise a horn last time. He walked away."

Nathan bristled. "He walked away because he was uncertain. Not because he was harmless."

"But he doesn't know you," she said. "He doesn't know the child is yours. If he suspects anything, it's me. And he left. He gave supplies. If this dinner is what they say it is—a peace offering—then why provoke him with another disappearance?"

Lois stepped forward. "Because peace with Rome has teeth. It smiles as it swallows. You know that."

Benaiah shifted against the wall, his voice low. "And rumor moves faster than truth. I've heard whispers—travelers saying a Samaritan woman, once gone, has been seen again near these ridges. No name. Just fragments. But fragments are enough to make men like Mordecai suspicious."

Mara pressed her hand into her lap, her eyes darting between them.

"I do know," she said finally, her voice rough. "But I also know that running makes us look guilty. If I vanish before the meal is served, I become a secret worth chasing."

Benaiah's voice was quiet, but steady. "You think staying makes you safer?"

"I think staying might keep the others safer. If Mordecai has any humanity left—and I'm not convinced he doesn't—he won't ignite violence at a meal staged as a gesture of goodwill. Not when villagers are watching. Not when he still needs to win them."

Lois opened her mouth, then closed it.

Nathan stepped closer, hand resting on the table. "What do you want to do?"

Mara looked down at her son. "I want you to go with Lois and Caleb. The Romans don't know your face, only your name. If they search, they'll search for me."

Nathan's face tightened. "I won't leave you."

"Yes," she said gently. "You will. Just until morning. Benaiah stays with me. The trapdoor remains open. If something turns…" She didn't finish. She didn't need to.

Lois exhaled sharply. "You don't need to be brave to prove anything."

"I'm not trying to prove anything," Mara said. "I'm just… tired of being hunted. And tired of the fear deciding every hour of this child's life."

Lois studied Mara's face for a long moment. Then, without a word, she lowered the infant into Mara's waiting arms. The baby stirred, rooting against her chest until he settled again.

"You're his mother," Lois said quietly. "Let him feel that strength, even when you don't." Mara bowed her head over the child, her tears falling silently into the folds of the linen.

The room held its breath.

Then Benaiah nodded. "One night. We watch. We wait. If it's smoke and nothing more… we breathe. If it's fire—"

"We run," Nathan finished.

Mara nodded, one hand holding her child, the other gripping the table like an anchor.

Outside, the first strains of lyre music drifted through the square.

And inside, hope began—just barely—to outweigh dread.

In the village center, the long table stretched under woven canopies in the town square, flanked by Roman guards and nervous villagers dressed in their best tunics. The scent of roast lamb mingled with olives, figs, and the heavy hush of caution. Mordecai sat at the center, regal in his courier's sash, but without his armor.

Nathan took his seat beside Lois, eyes flicking between soldiers and exits. Caleb sat between them, his small hands folded obediently, but his wide eyes missed nothing. Leah was there too, settled on a low stool close to Lois, a cup of watered wine cradled carefully in her trembling hands. She stared at the table with a vague smile, nodding now and then as though she heard echoes from another meal long ago.

Mordecai lifted his goblet. "To community," he said smoothly. "To order. To shared bread in uncertain times."

The soldiers echoed him with a murmur, some raising their cups, some only shifting in their seats. But Mordecai's eyes did not linger on them. They slid across the table, pausing first on Lois, then on Leah, but still carrying that soft, unnerving light.

And then his gaze caught on the others.

A man sat beside Lois. Not a neighbor he knew. Not kin. A Galilean by the look of him—broad-shouldered, watchful, his hand always near the knife at his belt. Mordecai's jaw tightened almost imperceptibly.

Beside the man, a boy sat straight-backed, his small hands folded on the table. Caleb. Mordecai's gaze lingered longer than it should have. The child's hair, the tilt of his jaw—something there pulled like a hook through memory.

The man—sat too close, too familiar. His arm brushed the boy's as they reached for the bread, as if he belonged there. Jealousy burned sharp in Mordecai's chest, cloaked quickly beneath a smile that never touched his eyes.

He had heard a wail earlier in the day, the unmistakable cry of an infant. Yet here was no child in sight. Only Lois, steady as stone; Leah, humming to herself with her cup in hand; a man he does not know, watchful as a wolf; and Caleb, whose wide eyes flicked from face to face, trying to understand the weight of the evening.

Mordecai masked the surge of suspicion, lifting his goblet once more as though nothing had stirred within him. But his eyes, sharp as hooked iron, lingered on the trio.

"To peace," Lois echoed, voice even.

For a while, the charade held.

Wine was poured. Bread passed. The flicker of torches played on polished bronze and tired eyes.

Leah, frail but alert, laughed softly at a Roman's clumsy attempt to praise Akrabbim's olives. Matthias nodded along, regal despite the weight of age, propped carefully on a cushion with folded hands.

Caleb leaned into Nathan, whispering something about the food, and Nathan gently reassuring the boy with a smile and a hand on his shoulder.

That was the moment Mordecai's eye caught it—Nathan's hand. Caleb's ease. Lois's glance toward them both.

His goblet paused in mid-air.

"Lois," Mordecai said, voice smooth as oil but thinner than before, "I must say, the child is… quite attached to him." He tilted his head toward Nathan, eyes sharp. "Does he always sit so near? Or is this a special occasion?"

Lois didn't blink, hiding Nathan's true name was imperative she calmly replied, "*Nathan* has been helping around the house. Caleb can't yet lift the heavy jars nor render repairs." Then she added without thought, "and Caleb is drawn to steadiness."

"Mm." Mordecai's gaze lingered on Nathan. "And you—I didn't catch your name. You have the time to travel, stopping to assist another man's family?"

Nathan met his stare without flinching. "The name is Nathan, I go where I'm needed."

"That's convenient." Mordecai smiled, but it didn't reach his eyes. "And what is it you do, exactly?"

"I fix what's broken," Nathan replied, evenly.

Something flickered in Mordecai's jaw. "Do you?"

Caleb, sensing the shift, leaned a little closer to Nathan, instinctively seeking protection. The gesture did not go unnoticed.

"I see," Mordecai said, sitting back. "Well. I suppose broken things find each other."

The air thinned. A soldier coughed. Somewhere beyond the canopy, a dog barked once and was silent.

The tension curled like smoke beneath the canopy, barely visible but still choking.

Mordecai lifted his goblet but did not drink. His eyes, unreadable to most, flicked again to Nathan, then to Caleb. He tapped the rim of his cup with one finger—once, twice. Then he looked toward Leah, his voice casual, almost warm.

"Em," he said. "It's good to see you well enough to join us."

Leah smiled, ever gracious, though her words tumbled one over the other. "The warmth helps my joints—yes, yes, I feel it all the way to my fingers. And the wine doesn't hurt, not at all. Haven't had wine like this in… oh, since the harvest feast, before…" She trailed off, her eyes darting to Lois, then back to the cup in her hand. She laughed softly, almost giddy, and lifted it as though toasting no one in particular. "It's good to be out. To see faces. To remember what the world looks like beyond the courtyard."

He chuckled softly. "I imagine the quiet of the house has helped, too. Fewer feet running across the courtyard these days."

"Oh yes," Leah said, patting her shawl with a dreamy smile. "Though it isn't too quiet, not with a baby in the house."

Mordecai's brow lifted, the faintest curve of curiosity. "Ah, yes, your neighbor's baby, is it?"

Leah nodded brightly. "Such a sweet child. Doesn't fuss much at all."

"I wasn't aware anyone in the village had a newborn," Mordecai said, his tone light but sharpened with interest.

Lois's knife paused mid-cut, pressing against the fig without breaking its skin. She didn't look up. "She means the child of a trader passing through last week," she said quickly. "They stayed one night, left before dawn."

But Leah shook her head, stubborn in her half-cheerful fog. "No, no. She's still here. Her mother's resting in the back. Poor girl's been through so much—"

Lois set her fork down with a sharp clink and reached for Leah's cup, refilling it before it was half-empty. "Enough, Mother," she said smoothly. "You'll wear yourself out with too much talk."

Mordecai's eyes did not move from Leah's face. "Still here, you say?" His voice was almost tender, but Lois heard the steel beneath. "And what poor girl might that be?"

Leah blinked, forgetting the thread of her own words. She looked down at her lap, muttering something about shawls and figs.

Lois leaned in quickly, her hand firm over Leah's. "Eat," she urged gently, her smile wide enough for the soldiers to see. "The food will do you good."

But across the table, Mordecai was still watching. Not Leah. Not Lois. Nathan.

"I see," Mordecai said, setting his cup down gently. "And this mother… does she have a name?" Leah blinked, "Photine," she replied.

The table fell still.

Lois's hand closed slowly around her knife.

Caleb stopped chewing.

Nathan's jaw tightened, but he forced himself to remain still.

Mordecai stared at Leah, and for a moment the world narrowed to a single pulse behind his eyes.

Leah, suddenly unsure, looked to Lois. "Did I say something wrong?"

Lois reached quickly for her hand. "No, Mother," she said softly. "Your mind wanders sometimes, that's all. We all know it. You confuse days, confuse people. It's nothing." She turned to Mordecai, meeting his gaze with forced calm. "You can see how she is. Age and strain… her mind isn't what it was."

Mordecai stood, his goblet in hand, the smile on his lips tight as a noose. "Not at all, Em," he said to Leah. "You've said just enough."

Then he turned his eyes on Lois, the mask slipping, his voice edged now with iron. "But you—" He set the goblet down deliberately, the thud carrying through the silence. "You always were a poor liar."

Lois's knuckles whitened around her cup. Nathan kept his smile in place, but his jaw was clenched hard enough to ache. Caleb's small hands tightened on the edge of the table, his wide eyes darting between them.

The air shifted—thick, taut.

Mordecai sipped his wine. "So quiet here," he remarked. "No signs of the unrest they whisper about in Caesarea. No rebels. No hidden prophets. No fugitives." The last words hung heavily in the air.

Lois responded evenly, "We are a simple people."

"And yet," Mordecai said, turning to Leah, "Em, reveals so much."

A long pause.

The color in Lois's face drained, but she willed herself still.

Ezra glanced down, then up again, feigning interest in a serving dish.

Mordecai set his cup down with perfect calm. "Photine," he repeated, as if tasting the syllables.

His voice dropped low. "She's here? And the man who stole her, Ezra, is he here as well?"

The breath in Mordecai's chest turned to stone. His thoughts raced—Lois's defiance, another man's presence, the child's cry that morning. It clicked into place with a cruel, elegant finality. Nathan…Ezra. The stranger sitting at his table. The husband. The protector.

"The governor will be most interested to learn of this," Mordecai said, too calmly. "You've harbored fugitives. Interfered with Roman justice. Lied to an envoy."

Lois locked eyes with him. "She is my family."

Mordecai rose. "She is my property."

Ezra stood now too, quiet but unyielding, shedding his cover without regard. "She is not."

The silence at the table grew tense, brittle.

Mordecai turned to the nearest soldier, voice flat and cold. "Take him," he said, nodding toward Ezra. Then, with a flick of his hand toward the doorway, "Seal the court. Let no one leave."

"Don't," Lois said sharply. "You'll bring war to your own door."

He hesitated because of Caleb. The boy was staring up at him. So familiar. So unbearably *his*.

And for just a second, something old and wounded flickered in Mordecai's face. Then it vanished.

He looked at Ezra and, for the first time, saw clearly what role he played. Not a protector. A rival.

A thief.

"I'll handle this myself," Mordecai said coldly and stepped into the night.

The house was dim, lit only by the orange flicker of a dying oil lamp near the hearth. Photine paced in slow circles, the baby bundled tightly against her chest. Her movements were deliberate, rhythmic— more to keep herself steady than to soothe the child.

Benaiah stood near the back door, arms crossed, watching the shadows stretch across the floor. He hadn't spoken much since the others left for the Roman gathering. But now, as night pressed closer, the silence between them cracked.

"He's not just here for food and wine," Benaiah said finally, his voice low, certain.

Photine didn't look up. "I know."

"He'll ask questions. He already is."

"I know that too."

Benaiah turned toward her. "And when he doesn't like the answers, he'll come here."

Photine stopped pacing. "He won't find me easily."

"He won't need to." He stepped forward. "If he sees the child, it will be enough."

She looked down at the infant, who slept soundly against her heartbeat. "Do you think he'd hurt a child?"

"I think Mordecai has convinced himself that you are still his, and the child is an assault on him. And that makes him dangerous."

Photine walked to the far corner where a satchel lay open. She pulled out a length of cloth, wide and strong, and wrapped it around her shoulders and waist with practiced care. The infant stirred as she lifted him, tucking him against her chest, then drew the cloth snug until he was bound securely to her. She tested the knot, tugging once, twice, until she was sure it would hold. Her arms were free now, ready for whatever came.

"Then we prepare to run," she said, her voice steady.

Benaiah nodded. "Tonight, if it comes to it. You'll take the ravine path west—fewer patrols, and it cuts behind the grove. Ezra marked the route."

A long pause passed between them. Then Photine asked, "Do you think Ezra's safe?"

Benaiah's jaw tightened. "He knows how to mask fear. But Mordecai—he knows how to smell it."

She crossed to the window and pushed the curtain aside. The village shimmered in the starlight, still deceptively peaceful. Her voice was barely a whisper. "Maybe he's not coming." Benaiah didn't answer.

Instead, he checked the latch on the back door, then pressed his hand to the hidden compartment in the cellar, just in case. "Sleep if you can," he said. "I'll watch." But neither of them would.

Not tonight.

The night had deepened.

Even the cicadas, once humming loudly in the olive trees, had fallen quiet.

Benaiah sat at the edge of the hearth, sharpening a short blade with steady, silent strokes. The sound was faint, deliberate. He paused, every few minutes, to listen.

Then he felt it. Not noise, not movement—just a shift. A pressure in the air, like the sky itself, was lowering.

He moved to the door without a word.

Photine watched him, the baby still against her chest, now stirring.

"What is it?" she asked.

He didn't answer at first. He slipped the knife into his belt and reached for the clay jug near the door. He poured water slowly, calmly, then set it back down.

"Outside," he said, "a lantern. Moving slowly. Too smooth to be a villager. Too late for a neighbor."

Her breath caught. "Is it him?"

He nodded once. "Or his men."

She backed into the shadows, her hand covering the child's head. "Maybe it's nothing."

"No," Benaiah murmured. "This night's too quiet for nothing."

He stepped back from the door, motioning her to move to the rear chamber. "We go if he knocks.

We run if he forces the door. You don't stop for anything."

Photine looked at the child. "Not even for Ezra?"

A knock. Not loud. Not rushed.

Just certain.

Photine's body froze. The baby stirred again, lips parting with a soft mewl that might become a cry.

Benaiah's eyes flicked to the floor trap. "Now."

He crossed to the door, resting his hand on the latch.

Outside, the voice came, muffled through wood and iron.

"Photine," Mordecai said.

Not a question. Not a request.

A memory, returned.

Photine disappeared into the shadows.

Ezra darted down the narrow alley behind the olive press, Lois at his heels. They weaved through carts and scattered chickens, breath sharp in their lungs. Behind them, a pair of soldiers hesitated at the crossroads. Mordecai's orders had been fractured, half-spoken. He had claimed he would handle the house himself, leaving the apprehension of Ezra in uncertain hands.

That hesitation was all Ezra needed.

Ahead, the familiar outline of Lois's home came into view, half-shrouded in evening mist. And already—too close—Mordecai's voice was rising like smoke through the streets. "Photine…"

The sound of it struck like a gong in Ezra's chest.

Lois didn't speak. Her breath came short and ragged, but her legs never faltered. The hem of her tunic caught on a splintered fence post; she yanked it free without slowing.

They rounded the last bend just as the house came into view, Benaiah's tall form a silhouette through the slats of the front window. Ezra's fingers closed around the hilt of his blade—not drawn, not yet.

Behind them, a shadow slipped between two stalls and ducked beneath the awning of an abandoned fig vendor. Caleb. He was supposed to stay behind with Leah, but the boy had inherited more than just Mordecai's eyes.

He crept along the side of the building, low and silent, close enough to see the front door, but hidden from the street. His small chest rose and fell rapidly, fear and determination etched across his face.

At the house, Ezra reached the back door just as Benaiah cracked it open, his expression grim.

"Too late," he said. "He's outside."

Inside, the air was tight with waiting.

Photine had vanished into the cellar, the baby bound close against her chest. Down in the cool dark, she moved with care, shifting aside the tall water jugs stacked against the far wall. Behind them, the outline of a narrow opening revealed itself. A tunnel carved painstakingly over months, dug for this very purpose. She crouched low, steadying the infant with one hand as she pressed her shoulder to the edge of the stones.

The passage yawned black before her, no wider than her body. She knew it would force her to crawl, to inch forward until she reached the outlet near the olive grove beyond the ridge. A way out. A way to vanish if the house above gave way to soldiers.

She crouched there, poised, listening. Above, the trapdoor had been closed and sealed, the rug dragged back into place. The lamp was snuffed. Only the faint glow from the hearth leaked through the cracks in the floorboards, a reminder of the life they clung to even as escape pressed like a shadow at her back.

Lois crossed the threshold, stepping into the house she'd once ruled and now defended.

Ezra followed, pausing for a breath as Mordecai's shadow darkened the window.

Outside, on the road, Caleb pressed himself into the crook of the fence, eyes wide, watching as the man everyone whispered about raised his hand and knocked once again.

Then silence.

A pause.

And Mordecai's voice came again, lower this time. "Lois. Ezra. Shall we speak plainly?"

Lois turned to Ezra, her voice barely a whisper. "He knows."

Ezra's grip on his blade tightened. "Then we stall. You open the door. I'll take the rest."

And as Lois reached for the handle, steady despite the tremble in her bones, Caleb inched close enough to see the shape of his father's face.

The boy did not yet understand what he was seeing.

But he would.

He would remember this night for the rest of his short life.

The door creaked open.

Lois stepped into the cool dusk, hands visible, gaze level. Ezra lingered behind her, partially obscured by the shadows inside, blade hidden but ready.

Mordecai stood alone in the courtyard, hand resting on the hilt at his side. The air around him trembled—with the weight of something fraying at the edges.

"You've housed fugitives," he said evenly. "Harbored a man condemned by Roman decree.

Shielded a woman and child born of betrayal." His eyes narrowed. "Tell me I'm wrong."

"I'll tell you nothing," Lois said.

Ezra stepped into the light beside her. "Then I will."

Mordecai's jaw clenched. His gaze locked on Ezra like a tether pulled tight.

Ezra stood meeting Mordecai's eyes and contempt.

"They said you were clever," Mordecai muttered. "But not clever enough."

He stepped forward, drawing his sword in one smooth motion. "The penalty for harboring fugitives is death."

And then—footsteps.

Light. Too light.

Caleb.

He had crept through the alley behind the house, slipping from shadow to shadow, drawn not by orders or tactics, but by instinct. By love.

He saw Mordecai's sword. Saw his mother tense. Saw Ezra plant his stance like a wall. And something in him surged—fear, fury, a child's fierce courage.

He cried out and rushed forward.

"Leave them alone!"

Mordecai spun.

Too fast.

Too practiced.

Too afraid.

His sword arced before recognition could stop it.

The blade struck flesh.

The cry that followed was not Photine's. Not Lois's. Not Ezra's.

It was Mordecai's.

The boy collapsed at his feet, wide eyes blinking up at a sky that no longer held promise. His small hand clutched the edge of Mordecai's cloak, then released.

Lois screamed.

Ezra moved—too late.

Mordecai staggered back, sword falling from his fingers, clattering against stone. "No," he breathed. "No—" But there was no undoing.

Caleb lay still.

And in that stillness, everything else shattered.

Behind them, Photine emerged into the doorway, the child clutched tight against her chest. Benaiah appeared at her side.

Ezra knelt, scooping the boy's small body into his arms. Lois fell beside him, her hands shaking as she touched her only son's face.

Mordecai stood paralyzed.

Not a conqueror. Not a courier. A man who had killed his own son.

Mordecai staggered back a step. His sword arm was limp, his eyes fixed on the still form at his feet.

The world spun—Lois's scream, Ezra's broken cry, the child's blood staining the dust.

Then something inside Mordecai snapped.

He reached for the sky, lips curled into a snarl of denial and command, and shouted a single, guttural word:

"SEIZE THEM!"

The Roman soldiers reacted without pause—without clarity. Orders blurred. Authority fractured. What began as a maneuver turned into slaughter.

A soldier lunged toward Ezra. Ezra turned, blade flashing, parrying the first strike. But the second—he didn't see it.

It slid through his side.

Ezra's mouth opened, but no sound came. He collapsed beside Caleb, his fingers twitching once, then stilling.

"No—!" Lois flung herself toward him, but another soldier intercepted her. She struck him with the heel of her hand, fury giving her strength. He stumbled, stunned, but not out.

From the doorway, Benaiah shouted, "Photine—run!"

The baby wailed in her arms, tiny lungs drowning in the noise. Photine turned, eyes wide with horror, but obeyed. She slipped down into the cellar and through the rear passage, Lois right behind her, blood on her sash, grief in her bones pulling the trapdoor closed behind her.

Behind them, Benaiah drew his dagger. One Roman fell. Then another. But there were too many.

The fire began when a lantern was knocked from a soldier's belt. Oil spread across the floor, up the wooden wall, into the rafters. Screams mixed with crackling flame.

Mordecai stood frozen. His sword, slick with his own son's blood, hung useless at his side. He stared at the lifeless boy—his boy—as if the world had tilted and left him behind.

He fell to his knees. And then a blade caught him from behind.

Benaiah, bloodied and burning, had come through the smoke. His strike was clean, fueled by necessity.

Mordecai turned, staggered, looked at him—with a terrible, broken recognition.

"Jotham?" he rasped. "Brother…?"

Benaiah said nothing. Just held him as he sank, the torchlight flickering across Mordecai's eyes one final time—eyes chasing ghosts that would never come home.

Outside, the street was filled with smoke. Blades. Shouting. Villagers fled into the shadows. The soldiers no longer waited for orders. They struck at anything that moved.

Photine, Lois, and the baby were already in the grove, stumbling through underbrush. But the fire behind them illuminated their path— and made them visible.

"There! In the trees!" a soldier shouted.

Arrows flew.

Lois screamed as one grazed her thigh. She fell, Photine turned back, helping her to her feet. The baby cried, confused and terrified, face streaked with soot and dirt.

They ran. Deeper into the grove. Then down toward the dry ravine.

But the soldiers followed. Two of them. Fast.

Photine spotted a rock ledge and pushed Lois toward it. "Climb! I'll lead them off!"

"No—don't you dare!"

But Photine was already gone, ducking through the trees with the baby strapped to her chest.

Lois, bleeding, pulled herself up and watched from above.

Photine ran until her breath gave out. Then she doubled back, hiding behind a low ridge of stone.

The baby whimpered.

The soldiers came into view—slower and cautious.

Photine gripped a stone, her hand trembling. She was ready to fight, to die, to—

A sharp, awful thud.

She gasped. Looked down. The baby was still.

For one terrible second, she thought the child was asleep. But there was blood. A red bloom across the baby's side—an arrow meant for her had found the child.

"No..."

Her voice cracked, strangled in her throat.

"No, no, please—"

But the tiny chest no longer rose.

She held the baby close, rocking, whispering prayers.

The soldiers passed by without seeing her. Perhaps the shadows protected her, or perhaps they believed their work done. Either way, they vanished.

Later, she didn't know how much later, Lois found her.

Photine was still curled around the child's body, her face streaked with ash and salt.

Lois knelt beside her, pulling her close, cradling both mother and child.

For a while, there were no words. Only the distant crackle of fire, and the silence of a broken world.

At dawn, two cloaked women walked out of the olive groves, down the road to nowhere, carrying one less heartbeat than the night before.

CHAPTER 14
ONE LESS HEARTBEAT

The way out of Akrabbim was not the main road. Benaiah had made certain of that.

He had traced the path weeks before, knowing what might come—marked by a shepherd's cairn here, a bend in the wadi there, narrow places where brush could be cleared for passage. It was not safe, not truly, but safer than the Roman road curling north and east like a noose.

So they walked where soldiers would not: the ravine that edged the olive groves, the terraces cut long ago for vines now half-wild, the goat tracks that wound between limestone outcrops. It was slower, harder, the way meant for those who carried burdens too precious to be seen.

Lois walked as if each stone were heavier than her own body. Her silence was its own language—the hollow left by those she could not carry with her. Photine matched her pace, the swaddled bundle against her chest heavier than breath. She bore it anyway. To set it down would be a second betrayal.

Behind them, Akrabbim smoldered—grain silos cracked, olive oil fires still licking the blackened walls, the air thick with smoke carrying both grief and warning. They did not look back.

The land itself seemed scarred. Dust clung to their ankles. The hush between the hills was too deep, too listening. Even the birds had gone quiet, as if the world knew that what walked there now was not just women and children, but survivors carrying the ache of a city undone.

Hours passed, maybe more. Neither woman counted them.

The hills grew steeper, the stones sharper beneath their sandals. Dust clung to their hems, and every breath carried the bitter smoke of Akrabbim.

Lois had walked away before—when soldiers came and took Mordecai—but never like this. Never leaving her own blood behind.

Her mind replayed it without mercy: Caleb's small body crumpled at his father's feet, the sword stroke that cut through innocence. She saw the spattered earth, the pool of blood darkening faster than she could cry his name. She saw Mordecai's face—not triumphant, not even remorseful, but fractured, as though he too was startled at what his hand had done. None of it mattered. The boy was gone. And she, his mother, had fled without laying him to rest.

Every step since had been half-ash, half-betrayal. What kind of mother leaves her child on the ground where he fell? Even if the ground was poisoned by Rome and stained by his father's blade?

When the last olive trees faded behind them, and the first wild fig branches stretched above their heads, Lois finally spoke. Her voice was low, trembling.

"We don't have to leave him without a remembrance," she said. "We can give him a resting place. One made with love. With our hands."

She did not look at Photine when she said it. She could not. Her eyes were fixed ahead, on nothing, on everything—the thought that if she stopped moving, she might collapse into the dirt and never rise again. But she pressed on, clinging to the only act of defiance left to her: to remember. To make a space in the world where Caleb's name could still be spoken.

They stopped beneath a cairn of stones, half-fallen, half-swallowed by thorn and sand.

Once it had marked the boundary of a tribe, or perhaps the place where a shepherd raised an altar to give thanks for water. No prayers had been spoken here for generations, yet the stones held their silence as if listening still.

They stopped at the cairn of stones—ancient, half-fallen, their silence heavier than the stones themselves. A marker of some forgotten boundary, or maybe just the place where a weary shepherd once gave thanks for water. It didn't matter. To Lois and Photine, it was enough. A witness in the wilderness. A place to set memory down, even if no one else would ever remember.

Photine knelt, her body folding as though the earth itself pulled her down. With trembling fingers, she unwrapped the linen and kissed the baby's brow one last time. His skin was already cooling, yet she pressed her lips there as though her warmth might call him back. Then, gently, she laid him in the hollow she and Lois had dug and lined with cloth and fig leaves.

Her hands lingered at the edge of the stones, fingertips scraping against their roughness. Her voice broke in the stillness.

"I thought I would sing to him. I thought I would teach him to walk—watch him run in the press yard, climb fig trees, chase after Caleb." Her breath caught. "I thought he would have his loving hand to steady him."

Lois crouched beside her, her face drawn, her body trembling under the weight of what she carried.

"I didn't get to lay Caleb to rest," she whispered. Her words scraped the air like broken glass. "I left him where he fell—my son, my boy. Slain at the sword of his own father, left in the dust at his killer's feet." Her hands clenched at her robe until her knuckles ached. "I should have covered him. I should have… something."

Her chest heaved, but no sobs came—only a dry, gutted sound that might have been her heart breaking all over again.

Photine turned, grief folding into grief. Their tears mingled, their silence bound.

Lois forced her breath steady, her voice ragged but fierce.

"But this child… this child will not go nameless. He knew your heartbeat. He knew your warmth. He goes into the earth wrapped in love, not abandoned to the sword." She reached forward and touched the swaddled bundle, her fingers reverent. "May the God who sees remember him. May He gather both our sons—the one torn from this world, and the one who never took his first steps—and hold them in the place Rome cannot reach."

Photine bent lower, pressing her forehead to the stones. Her whole body shook with the effort of letting go.

"I hoped, I prayed there would be time," she said through sobs. "Time to see him grow. To hear him laugh. To watch him live. And Ezra—" Her voice cracked. "Ezra should have held him. He should have grown old beside me."

Lois knelt beside her, steady and unyielding. Her hand rested on Photine's back.

"He has our tears, Photine. And he has Ezra's name carried in our breath. That is their cry in the world now. Not silence. Never silence."

She bowed her head to the cairn, lips moving in prayer. "And Benaiah too—his strength, his loyalty. May the God who sees bind them together in memory. May the earth keep what Rome could not destroy."

Photine lifted her trembling hands, palms open to the desert air. "Elior, Caleb, Ezra, Benaiah—may their names rise like incense. May the wind carry them. May the world remember what was taken."

Together, beneath the wilderness sky, the two women sat in remembrance—an offering of breath, of grief, of love stronger than empire.

The wind stirred the fallen leaves around the stones, carrying their voices into the barren hills as if the desert itself agreed: Rome could steal their children's lives, but not their remembrance.

They stayed on their knees until the silence pressed too heavy to bear. Then Lois lifted her gaze to the loose stones scattered around them, the ones weathered by ages of sun and wind. Slowly, deliberately, she picked one up and set it atop the hollow where Elior lay.

Photine's swollen eyes followed her, uncomprehending at first. Then she, too, reached for a stone—her hands shaking, her breath catching—as she placed it with trembling care.

One by one, they gathered rocks from the dust, stacking them into a cairn. Not hurried, not careless. Each one chosen, each one laid with the weight of love.

"This one for Caleb," Lois said softly, her hands rough against the granite. "My son. My lastborn, who breathed the breath of life. Taken before I could even bless his body."

Photine's fingers pressed another stone into place. "This one for Elior," she whispered. "For the life he was meant to have, the songs I never sang, the future I will never hold."

Back and forth they went, stones and tears, grief and memory, until the cairn rose high enough to be seen from the path—yet not so high it would draw Roman eyes. A secret shrine. A mother's silent defiance.

Lois smoothed her palm across the top stone. "Now they are remembered together," she said.

"Two sons, one blood, one hope. Rome could not erase them."

Photine bowed her head, pressing her lips to the cool surface. "Let this be their resting place," she whispered, "and our vow."

The wind stirred, brushing over the cairn, rattling the fig branches above. It felt like a witness, like a seal.

Side by side, Lois and Photine rose. Their faces were streaked with ash and salt, their hands raw from stone, but their backs straightened. They had built something no empire could tear down: a monument of love, small yet unshakable.

Without looking back, they turned toward the hills. Behind them, the cairn cradled not only the bodies and memories of their sons, but also a defiance carved in stone—the promise that Rome would never speak the final word. Hand in hand, they walked on, each step an act of steadiness and solidarity, toward the waiting home where two daughters still breathed hope into the shadows.

The wind picked up.

And then something shifted.

It wasn't hope—not yet.

But it was a movement.

And in movement, there is breath.

By dusk, the walls of the women's house came into view, set against the mountains like a shelter carved out of stone itself. Its rooflines were simple, its courtyards small, but to the weary it looked like a fortress of mercy. Photine's legs faltered beneath her, and Lois caught her—steady as always, the same hands that had laid a son to rest and still found strength to carry the living.

For a moment, Lois stood still, her gaze fixed on the refuge ahead. Would they be welcomed, or turned away for bringing danger into their shadows? Could this place truly hold safety, or would Rome's echo find them here as well? The questions pressed heavily, but she set her jaw and leaned closer to Photine.

"Come on," Lois said softly. "Our girls are waiting."

They reached the gates with the moon behind them and smoke behind that. And though Photine's heart was broken in a way no mother should endure, she felt the faintest ember stir in her chest.

Grief had marked her.

But it had not ended her.

The wooden gates groaned as they opened, revealing the stone courtyard veiled in violet dusk. A nun greeted them, solemn and silent, her eyes scanning their faces before settling with reverence on the empty swaddle in Photine's arms. She stepped aside without a word.

The sisters did not speak. The walls of the women's house held more than vows; they held space.

Space for sorrow. Space for rest. Space for what words could never repair.

Photine crossed the threshold last, and something in her cracked as the gates closed behind them—like a release. All her life had been a series of leavings and takings. A father who vanished into the hills and never came back. A brother who sold her like a burden too heavy to bear. Jotham, who had offered her safety but not love, and Mordecai, who had turned her body into a battlefield. Even Ezra—her Ezra—who had given her joy for the first time, had been ripped from her arms along with the son they had made together.

Her hands curled into her robe, feeling the faint edges of the olive-wood shard pressed against her side. She had carried it for years, and now it was joined by the twin that her father once carved, and she still didn't know if it was a curse or blessing. Maybe both. Maybe it was the weight tethering her to a past she could never outrun, and the spark refusing to die no matter how many times Rome or men tried to crush her.

She was angry—furious, bone-deep, the kind of anger that could salt a field bare. But beneath the fury, a pulse stirred. Small, fragile, but alive. A knowing that all she had endured had not ground her into dust, it had lit a coal.

She was still bleeding inside. She still ached with loss. But now, within these walls, her feet found ground that did not collapse. For the first time in what felt like a lifetime, she could breathe without immediately choking on fear.

And somewhere in the quiet of her chest, a spark flared, not forgiveness, not yet, maybe not ever. But fire.

The girls saw them before they were ready to be seen.

Miriam, now thirteen and already taller than Lois, rose from where she had been kneeling beside the herb garden, hands stained with sage and soil. Over a year in the women's house had sharpened her edges: her braids were tighter, her posture straighter, and the softness in her face had given way to something quieter, older.

Beside her, Ruth, eleven, clutched a clay bowl of olives, her movements careful, her wide eyes scanning the path with cautious hope. The childish roundness in her cheeks had thinned, but the light in her gaze remained—flickering, but not gone.

"Em?"

Lois didn't answer with words. She just opened her arms.

Miriam dropped everything and ran, the time between them collapsing in an instant. She threw herself into Lois's arms, sobbing without shame, the sound raw and young despite the woman she was becoming. Ruth followed close behind, olive pits scattering across the stones like beads torn from a broken cord.

Photine lingered at the edge, her breath caught between longing and dread. The last time she had seen them, Miriam had been eight, Ruth barely six, still girls with soft braids and questions that tugged at her hem. Now they were taller, faces lengthened, eyes carrying shadows no children should hold.

She almost stepped back, afraid to press into a place that wasn't hers anymore. But Ruth's gaze found her. Recognition flickered— hesitant, searching—and then, Ruth turned and closed the distance. Without a word, she wrapped her small arms tight around Photine's waist, burying her face against the woman she had once lost.

Photine's hands trembled as they came down over Ruth's back. The embrace was fragile, awkward, and yet it tethered her, binding the broken threads of years into a knot of grief and grace.

"I knew it," Ruth murmured against her. "I knew you'd come back."

Photine closed her eyes and held her.

She didn't know how to tell them about the baby. About Ezra. About their home, lost again. The words were boulders she wasn't strong enough to lift.

They had barely crossed the threshold of the women's house when the questions came. Miriam's eyes darted past Lois, scanning the shadows behind her as if Caleb might stumble in, dirty and laughing, the way he had after climbing too high in the fig tree. Ruth clutched her mother's sleeve, her small face pinched with something between hope and fear.

"Where is he?" Miriam asked, voice sharp with the urgency of not knowing. "Where's Caleb?" Lois froze, her breath catching like a thread pulled too tight. She sank to her knees, gathering both girls close. "My loves," she began, her voice already breaking. Lois gathered her daughters close, her breath ragged, "…Caleb is gone."

The words fell heavy as stone. Miriam's face collapsed, her sobs tearing loose before she could stop them. Ruth blinked rapidly, her small hands fisting at her sides. "Gone?" she whispered. "Where is he? Where did he go?"

Lois pulled her in, holding both of them against her. "Not gone away. Gone from this life. He… he was struck down."

Miriam's sobs broke into jagged questions. "Struck down? By who? Why would anyone—he's just a boy!"

Lois pressed her lips to her daughter's hair, her own tears streaking her cheeks. "By your father," she whispered, steady though the words burned. "Mordecai's sword took him. He was not the man we once knew—he was Rome's shadow. And Caleb… Caleb was in his path."

Ruth let out a sound between a cry and a scream, clinging to Lois as though she could anchor him back into the world. "Papa… killed him?"

Lois held her tighter, rocking her gently. "Not out of love. Not out of the man he once was. Rome had hollowed him, filled him with rage not his own. In the chaos, Caleb came up behind him, and Mordecai turned with his sword already drawn. He didn't see—it wasn't even him anymore. It was the fury Rome forged in him. And our Caleb… he was caught in its path."

Photine knelt beside them, tears shining. "Your brother's courage was greater than his years," she said softly. "He will not be forgotten."

Miriam pulled back just enough to search Lois's face, her voice raw. "Did you see him? Was he alone?"

Lois's throat tightened. She drew in a gravelly breath. "I was with him. It was a battle all around—fire in the streets, the town falling to ash. Your father has fallen, and Rome's fury left nothing standing. We barely escaped at all, only because Ezra and Benaiah fought to give us the chance. They did not make it out, but their courage carried us here."

Miriam sobbed, while Ruth pressed both fists against her mouth, shaking her head as if she could shove the truth away.

Photine, standing near, could no longer hold herself back. The despair tore from her like a wound reopening. She sank to her knees beside them, voice breaking. "Ezra… Benaiah… and now the child. All of them—taken." Her hands clutched at her chest as though the ache inside might split her apart. "How much more must be asked of us?"

The four of them folded together, a knot of grief that no words could untangle, their weeping rising into the rafters of the women's house until it seemed the walls themselves would remember their sorrow.

Lois pulled them tighter, rocking them even as her own chest heaved. "He was brave. So brave. He tried to protect us. But…" Her voice trailed into silence, swallowed by their sobs.

For a long while, the four of them stayed there on the stone floor, grief pooling around them like water with no shore. When at last their cries broke into hiccupped breaths, two of the elder women of the house came quietly, carrying lamps. They did not speak, only knelt to gather cloaks around the girls' trembling shoulders and guide them gently down the corridor.

Photine and Lois followed, arms steadying daughters who could hardly walk for the weight of loss. In the small guest room, warm mats had been laid out, and the sisters left a loaf of bread, bowls of water, and a sprig of thyme for calming. Miriam and Ruth curled between their mother and Photine, clutching them like fragile bridges toward tomorrow.

When the girls had finally drifted into exhausted sleep, faces still streaked with tears, Lois whispered into the dark, "We have to decide what's next."

Photine looked at her through swollen eyes. "There's nothing left to go back to."

"No," Lois said. "But there might be something worth building forward."

And somewhere in the women's house, a bell rang softly for midnight prayer. The chant echoed like a lullaby for the broken, carried on mountain wind and faith deeper than ruin.

Photine didn't rise to pray. But she listened. And for the first time since the cellar, she breathed without pain.

Time passed with a healing rhythm; they had been at the women's house long enough to know the sound of the second bell meant water was being drawn for the midday meal.

Long enough that Photine could go a full hour without weeping.

The stone walls were cool during the heat of the day, and the air was thick with thyme and myrrh smoke from the morning offering. Lois was in the lower cloister garden, tending a stubborn patch of yarrow. She had begun helping with the birthing room as well, where the sisters received women from nearby villages—some too young, all too tired.

Photine, however, had found no place to rest her spirit. She chopped vegetables, sorted grain, folded linen, but each task felt borrowed, like trying to write her name with someone else's hand.

Today, she sat near the apothecary alcove, grinding dried rosehips into a fine powder while Ruth read aloud softly beside her. "'…and the herb shall be steeped at sunrise, strained by moonlight, and offered with a word of blessing to calm the womb or quiet grief…'" Ruth's voice trailed off. "Do you think herbs really listen when we bless them?"

Photine smiled faintly. "If they didn't, I don't think any of us would be here."

Ruth went quiet, the way children do when they're thinking very big thoughts.

Before she could speak again, a murmur stirred beneath the courtyard arches. A small band of travelers had arrived, dust on their sandals, skin darkened by the Negev sun, their laughter edged with the relief of finding water and shade. Merchants, messengers, perhaps even pilgrims, most bound north along the trade road that would, in time, wind all the way to Jerusalem.

The sisters greeted them with bowls of figs and skins of water, reminding them to keep their voices gentle within the house. The clatter of foreign tongues and the smell of leather packs filled the air, a sharp contrast to the quiet grief that had settled over Lois and her daughters.

For Photine, it was jarring, the collision of her shattered world with the steady pulse of life moving on. A day's walk had carried them from the smoke of Akrabbim into this refuge, yet already the road was reminding them: the world beyond their sorrow had not stopped.

One man caught Photine's eye, not for anything strange about him, but for what he carried: a small wooden flute tied to his sash, smoothed from years of use. Something stirred in her memory, unbidden. Ezra's gentle hands, playing with the rhythm of the evening sounds in a time that seemed so far away. She shook the thought away.

Later, while refilling the grain bins in the storehouse, she overheard him speaking to one of the sisters.

"No, I swear it was him. Eyes like riverstone. Spoke with a priest's cadence, but he didn't belong to any temple. Called himself Elisar, I think, or something like it. Disappeared after the raid in Capernaum, took half the scrolls with him, they say. Been hiding out in the cliffs east of the Galilee. Some say he was a ghost. Or a prophet. Or both."

Photine froze, the scoop of barley trembling in her hand.

Elisar.

It wasn't his name. Not exactly. But it was close enough to strike her like a whisper through stone.

Her father's name, Eleazar, had not been spoken aloud in years. She had buried it somewhere between her mother's silence and Zimri's anger.

Photine's hand slipped into her satchel as the man turned to leave. Her fingers closed around the familiar weight, two small shards of olive wood, worn smooth by years of keeping and carrying. She hurried after him, her voice catching.

"Wait."

He paused, more out of politeness than interest.

She held the pieces out to him, palms trembling. "Do you know these? Have you seen their like?" They belonged to," Her throat tightened. "To someone I lost."

The man glanced at them, barely. His brow furrowed, not in recognition, but irritation. "Wood is wood, woman. Broken scraps mean nothing. Best burn them for kindling." Photine's jaw tightened. She pulled the shards back as though scorched.

"You don't understand," she whispered.

He gave her the kind of look reserved for madwomen or beggars, pity mixed with dismissal. "No, I don't. Nor do I care." With that, he adjusted his cloak and moved on, already calling for water from the sisters.

Something in Photine snapped. She clutched the shards back to her chest, her eyes burning hot.

"They are not nothing," she hissed. Her voice cracked like flint against stone. "They are all I have left. A name. A vow. A life Rome could not erase."

For the first time, the man blinked at her, taken aback by the fire in her voice. He shook his head, muttered something about grief making people mad, and turned away.

Photine stood rooted, chest rising and falling, the olive shards digging into her palm until they hurt. She welcomed the pain. It was proof she was still alive. Proof that the memory still lived.

That night, when the sisters chanted psalms under the stars, Photine did not join them. She sat alone under the olive tree at the edge of the women's house wall, her fingers tracing the edge of a dried fig leaf.

She did not know what the man's story meant, nor why his dismissal stung so sharply. Yet when she tucked the olive shards back into her palm, something stirred in her chest. The grief was still there, jagged and unrelenting, but the weight of not-knowing had loosened, just enough to let a breath slip through.

And in that space, something else flickered. Not comfort. Not peace. Something more dangerous. More alive. It frightened her even as it steadied her spine. Whatever it was, it refused to die, no matter how many times the world tried to bury it.

From that day, Photine's ears sharpened. She began listening not as a guest among the sisters but as a hunter in plain sight. Every trader's boast, every pilgrim's sigh, every whispered tale of raids or ruins—she sifted it all for fragments, for anything that might lead her closer to what she could not name aloud.

The sisters noticed her quietness but did not press. To them, she was simply weary, hollowed by grief. But inside her, a different hunger grew. She took the chores that kept her near the gates, the kitchen where travelers paused for water, and the courtyard where stories unraveled at dusk. She gathered them like seeds, tucking them into memory where no one could see.

Months passed. The seasons turned. Wildflowers burned out and returned, figs ripened and fell. And Photine, though her hands kept busy with grinding grain, mending cloth, tending children, was no longer still. Her mind moved with the caravans, with the fishermen, with the shepherds who drifted down from Galilee.

Sometimes she fingered the olive shards in her sash, the wood smooth from her touch. They were proof that her past was not as simple as loss, that someone had once meant for her to remember. And though no story gave rise to certainty, the not-knowing had become unbearable.

Her grief for Ezra, for her only child, for all she had lost, did not lessen, but it sharpened into something else. Restlessness. Fire. She felt herself pressing against the walls of the women's house, like a vine that could not stop growing.

She did not say it aloud. Not yet. But she knew: she would not remain here forever.

CHAPTER 15
A NAME TO TRAVEL WITH

The travelers were gone. Their dusty footprints had been swept from the courtyard, their laughter faded like a song no one remembered how to finish.

In their absence, life at the women's house returned to its still, sacred rhythm, prayers at dawn, work at noon, rest beneath olive branches in the heat of the afternoon.

Lois had begun to smile again. Not often, but enough. She had taken to teaching the younger sisters how to pack tinctures for travel, and the older ones how to manage a laboring mother with both steadiness and gentleness. Her grief over Caleb, though carved deep, had settled into her bones like something known and carried.

The girls were thriving in the quiet. Miriam had found purpose tending the herb beds. Ruth sang again—softly, only when she thought no one was listening.

But Photine...

Photine was not made for stillness.

Not now.

She moved through the house and courtyard like a shadow tethered to breath. She worked, she ate, she prayed when she could. But every step was leading away.

She carried the unease like a stone in her chest, turning it over day after day without release. The travelers had gone, yet the fragments they left behind refused to leave her. At night, when the courtyard stilled, and the sisters' lamps burned low, she found herself wondering where her mother might have walked when she was young, what hills she had called home, and whether the olive groves still bent with the same wind. She had come farther from those beginnings than she had ever meant to, and though she did not yet name it aloud, something in her ached to turn back.

That evening, beneath the fig tree where the girls sorted lentils and Lois mended a torn sleeve, Photine sat with her hands idle in her lap. The hum of ordinary life pressed around her, but she could not join it. The weight in her chest grew heavier until silence itself felt unbearable.

The words slipped out before she could shape them, sharp and uninvited.

"I need to go."

Lois looked up, needle frozen mid-stitch. "Go where?"

"I don't know exactly. North. Toward Samaria, or Galilee. Maybe beyond."

The girls stirred beside them, but Photine's gaze stayed fixed on the horizon. The fig leaves above rattled in the wind, like a question no one wanted to ask.

Lois set her mending down. "You're not hunted anymore, Photine. But, the Romans still remember your name."

"It was Mordecai who etched it on their tongues," Photine said, her voice sharp. "And Mordecai is gone. His power drained like the blood he spilled, almost a year past. Rome has other enemies now."

"That doesn't mean you're safe."

Photine's laugh was bitter, without joy. "Safe? Lois, I've been carried from one house to another, one man's will to another, one cage after the next. My father left. My brother sold me.

Jotham…" Her voice faltered, caught between longing and anger. "Jotham gave me safety—yes. Even a kind of quiet, steady love. But he never let me in. He carried his burdens in silence, as if my hands were too weak, as if my mind were too small to bear them. I could have helped him. I would have. But he never asked. Never trusted me with who he really was. And then he got himself killed, and with him went the fragile shelter I thought I had."

Her hand shook as she pressed the olive shard tighter, her breath sharp. "Mordecai broke me. Ezra was the only one I ever truly chose—and Rome crushed him too. Now, even here, every choice is made for me. Is this safety? Or just another prison with kinder walls?"

Her hand trembled as it found the olive shard in her sash. She pressed it tight, as though the wood itself could anchor her.

"I feel more danger to my spirit if I stay than if I leave," she whispered. "This is not my life. Not the one I was meant to carry."

Lois's lips parted, but she closed them again. She saw it, the fury, the hollow grief, the woman scorned yet unbroken, ready to rise or burn.

The fig leaves rustled once more, as if in witness.

"You'll need protection," Lois had warned. "A woman traveling alone—"

"I know."

His name was Barshai. Once a wool trader, then a caravan broker, now little more than a frail shadow of a man bound by debts he no longer had the strength to pay. His skin was darkened like leather from decades under desert suns, his eyes rheumy, his fingers stiff with old injuries. When he first came to the sisters' house, he shuffled bent-backed, clutching his knees, asking only for herbs to soothe the pain. His voice rasped, his breath sour with fermented dates, his chest rattling like a half-empty gourd.

Photine saw him, and something in her hardened. Not compassion, at least not in its pure form. It was a calculation. For once in her life, she would not be bartered, abandoned, or thrust into another's plan. She would make the choice, however unsavory it seemed.

She began small. A warm cloth pressed to his joints. A steady hand guiding the cup of willow tea to his lips. She sat close, too close, when she spooned broth to his mouth. She let her fingers linger when she adjusted the pillow under his head. She spoke softly, low, letting her voice curl like smoke in the dim lamplight. "You're strong still," she told him, brushing back his wiry hair. "Stronger than they know. You just need someone who sees you."

The old man's breath quickened, more from her presence than his failing lungs. He had lived long enough to know when he was being courted, but not long enough to resist the promise of warmth pressed against his fading years.

In the days that followed, she fed him promises alongside herbs. "If you were my husband," she whispered once, leaning so close her breath stirred the hollow of his ear, "you wouldn't be alone. I would see to your comfort. And we could leave this place together. No one would laugh at your debts then. No one would dare."

He chuckled, a wheeze reeking of dates and decay, but his hand fumbled for hers anyway. The sisters shook their heads in silence, disapproval etched in every glance. But Photine pressed on, weaving care with seduction, pity with persuasion, her lips shaping the words while her soul recoiled.

Inside, she seethed. His skin was waxy, his fingers swollen and crooked, his voice a rasp that clawed at her nerves. Each touch made bile rise at the back of her throat. She loathed him. She loathed herself more. Yet beneath that loathing burned something hotter—anger and desperation rising like heat off a sun-soaked road. Anger at her father, who had vanished. At Zimri, who had sold her. At Jotham, who had never trusted her with his truth. At Mordecai, who had shattered her. At Rome, who had swallowed Ezra whole. And at the world itself, which had stolen Elior—her heart, her future, her fragile proof that love could survive the ruin.

Every man had taken something. Every choice had been stolen from her hands.

Not this time.

She tended Barshai until his color returned faintly, until he believed her touch had made him stronger, until the weight of her presence felt indispensable. Each stroke of the cloth, each murmur in his ear was a weapon disguised as care. She would not be left behind, not caged again.

On the third day, he spoke what she had already planted in him. "A man like me… should have a wife to keep him steady."

She smiled—soft, practiced, almost tender. "Then let me be that wife."

When Barshai finally dozed, mumbling her name, Photine slipped from the room. The air outside was cooler, though it did nothing to ease the fever in her chest. She nearly stumbled into Lois, who stood in the shadows near the doorway, arms folded tight across her middle.

"You think I don't see?" Lois's voice was low, rough. "The way you lean close, the way you let him believe your hands are more than they are?"

Photine's jaw tightened. "You don't understand."

"No," Lois said, eyes sharp with pain. "I understand too well. I've lost a husband. I've lost a son. I know what desperation can make a woman do. But this—" She shook her head slowly. "This isn't you."

Photine turned her face away, but her voice came hard, clipped. "Who am I, then, Lois? A widow without a husband? A mother without a child? A woman whose choices are always made by others? You want me to sit still and let Rome or hunger or grief finish me off?" Lois's silence cut deeper than words.

Photine pressed on, her tone fierce. "Barshai may be foul, but he's a door. A way out. If I have to crawl through it on my knees, I will. Better that than rotting here with memories."

Lois flinched, as though struck. Her voice was barely above a whisper. "And what will you be on the other side of that door?"

Photine's eyes glistened, but she refused to look away. "Alive," she said. "That's enough."

And so it was done. Not for love. Not even for companionship. But Photine, at last, had decided to shape her own path, even if it meant twisting another's weakness into her doorway out.

Barshai left the women's house with a new wife at his side, leaning on her arm like a man who believed he had won a final chance at life. Photine walked beside him, swaddled in vows she did not mean, her face unreadable.

No one believed it was love. Not even Barshai. Least of all Photine.

But he needed someone who could ease his pain and cook without poisoning him, and Photine needed something even more practical, a name to travel under. A man's name. A tether to freedom.

This was not her first marriage. Not even her second. But it was the first chosen completely by her, though not from love. With Ezra, she had chosen joy, partnership, the fire of being truly seen. With Barshai, she chose necessity. She chose survival. She chose a man she knew she could bend, manipulate, and bind to her bidding.

And yet when she closed her eyes, she could almost feel Ezra's gaze, steady, unwavering, the way he used to look at her when she argued too fiercely in the market or when she dreamed too loudly at night. He had never shown her disapproval, not once. Even when she had been reckless, he had only smiled and asked her to tell him more. But would he now? Would he look at her hands on this frail man's shoulders and see betrayal, or would he understand her raw, gnawing hunger of survival?

The thought burned in her chest. She could not bear the idea of Ezra's silence, not in memory, not in judgment. She told herself that necessity was not betrayal, that desperation was not faithlessness. But the shame still came, rising like heat off a sun-baked road, leaving her hollow and angry, a woman torn between the life she had lost and the ugliness of the life she forced herself into.

They had spoken no vows before a rabbi or judge. No one had exchanged coins or signed scrolls. But in the quiet sanctuary of the women's house, they had promised each other the only thing they still owned, faith. She would not be welcomed in every village. A woman with four husbands was not easily blessed. But Barshai never asked for her history, only her honesty. And with that, she was his.

Their agreement was quiet and clear. She would go where he went, manage what needed managing, and speak on his behalf when his voice failed. In return, she would have passage, protection, and the illusion of belonging to someone—at least long enough to find what she was looking for.

They departed at dawn, the morning mist soft around the base of the hills. Lois watched her from the monastery steps, Ruth clutching her skirt, Miriam holding back tears.

Photine didn't cry. She had no tears left, not yet.

She just nodded once, said "Thank you," and turned toward the road curving north like a question waiting to be answered.

Behind her, the gates of the women's house closed slowly, reverently.

Ahead, the road uncoiled without promise. She did not know what she sought, only that staying meant drowning. The weight of loss pressed on her from every side: Ezra torn from her, Elior laid to rest before he had even lived, Caleb fallen in battle not his own. Every corner of Akrabbim reeked of memory, and memory was a prison she could no longer breathe inside.

So she fled. Not toward, but away. Away from the ruin she carried in her chest, away from the ghost of Mordecai's shadow, away from the tender grave where hope itself lay buried. If something was waiting—whether legend or lie—it was less than what she had lost, and more than what remained.

Barshai sat beside her, coughing like a man trying to keep his soul from rattling loose. The sound punctuated every mile, a reminder that she was dragging another weight with her. His name sat like iron on her tongue, but she wore it anyway, because it opened gates, bought silence, and let her keep moving.

They left the northern skirts of Akrabbim at dawn, the air sharp with the last breath of night. The desert ridge gave way to stony wilderness, thornbush clinging to the earth, vultures carving lazy circles overhead. The road they took was no hidden path, it was the Roman trade route, rutted deep with cart wheels, the same road that carried salt from the Dead Sea and wine from Samaria. Every stone seemed to bear the weight of empire.

The donkey plodded faithfully, its hooves raising dust that clung to Photine's scarf. Beside her, Barshai coughed into his sleeve, bones rattling beneath sun-leathered skin. His cart creaked under dyed wool, amphorae of oil, and jars of over-brined olives. Trade was their mask; the road, their fragile protection.

They moved slowly—eight, maybe ten miles each day. By the third night, they reached the cisterns near Jericho, where reeds rattled in the wind, and jackals cried in the distance. From there, the road bent north along the Jordan Valley, climbing in places where the hills pressed in.

A week later, they passed the ruins near Archelais, Herod's abandoned palace half-swallowed by weeds. Barshai insisted they stop, his joints swollen, his breath ragged. Photine tended him with silence, offering no more kindness than duty required.

Another four days carried them into the lower slopes that led toward Samaria's hill country—fertile pockets where figs and olives grew stubborn out of stone, where villages huddled against ridges with smoke curling from their hearths. Here, the road forked. One way bent west toward Shechem, the other east toward Scythopolis.

Barshai's house sat on the edge of the village, stone stacked unevenly, plaster peeling where rain had carved grooves down the walls. The courtyard was overgrown with weeds, and a clay oven cracked from years of disuse. Inside, it smelled of damp wool, stale wine, and dust thick enough to write names in.

Photine set down her bundle and stood in the dim light, the air close and heavy. This was not a home so much as a relic, a place that had forgotten laughter, meals, children's voices. She pulled back her veil and set to work without asking. She swept the floor with a reed broom worn to nubs, righted jars toppled by rodents, and gathered what lentils and onions she could find to set bubbling in a cracked clay pot. By the time Barshai had sunk onto his mat with a groan, the house smelled of something other than rot.

The next day, a knock rattled the half-hinged door. A neighbor, broad-shouldered, with sun-browned skin and eyes always watching, stepped inside. Barshai brightened, pride flickering through his rheumy eyes at the chance to talk of more than aches.

"News from the road," the man said, lowering himself onto the stool Photine had scrubbed clean that morning. "Zealots again, stirring the cliffs east of the Galilee. Some whisper the Pharisees already have eyes on them. Rome does too. Trouble comes quick when swords meet scrolls."

Barshai coughed, waving a dismissive hand. "Idiots with swords and scrolls, that's how you end up nailed to wood."

The man shrugged, lowering his voice. "Not only zealots. There's talk of a Jew… a healer, some say. In Magdala, he's said to have driven seven demons out of a woman. Seven." He shook his head as if the number itself were hard to believe. "She follows him now, they whisper. A few others, too. Nothing large, not yet. But strange things—strange enough that Rome's eyes will turn if the whispers grow."

Photine, quiet in the corner, kneaded flatbread, keeping her head bent. But her ears caught every word. Her fingers stilled at the mention of the woman. Seven demons. A life torn apart and pieced back together. She knew something of that. She pressed the dough harder, trying to look small, invisible.

But the neighbor's gaze slid toward her anyway. "And this?" he asked, his tone edged with curiosity and scorn. "Your wife?"

Barshai puffed up, his chest rising, though his ribs wheezed with the effort. "Aye," he said, voice sharp with pride. "My wife. Young, strong, a blessing in my old age."

The neighbor barked a laugh, one hand on his knee. "A blessing, or a curse. She must be a shamed woman, to bind herself to a man with one foot already in the grave." He laughed again, as if it were a joke shared between men.

Photine looked up then, stepping forward from the shadows, meeting his eyes just long enough.

She almost laughed, a sharp, bitter sound caught in her throat. Shamed? Perhaps. Broken?

Certainly. But judged by yet another man? That, she no longer cared to carry.

Instead, she let her mouth curve, half amused, half dismissive, and dusted her hands of flour. Then she said lightly, "Some men are born old, neighbor. Some die that way, too—whether their breath has left them or not."

Barshai's smile faltered, pride pricked as if she had tugged at the last thread of his dignity. The neighbor chuckled, unsure if she was mocking Barshai or him, and the sound carried into the street, where other ears might twist it further.

Rumors had a way of growing in villages like this, Photine knew. But she did not look away. Let them talk.

That night, Barshai collapsed by the fire, grumbling about his hip and muttering that he should have stayed in Edom and married a woman with money instead of eyes like a jackal. Photine tended to him anyway—ground feverfew into paste, wrapped his joints with cloth soaked in elder vinegar.

She held the bowl steady as he coughed, the sound wet and rattling. His skin sagged like parchment over bone, and the sour smell of sickness clung to him no matter how often she washed the linens.

If he died here, tonight, the house would be quieter. No more groans in the dark. No more endless requests for water, for broth, for a back rubbed until her fingers ached. She might sleep through the night without being summoned, might walk in the morning without guilt gnawing at her heels.

But quiet was not the same as safety. A woman alone drew notice. Neighbors would come with their questions, their suspicions. Had she done enough? Had she tended him as a dutiful wife should? If they decided she had not, the blame would cling, and with it the risk of being cast out or handed over to another man with fewer obligations and less patience.

Even if no accusation came, what then? The roof would still need mending, the fields still turning. Without his presence, even frail as it was, her claim to this place might crumble. His sons, or his kin, if he had any, could arrive to divide the household, and she would be nothing more than a mouth to feed.

The thought dragged her back, unbidden, to the night Jotham died. She had been an innocent girl, married and widowed too young, when Mordecai stepped through the door, eyes already weighing her as if she were part of the inheritance. No time for grief, no choice in the matter. His claim on her had been swift, merciless, and final.

The memory burned. She had gone like a lamb then, stunned and pliant, telling herself it was survival. But she would not do it again. Not for another man's convenience, not for the comfort of kin who saw her only as labor and flesh.

If this one died, she would not stand waiting for the next hand to close around her. She would find another way—any way—from being seized like a prize.

She wrung the cloth hard enough for water to drip onto the mat, her jaw set. Better to keep him alive a little longer. His weakness shielded her, in its own way.

"You'll outlive me," he rasped, thin humor trembling in his throat.

"I'm not waiting for you to die," she said, steady, though her mind still echoed with Mordecai's shadow. "Just for the road to split."

He laughed until the cough took him, while she pressed the cloth firmly and kept her gaze on the bowl, vowing silently that she would never again be taken as spoil.

Her fingers tightened on the cloth, then eased. Each road carried its price. Better to keep him breathing for now, however heavy the care.

He regained strength slowly—first lifting the cup on his own, then walking a few paces to the doorway with her arm at his side. The rasp in his lungs never left, but his eyes cleared, and with them returned the habits of daily life: she rose before dawn to bake, carried jars to market, drew water at the well.

Life steadied, at least on the surface. His needs no longer bound her to the mat beside him, and the daily tasks fell back to her shoulders alone. Yet with her return to the market and the well came the eyes of others—curious, measuring, waiting for the story of her life to spill.

The market was thick with voices, the smell of figs and onions pressed into the air. Photine stacked the last of the bread loaves, brushing flour from her hands when two women paused by her stall. They weren't buying, just watching her the way sparrows eye a crust they don't intend to touch.

One leaned closer, her mouth pinched. "Strange, isn't it? A woman so young tied to a man half-buried already. What disgrace must she bring with her to settle for that?"

The other gave a quick laugh. "Perhaps she likes to see them weak. Easier than having them strong."

Heat rose in Photine's throat. She could have turned away, swallowed it. Instead, she let the words burn their way out.

"Better a sick old man than one who beats the breath from your chest," she said sharply. "Or a brother-in-law who claims you before the dirt is even settled. At least this one doesn't raise a hand or demand my youth for his gain."

Their brows lifted, and she knew at once she had said too much. One of them tilted her head, voice soft as honey but eyes sharp. "You've carried more sorrow than most, haven't you? So many losses for one so young."

The other clucked her tongue in sympathy, leaning closer. "It must be hard, starting over again and again. And now with…well, one already so frail. You must wonder how long this roof will last above you."

Photine felt the heat rise in her chest again. They wanted her grief parceled out like figs in a basket, for their amusement as much as their pity. She snapped before she could stop herself. "If men die, it is not because I wish it. I've buried enough tears to salt the ground."

Their faces softened further, almost sweet, but the gleam in their eyes told her she had given them exactly what they came for. One murmured, "So many losses… surely the burden is heavy."

Photine's throat tightened. She could have walked away, but the pity in their voices scraped like grit under her skin. "Yes, I've buried men," she snapped. "One lowered into the earth before I'd even dried my wedding veil, another claimed me before grief had cooled, and still another who lasted hardly longer than a season. Does that satisfy you?"

The women gasped, then exchanged a glance of quiet triumph. One leaned closer, whispering just loud enough for the stall beside them to catch: "Look at her—every man she touches ends up in the grave, and now she clings to one already halfway there."

Photine felt the heat climb into her cheeks. "Better that than a drunk who beats the life from his wife," she muttered, too sharp, too bitter.

But her anger only fed their delight. The second woman turned, voice pitched for the olive seller to hear. "Three husbands in the ground, and now tending a fourth. Poor old man."

The words spread as swiftly as dust in the wind, and by the time she reached the well, the story was no longer hers but the town's.

By evening, the story had multiplied. At the well, women muttered of poison in her bread, of curses carried in her womb. When she lifted her jar onto her shoulder, the laughter behind her was thick and sharp as thorns.

And at home, she found the old man sitting pale in the doorway, a neighbor's words still stinging his ears: *Be careful, friend. She'll be rid of you soon enough. Look what became of the others.*

It was there that the doubt began. A woman whose husbands died too young. A woman whose presence soured a house.

Barshai wondered how much of it was smoke, how much fire. He had taken her in with the thought of simple company, someone to steady his last years. But the market muttered, and the well carried stories faster than the stream. Already friends hesitated at his door, neighbors lingered with sidelong looks. He had not asked for such noise.

He told himself she was not to blame, that gossip had always fattened on women without kin, on widows who would not stay silent. And yet, when she snapped too quickly or let anger sharpen her words, the stories seemed to take shape around her. Around him.

He rubbed his hands together, dry as parchment. The food she set before him tasted the same, and yet he caught himself pausing before the first bite.

The lamp guttered low, throwing soft light against the walls. Barshai sat hunched on the mat, his hands folded as if in prayer, though no words left his lips. Photine set the bowl aside and waited, sensing the heaviness in his silence.

At last, he spoke. "They talk. You know it. At the market, at the well. I thought I could ignore it, but the words follow me home. They make me…look at the bread in my hand before I taste it.

Not because I believe them, child, but because I crave peace. And this noise is no peace."

Photine lowered her gaze. The air seemed to press around her chest. "I never asked for the stories," she said, her voice thin. "But I have buried too much. That part they know, and they twist it to their liking. I cannot cut the tongues from all of them."

Barshai's eyes flickered to hers. "Three husbands, they say. All gone. Is it true?"

Her lips parted, then closed. She could not drag the whole weight into this room—could not summon Mordecai's shadow, nor speak the name of Ezra or Elior without splintering. "I have known loss," she said at last. "More than I can carry into words. That is enough truth for them to wound me."

He exhaled slowly, the sound more sigh than a breath. "I wanted company, not scandal. Quiet, not whispers at the gate. I am too old for battles, too near the end for talk of curses and poison."

Her throat ached. She wanted to tell him she was no curse, no dark hand. She wanted to pour out the years of survival and shame, but the words caught like thorns. Instead, she reached for the blanket at his shoulders, smoothing it with careful hands. "I never wished to bring trouble to your house. But wherever I go, trouble follows. Perhaps the fault is mine, perhaps not. Still—it clings."

He studied her face, weary and kind. "Then maybe it is time you begin again. Somewhere their tongues cannot reach. A new start before their stories choke us both."

Photine nodded, blinking hard against the sting in her eyes. "Yes. A new start. And until then, I will hold my tongue at the market, at the well. Let them whisper. I will not give them fire for their smoke."

Barshai settled back, closing his eyes. His voice drifted softer than the lamp's flame. "That is all I ask. A little quiet at the end."

She sat beside him, silent, her own heart restless with what she could not confess, and with the thought of roads not yet walked.

Barshai sat propped against the doorframe, the late light falling across his face. His strength had steadied, though his hands still shook when he reached for the cup. He held it a long while before speaking.

"There is a man I know," he said at last. "Donel. His wife was kin to me—her mother, a cousin on my mother's side. She's gone now, left him with five children, some grown enough, some still clinging to his robe. He has no hands to keep the house, no voice in it either. The children run wild. He needs…someone. And you need a place where tongues do not cut so deep."

Photine lowered her gaze. The market's echoes still stung, the laughter, the whispers, the cruel pity. She had answered too sharply, let her anger spill, and in doing so had fed them. Her silence now was the only weapon left to her.

Barshai's breath rattled as he went on. "Donel is not young. Not handsome. Not strong. But he is steady. And a steady man is a gift, though it does not glitter. He will treat you with respect, I think. More than I can give you in these last days of mine."

She swallowed hard, the grief pressing sharply at her throat. His kindness only deepened the ache of shame. How easily she had ruined herself with words, letting pain grow into rumor.

And worse, how easily she had learned to use words in other ways, bending them to win a scrap of bread or a night without a beating. At the women's house, she had smiled when she felt like weeping, feigned obedience when rage burned in her chest, and turned her gaze soft to disarm the men who came asking questions. She had manipulated them because it was the only weapon left to her, and part of her had grown skilled at it.

The memory sickened her now. Even when she spoke in anger at the market, it was the same weapon—her tongue. And always, it left her marked.

Barshai's trust felt undeserved. His blessing, unbearable. She could not tell him that her silence was not born of innocence but of exhaustion, that her shame was as much for the games she had played as for the stories they now told about her.

Barshai reached for her hand, his skin dry and paper-thin. "You are not cursed, child, though they say it. But you cannot root yourself where the ground has turned against you. Donel's house will be better soil."

Photine nodded, though her lips stayed closed. She could not tell him how heavy the silence in her heart had grown, how each memory pressed like stones inside her. She could not confess that she had given the gossip its seed with her own reckless tongue.

She bowed her head instead, letting Barshai believe she accepted. Shame burned in her chest, not only for the stories told of her, but for the way she had armed them herself.

Days later, Barshai leaned on his staff as they waited by the olive press, the afternoon light catching dust in the air. Photine stood beside him, head lowered, her basket resting heavy against her hip.

"There he is," Barshai murmured. "Donel."

The man approaching was broad-shouldered though streaked with gray, his step steady but slowed by care. Behind him trailed two of his children, arms full of kindling. His face was lined, not only with age but with the weight of too many tasks borne alone.

"Barshai," Donel greeted, clasping the older man's arm. His voice carried the evenness of one who had seen both joy and sorrow, and neither surprised him anymore. His eyes flicked toward Photine. "This is the woman you spoke of?"

Barshai nodded. "She has kept my house when I could not rise. She works hard, rises early, and holds her tongue when wisdom demands it." His glance at Photine held a quiet plea.

Donel studied her. "I heard only this much—that you have known loss. That is no crime. My house has known it too." He paused, shifting the weight of his words. "I do not ask for laughter or song. Only steadiness. My children need it. I need it."

Photine's throat tightened. She wanted to speak, to explain, to swear that she was not what the whispers made her. But the shame of her own sharp tongue silenced her. She dipped her head instead, eyes fixed on the dust at her feet.

Barshai's voice softened. "Donel is a better fit than I ever could be. He still has fields, a trade, a household. I have only had these last months, perhaps days. She will serve you well if given a fair chance." And as if in declaration to law and God, he proclaimed, "I release her into your care, and she accepts your roof and your name."

Donel inclined his head. "Then let it be so. Come, woman. My house is weary of silence."

Photine lifted her basket, following him without a word. Behind her, Barshai watched, his lips moving in a blessing too faint to hear.

Inside her chest, grief and shame tangled like thorns. A new start, but one already seeded with the doubts she could never uproot.

CHAPTER 16
A LAND REMEMBERED

His name was Donel. He had five children—four boys and one girl—most under the age of ten.

His home was in the outer hills near Sychar. Isolated, practical, unadorned.

There was no ceremony. No monetary exchange.

No priest, no scroll, only undeserved blessing and arrangement from Barshai, the husband who lived.

No priest to bless, no scroll to bind.

Only the frail voice of Barshai, the husband who lingered still, speaking an undeserved blessing and arranging what life remained for her.

The road wound slowly through the valleys, climbing toward the Samaritan hills. With the two children at their side, the pace was steady but unhurried, each mile stretched by rest and chatter. By the time the shadows lengthened, the ridges of Sychar rose before them. They reached the outer hills at dusk. Nine years had passed since Photine last set her feet on this soil, her homeland. Yet the years lay across her like lifetimes, each marked by loss, by wandering, by the endless work of survival. The hills rose familiar, but she no longer felt the girl who had once walked them.

The hills sloped gently here, softened by seasons of harvest and the trudge of tired feet. Scrubby olive trees clung to stone terraces like old regrets. Wild thyme grew in tufts along the roadside, scenting the air with faint memory. A few goats wandered loose, meandering with the casual authority of those who knew they belonged.

Donel said little on the road. He pointed instead—the fields needing sowing, the stream where goats were watered, the footpath leading to market. "You'll need to go soon," he told her. "Keep your head down. Don't speak too much." She nodded.

The boys, though, had no such restraint. Rambunctious, they darted ahead and circled back, their questions spilling into the air before she could shape an answer. *Why do the stones shine like that? Can we climb that wall? Will you bake bread as our mother did?* Their voices rose and tumbled over each other, leaving her to smile faintly at their restless energy, though inside she carried only the heavy silence of return.

She remembered Sychar differently—bustling, loud, bodies packed shoulder to shoulder around Jacob's well. But now the village felt hushed, withdrawn. Suspicious. The weight of Roman presence still clung to the air like soot, even without soldiers in sight. People here had grown wary. And it was not safety that silenced them, but survival.

Only a few here would remember her face.

But she remembered theirs.

Her mind flickered. Though it seemed a lifetime, and yet only moments, over a year had passed since she and Lois fled Akrabbim beneath a sky of ash and smoke. Since they buried Elior beneath a ruined cairn. Since Caleb fell to the sword. Since they hid within stone women's house walls, where whispered prayers offered brief refuge but no real rest.

And two years since she had known what it meant to have a home. A husband. A child growing within her.

Once, life had been full.

Easy. Or she thought it to be.

She had been happy—she knew happiness for a while.

And now she was here again, in the land of her youth, but not as herself. Not free. Bound again, this time not by marriage in name, but by necessity.

A servant-wife. A set of hands. A silence that could cook and sweep.

Donel's house stood a quarter-mile beyond the edge of the village, past a crumbling aqueduct and the brittle remains of a vineyard long claimed by drought. The structure itself was a squat square of sun-bleached stone, patched with clay where time had worn away its shape. Smoke curled lazily from a crooked chimney. Children's tunics fluttered from a frayed rope between two leaning posts. The place was not destitute. But neither was it whole.

Inside, the walls were bare. A shelf lined with chipped bowls. A woven mat with unraveling corners. A cracked jug sat half-full of wine gone sour, and in the shadowed corner a pair of clay dolls lay slumped together.

Photine paused at the threshold, the scent of firewood and stale bread brushing her face like breath from an old ghost. The air was thick with a life already worn into the walls, one she was expected to step into without invitation.

Inside, the children had watched her all evening—wide-eyed from shadowed corners, peering out from beneath furniture. The girl, maybe ten or eleven, offered her a dried date, then scurried off before Photine could thank her.

That night, there was no separate bed.

Photine lay beside Donel on a straw-stuffed mat pushed against the far wall. The house was a single long room divided more by use than by partitions. At its center glowed a clay hearth sunk into the packed earth floor, where smoke curled upward to escape through a small hole in the roof. Around it, low stones marked places for cooking pots and baskets of lentils, onions, and olives.

The ceiling beams were hung with drying herbs, strips of goat meat, and clay jars sealed with wax. Along one wall, rush mats were rolled for the children, tucked beside baskets of wool and tools for weaving. The opposite wall held the family's few valuables: a hand mill for grinding, worn bowls, and a narrow chest where garments were folded.

The air was warm with the mingled scents of smoke, oil, and animals, two goats penned in a corner behind a rough partition, bleating softly as they settled. It was no palace, but it was the beating heart of a household, crowded with life.

Near the only window, the children unrolled their sleeping mats and slept in a cluster—tangled limbs beneath patched linens. The youngest, no more than three, sucked his thumb and clung to a doll with one ear missing. The girl slept with her arm flung protectively across him like a gate. The eldest boy, taller than the rest, lay near the door with one eye half-open, as if always on guard. Between them, a pair of curly-haired boys twitched and kicked in sleep, caught between the edge of dreams and hunger. She had come to know their quick tongues on the journey—their questions spilling faster than answers, their laughter rolling like loose stones down a hill. Now, in the hush of night, their restlessness seemed only a softer echo of that same untamed energy.

Their names would come later. For now, they were shadows in the firelight, strangers she was expected to soothe, scold, serve.

Photine stared at the ceiling, watching the firelight twist into restless shadows. Something scurried in the corner. A mouse. Or just the wind.

There were no doors in this house but for the one at the front to shut out the night and the weather.

No place to be alone.

The room quieted one breath at a time, the children shifting on their mats, the goats sighing outside, the hearth collapsing into ash. Beside her, Donel's breathing already slowed, heavy with the day's labor. She had gathered enough to know his life was simple, unrelenting: wheat in season, limestone hauled from the northern quarry when the fields stood bare. Work that carved the body, work that left no room for softness. His words were as spare as his gestures, who needed washing, which child had strayed too far, what root to boil for cough.

And now, lying still on a mat that was not hers, in a house not hers, her mind spun restless. What was freedom but a mirage? Always just beyond reach, shimmering like water in the desert. One form of bondage traded for another, only quieter this time, shaped like usefulness instead of shame.

Dawn slipped into the room in a pale ribbon of light, brushing across smoke-stained beams. Photine woke to the sound of small feet scuffing against the floor and the faint whimper of the youngest stirring. The space beside her was empty—Donel was already out among the goats or in the fields, leaving the house to her and the children.

She sat up slowly, smoothing her tunic, watching the little ones watch her. Their eyes darted away when she looked back, as though caught in some secret. She forced a small smile. "Shall we start the fire?" she asked softly.

The twins were the first to respond, darting toward the hearth like sparrows let loose. They quarreled over the sticks to use, their voices tumbling over one another in questions they did not wait for her to answer. *Can we have dates? Will you bake bread? Do you know how to make the porridge sweet?* Their energy carried a strange warmth, and for a fleeting moment, she felt her chest ease.

But the older boy lingered at the doorway, arms folded tight, his eyes narrowing as though to measure her worth. The girl—tall for her years, her hair bound too severely for such a young face—busied herself with a water jar, her back turned in deliberate silence. Photine's heart pinched. They had known a mother's hand, and she was not it.

In the corner, the youngest child sat with his thumb pressed to his mouth, rocking slightly, gaze unfixed. He looked older than a babe but younger than a boy, and yet something in his expression told her he had been left too long without a mother's touch. He did not join the scramble of his brothers; he simply rocked and hummed under his breath.

Photine crouched beside the hearth, coaxing the embers back to life with a twist of dried grass. "Come, bring me the flour," she said, steady but kind. The twins leapt to obey, spilling half of it in their eagerness. The older boy snorted but did not move. The girl tightened her grip on the jar.

Photine swallowed her sigh. This was not her home, not her brood, and yet the shape of expectation already pressed itself against her. She had promised herself silence, but the ache of being measured and found wanting pressed heavily in her chest.

The fire crackled to life, and the smell of warming grain filled the room. Photine stirred slowly, careful not to let the pot scorch, while the twins hovered close.

"Will it be sweet?" one asked, tugging at her sleeve.

"If you want it sweet, bring me a date to chop into the pot," she answered, her voice even.

The boys scrambled to the basket, arguing over who had the better piece, pressing both into her hands before she could speak again. She smiled faintly, slicing them small, though her eyes drifted to the older two.

"You should sit. It will be ready soon," she offered.

The girl's chin lifted, her jaw tight. "We are not hungry yet." She turned back to the water jar, though her eyes flickered toward the pot.

The older boy gave a short, sharp laugh. "We eat when Father says. Not when you do."

Photine held his gaze for a breath, then lowered her eyes to the spoon. "As you wish."

A soft humming reached her from the corner. The littlest boy still rocked, his thumb pressed deep against his lips. She bent, ladling a spoonful of porridge into a small bowl, cooling it with a breath before setting it gently in his lap.

"For you," she whispered.

He blinked at her, eyes round, then dipped his fingers into the bowl, smearing the grain across his lips. His hum quietened.

The twins clapped as though it were a trick. "He eats! He eats for you!"

The girl shot them a sharp look. "Be quiet. Father will be home soon."

Photine stirred the pot again, keeping her face calm though her chest twisted. She had stepped into a house heavy with memory, and every kindness seemed both welcome and suspect. Still, she said softly, "Then let us be ready for him."

Photine set the ladle aside and crouched low to the twins' level as they circled the hearth. "You're quick as hares," she said, her smile small but genuine. "Do you always rise with the sun?"

"Yes!" one shouted before the other elbowed him. "No, not always. Sometimes Father pulls us up by the ears." Both burst into laughter, falling against each other.

Photine let their noise wash over her. "And which of you runs faster?"

"Me!" they cried together. The boys glared at each other, ready to argue, until Photine raised a hand. "Then show me. After breakfast. We'll find a clear stretch outside, and I will judge for myself."

Their eyes widened. "You'll watch?"

"I will watch," she said. "But only if you eat all you are given."

One snatched the bowl eagerly. The other sniffed it first, as though testing her promise, then dug in. Their chatter spilled again, questions tumbling over one another: *Will you bake bread? Will you come to the market? Do you know stories?*

Photine answered carefully, her voice warm but measured. "Bread, yes. Market, if your father wills it. Stories…perhaps."

The older boy at the doorway snorted. "You'll tell no stories like our mother. She sang them, and you are not her."

The words landed sharply, but Photine only bowed her head. "No," she said quietly. "I am not her. And I will never take her place. But perhaps…I might still tell a story when the time is right."

Her voice faltered, weighted with something the children could not name but felt in their bones. She knew loss—had worn it like a garment—and in their defiance, she recognized her own reflection.

The girl's eyes flicked toward her then, caught between suspicion and longing, the faintest softening before she turned back to the water jar. The littlest rocked in silence, but when Photine set her hand gently on his shoulder, he did not flinch.

The twins leaned close to the hearth; their questions as restless as their feet. In them, she saw the hunger to be known, to be steadied, though they hid it in noise and play.

For the first time since crossing Donel's threshold, she felt a fragile thread of possibility, woven from shared grief as much as hope.

The porridge was ready when the doorway darkened. Donel stepped inside, the scent of earth and animals clinging to him—goat's milk, damp straw, the sharp dust of turned soil. He paused, taking in the sight of the children clustered around the hearth and Photine crouched with the ladle in her hand.

Something flickered across his face—perhaps memory. Two years had passed since another woman had stood in that same place, her hands sure at the pot, her voice weaving songs between the crackle of the fire and the chatter of the children. The hearth still bore her absence like an unhealed scar.

He drew a breath, steadying himself. The house needed order, not ghosts. Still, the shadow of her lingered as he set his gaze on Photine, weighing the shape of what she might become in this house that was still, in part, hers.

The twins darted toward him at once, voices tumbling over each other: *"She made breakfast!"*

Donel raised a hand, and the boys stilled as though the air itself had hushed them. His gaze moved from the pot to Photine, unreadable, before turning back to the children. "You will listen when she speaks," he said firmly. "She will care for this house, and you will honor her in it. Do you understand?"

The older boy gave a grudging nod. The girl's lips pressed into a line. The littlest still rocked where he sat, thumb still in his mouth.

Donel gestured toward each of them in turn. "This is Tomer," he said of the boy by the doorway. "Nessa," with a nod to the girl at the jar. "The twins—Jonah and Markus." The boys grinned, elbowing each other. He bent briefly to touch the youngest's head. "And Levi."

The names fell like markers in Photine's mind, the beginning of a map she would have to learn.

Donel straightened. "Nessa, you will take her to the stream after the meal. Show her where to draw water and where to keep away. There are paths she must know."

Nessa hesitated, her eyes flicking between her father and the stranger at the hearth. At last, she bowed her head. "Yes, Father."

Donel moved to the chest by the wall, setting down his tools with the weight of one who had no time for ceremony. "The house will run as it has," he said. "But now there are two hands where there was one. Let them not war with each other."

Photine bent over the pot, her face hidden by the rising steam. The children's names echoed in her mind. She had been spoken into their lives as a necessity, nothing more. Yet even necessity could take root.

Breakfast was a quiet, awkward affair. The twins slurped their porridge with little regard for silence until Donel cleared his throat, and even they settled. Tomer ate in deliberate, measured bites, eyes cast down, while Nessa fed Levi small spoonfuls from her own bowl, her arm wrapped firmly around him as if shielding him from all else. Photine said little, her hands steady on the pot, but her throat tightened with every glance in her direction. She felt like a shadow seated among them, tolerated but not yet belonging.

When the bowls were scraped clean, Donel rose, his joints stiff from years of work. "Tomer, with me," he said. The boy pushed to his feet at once, proud to be chosen, and followed his father out into the morning light, where the fields waited.

The twins lingered long enough to glance at Photine, mischief already twitching in their shoulders. With a wink at each other, they darted off into the yard, their voices carrying in bursts of laughter.

Nessa stood slowly, balancing Levi on her hip. His thumb pressed deep into his mouth, his head against her shoulder. She looked at Photine without smiling. "Father says you need to know the stream."

Photine nodded. "Show me, then."

They walked in silence, Nessa steady with Levi's weight, Photine carrying the jar. The air was cool under the trees, the murmur of water growing stronger as they neared. When they reached the bank, Nessa knelt to dip a finger into the stream for Levi to splash, while Photine bent to fill the jar.

She caught herself staring at the boy—the softness of his curls, the way he leaned into his sister's chest with a trust so complete it ached to see. Her arms remembered another weight, smaller but just as clinging. Caleb had been that age when she fled Akrabbim—wild, tender, and far too young to understand why she vanished. His voice still haunted her in dreams, calling after her as she slipped into the dark.

And Elior—she could only imagine at this age. The curve of his cheek, the way his hand might have wrapped around her tunic, the small laugh she would never hear. The ache for him was different, sharper—memory gave her no anchor. Only absence.

She pressed her lips together until the sting in her eyes eased. Levi stirred against Nessa's chest, and she looked away, steadying her breath, willing herself not to crumble.

Nessa noticed her stare and drew Levi closer, as though protecting him. "He's slow," the girl said flatly. "But he's ours."

Photine swallowed. "All the more reason he is precious." Her voice wavered, though she forced it steady. She turned back to the jar, watching the ripples smooth.

Nessa's arms tightened around Levi, her expression unreadable. Photine straightened, adjusting the jar to her hip.

Levi shifted in her arms, and Nessa rocked him absently. "You won't have to fuss over him," she said at last, her tone cool but not unkind. "Between Tomer and me, we've managed well enough. We keep the house, we keep the little ones. We've done it since Mother died."

Photine let the words settle, heavy as stones.

Nessa's jaw tightened, and she adjusted Levi higher on her hip. "I don't know why Father thought we needed you. We aren't helpless." Her gaze flicked to Photine, sharp with something that was equal parts pride and fear. "He should have asked us first."

Photine could not argue—the girl's strength was plain, her wariness justified. She only said softly, "You have carried more than most women twice your age. That shows."

Nessa's eyes softened for a moment, then she turned away, splashing her hand in the water for Levi to grab at. The silence that followed was not warm, but neither was it closed.

Photine lifted the jar from the stream, her arms straining at its weight. A sudden rustle from the reeds cracked the stillness. The twins burst out with a wild shout, arms flailing, their laughter shrill as they leapt into the clearing.

Startled, Photine turned too sharply. The jar tipped, and a rush of cold water splashed across Nessa's skirt, soaking the fabric and dripping down to Levi's dangling feet.

Nessa gasped, her face flushing hot. "Careful!" she snapped at Photine, clutching Levi tighter as he whimpered at the sudden chill. "Have you no sense?"

Photine opened her mouth, then closed it again, the shame sharp as a slap.

The twins doubled over with laughter, pointing, pleased with their trick.

"Enough!" Nessa turned on them, her voice cracking with authority far beyond her years. "Do you think this is a game? He's a baby, not your plaything!"

The boys' laughter faltered, fading into sheepish grins, but the damage was done. The air was thick with irritation—Nessa's anger, Photine's humiliation, the twins' restless mischief. Levi whimpered again, and Nessa hushed him fiercely, casting Photine a glance that said she was more burden than help.

They made their way back in silence, the jar heavier on Photine's hip for all she held it steady this time. Water still clung darkly to Nessa's skirt, dripping against her legs with each step. Levi whimpered off and on, his thumb pressed to his mouth, and Nessa rocked him with a rhythm that felt more like defiance than comfort.

The twins trailed ahead, darting in and out of the path, whispering to each other but glancing back often, their laughter curbed by their sister's sharp rebuke.

Photine kept her eyes on the ground, the ache in her chest heavier than the jar. She had meant no harm, yet she had felt the weight of judgment—another failure, another reason to be whispered about.

By the time they reached the low doorway of the house, Nessa's arms were stiff with carrying, her voice clipped as she barked at the twins to fetch kindling. She did not look at Photine as she crossed the threshold.

Photine lingered a moment outside, adjusting the jar against her hip. The voices of the children rose inside, restless and tangled. For an instant, she wished she could turn and keep walking, past the yard, past the fields, past all the eyes measuring her. But the jar was full, and the house was waiting.

So she stepped inside.

Nessa peeled off her damp skirt, muttering about the stream. She balanced Levi on one hip, his head pressed against her shoulder, and shoved a satchel into Photine's hands with the other.

"For market," she said curtly, her voice flat with authority.

Photine blinked, fingers tightening on the strap. "With who?"

"The twins. They know the way." Nessa bent to tie one of their tunics, the motion so practiced it looked like second nature. "Dates and honey. Don't speak to Asa."

"Who's Asa?"

"Doesn't matter. Just don't."

Nessa turned her back, busy with Levi and the fire as though the matter were finished.

Photine stood, the satchel heavy against her side. She had no idea where the coins were kept, whether Donel would return before evening, or whether she was even trusted to barter for the family. Nessa's commands echoed more like orders given to a servant than instructions for a new wife in the house. The sting of it lodged deep, but she swallowed it down.

She caught her reflection in a shallow basin of water—a hollow-eyed woman with tangled hair, smoke still clinging to her clothes, silence pressed into her bones. A wife again. A mother of sorts. A stranger with no map, surrounded by names she hadn't chosen and silences she didn't deserve.

Photine dipped her hands into the basin, splashing cool water over her face. She smoothed the stray curled strands of hair, twisting them back beneath her scarf. She rubbed at the smudge of ash on her cheek, straightened the belt at her waist, and shook the wrinkles from her tunic until it hung more evenly. None of it made her beautiful, but at least it made her orderly—fit to stand in the press of a market without drawing stares for slovenliness.

Her fingers lingered on the rim of the basin. Her stomach knotted. To walk again into Sychar after so many years, to face the weight of a town's eyes—would they see only a stranger, or would the stories have already run ahead of her?

Behind her, the twins' laughter rang out, impatient, urging her forward. Photine drew one more breath, squared her shoulders, and lifted the satchel. If she trembled, it would be on the inside.

But she would carry the satchel.

She would follow the twins.

She would learn the faces.

And she would walk into Sychar—head down, but eyes open.

The road into Sychar wound between olive groves and vineyards, the dust rising around their ankles. The twins ran ahead, darting back now and again to ensure she followed. Photine kept the satchel pressed against her side, her pace steady though her stomach twisted.

By the time they reached the outer stalls, the hum of the market wrapped around them—voices haggling over olives, the bray of a tethered donkey, the smell of figs ripening too quickly in the sun.

It did not take long for eyes to follow them. People knew Donel's boys—everyone did—and now here they were, flanking a woman no one recognized. Whispers rose like gnats in the heat.

"Who is she?"

"Another cousin?"

"No, not kin—look at her hands, not a farmer's wife."

"Donel's woman, then?"

Photine kept her gaze on the baskets of dates, nodding politely to the seller as the boys argued over which figs looked sweetest. The murmurs grew, soft but sharp, trailing her every step.

Near the honey stall, a woman leaned toward another, her voice carrying just enough: "Donel's been two years without his wife. Perhaps he's found himself a new one. Poor children."

The twins froze, their heads whipping around. "She's not 'perhaps,'" Markus blurted, puffing his chest. "She's our new mother!"

Jonah echoed him at once, louder still: "Yes—our mother! Father said!"

Photine's breath caught. A hush rippled through the nearby stalls. The honey-seller raised his brows but said nothing. A fig-merchant smirked into her sleeve.

Photine bent quickly, smoothing Jonah's curls, her hand steady though her heart raced. "That's enough," she whispered, forcing a smile. "Help me choose, and then we'll be on our way." The twins grinned, proud of themselves, oblivious to the storm they had stirred.

The whispers did not fade. They followed, sharper now, naming her without knowing her, grafting rumor onto her silence. By the time she lifted the satchel again, Photine knew her face was already being sewn into Sychar's fabric—threaded with suspicion, stitched with pity.

And she had not even spoken a word.

CHAPTER 17
STONES AND BREAD

It had been three months since she returned to Sychar.

The days had fallen into a predictable rhythm. She rose before dawn to knead barley into loaves, then carried water from the near-dry stream behind the ruined vineyard. Midmorning meant sweeping dust from the floor only for it to drift back again, and afternoons were spent tending to the younger children, whose hunger for attention was more constant than their hunger for food. She washed linens when she could find clean water. She traded goat cheese for vinegar. She kept to herself.

But the house bore years of neglect, and her hands found work in its corners. She patched a cracked wall with clay from the streambed. She reset stones that had slipped from the hearth. She stitched torn mats and mended the roof where rain had slipped through, catching the drips in a clay bowl until the work was done.

And when the repairs were finished, she took a small knife and pressed its edge into the wood of the doorway, tracing slow lines that curled and twined. Vines grew there beneath her hand—spirals and tendrils, leaves that bent as if to follow the sun. A mark of care, a small rebellion of beauty.

Nessa scoffed when she saw it. "We don't need vines on the door. We need oil and flour, not scratches in the wood." She turned away sharply, her voice clipped, as though to shame Photine's indulgence.

But later, when she thought no one was looking, Photine saw the girl's fingers drift across the carving, tracing the curves of the leaves with the same absent tenderness she used to smooth Levi's hair.

The village had not forgotten her—not entirely. Whispers followed, buzzing from lips that half-remembered and half-invented.

"That's the one—she lived in Shechem as a girl."

"I knew her name once. Didn't her father get arrested?"

"I heard he was working with the rebels."

"Wasn't she tied to the rebels there?"

At first, it was only whispers at the market. But soon one voice rose louder, steady enough to be heard three stalls away.

"I knew her in Shechem," the man declared, pointing with a skewer of figs as though it were proof. His face was leathery with age, his beard thin, his eyes sharp with the satisfaction of being listened to. "She was married to the old man Barshai—nearly killed him! He had to get rid of her before she did away with him altogether."

Photine froze, her hand hovering over a basket of lentils.

The crowd leaned closer. A woman clucked her tongue. "I heard this is her fifth marriage!"

"No," another interrupted, savoring the scandal. "She was sold. Twice. Maybe three times.

Passed from one man to another like an unwanted goat."

The man with the figs nodded solemnly, as though confirming every word. "I saw it with my own eyes. She brought nothing but ruin wherever she went."

None of it was fully true. And yet, parts of it brushed close enough to sting. Yes, she had been given, taken, and left. Yes, Barshai had grown sickly under her care. But the rest was smoke—rumor woven into story, story hardened into fact the moment it left another's mouth.

Photine lowered her gaze, her heart thudding in her chest. It didn't matter what was true and what was a lie. The shape of her past had traveled down the road from Shechem, carried on the tongues of those who had known her long ago—or claimed they had. And now, here in Sychar, it was taking root again.

No one said it to her face. They rarely said anything to her face. But she felt it, the way eyes slid over her, the way laughter bent when she passed.

She bore it like a pack mule bears its load—not by strength, but by habit. Her silence became a kind of shield. Her lowered eyes, an armor.

Donel spoke little, and when he did, it was only to direct:

"Don't forget the east field," or "They like the lentils with garlic."

He kept his distance for the most part. But there were times he reached for her—brief, unadorned, without tenderness or cruelty. A husband's right, a wife's duty. When it was done, he turned to sleep as if nothing had passed between them.

She had expected worse. She felt nothing.

One morning at the market, Photine kept to the edge of the stalls. She moved like smoke, there and not there, but still the stares pressed against her back.

She was weighing a bundle of onions when a voice cut through, dry and sharp as flint.

"They'll cheat you for those. Twice the price for half the weight. They think widows don't count their coins."

Photine turned. The speaker was tall, her hair threaded with silver, though her face was not yet old. A scar traced from her ear to the corner of her jaw, a mark that might have silenced another woman but had given her a cracked, lopsided smile instead. She carried herself with the confidence of one who had been named worthless and lived anyway.

Behind her stood two others. The older of the pair, broad-hipped and strong, shifted a basket of lentils against her hip. Her hair was tightly bound, her face stern, her eyes watchful. The youngest was hardly more than a girl, with dark curls escaping her scarf and hands that fidgeted with everything she touched—her sleeve, her basket, the strap of her sandal.

"We're with Ephram," the tall one said, as if that were explanation enough.

Photine frowned. The name stirred something—half-buried, half-forgotten. Ephram. A boy from Shechem, nearer Zimri's age than hers. She remembered him trailing at the edges of games, never quite fast enough, never loud enough to keep up with the others. He had carved shapes into wood when the rest chased each other through the vineyards. Not cruel, not sharp like some boys—but apart.

She hadn't thought of him in years. And now, here his name was, carried on the lips of women who wore no shame yet bore the weight of every whisper the village cast off.

Her frown softened. "Ephram," she murmured, as though testing the memory against the present.

The older woman spoke next, her tone flat, almost protective. "Ephram keeps a house. Brings us what he earns at the market, and we keep the rest. We share the work. Folks don't like it. Say it isn't proper. But we eat, and we aren't turned out to beg."

The youngest snorted and glanced at Photine with a spark of mischief. "They say Ephram can't father children. We say he's too kind to try. And anyway, he'd rather weave cloth than chase skirts." She grinned widely, showing a gap in her teeth, then shrugged. "Better for us."

Photine studied them—three women cast off by their families or husbands, gathered under one roof not by law or ceremony, but by need. Not wives, not servants. Something else. Something freer, though the town despised them for it.

It wasn't mockery. It was survival. And for the first time in weeks, Photine's lips curved into a laugh, soft and cautious, but real.

The tall woman's scar pulled as her smile deepened. She pressed an onion into Photine's hand. "Come to us at dusk. We eat together— always. No titles. No husbands. Just women."

Photine hesitated, then nodded. The air in the market was still heavy with stares and whispers, but in that moment, she felt welcomed. It was the first kindness she had been offered since stepping back into Sychar.

She wasn't entirely sure it was an invitation; maybe she hoped it was. She didn't say yes. Not yet. But the onion in her palm was warm.

Three more months passed, and the house ran differently now.

Bread rose at the right time. The hearth stayed warm, even in the wind. The children knew when to help and when to scatter. Photine had arranged the home like a weaver at her loom—each task a thread, each moment a knot drawn tight. Nessa had become a true second hand. Markus and Jonah hauled kindling without needing to be asked. Even Levi, now four years old, had begun sleeping through the night.

Donel said little, but he noticed. He left earlier and came back later, trusting that things would be in place. Their dynamic was functional—like stone placed atop stone. What was built between them was not affection—it was survival.

Photine rarely went to the village. Her errands were sparse, discreet. When she needed water, she walked the half-mile to a small stream beneath the scrub hills. It was less convenient, but it kept her invisible. And invisible meant unbothered.

She thought sometimes of the women she had met at the market—the tall one with the scar, the stern one with her watchful eyes, the young one with restless hands. There had been laughter in them, a kind of stubborn light she hadn't felt in years. For a moment, she had nearly stepped into it, nearly let herself believe that friendship might soften the edges of her days.

But already the village's eyes were too sharp on her back. Already whispers curled in every shadow, twisting her story into something she could not control. To join those women, to linger in their company, would only feed the tongues wagging against her.

Better to be silent. Better to be unseen. Better to keep her world small.

So she chose the scrub hills, the quiet stream, and the safety of her own shadow.

But then the rains came late. And the goats upstream multiplied. And the water, once clear, began to smell of rot and dung.

So she was forced to go to the well.

Jacob's Well still sat at the center of the village like a relic too sacred to abandon. Women still gathered there in the cool of morning—baskets in arms, tongues sharp, eyes sharper. Photine had hoped that after so many years, her face might go unnoticed. But Sychar did not forget what it condemned.

The whispers began before she reached the stone lip.

"Donel's wife—that one. The one with the past."

"She wasn't his first. And he wasn't her first, or second, or third, or fourth…"

"Her kind always returns. Like bad debt."

Snickers followed, sharp and thin, rattling louder in her ears than the creak of the rope.

She said nothing. Lowered her jar. Counted the turns of the rope.

But in the silence of her chest, the words clung. She began to wear them, piece by piece—shame-shaped garments stitched by rumor, draped heavy across her spirit. No matter how she tried to walk lightly, they hung from her, whispering with every step.

She learned to linger in her tasks, to draw out the kneading of bread or the mending of clothes, until the midday heat pressed the village into silence. Only then would she take up her jar and walk the dusty road to the well. Fewer eyes, fewer whispers. Or so she hoped.

Thankfully, she was not alone.

The other women were already there—Sarah, Mara, and Ketziah—the co-wives of the man known as Ephram the Clothier. None of them wore rings. None of them wore shame. They laughed as they pulled the rope together, their sleeves rolled high, water spilling onto their skirts without apology.

Sarah, tall and scarred, caught sight of Photine first. "There she is—the quiet one," she said, her voice carrying both welcome and challenge.

Mara, broad and sharp-eyed, nodded toward the jar at Photine's side. "Best time of day for water. Let the gossip bake in the sun while we draw in peace."

And Ketziah, youngest, grinned as she balanced her own jar against her hip. "Peace? Not with me around." She winked, then laughed at her own mischief.

Photine's lips trembled, caught between wariness and something dangerously close to relief. She had carried the village's whispers like stones in her belly, but here stood women who refused to bend beneath them.

None of them asked her to explain herself. None of them looked at her with suspicion. They simply made room, as though she had been expected all along.

As the jars dipped and the water sloshed, she caught their names in passing. Sarah—the tall one with the scar. Mara—the broad-shouldered, watchful one. Ketziah—the youngest, quick with a grin.

At the sound of *Mara*, Photine's chest tightened. Once, in the raw days before Ezra's death, she herself had chosen that name. *Call me Mara,* she had whispered to Lois, *for the Lord has dealt bitterly with me.* A name for emptiness, for a soul too heavy to lift its head. She had shed it later when she no longer could hide, but the taste of it lingered even now.

Her gaze flicked toward the woman who bore it without apology, her hands steady on the rope, her posture strong. Photine wondered what kind of bitterness Mara had survived—and whether wearing the name had made her stronger.

For the first time in years, she did not feel like the only one carrying shadows.

They greeted Photine as if her place had been waiting all along. Ketziah grinned and pressed half a fig into her palm. "You look hungry," she said. "Best eat before the flies do."

Photine's fingers curled around the fruit, surprised by the simple kindness.

Mara gave a sharp tug on the rope, water splashing against the stone lip. She muttered just loud enough for all of them to hear, "It's always the dried-up ones who talk the most." Her eyes flicked toward the cluster of women who had paused to watch.

Sarah smirked, wiping her hands on her tunic. "We're the thorn bushes they can't prune," she said. "So they circle us and whisper instead."

A laugh caught in Photine's throat—real, wide, untethered. The sound startled her as much as it seemed to surprise them. For the briefest moment, the heaviness inside her loosened, and she remembered what it felt like to breathe without fear of judgment.

But the moment did not last.

Old Malcah—the butcher's wife—swept past with a bundle of leeks in her arms, muttering prayers under her breath. She drew her shawl tight across her nose as though the mere scent of them were unclean. Two younger women trailed behind, their faces half-hidden by hands that tried and failed to muffle laughter. One mimed spitting, the gesture sharp as a slap.

Photine stiffened, the fig still sticky in her hand. The laughter rang in her ears, louder than it should have. *Shame-shaped garments,* she thought. She had worn them so long she feared they had become her skin.

Sarah nudged her shoulder, voice low but firm. "Let them choke on their own dust. We've no time for it."

Photine swallowed, nodding, though her heart throbbed in her chest. She wished she could wear defiance as these women did. But all she could manage was silence, her smile already fading into the shadows of her spirit.

And later that night, Donel came home early.

He didn't shout. He didn't strike.

He simply closed the door harder than usual and set his sandals too precisely by the wall.

"I heard where you were," he said.

"I needed water," she replied, steady.

"From Jacob's Well? With *them*?" She held his gaze, unflinching.

"It was either that," she said, "or make the children drink sickness."

He looked at her then—not angry, but calculating. Measuring how visible she had become. How visible *they* all had become.

"I don't want them around here," he finally said. "You draw enough eyes as it is. You want to talk, do it with Nessa. Or the old woman by the fields. Anyone but them."

Photine's jaw tightened. "I have mended your roof. I've patched your walls. I've kept the children clothed, fed, and tended when fevers come. I ask nothing in return. Nothing. Not even kindness."

His mouth pressed into a line, but he did not interrupt.

"And yet," she continued, her voice low, "the only time I feel myself—like I am more than hands and bread and silence—is with them. They see me. They don't spit when I pass."

For a moment, the room was still, save for the faint sound of the twins laughing outside.

Donel exhaled, slow, heavy. "It is not about spit, woman. It is about survival.

Every whisper touches me, and the children. Do you think your shame is yours alone?"

Her throat burned, but she forced herself to answer. "Then let me carry it where I will. I have no family left but this house, and even here I am a stranger. Will you take the only friends I have?"

His gaze faltered, shadowed with the weariness of a man who had carried more than his share. At last, he shook his head. "Do as you will. But don't mistake their company for safety. When the village casts stones, they will not ask whose door they hit."

She nodded once, though inside something curled tighter than before. She had not chosen this life. But she would choose where to draw her breath, and with whom to share it.

Even if it cost her.

Even if it meant drawing water beneath scornful eyes—because even in disdain, she was seen. And sometimes, being seen was the first step back toward being known.

Donel didn't like her going to the well. He said he'd fix the path to the farther spring when the barley came in. But until then, Photine would have to continue to use the well.

She hated the way her feet felt heavier the closer she came to it. As if the ground knew her weight. As if the dust remembered.

The other women gathered there in the mornings—some were faces she once knew by name, now older and hardened by rumor. They did not speak to her. Mostly, it was the younger wives or daughters who were tasked with getting water for the day, and they reveled in gossip. But the ones on the fringe, the ones who came later or stayed quiet longer—those were the ones she noticed. A nod here. A glance held half a second too long. A sleeve adjusted in a pattern she began to understand.

Like Esther, the potter's widow, who never married again but somehow always had bread. Like the women, she was told to stay away lest she bring unwanted attention to the family.

They never lingered all at once. Sometimes only one would speak to her, offering a fig or a crooked smile in the shade of the market stall. Another would press her shoulder as they passed at the well, as if steadying her—but it was a language, a code. Quiet survival.

It was a strange comfort to be invisible together.

At home, things were not so quiet.

Nessa had grown into the role of woman-of-the-house with a precise, possessive energy—the kind born of necessity. She was twelve now—the same age Photine had been when her father disappeared. That memory alone softened Photine's judgment, even when Nessa snapped orders or corrected her folding methods with an edge too sharp for a child. She ruled the home with the fierce loyalty of a vine that clings so tightly it chokes what grows beside it.

Tomer, just two years older, was already learning the weight of his father's work. Photine had grown quietly fond of the way he bore his tasks without complaint. He reminded her of what Zimri could have been—what he wasn't. A boy who stepped forward when the family needed someone to fill the space of a man.

But it was Nessa who saw her as competition.

The house no longer needed Photine. Not really. Between Tomer's steadiness and Nessa's sharp eyes, the cooking and cleaning ran without her. And the younger ones—still warm and affectionate—knew better than to cross their sister's gaze.

It drove her outward. To the market. To the well.

At first, she drew water early, alone. But over time, she began to cross paths with Mara… then Ketziah… then Sarah. Never all at once. Only one at a time. Each with a glance, a brief smile, a passing comment that meant more than it seemed.

There were no meetings. No plans. Just small convergences.

But the whispers followed them.

"Defiled," she heard one woman hiss.

"Leftover men and women," muttered another.

She tried not to care. But Donel did.

He came home from the market that day with a clenched jaw and a warning in his tone.

"You don't speak to those women anymore," he said. "People are watching. They talk.

About you. About me. About the children."

Photine held his gaze but didn't argue.

That night, she watched as Nessa portioned out the lentils and told the younger boys where to sit. Tomer fixed a cracked bowl with resin while Markus and Jonah fetched more firewood without being asked. Even little Levi, half-asleep in her lap, was gently pried away by Nessa and tucked in with surprising tenderness.

She was no longer needed here. At least not by them.

And so she began to need something else.

Something outside the house. Beyond the silence. Beyond the names they called her. Beyond the life that had been chosen for her, instead of the one she would've chosen.

She didn't know what it was.

But it started at the well.

Nessa moved swiftly after supper, clearing dishes before Photine could even reach for the washing bowl. She barked orders at the younger boys with command. When bedtime came, it was Nessa who gathered the little ones, tucked them in, and dimmed the hearth. And when Donel returned, it was she who brought him water, who recited the day's chores like a steward, who smoothed the wrinkles from her tunic and stood beside him—not like a daughter, but like a wife in miniature.

Photine did not protest.

She noticed it first with the laundry. Nessa had already scrubbed it by the time she returned from the well. Then it was the mending, then the oil, then the accounts.

One morning, Photine rose early to knead the bread—only to find Tomer already shaping the loaves. His hands were clumsy but proud.

"Papa said I could try," he mumbled, not meeting her eyes.

And so, slowly, she began to leave.

The market. The olive groves. The far ridge near the dried vineyard. Any place that wasn't the walls of Donel's house. Any place where she didn't feel like a leftover guest wearing out her welcome.

One afternoon, as she returned from the well, her skirt dusty and her water jug sloshing against her hip, Donel met her at the gate.

"You were seen with them," he said. His jaw was tight.

"With who?"

"The ones at the well. Sarah. Mara. That crowd."

Photine said nothing.

"They're not good for business," he added. "People see you with them, they think I don't keep my house. They think you're… like them." He didn't finish the sentence. He didn't need to.

She didn't answer. Just moved past him into the house, where Nessa was already setting the table, the sleeves of her tunic rolled with the confidence that Photine had once possessed.

She no longer knew where to place her hands.

She was neither a guest nor a wife. Not a servant, not a sister. A useful ghost.

That night, when the younger children were settled and Donel's breathing had already thickened into sleep, Photine found Nessa by the hearth. The girl was mending a tear in Levi's tunic, her fingers quick and sure in the firelight.

Photine lowered herself to the mat across from her. For a moment, she only watched the needle flash through the cloth. Then she said softly, "I was not much older than you when I lost my father. One day, he was there. The next…gone. I never saw him again." Nessa's hands stilled, though her eyes stayed fixed on the fabric.

Photine continued, choosing her words carefully. "And not long after, I was taken from my home. Married off before I knew what marriage meant. Everything familiar—gone in an instant. You are stronger than I was. You've kept your family together. But I know how it feels to have the ground taken out from under you."

The girl drew the thread tight, her lips pressed thin. She did not speak, but her shoulders had lost some of their rigidness.

Photine hesitated, then added, "I worry sometimes…that you and the children will believe what the village says about me. That their laughter and whispers will plant roots. I would not wish that shame on them or you."

For the first time, Nessa's eyes lifted to hers. The firelight flickered between them. She said nothing, only knotted the thread with a quick twist and folded the tunic into her lap.

But when she rose to leave, her step slowed—just for a breath— beside Photine. It was not forgiveness, nor welcome. But it was no longer pure rejection either.

Photine sat in the hush of the embers long after she was gone, wondering if words could ever bridge a gulf this wide.

In the still of night, she went out into the dark, sat near the crumbling aqueduct, and traced the grooves of a clay jar left behind by someone else. She wondered how long something had to be broken before it could stop trying to be whole.

CHAPTER 18
THE HOUSE ON THE HILL

She waited until late morning, after the children were bent to their chores and Nessa commanded the house. With a basket slung over one arm and a shawl pulled low over her hair, Photine slipped out under the pretense of gathering herbs near the ridge. But her feet knew the truth. They turned toward Shechem.

The path wound across the valley floor and up into the lower hills. It was not a long walk—an hour at most if her pace stayed steady—but every step pressed old dust into her sandals. The land was both familiar and strange: the same terraces of olive trees she once climbed, now smaller, thinner, as if they had shrunk without her. The stream from the hillside was where she and Zimri once skipped stones, swearing they would see whose landed nearest the reed bank. Even the bend in the path where they had raced to the gate lay waiting for her, unchanged, though her breath caught as she slowed there.

She rounded it, heart tight, and stopped.

The house was no longer theirs. A new door, well-painted, gleamed against the stone. Flower pots lined the wall, bursting with marigolds and basil. A clay dove swung from the lintel, flashing in the sunlight. From within came the soft hum of a woman's voice, the clatter of dishes, and children's laughter spilling out of the back garden.

It wasn't an empty ruin. It was a home—lived in, loved, and layered over her own memory.

She pressed her palm briefly to the gatepost, the same place her mother once leaned while calling them in from play. Her throat tightened.

"Photine?"

The voice startled her. She turned, and there—older, stooped, carrying a bundle of firewood—stood Yaron, once her neighbor. His brow furrowed, then cleared. "I thought that was you. From the back, I almost mistook you for your mother."

Her tongue felt thick. "Peace to you, Yaron."

He shifted his load, eyes narrowing. "I heard you were…gone. Some said taken east, others said south to Akrabbim. Word reached us from travelers—Jotham's name was spoken, then Mordecai's after." He clicked his tongue. "The village said many things."

Photine stiffened. "Villages always do."

Yaron's gaze softened, just slightly. "Zimri went north, years ago. Never came back. Some say he fell in with rebels, others that he married in the hills. No one truly knows." He shifted the bundle of wood against his hip, his eyes moving past her to the house. "Your mother…she didn't go with him. She'd already been broken by too much loss. After Eleazar left, after you were taken, she carried on a little while. But sorrow wears the body thin. She faded. We buried her by the almond tree, just outside the vineyard."

Photine's throat closed, the image striking her sharper than any rumor. Her mother's hands scrubbing the steps, her voice calling them in from play—now quiet beneath the soil she once tended.

"It is strange," Yaron said, studying her face. "Seeing you here again. Like a ghost at the gate."

Her chest clenched. "This is no longer my home."

"No," Yaron agreed, almost kindly. "It belongs to others now. Best not to stir old dust, Photine.

People remember more than they should—and less than what matters."

She inclined her head, unable to speak, and turned away before her tears betrayed her.

The road back to Sychar seemed longer, heavier. She had gone searching for traces of Zimri, of herself, but found only someone else's laughter in the doorway.

Her steps slowed near the vineyard. The almond tree rose at its edge, branches pale against the afternoon light. Yaron's words rang in her ears: *We buried her by the almond tree.*

Photine's feet carried her there before she had chosen it. She laid the basket down and pressed her hand against the trunk, rough bark flaking beneath her fingers.

Memory came in pieces. Her mother's laugh when she was small, warm as bread rising in the oven. Fingers threading Photine's hair by lamplight, smoothing it into a braid. The smell of crushed thyme in her apron, the gentle cluck of her tongue when Photine skinned her knee. And then, years later, the tired lines around her eyes when Eleazar did not return. How quickly her mother had seemed older, worn thin by waiting.

Photine sank to her knees at the tree's roots. She let her fingers trace the soil as though she could feel her mother's hand there still. Her throat ached, but she forced her words to steady.

"Mother," she whispered, "I found you. I am here." She pressed her lips together, fighting the sting in her eyes. "I wanted to tell you…I am well. I have a home. Children around me. Work for my hands. You don't need to worry about me anymore."

The words caught, too sweet to swallow. She shifted, covering the break in her voice. "I'm strong, Mother. You always said I would be. You'd be proud."

She bowed her head low, so the soil would not see the lie in her eyes. For if her mother had been able to look into her, she would have seen the raw wounds, the shame, the years of being passed from one man to another like a garment torn and mended too many times.

Photine rose quickly, brushing the dust from her knees. She touched the tree once more, brief and fierce, and whispered, "Rest now. I'll be all right."

Then she turned back to the road, her basket light, her heart heavier than before. Each step felt like walking out of one world and into another, leaving the quiet of the almond tree for the noise of barter and bargaining. She wiped her face quickly with the edge of her shawl—no trace of tears could follow her into the village.

By the time she reached the outskirts, the market was already bustling. Baskets overlapped in narrow walkways, and the scent of cumin and fish clung to the air. She moved through it not like a customer but like a shadow.

Near the far end, under a weathered canvas tent, she spotted a familiar profile. The tall woman's words came rushing back—*We're with Ephram.* At the time, the name had tugged faintly at her memory, but now she knew. It *had* to be him. Older now, broader, but still with that hawkish nose and that merchant's poise.

He stood with his arms crossed, inspecting bolts of dyed fabric while two younger men scribbled notes and weighed copper weights. Not the awkward boy she half-remembered, carving sticks in the dust while Zimri and the others ran ahead—but the same Ephram, grown into the work of his hands.

She hesitated. For years, hearing a name from her past meant danger. But something in Ephram's posture, the way he lifted his chin while bartering, told her he would not flinch from a ghost.

"Ephram?" she said, voice low but steady.

He turned, squinted into the sun, then blinked in recognition. "By the prophets… Photine? Is that you?"

A smile touched her lips, thin but true. "Apparently, I'm hard to forget."

He laughed, and for a moment, his whole frame softened. "You look…" He stopped himself, eyes searching her face. "Well. It's been a long time."

"A lifetime," she agreed.

They stood in the space between old memory and present strangeness. Neither fully friends, nor fully strangers.

"I'd heard you returned," Ephram said. "With Donel, yes?"

She nodded. "I've been helping with the house. The children."

His brow furrowed, then eased into something gentler. "Donel…he was never much for chatter. A private man. But steady. I know he's carried more than most since his wife passed. I see his name on cargo slips now and then—grain, stone, wool. Reliable work."

"You still trade?" she asked, adjusting the shawl on her shoulders.

"Spices. Textiles. Some fruit from Tyre when the roads behave. Less than I used to, but enough to keep the house in motion—and the women busy."

He said it without apology. Not "wives," not "servants." Just "the women."

Photine tilted her head. "Sarah, Mara, and Ketziah told me you were a clothier."

Ephram smirked. "They also probably told you I can't father children and don't try very hard."

She laughed despite herself. "They did."

"Well, they're not wrong." He scratched his chin. "But I make a fine curry, and I can recite five psalms without looking, so they keep me around."

She didn't expect that kind of honesty. It disarmed her.

"I used to run markets," she said, voice quieter now. "With Ezra. He was from En-Dor. We traded everything—spices, tools, woven goods, herbs, when we could find them. I learned the craft from him."

Ephram's eyes lit with recognition. "Ezra of En-Dor—of course. I remember him. Sharp mind, fair tradesman. A bit too honest for his own good sometimes." His gaze lingered on her, thoughtful. "And you—" a smile pulled at the corner of his mouth—"you haven't changed as much as you think. I can still see the girl who used to outpace Zimri in bargaining, stepping in before he could finish a sentence. You never lacked for confidence, even then."

Heat rose to her cheeks, unexpected. "I was just stubborn."

"Stubborn," Ephram chuckled. "That's one word for it. I always thought you'd end up running your own stall one day. Seems I wasn't far off."

She smiled faintly. "Ezra preferred clarity over coin. But he knew how to stretch a haul across three towns and never get swindled."

"And you were his partner?" Ephram asked, intrigued.

"We built it together. I know the weight of a fair measure, how to read a buyer's silence, how to set a stall to draw the eye. Ezra handled the trade routes. I handled everything else."

Ephram whistled softly. "Then you'd be more useful to me than half the boys I send to market." Ephram paused, noting a sadness that hung over Photine like an old, well-worn tunic.

Ephram's expression shifted, the easy humor giving way to something steadier. He leaned an elbow against the stall, lowering his voice. "Tell me what happened, Photine. How is it you're here now, with Donel? Don't give me the scraps the market chews on. You tell me. I don't pay weight to rumors."

Her breath caught, the directness pressing against years of silence. She hesitated, then said, "Ezra…he's gone. But before that, we built something together. I know weights, bartering rates, how to stretch inventory, and sweeten a deal without losing coin." She lifted her chin, just slightly. "If you're ever short on help—"

"You'd work again?" he interrupted, eyebrows raised.

"I need to," she said. "Not for coin. For clarity."

Ephram raised a brow, studying her face as if seeing the girl behind the woman. Then, unexpectedly, he chuckled.

"You remember when old Haran caught you climbing the olive tree outside his fence?"

Photine blinked, surprised. "I do. He shouted like I was stealing from the Temple."

"You were what—eight? Nine?"

"Nine," she said with a wry smile. "And I wasn't stealing. I was investigating. He'd carved those odd marks in the trunk, remember?"

Ephram laughed again, the sound soft and genuine. "You told him you were 'keeping record for the scribes yet to be born.' Used those exact words."

"I did?"

"Yes. And then you scolded him for not protecting the tree's bark properly. Said it was sacred."

He shook his head fondly. "He didn't know what to do with you. None of us did."

There was a pause, the quiet weight of shared time.

"You were always a force," Ephram said, more gently now. "Even then. Smart, relentless. Half the boys were scared of you, the rest just followed you around hoping to be picked for your next scheme."

She glanced down, suddenly feeling the years between then and now like a thread pulled too tight.

"I miss her," she murmured. "That girl."

"She's not gone," Ephram said, voice steady. "She's just… been waiting. Maybe it's time you let her out again."

Ephram considered her for a moment, then nodded. "Come by after the feast day. We'll start small.

You can help me with inventory and prep for the market. No pressure."

"I prefer pressure," she said, then immediately softened. "But thank you."

He waved her off. "You're sharper than most I've hired—and not just because you remember how to haggle with the fishmongers." She turned to leave, then paused. "I went to see my old house today." He stilled.

"A new family is living there. It's bright. Blooming."

He didn't speak for a while.

"Zimri?" he finally asked.

She shook her head. "Gone, I think. Long gone." Her voice faltered, and then, softer: "My mother too. They said she rests beneath the almond tree."

Ephram exhaled, the sound heavy. "I'm sorry."

She drew her shawl tighter, eyes tracing the dust at her feet. "Sorry changes nothing. Time marches on, whether we will it or not."

He nodded slowly. "Maybe it does."

As she walked back through the thinning market crowd, the sun high and golden, she did not pull her shawl low over her face. She walked upright. She carried an empty basket, but her hands felt full.

Tomorrow, she would rise early—not for Donel, not for Nessa, not even for Levi and the others—but for herself.

She would go to the market. She would remember the weight of scales, the tones of barter, the joy of exchanging more than goods. And in the hours between silence and ridicule, she would find something sacred again. A purpose.

The thought lingered with her long after the market noise had faded and the house fell silent.

By morning, it had hardened into resolve. She rose before the birds, before even Nessa stirred, the sky still heavy with the last shadows of night.

The morning after the feast day, she woke before the birds. Sleep had come in fits, broken by memories pressing like stones against her chest.

Her body rose before her thoughts caught up, already moving toward the small bundle she'd prepared the night before: a clean tunic and her best sandals. She was ready to feel something of herself again, the self she knew when she was free and happy.

She packed a fig and a heel of bread into her satchel, brushed the dust from her sleeves, and stared at herself in the warped bronze mirror near the door. The woman looking back at her wasn't a wife. Wasn't a servant. She wasn't sure what to call herself, but for the first time in a long time, she didn't flinch from her own gaze.

When she stepped into the courtyard, the sky was still stretching from blue to gold. The air carried the scent of clay and promise. She moved quietly, careful not to wake the others. Even Nessa had let her guard down in sleep, her brow uncreased, her fingers still curled in command. Tomer's arm draped over Jonah, and Levi murmured something wordless from his mat in the corner.

Photine paused. For them, she felt a pulse of something close to tenderness. But it no longer held her captive.

She slipped out before the rooster crowed.

The walk to the market felt different this time. Her feet knew the way, but her thoughts danced ahead of her, already organizing Ephram's inventory, planning which bolts of cloth to place near the front, remembering which merchants liked to be flattered and which preferred quiet competence.

By the time she reached his stall, the sun had only just lifted over the rooftops. Ephram was already there, sleeves rolled, muttering at a shipment of poorly dyed linen.

"You're early," he said, startled but pleased.

"I didn't sleep," she replied, grinning. "Too many ideas."

He laughed. "Good. I've got twice the work and half the patience."

Photine stepped inside the tent, her hands already reaching for a bolt of wool. "Then let's begin."

And just like that, she had a flicker of the girl she thought the world had stripped away.

By the end of her second week working alongside Ephram, the market began to shift. His cloth tent, once overlooked, had started to draw steady attention—because of how Photine arranged them. Colors flowed like water, warm tones to one side, cool shades to the other. She rewrote the signs to include measurements and barter equivalents. She knew how women shopped—what they touched first, what they feared overpaying for, what shade made them hesitate before walking away. And she used it.

Ephram had always been a decent merchant. But Photine made the stall a place where people lingered, where they smiled before they bartered. She knew which gossip to entertain and which to steer elsewhere. The quiet ones, she asked about their mothers. The loud ones, she flattered, until they dropped their guard. The old woman gave extra fabric when no one was watching. By the end of the month, they had doubled their trade in dyed wool and added two new buyers for linens.

But the more her presence was noticed, the sharper the whispers grew. They clung to the edges of the market like smoke.

"She's already had three husbands. Maybe four."

"Donel must be desperate—bringing that curse into his house."

"Those poor children, living under her roof. What chance do they have?"

It was never said to her face. It was never shouted aloud. Just muttered in passing, traded with onions and oil, wrapped in feigned pity. *Poor Donel. Poor innocent children.* As if her usefulness in the home, the meals she set on the hearth, the chores she carried without complaint, were invisible.

And still the words spread—rising louder with every smile she coaxed from Ephram's stall, every coin he counted into his ledger.

And Donel noticed.

At first, he said little. He came home and found the hearth fire low, the house swept but not shining, the lentils cooked but slightly over-salted. The children were still cared for, but by Nessa's command and Tomer's growing hands. Photine's absence was not felt as a loss, but as a quiet space someone else had filled.

Then, one morning, he waited for her just inside the gate.

"You don't belong there," he said, voice low but steady. "The women. That man."

"I belong where I'm useful," she replied, shifting her basket higher on her hip.

He closed the low door behind him with the careful gentleness of a man who feared waking ghosts. When he spoke, it was soft but edged. "I heard you've been working with Ephram."

She had just reached for her shawl. "Yes. At his stall. He needs a hand. I can measure, mend, mark cloth——"

"Ephram?" His voice tightened. "You'll be seen with him in the market."

"I am already seen," she said. "Seen and named. My presence there brings trade. It helps the house."

Donel's face folded like a page. "It brings talk," he said. "To our door. About you, about me, about the children. People are not kind with their tongue, Photine. They will not spare the boys or Nessa."

"I'm trying to be useful," she answered, the word a kind of prayer. "I cook, I mend, I keep this place. With Ephram, I can do more. I can bring coins. I can learn—help in his trade—and bring that skill back. We need that."

He stood very still. The room seemed to listen to them. "You are not his wife," he said finally, not accusing so much as naming. "You are here under my roof. You are wed by law and by what has been done between us. That is how the world will see it."

She laughed then, short and dry. "Wed by law, perhaps. Wed by kindness? No. You did not choose me. You took what you needed and then…we lived. I am no wife in the way the word should mean. I serve your needs."

He flinched at the sting but did not argue the point. "That is not what I meant." His hands were folded, precise. "My concern is not for myself. It is for the children. They are small. They will be cut down by rumor the same way a reed is snapped. If the market talks, merchants will not come as readily. Buyers will ask questions. People who might help us will step back when the story is loud."

Photine's face went hot. "So I must hide? Stay in a corner and be invisible so your name stays clean?"

"It is not about cleanliness," he said. "It is about survival. When you draw eyes, those eyes come to the house. They measure its worth. They decide whether it is safe to trade with us, to take on our grain, to lend us seed in the spring."

She stepped closer, the basket clutched at her hip. "Let me work in your trade. I know weights; I know how to stretch a bolt of cloth so a poor woman leaves covered. I will shoulder the hard hours, Donel. I will rise before dawn. Let me prove it."

He looked at her then with a tired sort of sorrow. "You do not belong in the quarry. You do not belong in the sacks. Women in my trade take what they can at the market and come home. The work I do—haul stone, negotiate with foremen—is not for you. It would expose you to more harm than good."

"You think Ephram is a risk and my helping you is not?" she shot back. "Ephram keeps cloth and counts coins. He is no threat to this house."

"No," Donel said. "Ephram is a merchant. He is what he is. My fear is not him. My fear is the way people will twist things. They will say you slept with merchants for gain, that you invited ruin to our door. I won't have that for the boys. I won't have their lives narrowed because of whispers."

She pressed her lips together so hard they whitened. "I have given this house my hands. I have given it work and watch and meal, and night. I ask nothing—only to be allowed to help in a way that keeps us fed."

"You already help," he said. "Enough that the house stands. But you must not add fuel to the fire." He stepped forward, and the quiet in his voice cut clean. "No more market. Nessa and Tomer will handle what's needed at the stall and the well. You will stay here with the younger children. Keep the house. Keep them. Do you understand me?"

Her heartbeat hammered in her throat. "You can't order me like a servant."

"You are not my child," he said flatly. "You are something different and more complicated. A liability I did not ask for."

The phrase struck like iron. Photine's hands trembled; she imagined herself folding up small and fitting the shape of his decree to survive. She pictured the children's faces, the way Levi's thumb found his mouth when he was afraid. She saw Nessa's sharp jaw, the way the older two measured people before they spoke.

Anger rose, hot and humming. Humiliation rose beside it, pricking like thorns. She could shut down—curl inward and let the town's story flatten her until she was a shadow in her own house. Or she could push back: learn the trade anyway, argue for a place at the stall, force the world to see her usefulness as fact rather than rumor.

Her voice came out low, steel-hidden. "You think hiding me will keep them safe. But the house was never only yours to protect. I have done enough to keep this roof over your head. I will not be locked away for their comfort."

He moved his chin in a final statement. "Then you leave me little choice. For the good of this household, I set the rule. No market for you. You remain within these walls with the young ones. That is my command."

She turned away, and the room suddenly seemed too narrow. She breathed shallowly, rage curdling into something hard and quiet beneath her ribs. She said nothing more. But her silence was a promise—either to yield, or to rise.

The next morning, she rose early. The house was still; shadows clung to the walls as if reluctant to leave. She moved with the careful economy of someone who had learned to make a few small things last.

She gathered her few possessions — a fold of cloth, the thin necklace Ezra had once given her, the smooth stone from Lois's garden — and from the bottom of a drawer she drew out two shards of olive wood, worn by years of handling. She had kept the promise they held through journeys and marriages, a fragment of his hand left behind when he vanished.

She wrapped the lot in a stained scarf, tucking the olive shard close to her heart where its grain pressed like a promise. Then she moved through the dim room: kissed Levi's forehead while he still slept, pressed her fingers into Jonah's small, callused hand, smoothed the blanket over Nessa. For a moment, she listened to the soft rise and fall of their breathing, as if memorizing the rhythm of the house one more time.

Before the sun had climbed the hill, she slipped out, the scarf knot tight at her shoulder. The shard of olive wood bumped faintly against her breastbone, a weight and a map both, as she stepped into the cool morning air.

She didn't look back.

CHAPTER 19
THREADS AND THRESHOLDS

Ephram didn't ask questions when she arrived. He saw the bundle, the bruised pride, and opened the gate. Mara cleared space beside her own mat. Ketziah made tea. Sarah said only, "About time."

People talked, of course. Louder now. She had traded one house for another, one man's name for another's ambiguity. To the villagers, it was confirmation of everything they had whispered. A sixth man. A shared home. A woman who couldn't stay where she was put.

But inside those walls, Photine flourished.

She rearranged Ephram's storehouse and tripled his inventory record-keeping. She taught Ketziah how to weigh thread against a coin without the balance. She helped Sarah mend trade relationships with two vendors from Jericho. She mapped out the travel times for the spice caravans and made a list of buyers in Sebaste she could reach with a donkey and a day's journey.

She laughed more now, sometimes loud enough to startle herself.

Still, the judgment lingered like smoke. Women pulled their daughters closer when she walked by. Men averted their gaze or watched her too closely. But Photine had learned—being scorned was survivable. Being silenced was not.

It was Mara who first mentioned the traveling prophet.

Ephram shrugged. "A Jew," he said, mouth full of figs. "From the Galilee."

Photine rolled her eyes. "They're always from Galilee," she muttered, a half-smile slipping through. The remark sounded like a joke until the memory of Ezra's laugh made it ache.

"No, this one's different," Ketziah added. "He doesn't charge for healing. He doesn't turn women away."

"They never do at first," Photine muttered, sorting bolts of linen.

Sarah leaned in. "They say he reads people's hearts. That he healed a woman of her demons."

"Sounds dangerous," Photine replied. "And convenient."

But the rumors kept coming.

A crowd in Cana. A blind man in Nain. A widow's son was restored. Women—actual women—speaking in public, beside him, not behind him.

Photine tried to ignore it. She had no room for dreams. She'd built her life on the bones of men who claimed too much and gave too little.

And he was a Jew.

That was enough for her to close the door.

Still, something stirred. Quiet, unwelcome. Like the first wind before a storm.

Days had turned into weeks, and weeks into months since Photine left Donel's home and stepped across the unseen, new life. At first, there was silence. No sandals scraping the road behind her. No summons, no pleas. Just the sound of her own feet carrying her forward, toward the dye vats and Ephram's cluttered storeroom, toward the hushed laughter of women who had also refused to disappear.

She had not seen the children. Not really. Not up close.

Until one morning, in the market beneath the striped awning of a fig seller's cart, she heard a sound, high, bright, breathless, a little squeal that had no words, only pure surprise and delight.

Before she could even find its source, a small body slammed into her legs with the force of unrestrained joy. He didn't call a name so much as make a pleased, urgent noise, half-laugh, half-wail, the way children do when they have found something they thought lost.

Photine froze. The ache folded over her so sharply she almost let the bolt of cloth tumble from her hands. She crouched, breath shallow, and settled her palms at his shoulders as if to steady both of them. He pressed his forehead into her tunic, fingers clutching at the hem, and made that same bright sound again. No sentences came, only the small, sure weight of him against her.

"Levi," she whispered at last, voice breaking on the single name. He answered with a grin splitting his dusty face and a bright, eager clap—no words, only joy. Photine laughed then, a sound half-choked and raw with relief, and smoothed the wild hair from his brow.

For a long moment, she simply held him, feeling the steady rise of his breath and the small, steady proof that she was, for now, where she was needed.

That's when she saw the others. Jonah and Markus were standing stiffly by the spice stall across the row. Markus had one hand on his brother's shoulder, the protective stance of someone who wasn't sure what would happen next. Jonah looked as though he wanted to run to her, too, but his feet betrayed his heart. He stayed still.

Photine stood slowly, one hand resting gently on Levi's head. "Your brothers are waiting."

She lifted Levi into her arms and walked him over to where the older boys flung stones at a cracked jar. They straightened when they saw her, Tomer with the careful look of someone used to being chosen, Jonah with his shy glance, Markus already folding his arms like a little man who expected the world to be blunt.

Photine set Levi down between them. He stayed close to her skirts, more a shadow than a speaker. She smoothed his tunic and let her fingers linger on the soft nape of his neck.

Tomer was the one who spoke, the question coming out like a matter-of-fact, "Are you coming home?"

The words hit like a cold wind. She could have stepped around them, lied, said errands, work, or duty. Instead, she met his eyes and kept her voice simple. "Not this time," she said.

"Why?" Jonah piped up, rubbing his thumb against his lip the way he always did when he worried.

She crouched to be level with them, folding her hands on her knees so they could see she was steady. "Because sometimes grown-ups promise more than they can keep. Sometimes things break and can't be fixed the way we want." She swallowed, then added, softer, "Like when Nessa dropped the plate, and we had to glue it together."

Markus snorted—a small, fierce sound. "That was Nessa's plate. We fixed it." He jabbed a thumb toward the yard as if the act proved everything.

"It was fixed," she agreed. "But you remember the crack." Her gaze found each of them in turn. "I did what I could for this house. I will keep doing what I can. But I won't pretend I can put everything back the way it was."

Jonah looked down, then up at her, and for a second his eyes were very old. "Can we come to you?" he asked.

She let out a tight sigh, more feeling than pain. "If you see me in the market, wave. That's always allowed."

They considered that like a solemn treaty. Tomer nodded once, satisfied; Jonah's face relaxed a fraction; Markus shrugged and turned back to the jar. Levi, who had said nothing, shuffled after his brothers and darted off with them across the yard.

She watched them go, their shoulders bunched, the way they moved as if carrying more than boys should. The moment was small and ordinary. It was, she thought, more than enough: enough to remind her that she had loved them, and enough to make her feel the cost of leaving.

She stood frozen. The market's clatter and the rattle of scales spinning around her like wind-blown leaves. The bright colors, the shouted prices, the small, sharp bargains felt distant, as if she were watching through a pane of glass. Then, almost against her will, she turned back toward Ephram's stall. Her chest ached in places she had thought sealed; beneath that ache, something else stirred—quiet, unwelcome, but undeniably there—and it had her listening again.

The first sign came in the way Ephram's voice clipped at the edges. He returned then from Sebaste, a bolt of indigo-streaked wool thrown over his shoulder, the dye still dark at the hem.

He had been gone only a morning, bargaining at the dye merchant, checking colors and weights. Now, he crossed the courtyard with the gait of a man who knows his goods and his gains. Where his greeting would usually have been easy and warm, it faltered, tightened around a caution he didn't bother to hide.

He stopped when he saw her, no performing merchant's laugh, no easy barbs. Instead, he let the bolt rest on the stall frame and studied her as if measuring an unseen thread. "Back so soon?" she asked, hearing him enter and turning around, with concern she noted out loud, "You look…tired."

Photine met his eyes and, for the first time that day, did not look away. The market's murmur narrowed to the small exchange, the indigo at Ephram's sleeve, the stall's half-shadow, and the place she'd been pulled from by memory and loss.

Ephram's voice dropped. "There's a man asking after you."

She looked up, slowly. The world seemed to have thickened. Her question came out smaller than she meant, a tremor threaded through it. "A Roman?"

The single word carried the sharp, sudden fear of someone who knew what a Roman's curiosity could cost. Her fingers tightened on the basket at her side; the breath left her like a small surrender.

Ephram shook his head once, grim. "Worse."

She didn't wait for him to say the name, she already felt it, heard it in the markets and at the well, in the hush that followed a passerby. "Donel," she said, and the name landed like a stone.

She stood, brushing unseen dust from her sash. The air around them thickened with the weight of a truth that had been circling for months. Donel had stayed away when she left. No protests. No retrieval. Just silence. But silence was never surrender.

Ephram crossed his arms. "He's in the lower market. Not shouting, not threatening. But making himself known. He wants a word. With you. And with me."

She nodded. Her heart wasn't racing. Not yet. It simply sank lower in her chest, heavy and resigned.

"Let's not keep him waiting," she said.

They found him by the olive press, one hand on his belt, the other gripping the edge of a stall as if anchoring himself. He was leaner than before, jaw tighter, beard streaked with more gray. But his presence still carved space, still demanded notice.

He straightened when he saw them approach, shoulders squaring as if to make himself a smaller, steadier shape in the crowd.

"Photine," he said, even and careful. His glance slid to Ephram and back. "Merchant."

"Donel," Ephram answered, flat as a slate.

She waited for the rest. The market noise shrank to a ring of distant sound.

"I didn't come to argue," Donel said. "Not here. I'm not here to drag anyone through the streets." "That's thoughtful of you," she said, cool.

He didn't smile. He took a breath as if measuring each word. "Tomer told me this morning. He saw you at Ephram's stall yesterday. Jonah saw you, too. They said people watched. They whispered."

The name of the children in his mouth made the complaint heavier. "Do you know what the market does with that kind of talk? It turns it into a ledger, who will trade with us, who will lend us seed, who will look twice at our boys when they come to court for work. People begin to say a man cannot manage his house if his wife keeps company with other men in the market. They say he's weak. They say the children are ill-kept."

He said it plainly, without venom. It was fear, practical and raw. "I am not comfortable with that. I will not have their mouths sell my sons short."

Photine's hands tightened on the basket. "I go to work," she said. "I bring coin. I teach numbers.

I make Ephram's stall more than it was."

Donel's jaw tightened, not with anger now but with a tired, stubborn kind of care. He leaned in, lowering his voice so the market's noise might not snag what he said.

"Come back with me now," he said. "We'll tell them, at the gate, where the elders gather. I'll say you were only helping Ephram for a time, that it was work for the house, nothing more. I'll tell them you will remain at home to tend the children. It will stop them talking."

Photine's fingers closed harder on the basket strap. The idea of parading herself as something she was not, an obedient woman who slipped away from work at her husband's word, felt like a small, public death. "You'd have them believe I left my hands idle so the story is easier to sell?" she asked. "You'd have me lie so people will be quiet?"

"It isn't a lie," Donel said bluntly. "You did help. Say we set a time, this is the end. You go home, we keep the honor of the house, and the market loses its hymn to your name."

She shook her head. A laugh, low and hard, escaped her. "You think the whispers stop because you tell them to?" Her voice dropped, sharp despite herself. "They will plant their own truth in the rows of the stalls, whether you speak or not. You cannot buy back what they want to believe."

Ephram watched the exchange from under his awning, fingers idly untying a bolt of cloth. He did not speak, but his eyes kept her.

The younger men at his side shifted, uneasy; a woman at a nearby stall pretended not to listen but kept her hands poised on her scale. The market was all ears.

Donel's voice softened. "I only ask you for the children. For them, I'll stand in the square and tell whatever needs telling. I'll say what will quiet the tongues. You can stay out of the market. We will not need that extra coin if it costs my children their chances."

Photine felt the words like small stones in her palm, each one an offer, each one a demand. It would be easy, she thought. It would be safe. She could go home, fold herself back into the quiet of hearth and small hands, and let rumor pass like wind over a field. But quiet had a price she could feel already: a slow erasure, a woman measured only by what she did not speak.

"No," she said at last, and the single syllable carried more than she meant. "I will not make myself invisible for the comfort of others. I will not be the thing you set down when you want the house to look neat."

Donel closed his eyes for a beat, then opened them. "You choose then." There was no malice in it, only the bluntness of a man who knew what a bad impression could do to a boy's life. "If you stay in the market, I will have to do what fathers do. I will speak to the elders as it is. But I will not lie for the sake of comfort."

Around them, the market hummed, and then, as if some invisible cue had been given, a woman by the oil stall nudged another, and both dipped their heads to listen. A child who had been chasing a goat slowed, sensing the hardness in the air. Ephram folded the bolt of cloth and kept his hands where any man would see them.

Photine drew a breath that felt like a tally. She could feel all the small things she had done for this family, bread baked before dawn, nights spent watching a fevered forehead, and the market's talk tried to reduce them to nothing. She straightened, lifted the basket, and met

Donel's eyes. "I will not be hidden," she said, quieter now but fixed. "I will not be your silence."

He said nothing more. His face did not shift toward triumph or anger; it took on the worn line of a man giving himself over to consequence. He turned away first. Photine stayed where she stood, the market moving around her like a tide—some heads turned, some voices quieted, and the stall became an island of two people who had made a choice neither wanted to celebrate...

He turned back to her, not angry, but resolute. "I will dissolve the union. Publicly. You want freedom, fine. But I won't have it said that I was cast off. That I was cuckolded or weak."

Ephram shifted his stance. "What does dissolving it mean? You going to write a bill of divorce and pin it to the temple gate like some Pharisee?"

Donel didn't rise to the bait. "I'll go before the council. I'll say she was unfit, that the match was a mistake. That I release her from obligation."

Photine's lip curled. "But not from the shame."

"No," Donel admitted. "Shame's not mine to give or take."

For the first time, something almost like sorrow flickered in his face.

He took a step closer, voice lowering. "You were good with the children. Even Nessa sees that now. She told me the lentils taste worse without you."

Photine blinked.

"I should've seen it sooner," he added. "That you didn't belong there. That you were already elsewhere."

"I never hated you," he said. "But I didn't know how to need you without swallowing you." She said nothing.

He straightened, the softness retreating. "I'll go to the elders before the feast day. You'll be free before the week ends."

He turned then. But before walking away, he looked once more at Ephram.

"You never touched her, did you?"

Ephram shook his head. "Not once."

Donel nodded. "Stranger things have happened."

Then he was gone.

That night, the house felt stiller than usual. Sarah lit the lamps early. Ketziah hummed a strange lullaby from the east hills. Mara roasted almonds and set them out without comment.

Ephram sat beside Photine near the hearth.

"Are you relieved?" he asked.

She stared into the flame. "I don't know. It doesn't feel like relief. It feels like… the closing of a door I never opened."

He nodded. "Sometimes, that's enough."

She leaned back, head against the clay wall.

"I thought I'd feel clean," she whispered. "But I just feel… like ash."

Ephram reached for the poker, stirred the coals.

"Well," he said softly, "ash still burns."

Photine didn't answer. She just watched the embers pulse, shrinking and flaring like the breath of something too weary to rise.

After a long silence, she whispered, "Nessa said the lentils taste worse."

Ephram looked up.

He didn't press.

"She was twelve," Photine went on, voice tight. "The same age I was when my mother… stopped being my mother. After my father disappeared, she just… dimmed. Like the light went out, and everything else was memory. And I hated her for it." Her throat closed, but she pressed forward. "I needed her, and she was gone. Not dead, just… unreachable."

She rubbed at her knuckles. "I swore I'd never be that kind of woman. I swore I'd stay awake."

Ephram didn't speak. He just waited, which was its own kind of tenderness.

"And now here I am," she said, almost laughing. "Another woman who walked out. Another wound Nessa will carry. I thought I was saving myself, but maybe I was just handing her the same silence I lived through."

She let the fire speak for a moment. Its pop and sigh answered more honestly than words could.

"I don't want to go back," she finally said. "But part of me wonders… could it be different now? If I went back for the right reasons? Not to vanish, not to disappear into duty—but to stay awake? To bring something new into that house instead of letting it swallow me?"

Ephram turned toward her then. "You'd go back to him?"

"No," she said quickly. Then softer, "Maybe."

She sighed, shifting the pooled fabric around her legs. "Not as a wife. Not like before. But… the children. They didn't ask for any of this. And Donel—he didn't grab me. He didn't call me a whore. He let me go. I think maybe… he wanted to punish me with absence, but now that he's had it, he doesn't know what to do with the silence."

Ephram stirred the fire again, careful not to let his own feelings cloud the air between them.

"What would you need to even consider going back?"

She thought for a long moment.

"My own work. My own self. A say in how the home is run. No more touching me like I'm owned. No more being seen only when I'm useful."

"And would he give you that?"

She thought of Barshai then, not as a man she'd loved but as a choice she'd made to survive. That union had never fit. She had known it the moment she bent his pity and fear into a vow, persuading the old man to call her his wife so she could leave the women's house with a roof over her head. He had taken her because convenience and companionship were different things to him. He wanted someone to steady his days, not to rattle the quiet he craved. Rumors had made even him uneasy. Barshai, for all his kindness, began to wonder if he was safe in her company. In the end, wanting only peace in his last years and knowing Donel needed help, he arranged the match that sent her on again. Leaving Barshai had been a hurt, yes, but it was also a motion forward—survival braided with compromise.

This was different. Donel's refusal felt like a shutter slammed in her face. It was not the steady absence of someone who walks away, nor the sharp escape she'd once made, this was exile performed in polite language. To be told, finally, that you are unwanted in the place you thought you could belong. There was a cruelty to it that cut through whatever armor she had cobbled together. Rejection did not rip a woman into motion; it left her to stand and watch the pieces settle on the floor. That settling lit the old shame like glass underfoot.

"I don't know," she admitted then, surprising herself with how small the words sounded. "But if I were different—if something in me had changed—maybe it would change something in him. Not for his sake. For theirs." She thought of the boys' faces, how quickly the town's talk could carve a hard line around their future, and her voice tightened with the weight of it.

Ephram didn't argue. He simply nodded, slow and thoughtful. "Just… don't lose yourself to save someone else," he said.

Photine looked into the low coals of the hearth. The heat touched her cheek, but did not warm the hollow in her ribs.

"I don't plan to lose myself," she said at last, the words steadier than she felt, "I plan to become someone worth finding."

She rose slowly, as if a thin skin of weariness fell away behind her. The hearth clicked and sighed. She moved to the wall, running a hand along the clay jugs. The market's muffled life pulsed beyond the awning.

"I'll go for water tomorrow," she said, voice measured. "I need time to think."

Ephram watched her, then returned to his bolts and weights. Outside, the market turned like a wheel—loud, indifferent, hungry for its next thing to chew on. Inside, Photine folded her thoughts like cloth, one careful crease after another, preparing to stitch whatever came next out of the ragged pieces she owned.

She didn't say where. She didn't need to.

But the well was waiting.

CHAPTER 20
THE WELL BETWEEN WORLDS

She did not know what would happen next.

But even before he spoke, before the water stirred in its depth, she knew:

Her life would never be the same…

The silence stretched between them like a thread drawn taut.

She stared at him. Dust clung to his feet. His robe was plain, travel-worn. His hands rested lightly on his knees, palms open.

He had not moved since she arrived. It was as if he had been waiting—not just here, but across years. Across lives.

"I don't talk to strange men," she said at last, her voice dry.

He didn't flinch. Didn't retreat. Just watched her the way the sky watches sea, without judgment, without end.

"You're not a Samaritan," she added, chin rising.

"No," he answered. "But I was thirsty."

His voice was low, but it rang in her chest like a bell.

She narrowed her eyes. "So you sit at our well, waiting for a drink, without a jar or rope?"

He smiled then—not mockery. Something sadder. Gentler. As if he had seen this moment coming and still dared to show up.

"I have water," he said, "you don't know."

Her lips parted. A scoff rose to cover the tremor in her spine. "You? You'd give me water?"

"I would."

"And I'm just supposed to believe that? A Jew, offering me something better than Jacob's well?" He didn't answer right away.

Instead, he leaned forward slightly, as if to speak into the very marrow of her.

"If you knew who was speaking to you," he said, "you would ask. And I would give you water that lives."

Her breath caught—because of what had filled the air around them the moment he said them. Not a threat. Not prophecy.

Presence.

It wasn't loud.

It didn't blaze like fire or quake the earth.

It moved through her like breath she hadn't known she was holding—ancient, impossible, familiar.

Something within her gave way. Not like a breaking. Like a door—sealed for years—quietly unlocking.

She felt it in her ribs first. Then her spine. Then behind her eyes, where old prayers had gone to die.

It was not fear that took her breath. It was recognition.

She didn't know this man. Not in the way the world defines knowing. She didn't know where he was from, what tribe claimed him, what rabbi trained him. She couldn't name his lineage or his politics.

But she knew the way he looked at her.

Not as a Samaritan.

Not as a woman.

Not as a scandal.

Not as a body to barter or a soul to fix.

He looked at her as if there were no cracks in her at all.

And in that seeing, something began to stir beneath her skin— something older than law, older than shame.

A presence. Not just around her. **In her.**

She wavered. From the sudden awareness of just how long she'd been surviving on fragments.

Her mind tried to outrun it:

Is he a prophet? A spy? An angel cloaked in skin? A trick of thirst and heat?

The questions came fast, like wind through dry reeds.

But her soul whispered slower:

He is stillness before the word.

He is water before the cup.

He is the space between the wound and the healing.

And somehow, impossibly, she wasn't afraid.

She was exposed, yes. Known.

But not undone.

No finger pointed. No shame declared. No righteousness weaponized.

Only presence.

Only truth, spoken like a song she had once known by heart and forgotten—until now.

A tear slipped down her cheek and landed on the lip of her jug.

Not grief. Not joy.

Release.

She had spent years hiding in plain sight—behind men, behind roles, behind obedience, defiance and silence.

But this man had walked straight past all of it.

Not to tear her open.

But to call her whole.

And something in her—bruised but breathing—was beginning to rise.

She took a shaky breath. Her world felt off-kilter—like it had tilted toward something too wide to see.

"I can see you are a prophet," she said, cautiously. "So tell me this… we worship here, on this mountain. You say Jerusalem. Who's right?"

It came out sharper than she meant, more accusation than inquiry. But she needed to know. If he truly saw her, he would see her people too.

Jesus looked toward the rise of Mount Gerizim behind them—then past it, to something farther still.

"Believe me," he said gently, "the hour is coming when you will worship neither on this mountain nor in Jerusalem."

Photine's brow furrowed. Her whole life had been framed by where holiness resided, by who was allowed in, by what made one clean.

He went on, "You worship what you do not know. We worship what we know—for salvation comes from the Jews."

She bristled—but then he added:

"But the hour is coming—and is now here—when the true worshipers will worship the Father in spirit and truth. The Father seeks such as these." He looked directly at her.

"God is spirit. And those who worship must worship in spirit and in truth."

Spirit and truth.

Not ritual. Not gender. Not tribe. Not purity by men's definition.

Her chest tightened. This… this she could believe in. Not another priest dictating access. Not another system built to keep women low and out of reach. But a God who searched hearts, not lineages. A God who didn't demand sacrifice, but honesty.

She stared at him again—parched in a way that had nothing to do with the sun. The thirst was older than the morning, older than the bargains and the market clatter; it lived in the hollow behind her breastbone, the place her mother once cupped with hands that smelled of thyme and oven smoke. It was the longing that had kept her going through barter and beds she never chose: not merely for water, but for a place where shame could be set down like a burden and not followed, for a voice that would meet hers without measuring it. She had carried that need so long it felt less like hope and more like truth.

"Sir," she said slowly, the words strange and careful on her tongue, "give me this water. So that I won't thirst again. So I don't have to keep coming here—dragging my shame with every step."

He tilted his head slightly, listening not only to the syllables but to the tremor beneath them. He did not hand her water. Instead, a breeze slid down the lane, cool and sudden, lifting the edge of her shawl and tasting like fig smoke and distant rain. It brushed her face and eased the rawness in her throat as surely as any cup. Photine closed her eyes and let the wind be the answer she had been asking for.

"Go," he said softly. "Call your husband, and come back."

Photine froze. Her breath snagged in her throat, small and ragged as a fish's gasp. For a breathless second the market blurred—the shouts, the clatter of scales, the bright cloths folding into one colorless smear. Beneath it all, something vast and old seemed to yaw open, a hollow in the world that wanted to swallow her shame whole.

Her shame rose up like smoke, quick and hot. Images crowded the hollow: faces at the well, mouths forming a story she could not correct; Levi's small body holding tight to her the other morning; Donel's flat, finished voice telling her she would be free before the week ends. If Donel no longer wanted her—if he had chosen the house without her—what then?

The shard of olive wood at her breast pressed the shape of her fear into her ribs. Her fingers found it without meaning to, thumb tracing the worn seal her father had whittled. The motion steadied nothing. Her mouth went dry.

"I… I have no husband," she said, eyes narrowing, defenses rising.

He nodded slowly, never breaking her gaze. "You have spoken the truth. You have had five husbands—and the man you live with now is not your husband. What you say is true." The world tilted again—but this time, inward.

A lifetime opened behind her eyes: names, hands, nights, rooms, silences.

And through it all, no one had ever seen her whole.

But he had.

And still, he stayed.

"I know…" she said, barely louder than a breath. "I know the Messiah is coming. The one they call the Anointed. When he comes, he will explain everything." Then—he did move.

He straightened, his back no longer bowed in rest, but poised with intention.

And he said, as a truth too bright to deny:

"I am he. The one who is speaking to you."

Silence. But it was a different silence now.

Not the strained kind that lives in unsaid pain.

This was the stillness of holy ground.

She couldn't speak—not because she didn't believe him.

But because somewhere in her deepest knowing, she already had.

She looked down at the jug in her hands, heavy with what no longer mattered.

She set it down—in release.

And then the sound of footsteps broke the quiet—shuffling and uncertain.

The disciples had returned.

She saw their confusion—the glances, the murmurs.

Why was he talking to her? Why here? Why her?

She ignored them.

She ran.

Not from shame.

Not away.

But toward something.

Back through the dry fields. Past the skeptical glances. Past the ruin and the rumor.

She ran with her head high and her hands empty—for the first time in years.

By the time she reached the village, her breath was ragged with joy.

"Come," she said to the first faces she saw. "Come see a man who told me everything I ever did."

She laughed—a wild, unguarded sound.

"Could he be the Anointed One?"

And even those who once crossed the street to avoid her… followed.

When Photine crested the hill, breathless and dusty, the sun was already sliding westward, turning the world gold. Behind her came a scatter of townspeople—curious, skeptical, a few wide-eyed with something like hope. Most had never followed her anywhere before.

Now they could barely keep up.

She slowed only when Jacob's well came into view, her pulse drumming like sandals on dry earth. But instead of finding the stranger alone, she saw a small gathering.

Jesus sat beneath the olive tree's shade, surrounded by a handful of men—his disciples, she assumed. They were laughing softly, rinsing dust from their hands and faces, pouring water from her jars. One of them—young and wiry—was drinking straight from the ladle with abandon, eyes closed in delight.

And there, lined neatly beside the well, were her jugs. Filled.

The same vessels she had abandoned were no longer empty. Someone had drawn the water for her. More than that, someone had noticed her leaving and chose not to let her story end in unfinished labor.

She stood frozen, heart thudding—not with embarrassment, but something else.

Something strange and unfamiliar.

Honor.

She had not been forgotten.

A few townspeople murmured behind her. A man squinted toward the well. "That's the Jew she was yelling about?" he said under his breath. "The one who told her everything she's ever done?"

"Looks like he's just… drinking water," said another.

Photine stepped forward, slowly, as if crossing the threshold into a dream. Jesus looked up and met her eyes.

There was no surprise in his gaze.

Only welcome.

Beside him—half-reclining by the water, a cup of water at her knee—sat a woman whose ease seemed to slow the market's hurry. Her hair fell free and heavy over one shoulder, dark as wet olive leaves; a simple twisted bronze earring caught the light at her lobe. She wore a linen tunic patterned with a narrow dyed border at the sleeve and hem, a woolen wrap pulled loosely about her shoulders against the morning breeze, and a woven belt cinching a pouch at her hip. Her hands were not idle: the nails were callused, the fingers nimble from work and not from ornament.

She met Photine's gaze and gave the smallest, steady nod—an acknowledgment, the courteous currency of women who had learned how to hold their ground. Photine did not know her, not truly. She had only heard the whisper of the woman's name in the market before, a rumor of competence and sharp humor. The nod, the posture, the way the woman rested as if the world were expected to wait. Those things were enough.

Jesus rose, dusting his hands lightly. He glanced at the people crowding behind her, men who had never spoken to her, women who had avoided her eyes in the market, children who had mimicked their parents' disdain.

He looked at them as seekers.

And then, he spoke.

Stepping forward, water still glistening on his hands, and looked out over the gathering. No one spoke.

The well, the hill, the sky—everything seemed to hold its breath.

"You came to see for yourselves," he said, voice steady, rich with calm. "You heard a woman's cry and followed it."

A few townsmen shifted uneasily. One cleared his throat, unsure if this was praise or rebuke.

He went on, "You think the kingdom of God is far away. In temples. On mountains. Hidden behind laws or spoken only by men who wear robes and rings." He gestured to the well, to the earth beneath their feet.

"But the kingdom is within you. And around you. When you know yourselves, you will be known. And you will understand that you are children of the living One."

A murmur rippled through the crowd—disbelief, wonder, something in between.

He continued, "What you seek is not locked behind walls of power. It does not wear a crown or carry a sword. It is not purchased by blood or earned by purity. It is breathed." His hand pressed to his own chest.

"It rises in you when you forgive, when you remember, when you see the light in your neighbor's face and do not look away."

He turned his eyes toward a woman at the edge of the group, one who had whispered about Photine in the market just days before.

"When you divide the world into clean and unclean, worthy and unworthy, male and female, Jew and Samaritan—you forget the breath that made you all."

The crowd stilled. It wasn't condemnation they felt. It was exposure. Not cruel, but holy.

And yet, none turned to leave.

A child, maybe seven or eight, moved closer to Jesus, drawn by something he didn't understand but trusted. Jesus smiled and crouched beside him.

"Let the little ones come," he said gently, ruffling the boy's hair. "For they remember the truth you've forgotten: that love is not earned. It simply is."

Photine felt her throat close, her vision blur. The water jars at her feet shimmered like offerings.

She had run. She had hidden. She had cursed the sky and the men who ruled beneath it. But here, between shame and grace, she saw what she never thought she'd see again.

Hope.

And then—his eyes found hers again.

Jesus stepped closer, and his voice, though quiet, carried across the hush like a sacred wind.

"Thank you," he said to her, his tone neither grand nor performative. Just real. Grateful.

"For bringing your husband."

Photine turned, startled. The crowd shifted.

And there, standing just beyond the others, at the edge of the olive tree's shadow, was Donel.

Dust on his cloak. Sweat at his brow. His eyes locked on hers, not angry. Not even confused.

But shaken—as if something inside him had just cracked open.

She hadn't seen him follow. Hadn't expected him to.

But something in him must have stirred—curiosity, pride, or perhaps something older.

Something like longing.

He didn't speak. He didn't need to.

Photine looked back at Jesus.

And in that moment, something passed between them, wordless but alive.

The well was no longer just a place of water.

It was a place of crossing.

Of endings and beginnings.

Of being seen.

The air shifted again—soft, like a breeze not felt on the skin but in the soul.

Jesus turned his gaze toward Donel, still standing at the edge of the crowd, half in shadow.

"Come," he said simply, extending a hand.

Donel hesitated. His fingers twitched slightly at his sides. The children, the work, the years—it all lived in his shoulders. But something stronger moved his feet.

He stepped forward.

When he reached Jesus, he kept his eyes low.

"I don't know what I'm doing here," he said hoarsely.

Jesus didn't answer right away. He placed a hand lightly on Donel's shoulder.

"You loved a woman," Jesus said, "and she died. Not because you failed her. But because even love cannot hold back time. She trusted you with her children, and you carried that weight the only way you knew how."

Donel's brow furrowed. His jaw clenched.

Jesus continued, "But somewhere along the way, you forgot that you were not meant to carry them—or your grief—alone."

Donel's breath shuddered out.

"She would tell you," Jesus said softly, "that you were a good man. That you did not fail. That she sees how tired your heart has become."

A sound escaped Donel's throat—half sob, half disbelief.

"She would tell you," Jesus added, "that Photine is not her replacement. She is a woman of fire and flesh and wisdom. And she is not here to be controlled or cured. But chosen. And if you choose her, not for what she can do or how she serves, but for who she is, you will see what blessing means."

Photine's breath caught. Donel slowly lifted his eyes toward her.

Something in his expression had softened. Not defeated. Not ashamed. Just… open.

Jesus smiled, hand still on Donel's shoulder.

"Your marriage," he said, "has not ended. It was waiting to begin."

The crowd said nothing. Even the wind was still.

Jesus turned to Photine now.

"She is the well you feared was dry," he said. "But love does not draw from empty places. It digs deeper."

Then, with a voice like both thunder and balm, he raised his hand over them both.

"May your home be honest," he said, "not perfect. May your children be surrounded, not smothered. May your love be chosen, not owed. And may the past break open—not to wound—but to water the ground beneath your feet."

He let his hand fall.

And with that, Jesus turned back toward the filled jars.

"Come," he said to the crowd, as Mary Magdalene stepped beside him and began pouring water into smaller vessels. "Let everyone drink. Let everyone remember. No one is left behind."

That evening, the fire was lit early in Ephram's courtyard. Mara and Ketziah had prepared lentils with garlic and leeks, and Sarah had kneaded the flatbread thinner than usual so it would stretch further. The table was low and wide, borrowed from a neighbor. Cushions ringed the space, and the scent of herbs and roasted almonds filled the air. Even the wind felt softer—as if it, too, was resting.

Photine helped with the dishes, her sleeves rolled, her curls damp from drawing water. But her heart was light like it hadn't been in years—maybe ever. Donel had not spoken much on the walk back. He had only taken her hand once, when she stumbled on a rock in the path. And for the first time, she had let him steady her.

Jesus arrived just before dusk with his disciples, Mary Magdalene beside him. The men looked tired, sun-flushed, and dusty, but their eyes lit up at the smell of the meal.

Ephram welcomed them with a short bow. "There's room," he said, gesturing to the gathered space. "Not much luxury. But room."

Jesus smiled. "That's all we ever need."

Photine ushered the children forward—Tomer, Nessa, and the others—now scrubbed and uncertain, unsure if this was a feast or a reckoning. But when Jesus saw them, he greeted each one by name, as if he had known them all along.

Jonah leaned into Photine's side, whispering, "Is he really the one?"

She glanced at Jesus, who was already laughing at something Ephram said, then back at the boy.

"He's not what I expected," she said softly. "But yes. He is."

They sat in a loose, easy crowd around the low table—no formal order, only the knot of people who had been walking, talking, and sleeping in one another's shadows for years. Peter sat nearest Jesus on the left, sleeves rolled, fingers still smelling faintly of fish; his posture was ready to speak, to interrupt, to laugh. John leaned close to Jesus' shoulder, quieter, head tipped as if always listening for the tone that mattered. James watched the younger men with a broad, abrupt patience like a brother. Philip and Andrew sat mid-table, nudging an olive bowl to someone who had not reached. Andrew made the small, careful offer of food where it was needed. Matthew kept a folded tablet of papyrus and a stub of reed tucked under his arm, scribbling when the talk grew sharp. Thomas watched with slow suspicion, his brow knit. Bartholomew's eyes caught the details others missed, and Thaddaeus spoke rarely but with soft authority. Simon the Zealot's hands never stilled. Judas, quieter than most, stayed near a jar of wine, measuring what was given and taking his place without fuss.

Photine sat a little apart from that familiar knot between Donel and Mary. Ephram sat across the table with his household gathered near, and Jesus himself near the bread. He tore it with hands that had shaped the world and now broke it among outcasts and widows, fishermen and women who had bled; around them the pot hummed, bread crumbled, and the room breathed a mix of salt and oil and something like mercy. Each man and woman at the table was a gesture—one to speak, one to steady, one to question, one to note. Together, they made the ordinary miracle of a place where the hungry were met.

"Whoever you were before tonight," Jesus said as the meal began, "leave it behind. Not because it was shameful. But because it was never the whole of you."

Mary added, "What is sacred isn't who you've been told to be. It's who you are when you listen."

The room grew quiet, reverent but not somber.

Jesus lifted his cup. "This table is not for the pure," he said. "It is for the hungry."

He looked to Donel. "And the weary."

He looked to Photine. "And the brave."

He looked to Ephram. "And the open-handed."

Then, finally, he looked to the children. "And those who still believe in stories where miracles hide in the middle of ordinary days."

They drank.

And the bread passed again.

Laughter returned, hesitant at first, then strong. Someone sang—low and off-key, but welcomed. Mara passed the olives. Sarah wiped her hands on her robe and sat down. Even the disciples, so often guarded, relaxed. They listened more than they spoke.

As the bowls were cleared and the embers settled, a few of the disciples rose, drawing their cloaks close. With quiet nods and a murmur of thanks to Ephram, they slipped into the lane to make camp beyond the olive stand—Simon with a backward glance, John lifting a hand in promise of morning. Mary remained beside Photine like a small, steady flame. Matthew lingered near Ephram's jars, their low voices braided with talk of cloth and roads.

Later, as the stars emerged, Jesus leaned back on his elbows and said, "Do you know what the kingdom of God is?"

A hush fell.

"It's this," he said. "Not a throne. Not a temple. A table."

Photine blinked hard, the warmth in her chest nearly too much to bear.

A table.

A well.

A thread.

And a door flung wide.

CHAPTER 21
CONVERSATIONS BY LAMPLIGHT

The house had settled into that soft hour when dishes have been rinsed and set to dry, when lamps are trimmed low and the smoke of the hearth hangs sweet in the rafters. Outside, the moon rested on the ridge like a silver bowl. Within, quiet gathered in corners. The children had stopped chasing the last crumbs and now lay scattered on woven mats, bright eyes growing heavy, the older ones pretending not to yawn.

Ephram's courtyard held what remained of the evening: a half loaf of bread, a bowl of figs slick with oil, the hush following laughter. The men drew closer to the fire; the women leaned near the door to the small store-room where cloth was kept. Between them, Jesus sat on his heels in the sweep of packed earth, tracing gentle lines with a sprig of olive, letting the night breathe through the house.

Mary had taken her place near the threshold, where a seam of starlight ran along the floor. She held a fig in her palm but didn't eat it. Photine sat beside her, hands clasped around her knees. Ketziah, Sarah and Mara stood just behind, the curve of Mara's shoulder touching the wall, listening.

"They said I should not walk with him," Mary began lightly, her voice like a smile in the dark.

"That a woman belongs only to the inner room, not the road. But he did not summon me as a servant. He looked and said, *Come as yourself.* Do you know what it is to be wanted as yourself?"

Photine's breath hitched. "I have wanted it all my life."

Mary nodded. "When the Teacher spoke to us apart from the crowds, he gave us no yoke heavier than our own hearts. *Do not bind yourselves to new chains,* he said. *Do not make another law to replace the ones that harm. The path is within you—where your mind rests, there is your treasure.*" She tapped the fig. "Find the still place. From it, you will speak."

Sarah swallowed. "Stillness is hard to keep," she whispered. "Shame is noisy."

Mary's eyes flashed soft fire. "Then shame is a liar who shouts to be believed. Let it tire itself.

You do not owe it your voice."

Photine looked down at her hands. "In the market they will say what they have always said."

"They will," Mary agreed calmly. "Some will call your name wrong. Some will try to hand you their fear. Listen: *Do not accept what is not yours.*" She leaned closer, her words like thread drawn cleanly through cloth. "When the soul meets Desire, she says, 'I was not born of you.' When she meets Ignorance, she says, 'You have no root in me.' And she passes on. This is what he taught us, not to fight shadows with shadow, but to turn toward what is real and keep walking."

Photine felt the truth of it like a warm stone in the chest. "And sin?" she asked, voice almost inaudible. "He said once that we make sin when we do what is not our true nature. I do not want to make it."

Mary rested the fig on Photine's open palm. "You were fashioned to carry living water, not chains. What does not belong to you—fear, falsehood, the bending of yourself to please a lie—leave it. The rest, even your wounds, can become a mouth for grace."

Mara's hand slid to Photine's back. "He sees us whole," she murmured, as if reminding herself.

"He does," Mary said, and her tone shifted, tender and fierce. "He sees you as a witness. When you speak, speak from the still place. Some of the brothers will tremble because they misunderstand freedom. Let them. *Do not hand them your silence.*"

Photine let out a breath she'd been holding for years. "I am afraid," she admitted, "and yet—I am not."

"Good," Mary said, a smile curving in her voice. "That is how dawn feels before it knows its name."

Across the courtyard, Ephram lifted the lid of a chest and brought out a folded length of cloth.

The firelight slid over it like water over stone. "This came from a trader in Caesarea," he said, laying it across his arms. "Linen, fine-drawn. See the selvedge? Tight. No fray even if a child drags it through dust."

Matthew, who had been listening more than speaking all evening, leaned in. His fingers hovered just above the weave, reverent. "You can tell by the hand alone," he murmured. "I used to count bolts and think only of tally, not touch. After I left the booth… I noticed the way threads hold each other. A ledger lives in numbers. Cloth lives in the way it breathes."

Ephram laughed low. "Spoken like a man who has learned to read with more than eyes."

He reached for a jar of indigo cakes on the shelf and set one beside the linen. "This blue—if you cut it with too much water, it fades before the first washing. But if you feed it time, it becomes the color of the hour before night."

Matthew's mouth tilted. "The hour we live in now."

Donel had drawn closer, arms folded without threat, a man trying to understand the shape of a room he thought he knew. He watched Ephram and Matthew the way one watches a language one once spoke and suddenly hears again.

"You two talk as if you've known each other longer than an evening," he said gruffly, not accusing, simply bewildered.

Ephram met his eyes, the same gentleness he had offered Photine plain in his face. "Craft recognizes craft," he said. "He knows patterns. I know cloth. Between us there is a kindness." Matthew glanced up, the fire painting a small gold in his dark gaze. "And there is relief," he added softly. "To find a home for your hands."

They bent again over the linen, close enough that their shoulders nearly brushed, admiring the tight edge where the threads kissed and would not unravel. Matthew traced the path of a seam with a fingertip above the surface. Ephram mirrored, smiling. Donel watched the small choreography and felt a door quietly open in him. The thought rose without bitterness, simple and clean as a spring: *There was never anything between them but shelter and bread.*

Photine had not been Ephram's possession to lose. She had been a guest whose presence had brightened his house, a friend whose leaving would make the rooms echo for a time. Whatever flame lived in Ephram's chest tonight had kindled beside a different hearth. Donel stood very still and realized that his jealousy had been a cloak he could set down.

He cleared his throat. "If the blue holds as you say," he ventured, voice gentler than before, "it would make a good sash for Nessa when she comes to marry. She has her mother's way of tying a knot that never slips."

Ephram's smile widened. "Then she shall have it. I'll keep aside the best length." He looked back to Matthew, unhurried and unmistakable. Matthew answered with the briefest incline of his head, and the night became tender.

On the mats in the warm dust, the children drifted at the edge of sleep, alert as birds. Jesus had drawn a small boat in the earth with the olive sprig, and beside it a net like a web of moons.

Levi, the youngest, clambered without ceremony into his lap and pressed his cheek to Jesus' chest. "Tell a boat story," he demanded softly, the way small kings make laws.

"A boat story," Jesus agreed. He touched the little drawn boat. "There was once a fisherman whose net tore on a sharp rock. A good, clean net—ruined, he thought. He sat on the shore and wept, for he believed he had lost everything. But a woman came and knelt beside him. She took the torn strands and began to tie them to one another, small knots like prayers. The hole became a window, and the window let the sea breathe through the net. That night, when he cast it, the fish slid in as if they had been waiting. Sometimes," he said, looking at Levi, "what we lose becomes the opening where the gift enters."

Levi breathed a satisfied little sigh, as if something in him had been soothed that had never yet learned the word grief.

Markus and Jonah, the twins, propped themselves up on elbows, mirror images with different scrapes on their knees. "What about a race?" one asked. "A fast story."

"A fast story," Jesus said, smiling. "A man had two sandals. One fit and one did not. He threw away the one that pinched and ran in the one that fit, barefoot on the other foot. People laughed to see him lopsided. But he ran like the wind, because the good sandal taught the bare foot where to land." He winked. "Choose what is true and let it teach the part of you that is still learning." Jonah nudged Markus and whispered, "See? I told you, you don't have to be the same to run together."

Nessa had not spoken. She sat with her back straight, the posture of a girl who has been woman of her house too soon. In her lap, her hands were quiet, but Jesus saw how she kept them from wringing.

"And a lamp story?" she asked at last, trying to sound older than she was, and failing, blessedly, for a moment.

"A lamp story," he echoed, as if she had given him a jewel. "A widow had one lamp and very little oil. A storm came, and the night felt endless. She feared the flame would sputter and leave her alone with the wind. So she set the lamp in the window where all could see it. Her neighbors, seeing its small courage, brought a spoon of oil each, and soon the flame stood like a small tree. She thought she would lose her light by sharing it, but the sharing was how it lived." He paused, then added, "Some nights are long. You have made your lamp a window more than once."

Nessa ducked her head, and in that small movement a child peeked out from behind the woman she had been forced to play. She wiped at an eye with the back of her wrist and pretended the dust was fierce tonight.

Tomer, who at fourteen had learned to tie his jaw tight around a houseful of ache, spoke without looking up. "Is there a story where the mother comes back?" He made it sound like a joke that had not found its laughter yet.

Jesus did not flinch away. He drew another line in the dust, a curve that became a seed cupped in a palm. "A farmer saved one perfect seed from a harvest," he said. "He kept it in his pocket all winter. Sometimes he took it out and turned it in his fingers and wept, because what he loved was no longer in the fields. In spring, he knelt and buried the seed and walked away with empty hands. But in time, a green shoot rose. It did not look like what he had lost, and yet when the wind moved through it, he heard the same music. He learned that what is loved is never wasted, and that absence can be a kind of planting."

Tomer's mouth moved; the iron around his throat eased, and he breathed, really breathed, for the first time that day.

Levi, who had been tracing circles on Jesus' tunic with a finger, popped up with a small burst of courage. "Will Photine go away again?" he asked bluntly, because the youngest often holds the truth like a pebble they refuse to drop.

Jesus kissed the top of his head. "She will go where the truth calls her. But what she has given you will not leave. Love is like the sea— you cannot hold it in a jar, but if you stand on the shore, it keeps arriving."

Levi considered this, then nodded solemnly, as if a treaty had been made between him and the tide.

By the wall, Mary touched Photine's brow with two fingers, a benediction learned in no synagogue and older than any book. "When you are afraid," she murmured, "go into the quiet and ask, *What is mine to do?* Then do only that. Peace is not the absence of trouble. It is the root that holds when the wind rises."

Photine lifted her face. In Mary's eyes, she saw not a rival voice but a sister's lamp held out in a long corridor. "Will you walk with me tomorrow?" she asked, not meaning to sound like a girl and hearing the girl in herself anyway.

"I will walk beside you until your step remembers it was born to lead," Mary said softly. "Then I will walk a little behind, to guard your back."

Across the courtyard, Ephram set the linen aside, its blue deep as the coming dawn. Matthew's hand hovered. Their talk had moved from selvedge to pattern, from dye to design. They spoke like men who had found the sweet, unhurried edge of a new thing, and did not need to name it to be warmed by it.

Donel stood at last with his arms no longer crossed. His gaze turned from Ephram to Photine, and for once it was not a measuring look, nor a plea pressed into a demand. He saw the curve of her cheek in lamplight, the unguarded way she listened, the steadiness in her hands. He thought of his children, lighted tonight by stories that did not deny the dark, and he understood that he had tried to build a life with rope made of fear. Fear frays. He could choose a different thread.

He stepped nearer to Jesus and the children and lowered himself to the earth with the small grunt of a tired man. Levi crawled from Jesus' lap into his, satisfied to find that love could cross without falling. Tomer shifted closer until their shoulders brushed. Nessa's fingers sought Donel's sleeve and stayed there. Markus and Jonah lay back and looked up, twin constellations relaxed at last into their sky.

In the center of them all, Jesus closed his hand over the sprig of olive and let the drawn lines in the dust be what they were—boat, net, seed—then smudged them gently with the side of his palm so they became only earth again. He looked at Photine and Mary across the dim room and nodded once, a small, certain blessing.

He rose, gathering his mantle. "We've set our camp just beyond the olive stand," he said, warmth threading the words. "We'll leave you to rest."

Mary stood beside him, her touch light on Photine's arm. "At first light I'll return," she promised, eyes bright. "We'll walk together." Matthew, already drawing his cloak close, offered a quiet nod to Ephram. "Your table was generous. We won't forget it."

Ephram gave a grateful smile that lingered. "And I'll come back as well," he added gently. "There is more to speak, and perhaps…

more to make." Ephram's answering look was unhurried and unmistakably kind.

At the doorway, Jesus bent to the children. Levi, heavy with sleep, reached up without words. Jesus pressed a kiss to the boy's hair. "Little sailor, the sea will still be here in the morning." To Markus and Jonah, who were pretending not to be tired, he said, "Race the dawn only as far as your breath can laugh." Nessa met his gaze, trying not to wring her hands. He touched two fingers to his heart and then to hers, a quiet benediction. Tomer kept his jaw set, but Jesus' hand on his shoulder eased the iron there. "What is planted tonight will rise," he said simply.

They stepped into the night—Jesus first, Mary a soft flame at his side, Matthew turning back once with a small lift of his hand—then their figures thinned into moonlight and the hush of the road beyond the fig trees.

Donel rocked Levi into his arms and straightened. The twins collected their sandals with exaggerated sighs. Nessa fetched her shawl and draped it over her father's free shoulder. Tomer shifted close enough that their sleeves brushed. Donel looked to Photine—not a measuring look, but a clean one, as if a window had been opened in his chest. "We'll take the lower path," he said, voice steady. "The stones are kinder there." He tipped his head to Ephram and his companions. "Thank you for bread and for shelter."

To Photine: "We will see you in the morning." No claim, only the thread of kinship holding.

They went out together into the silvered lane—Tomer guiding, Nessa's fingers tucked in the crook of her father's arm, Markus and Jonah darting ahead and back, Levi's breath warm against Donel's collarbone—until their shapes folded into the slope of the hill and the soft dark kept them.

The house quieted to breathe and the soft rasp of the hearth. The last lamp made a narrow golden pool on the floorboards, where a moth turned slow circles like a prayer. Outside, the silver bowl of the moon tipped, and its light slid along the ridge.

Photine lay down at last, but sleep did not come quickly. She watched the crosshatch of roof beams cut a pocket of stars into the night and felt two things at once: the ache of all that had been taken, and the warmth of something given back without bargain. In the stillness, Mary had taught her to find; she asked what was hers to do. The answer rose quiet and entire, like a spring relieved after drought.

In the morning, voices would rise in the marketplace. In the morning, she would speak. But for now—here—this was the miracle: women who would not trade their voices for safety, men learning to set jealousy down like an outworn cloak, children held by stories that promised they were not abandoned to the wind.

The ember in the hearth breathed once and settled. The night held its long, gentle breath. In that fragile weave of hour and ember, something strong was being knotted—thread to thread, heart to heart.

The house had grown quiet, the fire reduced to coals, but Photine's mind would not quiet. Mary's patient firmness lingered in her ears—gentle, unyielding, a kind of authority rising from stillness rather than command. Ephram's and Matthew's laughter, their talk of bolts and patterns, still warmed the corners of the room like the last heat of the hearth. Even Donel, who carried his care in tight, careful lines, had softened, suggesting that the worst of the gossip might be only smoke after all.

Yet what held her most were the children—how Jesus had turned toward them with stories woven from their own lives, simple enough to hold in their hands, yet layered with truths they would carry for years. Tomer's eyes had widened at the tale of the seed hidden in the soil. Nessa had leaned forward when he spoke of the lamp and its shared oil, and Markus had straightened with pride at the parable of running together, not against one another. The twins had whispered to each other even as they listened. Photine could tell they, too, were caught by the rhythm of his voice.

She lay awake long after the others had drifted into sleep, staring at the low ceiling, her breath catching with a mixture of awe and dread. For if such stories could stir children, what would they do in the open square? What would happen when the townspeople, the merchants, the watchful Romans heard him speak with the same piercing clarity?

Morning came quickly, the first light stretching over the olive stand and spilling across the road. Whispers moved ahead of them into the marketplace: the prophet from Judea was still here, and he would be at the well. Photine tied her head covering with trembling hands, aware that this day was not hers alone anymore. Her story had become their story, her testimony a flame that could either draw or consume.

The morning light slipped through the cracks of Ephram's shutters, thin as threads drawn across the floor. Photine rose quietly. She found Ephram already awake, sleeves rolled past his elbows, carrying out the last of the jars to be rinsed at the basin.

Mara was humming softly as she gathered the bowls. Her movements were brisk, but there was a brightness in her eyes Photine had not seen before. Ketziah and Sarah knelt beside her, hands moving quickly as they scraped crumbs and stacked baskets, whispering to each other with the half-hidden laughter of sisters.

Photine joined them, sweeping the rushes from the floor into a neat pile. "It feels as if the air is different this morning," she said.

"It is," Mara replied, straightening with a jar in her hands. "The whole town will know by midday. Word spreads faster than fire when it is about prophets and wells."

Ephram set a jar on the bench with more force than needed, though not in anger. "They'll come with curiosity first," he said, wiping his hands on his tunic. "But curiosity is a short-lived friend. Romans don't care for crowds, and neither do our own rulers when they aren't the ones gathering them."

Ketziah stilled, her hands clutching a basket's edge. "Do you think they'll come for him? For us?"

Photine met her gaze. "They will come," she said simply. "But whether they come to listen or to silence, I do not know."

For a moment, the small room was quiet but for the sound of Sarah's sweeping and the faint clatter of pottery. Then Mara exhaled, long and steady. "If he speaks today, it won't be like last night. Everyone will hear. Not just children. Not just us. His words will either heal this place or divide it further."

Photine felt the truth of it settle in her chest. She remembered the parables he had woven for the children—the lamp that needed shared oil, the seed that had to vanish before new life could begin—and wondered how such gentle words could carry such danger.

Still, she found her lips forming the thought before she could stop it. "Perhaps division is needed before healing. A wound must be opened and cleansed before it can close."

Ephram turned toward her, his eyes shadowed with both admiration and fear. "Then may God grant us courage to bear the opening."

Ephram's warning about the Romans hung in the air, heavier than the dust they were sweeping from the floor. Photine's hands slowed on the broom, her breath catching as memory surged.

The broom shook in her hands. Fear coiled hot in her stomach, tightening her throat. But braided into that fear was anger, fierce and steady. And strangest of all—woven through both like a silver thread—was the lingering calm from the night before. The quiet gravity in Mary's words as she urged the women to find stillness. The way Jesus's gaze seemed to pierce through terror and kindle hope in the same instant.

It was dizzying, this tangle of peace and fury, grief and courage. She felt as though her soul itself had become a battlefield, one side urging her to tremble, the other urging her to rise.

Her thoughts turned, almost against her will, toward Donel and the children. She pictured Nessa with her serious, watchful eyes; Tomer trying to stand taller than his years; little Levi's eager embrace when he had seen her in the market. They had been part of the life she once thought she had lost forever. Yet here they were, drawn into the same story, standing on the edge of whatever this day would bring.

The sound of laughter drew her back. Sarah had said something wry, and Ketziah answered with a shake of her head, the two of them grinning in that sisterly way that stitched fear into something bearable. Ephram caught Photine's gaze across the room—and she wondered if he, too, carried this strange mixture of dread and peace.

Mara set down a jar with a firm hand. "The Romans may come," she said, as if naming the fear aloud would rob it of some of its power. "But we will not scatter. Not today. If truth is to be spoken, then let it be spoken in the open."

Photine pressed her lips together, not trusting her voice. A part of her still longed to run, to hide, to vanish before the iron boots closed in again. Yet another part knew that if she fled now, she would never stop fleeing.

And beneath it all, like the pulse of a far-off drum, came the echo of his words: *living water, springing up within.*

Photine's knuckles whitened against the broom handle. She felt the words rising in her throat before she could stop them.

"They've taken everything from me once already," she said, her voice rougher than she intended.

The others stilled, eyes turning toward her. "Romans—Mordecai with them—marched into Akrabbim and left nothing standing. My husband, my son, even the child Lois carried beneath her roof… gone."

The silence that followed was heavy, broken only by the shuffle of Sarah's feet as she drew closer.

Photine swallowed, forcing herself to go on. "I thought if I stayed hidden, if I kept my head down, maybe I could survive what was left. But even now, the sound of their boots…" She shook her head. "It is as though I am standing in that fire again, waiting for everything I love to be torn away."

Mara set down the jar she was carrying and stepped nearer, her eyes steady. "And yet you are still here," she said softly.

"Yes," Photine breathed. "Still here. And I don't know whether it is cowardice or courage that has kept me." Her voice cracked, surprising her. "All I know is that when I hear him speak—when I hear Mary remind us of the light within us—I feel something that frightens me more than the soldiers ever did. I feel as though I could stop running."

The words hung in the room, raw and unpolished, as though she had peeled her chest open before them all. Ephram's eyes softened, and Sarah touched Photine's arm, not with pity but with quiet solidarity.

Mara gave a small nod, her jaw firm. "Then hold on to that. Fear will come—anger will come—but if you have found even a drop of peace, guard it like water in the desert. Today, you will need it."

Photine lowered her gaze, blinking back the sting in her eyes. She had not meant to speak so openly, but now that the words had left her, she could not call them back. And perhaps that was the truest thing of all: she was tired of silence, tired of carrying the weight alone.

For the first time in many years, she did not feel alone.

The silence stretched, thick as the smoke that once hung over Akrabbim. Photine's chest rose and fell unevenly.

It was Ketziah who finally broke it, her tone gentler than usual, almost playful. "Well," she said, glancing toward the doorway where Matthew had passed earlier, "at least the Romans aren't the only ones marching about this place. Did you see the way Ephram and that disciple leaned together last night? As if the world could end and they'd still be talking about threads and dye."

Sarah let out a low laugh, muffling it quickly with her hand. "I thought the same. Ephram hasn't smiled like that in months."

Mara arched a brow, but her lips twitched despite herself. "It was more than cloth they were comparing, I think."

Photine looked up, startled at first, then found herself smiling despite the ache in her chest.

The memory of the two men bent over the table returned to her: Ephram's eyes lit with interest, Matthew's easy laughter answering him, the way conversation had flowed between them as naturally as water finding its path.

"It was… good to see," Photine admitted, her voice softer now. "Ephram has carried more weight than most know. To see him… lightened, even for an evening, it gave me hope."

"Hope," Sarah echoed, nudging Ketziah with her elbow. "Or something stronger."

The women laughed quietly, the tension in the room loosening like a knot undone. Ephram, returning just then with another jar in his hands, paused at the sound and eyed them warily.

"What mischief are you stirring now?" he asked, though his cheeks betrayed a faint color that only fueled their amusement.

"Nothing at all," Mara answered smoothly, her expression composed. "Only speaking of how well the threads of one life can be woven with another."

Photine bent her head, hiding her smile as the broom brushed across the floor again. For a brief moment, the fear of the morning lifted, replaced by something lighter, fragile but real.

Ephram opened his mouth to protest further, but before he could, the door creaked open.

Morning light spilled across the floor as Matthew stepped inside, Mary just behind him.

"Peace be with you," Matthew said, his smile easy, his voice still carrying the resonance of last night's laughter.

For the first time, Ephram lost his composure. He straightened too quickly, nearly upsetting the jar in his hands. "Peace—yes, yes— peace be with you," he stammered, his voice oddly high. His face flushed as he fumbled to set the jar back on the bench with exaggerated care.

Mary's eyes flicked between him and Matthew; Photine swore she caught the faintest glimmer of amusement in the tilt of her lips.

That was all it took.

Mara coughed into her hand but failed to disguise the chuckle rising in her throat. Sarah gave way first, laughter bubbling over until she doubled against the wall. Ketziah joined in, her giggles spilling bright as a spring. Even Photine's own laughter escaped before she could smother it, spilling into the room like sunlight breaking through a storm cloud.

Ephram turned scarlet, his gaze fixed firmly on the floor, but Matthew only looked puzzled and a little concerned. "Did I… interrupt something?" he asked.

"No," Mara managed, wiping her eyes, "not at all."

"Only everything," Ruth added, her laughter still shaking her shoulders.

Mary's calm presence seemed to settle the moment. Ephram busied himself with sweeping the same corner of the floor that had already been swept twice, his back stiff with both embarrassment and unspoken delight.

Photine's laughter softened into a smile, lingering long after the sound had faded. For a moment, the weight of Rome, of Mordecai, of the day to come, felt lighter. The walls of the room held not fear, but shared joy.

And outside, in the distance, the hum of the gathering crowd at the well began to rise.

CHAPTER 22
THE WELL AND THE HEARTH

Outside, the village breathed in the morning: vendors setting out bowls of figs, a boy shouting a price, the distant creak of a cart. A Roman patrol moved along the main way with that slow, confident stride of men; their helmets and straps picked up the light and slid past like an assertion. For a long blink, the market's chatter thinned — scales paused mid-tink, hands rested on wares — and a small, tight hush settled over the path.

Photine felt that hush the way a draught brushes the back of the neck. Old reflexes rose: the habit of shrinking when soldiers came, the careful folding of shame into the shoulders. Fear walked beside her then, obliging but not steering. She breathed, set her jaw, and stepped forward anyway.

Around her, the household moved with the soft precision of people who had practiced being ready. Ketziah wrapped a loaf; Sarah handed Photine a ladle; Ephram tucked extra cups into a basket. Mara slipped a fig into her palm, and Mary, meeting Photine's eyes, pressed her forehead once against hers — a private benediction in the middle of the street. They stepped into the lane with the calm of those who had learned how to prepare for a witness.

"We should go," Ketziah said without ceremony, folding the loaf into a cloth as if it were the only sensible thing to do.

Photine found herself watching the small economy of readiness. Sarah pressed a ladle into her palm. "We'll need supplies where we stand," she said. "Witnesses get thirsty." The words were practical and oddly tender, and Photine felt them sink like a cool stone in hot water.

"You're sure?" Mary asked quietly, not looking for permission but for company. Photine met her eyes, the same plain gaze that had steadied her at the stall. "I'm ready," she said. "Not because I'm brave. Because being small has made my feet ache." She folded the ladle into the basket, tightened the scarf at her throat, and let the heaviness of the morning settle into something like purpose.

They moved out together then, stepping into the lane with the calm of people who know their tasks and the courage to do them. The market's breath rose and fell around them; fear kept pace at Photine's elbow but did not lead.

Halfway to the well, a group of men idled in the shade and fell silent when Mary and Photine approached. "This isn't a woman's place," the steward said. "Nor a Samaritan's, to parade a Judean through our water."

"The well belongs to Jacob," Mary replied. "He dug it for thirst, not titles." She tipped her chin toward Photine. "She remembers being thirsty."

Photine met their scorn without apology. "I will not shrink for your comfort," she said, voice steady. They scoffed and moved on.

The well was filling. People stood in small knots, waiting for the rabbi. Jesus had not yet entered the shade, but the mood had shifted.

Photine stood where everyone would see her. Mary to her right; Sarah and Ketziah at the edges, making room; Mara where the nervous could stop and ask. From the lower path, Donel came with the children: Tomer alert at his side, Markus and Jonah bickering behind, Nessa holding Levi's hand. Donel carried a folded mat — the quiet message that they would stay.

He met Photine's eyes without claim. She nodded. The risk and the work of the day were agreed upon between them.

Hoofbeats, then again, the patrol paused nearby and watched as the crowd grew in number. Then Jesus arrived. No platform. No fanfare. He stood at the edge of the olive shade and let his voice find the dust.

"You search the sky for signs," he said. "But the harvest is not a star. It's your neighbor's face.

Lift your eyes."

Mary's hand rested on Photine's shoulder. Nessa watched like a girl choosing a door. Jesus spoke in plain, piercing stories. Those who had come to sneer leaned in.

When the murmurs fell, he looked over the crowd. "You've asked for signs," he said, "but the sign is near you. It looks like a neighbor you thought you knew." He turned and fixed his gaze on Photine. "Tell them what changed."

For a second, her name felt sudden in his mouth, not a question but a summons, and something in her tightened, a small, startled flutter beneath the ribs. She steadied herself against it, breathed once, and stepped forward.

She watched the Roman patrol at the lane's edge, helmets like small moons, the horses' flanks a slow, indifferent drum, and felt the square tighten. For a beat, she measured the air: too sharp to name an enemy outright, too full of truth to swallow it. She decided to let the story bear the shape of what had happened, not the names.

"So much was lost," she began, and the crowd leaned because stories travel the way bread does, shared and warm. "There was a night the fields smelled of smoke, and men came with torches. Things were taken that cannot be counted: a roof, a name, a child's laugh. We learned then how to bow our shoulders so the wind would not strike the lamp."

She let that sit, then spoke into the quiet. "There were hands that held coins and hands that pointed. I remember scales that clicked where my worth was named, and roads where faces I loved were led away. After that, hiding felt safer."

Her voice didn't accuse a troop or shout a governor's name; it placed the hurt where people who had seen it could find it. Those who had bartered, bought, or sold, or watched as others did, heard themselves in the language. Those who feared the soldiers heard what they needed to hear without being dragged into an open quarrel.

"I know the stories," she said. "Some I told myself. Yesterday, a man asked me for water. He asked truthfully about my life, and I spoke. He did not step back. So hear me: I am not a rumor. I am not only the worst thing I've done. I am your neighbor."

She looked across faces. "To the men who prefer me quiet: I'm not instructing you, I'm witnessing. To the women who watch from the sidelines: I see you; I was you. If I have wronged you, say it, and I will do what I can to set it right. If you carry a story that is not yours, put it down."

"I am still afraid," she added, "but I will not hide. Today I will draw water in the coolness of early daylight. Tomorrow I'll bring bread. If you've shied from the well as I did, come sit with me."

Jesus nodded. "That's what living water sounds like — truth that doesn't look away. If you want a sign, start small. Before sundown, do one thing you have avoided: give water to someone you've kept distant, return what you owe, speak true instead of slant. You don't harvest by staring at the sky."

A steward muttered, "Words are easy." Jesus answered calmly: "She told the truth and did not hide. That is where the kingdom begins." He motioned. "Stand here with Mary. Let them ask."

One of the women who had earlier challenged Photine stepped forward, cheeks damp. "I judged you," she said. "I'm sorry."

"Thank you," Photine answered simply.

Mary's hand at her back. "We're not moving her," she told anyone who still bristled. "We're making room."

The Roman officer watched, said nothing, and slowly eased his horse back. People began to move, jars, cloths, a strip of shade, practical kindness, unshowy and sufficient. Donel set Levi near and pointed where the children could sit. Tomer folded the family mat. Ephram and Matthew arranged a shade cloth and a pot. The work was practical and kind; therefore, enough.

When the crowd thinned to prepare a shared meal, Jesus spoke by the low lamp. "No one lights a lamp and hides it under a basket. If God gives you light, put it where it gives the house light. If you measure others by contempt, it spills back on you. Give mercy; you'll find you have more of it."

He nodded toward Photine. "Yesterday, she hid. Today she stands here. That is a lamp on a stand."

That evening, small reconciliations happened quietly: a trader returned a coin to a widow; two men who had not spoken in a year moved their mats together. Not everyone was there to witness, and not everyone would take the water offered that day. Still, love here was not a call to arms. Do not pick a fight where a hand can offer bread. Plant the seed; tend it; wait for its season. Often, the harvest comes after patience, not spectacle.

The Roman patrol turned its horses and left. As the light thinned, Jesus lifted his hand in blessing. "We go at sundown. Keep what began here at your well and your tables."

At the edge, Donel waited. "We're heading home," he told Photine. "You're welcome to come, if you choose."

She did not hurry. When she spoke, the words fell soft, part question, part claim. "I will come tonight—if you'll have me." She let the pause hang, then added, quieter, to Ephram, "I'll still work at the stall when I can." The first line sought permission; the second laid down a promise.

Ephram nodded. "There's room."

Mary's hand pressed against her back. "You're not trading one cage for another."

They gathered their things. Mary and Matthew would walk Jesus back toward the olives and the road beyond. Donel shifted Levi to the other shoulder; Nessa took the mat without argument.

Photine looked at the well, the lamp still lit on the stone, then followed her family down the lane.

They took the lower path beneath fig orchards where the stones were kinder, the air smelling of crushed leaves and warm dust. The town carried the day with it, women lingering at the well, men drawn near, a rabbi's voice threading the shade, so when Photine and Nessa fell a step behind the others, it felt like stepping into a quieter beat of the same song.

Nessa carried the mat's rough corner in her hand, the weight steadied against her hip; her shoulders squared as if she'd practiced courage. She kept her head down for a few paces, then blurted, the words tumbling out the way a twelve-year-old's apology sometimes does: "I didn't know it was—how much you lost. I thought you were…different. I'm sorry for the things I said. For the look. For making you hide."

Photine stopped; the apology landed small and bright. For a moment, she simply looked at the girl who had kept the house and then turned away from it to find a new truth. Her face softened. She reached and straightened Nessa's shawl with her trembling thumb. "Thank you," she said, voice low. "That helps more than you know."

They walked on, fingers almost brushing, and rejoined the family at Donel's door, where the room was the same in shape but different in its air.

Photine coaxed the cold coals back into a thread of flame with a reed fan, then slipped off her sandals and set them by the door. "You kept the house well," she said to Nessa, plain and true.

The girl bristled for praise and softened instead. "I did what needed doing," Nessa said.

Donel sat Levi down and loosened his sandals. The twins collapsed against the wall like sacks of lentils.

They ate a quiet meal: barley thickened to porridge, a smear of olive paste, a torn loaf shared round so everyone could take a piece. The twins spun half a story, then dropped it for the food.

Tomer stooped to test the table leg and, with a muttered complaint, set it right without being told. Donel found a small wooden comb tucked in a corner and laid it by the door like a small offering. Photine traced the tally marks in Nessa's ledger, tidy, careful, and met the girl's eye.

"Space is only for what you can count," Nessa grumbled, half-defensive, half-proud.

"And also for what changes you," Photine said, and the simplicity of the answer seemed to fit in the room like a second loaf.

When the plates had been cleared, the children moved into practiced motions: Tomer shepherded the twins to sweep, Markus and Jonah stacked the bowls, and Nessa handed out small flasks of water, eyes bright with the responsibility of it. Levi yawned and was tucked beneath a thin blanket while the others made the pallet neat. The house thinned to the soft sounds of work finishing and small bodies settling—murmured jokes, the scrape of a broom, and a whispered instruction over Levi's shoulder.

Photine stood, smoothing the edge of her tunic. "We'll speak plainly," she said to Donel, the words a quiet promise rather than a challenge. "I came because the children are mine to love, and because what was bent needs tending. I won't speak shame over myself, and I won't be treated as property. If I stay, it will be because I choose it — to work, to teach, to keep the lamp."

He came close to meeting her as an equal at last. His face, which had worn caution like armor, softened into something older and more honest. "I wanted less trouble," he said slowly, voice raw with an admission he'd long denied. "So I made rules and smaller places for myself—hard edges instead of work I was afraid to do. I blamed you for what I feared would befall the house, and in doing so, I failed the very people I wanted to protect." He swallowed. "I was frightened, and I let that fear become a shape I forced on you. I'm sorry for that."

He reached and offered his hand in the open space between them, not possessive but steady. "I don't want to own you or to paper over what's true. I want to see you — really see you — and learn how to keep this house together with your hands and your voice. If you stay, it will be because you choose it. If you leave, you'll go with my blessing, not my blame."

Photine looked at his hand for a long beat, then placed her own inside it. The contact was small and ordinary — warmth against warmth — and in that simple grip, something like a beginning settled between them.

They stepped out into the night together, into the fig-scented air. The children's laughter drifted behind the shuttered door like a ribbon. In the yard, the sky was a cold black bowl fretted with stars. Donel, holding Photine's hand, increased the pressure, not loud but steady. "I'm afraid," he admitted, low, "of the market's talk. Of the way people set value by rumor."

"So am I," she said. "But I won't be erased to keep you comfortable. I'll stand at the stall when it helps, sit at the well when we need water, and I will keep learning and seeking what makes us whole—because some things only change when we look at them squarely."

He nodded, and in the pause that followed, they made the small plan: who would fetch oil for a widow, who would mind the stall if she went north, how the twins would be taught to carry a burden and to share it. Nothing grand—just the careful map of a household learning to hold one another.

When they went back inside, the house smelled of cooling grain, and the lamp burned low. The children were tucked and breathing; Nessa lay already half-asleep, the twins curled at her feet. Photine eased down onto the straw mat beside Donel, close enough that their shoulders almost touched. He watched her for a long, quiet breath, the hard lines of the day softening, and then reached up to press one careful kiss to her forehead—a small, almost ashamed benediction. The night drew them close like a seam.

Before sleep, Photine lay awake a few breaths and listened to a psalm rising from the olives, to the distant scrape of a cart, to the road that never quite stopped moving. Mary's touch at the well still warmed her skin. Jesus's words turned over in her head like a coin she wanted to study — *lamp on a stand, start small, give water to the one you have kept at a distance.* He had pointed her toward the north, to a hillside near Capernaum: come if the road tugs at you, he'd said, and keep your ears open.

She thought of what she might find there — news of a man,
maybe, or an answer, or simply more of the truth she'd been learning
to speak. It was not a promise of reunion so much as a promise of
listening: to learn, to name, to be present where things were said aloud
and mended. For now, she would keep the lamp and the work; she
would teach the children to count and to care. But if the road called —
if a traveler bore a name she knew, or a trader spoke of a man from
her past — she would be ready to go—to meet what needed meeting.

Morning would come with bread and cloth and more chances to
be neighborly. For tonight, the house breathed around her, and the
small, true work of beginning again settled into her bones.

CHAPTER 23
THE HILLSIDE OF RETURN

It had been several months since the voice rose at Jacob's well. The market had settled into a new rhythm, and Photine's days were steadied by work: bread before dawn, a measure kept honest, hands that mended what was cracked. Ephram's stall was more than a trade now; it was a place where people learned to speak, then pay, then pass on. Mary, who had stayed with Jesus through his travels, was absent these weeks; her steadiness lived in the space she'd left behind, but her feet were on the road and not at the stall.

When word came that Jesus would teach on a hillside near Capernaum, it moved through the market like the wind. Ephram shrugged, shut the shutters, and said, practical as ever, "Come. It's a long road, but you'll come back with an answer or none — and answers are better than the same old grief." The line landed on Photine like a small permission she hadn't known she needed.

She did not tell Donel right away. Saying anything aloud felt suddenly dangerous, the risk of his voice closing around her like a rule, the memory of being told to hide so the house would look respectable. Fear sat with her like a second shadow: would he command her to stay, insisting the world be safe for his children? She folded the idea inward, let it warm, then offered it out the way you do with something fragile.

"Jesus will be teaching on the hillside near Capernaum," she said finally, testing the syllables. "There's a gathering. I thought—perhaps you should go…with me. Ephram will also travel to hear him speak." The sentence came out small, half an invitation, half a proposal. Donel blinked, the line at his mouth tightening. He opened to object, then closed it again.

Tomer, who had been listening from the doorway with the restless attention of youth, spoke up before Donel could frame a refusal. "Let me go," he said, sudden and earnest. "I want to hear him. I want to see. I can protect on the travel." His face was all forwardness; the offer was an honest wanting.

Donel looked from his son to Photine, and something in his chest that had been brittle seemed to give. The house was theirs to hold, he thought, but the children needed roots and reasons both.

"If you go," he said to Tomer, voice slow and steady, "you go with sense. Don't follow crowds.

Listen. Keep your head and your feet together on the road."

Tomer's grin was immediate and grateful. Photine let out a breath she hadn't realized she'd been holding, the small permission settling like a stone into place.

They left before the sun had pulled itself free of the hills, the air thick with the smell of crushed fig leaves and the dust that clung to sandals. Ephram walked beside Photine, Tomer at his shoulder — fifteen, all forwardness and questions — a small pack slung across his back. Their party threaded out of Sychar in the thin light: women with pitchers balanced on their hips, a shepherd with his staff, a trader leading a donkey burdened with bolts of cloth, a few traders leading donkeys afoot. The road did not march straight; it bent like a ribbon, curling around terraces and stone walls, climbing where the hills demanded and falling toward the valleys where streams still remembered rain.

On the first day, they moved through olive groves and terraces cut into the hill, much like steps. The ground underfoot was hard-packed limestone; loose stones rolled under a careless foot. At a wayside well, an old woman offered flatbread wrapped in cloth to the passing crowd; Tomer accepted it as if it were a feast. "Where are you bound?" she asked, squinting at their faces. When Photine told her, the woman's mouth made a small O of recognition. "He's a man who speaks straight," she said. "Good for the road. Keep your ears open and your tongue folded."

They passed shepherds with thin flocks, boys throwing rocks at goats, a handful of merchants with bolts of cloth, their packs smelling faintly of dye. People called the news to each other: "He's to teach on the lakeside!" "They say he heals!" "The Romans are steady as stones at the crossroads." A trader who had once bought cloth from Ephram leaned over his pack and gave the merchant a tight nod. "You'll find the road crowded," he warned. "Keep the boy near. Crowds pull on boys."

Tomer, who had heard some of Jesus' words at the well, peppered Ephram with follow-ups: "Will he tell the same stories again? Will he say the thing about giving water to the ones we avoid? Do people really change when someone says those things?"

Ephram folded the question into the rhythm of the road. "He returns to the same pictures until they land lamps, seeds, the neighbor at your door. He makes plain work into a kind of truth. Listen first; let it sink in. And keep your feet steady on the road."

Night fell the first evening under a sky like black cloth studded with dull coin. They slept in a rough fold beneath a fig tree, the children curled against one another, the donkeys huffing in the dark. Someone made a small fire, and men traded stories about fishermen who had come from the lake with strange reports. "He spoke down where the water meets the shore," one said. "Fishermen who've seen storms calmer than they expected say the man's words stick." The talk went round in sleepy circles; Tomer's eyes were heavy but bright with the promise of morning.

The second day, the high terraces gave way to gentler slopes. The groves thinned and the land opened; they crossed a shallow plain where farmers had planted barley in neat lines. The air grew warmer, and the scent shifted from fig to a thin, sharp perfume of wild sage.

Toward noon, they passed a caravan carrying salt and amphorae; a merchant with sun-browned cheeks traded a sliver of dried fish for news. "Capernaum is full," he said. "People sleep in the open where they can. Bring water and a mat; there's little shade near the shore."

Tomer listened to everything as if the words would stitch themselves into the story he wanted to tell later. "Do you think he remembers the ones he named 'neighbor'?" he asked suddenly, voice small with the weight of wanting to understand. Photine ruffled his hair, steadier than she felt.

"He remembers," she said. "That's what I think. He makes room where there was none."

They fell into a rhythm of walking and resting: one hour on, then a short break to fill waterskins from a clear trickle, then on again. Conversation broke into little clusters. An older man from the north, traveling alone, told them how fishermen spoke of the hillside gatherings near the lake:

"He asks hard things," the man said. "Not laws, exactly. He asks people how they live them out." His eyes were tired in a way that fit the road; his words planted a small caution in Ephram's mind.

On the third morning, coming up over a low ridge, the whole world opened. Below them, the Sea of Galilee shone like a blue plate set in a green bowl. The slope to the lake was dotted with people already spread out on rugs and stones, children running between legs, women shading infants with strips of woven cloth. The odor there was of water and sun and the oily tang of fish drying on racks. A chorus of voices rose and fell: vendors cried their wares, men called for space, someone laughed, sharp and clean.

They moved into the crowd, finding a spot on a warmed stone where the grass flattened to their knees. Tomer's hands were busy folding and refolding a strip of cloth; his face had the cavalry bravado of youth, but when he looked at the hillside and then at Photine, there was a steadiness in his gaze that matched the day's weight. Ephram set down their small pack with a soft thud and, standing, clapped Tomer's shoulder. "Keep your feet," he said. "Listen."

Around them, the people settled into waiting like birds roosting. The road behind had become a long thread of travel — traders and pilgrims, donkeys and children — and now the world here narrowed to the slope, the stone, the lake, and the man who would speak.

The hillside itself was a green bruise at the edge of the world. People settled on stones and rugs wherever they could find purchase. The talk softened into the waiting-breath of a crowd about to be taught: a string of voices, a rake of sandals, and the steady, patient shift of animals being tethered.

When Jesus stepped into the shade, he did not stand like a man who expected applause. He moved as if he were simply taking his place at a family table. He looked over the masses — at the fishermen, the women with children, the men who had come because a rumor nudged curiosity — and then he spoke plainly.

He taught with images anyone who had ever tended a lamp or a field would know: seeds cast into earth, lamps put on stands, eyes lifted to neighbors' faces rather than to the sky. People leaned; some folded their arms and tried not to lean at all. His words were spare and sharp, and at their edges they caught people who had long been used to hiding.

After a while, his voice softened, and he spoke in a way that turned a teaching into a summons. "Who among you carries lost things?" he asked. "Who among you has a wound that keeps you small? Come forward. We will not shame you for the place where the hurt begins, but we will name the work that mends."

A hush fell like a hand over the hillside. People looked at one another, and then, modestly, one by one, some rose — those whose burdens were public in a way that only neighbors knew. Some came because the invitation was too kind to refuse; some stayed because their shame lived loudest in their own chest.

Photine felt the call as a small tremor under her ribs. She had not planned to stand; she had not wanted eyes in which pity might be mistaken for understanding. Ephram's glance at her back was even and steady. Tomer stood at her shoulder, all forwardness and fierce small courage, his hand searching for the edge of her scarf as if to steady her.

She rose.

She did not walk forward alone. Ephram fell in beside her; Tomer fell just behind, the two of them a quiet guard. A few neighbors shifted closer, offering the brief, practical touches people give one another in marketplaces and courts—an adjustment of a shawl, a palm at the elbow—small acts that meant, *we see you*. When she reached the front, Jesus smiled in the way the sun does: not loud, only unmistakable.

"You have come, then," he said, and his look found her as if he had been waiting for that single footstep. There was no performative pause in his voice—only a clear, steady recognition. "You carry a long night in you," he added, softer, not asking for proof. "You have come with hurt and with courage both. Speak plainly; we will not let your words be turned into weapons or gossip. Tell us what ails your heart."

Photine breathed. At first, her voice was a narrow thread; then it widened with the memory of so many small humiliations and the one great fissure that had changed everything. She began where the ache began to have a shape — her father's leaving, the slow unmooring of a home that had been held together by hands too tired to speak. She told them how, in the hunger left behind, she had learned cunning as a tool: slipping a coin when no one watched, taking a favor and calling it payment, enjoying, with a secret and shameful flare, the small triumph of outbidding Zimri at market. She did not spare herself—she spoke of bending another man's pity into a vow so she could step away from the women's house, of words used as barter until they bought a roof. Then she spoke of the night the smoke came, of Ezra dying, and of Elior gone, names dropping like stones she could finally set down. The hillside held it all—no pity, no cruelty—only the plainness of what had been done and what had been lost. When she finished, she felt raw, like a wound rinsed with cold water, honest and aching in the open air.

Jesus listened as people listened in the open — patient, letting the air hold what she had let down. Then, he offered a word that was more balm than judgment: "Tell it plainly. Let the telling be its own easing; we will not turn your pain into a token for the market."

After a breath that felt like a small eternity, he added, "There are places where the road goes north and leaves people a long way from home. Sometimes roads carry men who are lost — and sometimes they carry those who go seeking. If someone here bears a name from your past, let them step forward."

The crowd stirred. A few heads swiveled, searching the sea of faces and the backs of shoulders. Photine's heart took a single sharp beat like a bird that had seen a shape it knew from childhood.

At the very edge of the people, a man stood, worn the way a traveler is worn, his jaw shaded with the unkempt beard, his hands callused from work, his cloak patched at the elbow. The years sat hard on him — a sunburn line, a freckle of scar at the knuckle — but his eyes were arrestingly the same. For a heartbeat, neither of them saw the other; then he half-bowed, and his voice found her name with the ease of something remembered.

"Photine?"

It was not a recognition born of rumor. It was a sound that carried small details home — the way she tilted her head, the nick in her left thumb from a millstone. Her hand went to the olive wood splinter in her scarf out of habit, and the man's gaze dropped to where the grain glinted like a secret between them.

"You," she said, and the word had the texture of gravel and of river—familiar, hard-worn, true.

It was Zimri. It was her brother, the boy who had once run the lane with her, and it was, somehow, in the way of the world, also a man who had been broken and remade by a road. He had heard of this rabbi; he had come because he had heard a rumor that a woman from his village stood in daylight and would not be hidden.

Their meeting was not cinematic. There was no sudden collapse in embraces. Photine crossed the small space and stopped a measure away. Zimri's hands trembled; he was older and newer at asking for forgiveness than the man Photine had imagined. He let his eyes do the talking first — a raw, pinched thing that held more than regret. When he spoke, his voice was flat with the memory of a boy who had been given too much to bear. "I was angry. Father was gone, and the house sagged. I was fourteen and full of blame. I thought I could fix it with a bargain. I arranged it, married you off to a man twice your age, sent you as far as the road would carry you. I thought distance would keep the shame out of our door. I was wrong. I did worse than leave; I helped to sell you into a life you did not choose. I have been wrong. I ask—will you hear me?"

Photine felt the hillside tilt under the weight of it. She had held her own catalogue of sins — the coins slipped into her palm, the bargains, the manipulations that had been both armor and vice. She stepped forward into the hush, measured and dry-eyed. "You banished me," she said, not a blade but a hinge opening. "You made a choice that hurt me. If we begin again, it will be with work. You will help. You will not excuse yourself with whatever you were given as a boy, and I will shed the cloak of shame received as a girl."

Photine felt, for a flinch of a moment, the old, foolish hope, that she might look out over the sea of faces and see her father there, that some prodigal return would fold the years up like a blanket. The hope faded as quickly as it came. Standing in the open air, with Zimri raw and steady before her, she understood she had already found what she needed: a reckoning, a heart willing to do the work, and a place that would keep asking for steadiness rather than excuse.

Without ceremony, she slipped one of the olive-wood shards from the knot at her throat and laid it into Zimri's open palm. He looked at it, puzzled, then met her eyes. "From Father," she said, the words small, "before he left." It was less a claim than a handing-over — a way to say the past had been held and that pieces of it could be used now to mend.

Zimri closed his fingers around the splinter as if feeling its grain could teach him how to be steadier. The action, simple, almost private, sealed something between them. Around them, the hillside breathed; the covenant they'd set down would be kept not by grand gestures but by mornings of breath and of repair.

The hillside held that exchange. It was not a wiping of the past; it was a ledger opened at last — entries to be paid in sweat and steadiness rather than in easy words.

Jesus stepped back a little — a small gesture of space and permission. Then he said to the hillside, "Where two have been separated by rumor and road, the first work is not to ask why, but to sit and listen. If you come with hurt, do not come to score it. Come to lay bread."

When the teaching ended and the crowd eased like breath out of a body, there were small acts: a pot of stew passed down a row, a fisherman offering a spare pan, a child given a scrap of bread.

Photine and Zimri slipped to the edge of the crowd and walked together in a small, deliberate circle to find a place out of the way— close enough that their voices wouldn't carry, far enough that they could speak without the hill eavesdropping. Their talk was slow and careful at first, the sort of sentences that stitch: where he had gone, what he had seen, what he would do now. Tomer fell in step a pace behind them, half-son, half-protector, his eyes flicking from the pair to the slope.

From the center of the gathering, Ephram caught sight of Matthew across a scatter of rugs and threaded through the crowd with the easy purpose of a man used to getting things done. He lowered his voice when he reached him. "There'll be work if this becomes a thing—more cloth, a proper place of shade for mothers. Can you put the word out? Tell the ones who keep lists, or write a note if you must."

Matthew's eyes brightened; he tucked the idea away like a new entry. "I'll tell those who keep records and a few traders who run the road," he said. The two of them bent close, heads together for a quiet plan, while the hillside hummed around their small conspiracy.

When the talk thinned and people began to fold their rugs and rise, the moment felt finished but not erased. The teaching had landed and now unhooked itself into ordinary plans: who would fetch extra cloth, who would lend a pot, who would make shade. As the crowd drifted down the slope and the last fingers of light slid off the lake, the road home already looked different. It was not that everything was forgiven; it was that the possibility of repair had been placed among them, and anyone who saw it could choose whether to carry it.

They left the hillside as the sun tipped toward afternoon, the crowd thinning into a long ribbon that unspooled back toward carts and donkeys and the slow beat of the road. The lake shrank behind them to a bright smear; the world narrowed, again, to feet and dust and the small business of moving on.

Photine kept pace at first, the talk of the hill still turning in her head. She answered Tomer's quick questions with short, careful sentences and let Ephram take the lead through a stretch of rutted track where rain had chewed the earth into a washboard. But halfway down a slope where a scrub of sage breathed up its scent, her steps lost the surety they'd had that morning. Her shoulders dipped; a thin sweat beaded at her temple. She paused and leaned one palm on a sun-warmed stone as if to steady herself.

Tomer, who walked a pace behind, turned and noticed first. "You okay?" he asked, the boy's voice edged with an alertness that had nothing to do with bravado now.

Photine forced a smile that felt brittle in her cheeks. "Just warm," she said, brushing at her sleeve, though the motion did little. "The road's heavier than it was coming out."

Ephram glanced back, eyebrows tightening. "You look pale," he said. "Sit. Shade's here." He pointed to a low scrub that would give them a dip from the sun. They eased into the small shadow, and the group spread like people who had agreed on a brief truce with heat. Photine sank with a small, grateful exhale. Her breath came a fraction faster than normal, and the dust tasted like tin.

Tomer sat close, his knee nearly touching hers, and offered the goatskin he carried. "Drink," he said, all the more urgent for his tenderness.

She took the skin with her trembling fingers and drank, slow and careful. The water went down too hot, or too cold; she could not tell which. For a moment, she let her eyes close and listened to the small sounds: a distant donkey bray, a man calling his boy, the hiss of wind through dry grass. The memory of the hill—the confession, the bargain, the way Zimri had given his promise—rolled through her again, and it pressed at her like a throng that wanted a door.

"You did well," Tomer said after a while. "You stood and told them. You made them see."

She laughed, small and without heat. "It was not a triumph," she said. "It was a thing I had to do. Saying it didn't make it tidy." The answer sounded truer than she had meant it to be.

Tomer's face knotted. "You shouldn't have pushed so hard," he said. "The hill and then the road—people get taken by the sun. Let me walk beside you. Tell Ephram if you need to. Don't—" His words stumbled; he did not have the grown man's language for care, only his blunt, fierce worry.

She looked at him, at the earnest line of his jaw. For the first time since leaving the house, she felt the fatigue not as a private thing but as an argument made visible. The urge to hide it, to shrug and keep walking, rose in her like a reflex. But Tomer's concern made the reflex stick like a thorn.

"All right," she said finally, the word a small surrender. "When we reach Sychar, I'll rest. Tell Ephram I might need to slow." Her voice was steady, but inside it was a landscape rearranging itself, the confession, the promise, the knowledge that she could not carry everything alone.

Ephram stood and brushed the dust from his knees, eyes assessing the rest of the route. "We'll take it easy," he said. "No long marches. We camp next spring." The plan folded around them like a practical blessing.

They rose and moved again, the pace gentled to match. Tomer kept close, his hand a quiet presence near hers, though he did not take it. In the heat of the day, with dust in their hair and the road for company, the small spare mercy of someone's watchfulness felt like its own kind of healing.

They reached home a week later than anyone had expected; the road back had stretched and folded into itself, and the village looked both smaller and kinder for the distance. The children ran before Photine crossed the threshold—Jonah first, breathless and grinning,

Markus tumbling after; Levi clinging to Nessa's skirts, then breaking away to hurl himself at her knees. Their mouths wanted questions, their bodies wanted proof she was real and not a story.

She let them have it: hands on heads, a dozen small complaints about dust and shoes, an urgent recounting of odd merchants and a man who spoke of lamps. For a little while, the house was all noise and feet and the simple jurisdiction of children glad to be fed. Photine laughed when they laughed; she let Tomer haul water, and Marcus show off a fig he'd been saving for her. The ordinary ministrations— someone stoking the coals, someone straightening a plate.

But Tomer watched her between the tasks, his eyes sharper than his years. After the supper's clearing, he sidled up to Donel in the doorway, voice low. "She's not herself," he said. "She did fine on the hill, but on the road back, she tired early and slept a lot. She ate less than she used to. I walked beside her most of the way." His words carried another weight — the memory of his mother's last days: the cough that came and stayed, the small meals she could not finish, the way she drifted while the house held its breath. "I don't want her to… be ill," Tomer added, blunt with the kind of fear only a boy who watched a mother die could have. The worry landed on Donel like a pebble thrown into still water.

Photine did not seem well. She moved more slowly than she had before the trip—small pauses that would have been nothing in another life but here read like a map. When the children bickered, she did not rise to quiet them with the old quickness; when Levi wanted a story, she closed her eyes for a breath before beginning. Night folded around them, and the house breathed toward sleep.

Donel found her later, standing at the back door where the olives threw long, dark fingers across the yard. The lamplight cut their faces in two. He came and stood beside her, not crowding but near enough that they shared the same thin warmth.

She spoke as if finishing a private conversation she had been carrying inside her, voice small and steady: "It taught me that asking for water and offering bread are the same work when many hands do it. It taught me that return can be a labor, and that hands will speak truths our mouths are afraid to form."

He listened. For a moment, his face held the hard, private worry of a man who'd tried to make smallness into safety. "You should not have gone if you were not well," he said finally, blunt and real. "Tomer said you were tired on the road. You look—" He stopped, searching for the gentler angle. "You look worn, Photine. I was afraid the trip would ask more of you than you can pay."

She turned to him; the fact had already settled in her like a small stone. "There's another reason," she said, the words slipping free before they could tremble. "I'm with child."

Donel's face eased as if something inside him had at last been set down. He took both her hands, holding them like a promise. "This child," he said, voice bright and steady, "is ours, a gift, not a burden. We will feed, name, teach, and keep this child safe from the fear that once nearly swallowed us. I will not make you small to make us look safe. We will protect you both, and we will do the work — morning by morning, together."

She let out a breath she'd been holding for days, and when he leaned to press a careful kiss to her forehead, it was a blessing. Outside, the olives whispered; inside, the house gathered itself to the small, ordinary work of keeping a family whole.

Photine watched the dim glow of the lamp play over the faces of the sleeping children and thought of space in ways that were practical as well as tender. There were seven of them under one roof now: Tomer, the near-man who carried errands and steadiness, Nessa, who was years from marrying and only now could explore as a child not yet thirteen years. Markus and Jonah, who wrestled in the doorway and who claimed corners for their games, Levi small and trusting, growing fast in his secure and steadfast care. Two adults did not make many hands for all that needed doing, but hands multiplied when they were given work to do and a reason to do it.

"We'll move the loom to the north wall," Photine said, testing of household order becoming plans. "We can lay another mat by the hearth when the rains come. Donel, teach Tomer how to measure barley—he'll be useful with the accounts. Nessa can mind the little ones by the fire when she's old enough; she's steady."

Donel's mouth softened into a small, rueful smile. "I'll build shelves," he said. "And a sleeping ledge for the twins so the youngest won't keep falling to the floor. We'll make the lean-to taller. Little things, steady things." He glanced toward Tomer, who stood at the threshold watching with the awkward patience of a near-man trying not to appear eager. "And when Tomer takes a wife, if that day comes, what then?"

Photine pictured it without sentimentality and with a quick, fierce tenderness: Tomer with a woman of his choosing, a small celebration of bread, the boys learning the work of two households folded into one larger table. "Then we will make room again," she said. "We will teach him to share labor and to keep his promises. We will tuck a mattress into the lean-to for a new woman until she stands steady. We will not pretend we know what another household will be, but we will show Tomer how to be the sort of man who keeps his word."

Photine reached for Donel's hand and squeezed. The plan was humble: raised shelves, a new mat, lessons taught over loaves, a neighbor who would barter time for a favor. It was not a grand promise, but it was daily fidelity. That night, as the children's breaths evened and the lamp burned lower, the future felt more like a room they were building together—one board at a time, one morning at a time.

Photine pressed her forehead to his for a single, private breath. She thought of the olive wood shard, one she kept for herself and one she gave to Zimri, with the recognition that they shared the pain of their father leaving. She thought of Lois and the girls back near Akrabbim.

Instead of a quick benediction, Photine did something steadier: she sat at the low table with a scrap of parchment and a stub of reed, took a deep breath, and made a letter.

Her hand trembled at first. The words came slow — part accounting, part apology. She named what could not stay unnamed: her father's leaving; the bargain a furious boy had struck that sent her away; the ways her cleverness, meant to protect, had sometimes wounded others. She wrote of the well and the hillside and of the man who had listened without turning her grief into gossip. Then, folding that private line into the same page, she wrote plainly: she was with child. She continued, *I am sorry for how I left you and for who I became before I left. If your hands can, forgive me. If your heart can, remember me as a sister still. If you can find a place for a small kindness, I will be grateful beyond words.*

When she was done, she pressed the olive-wood shard into the crease of the parchment as a seal something of the house carried in a thing to be given back — and tied the packet with a length of twine. At the market, she called Ephram over and, meeting his steady merchant's eye, handed him the note. "See, this gets to Akrabbim," she said. "The women's house, the one by the third cistern. Find a trader who goes that way. If it reaches Lois, tell her I asked for pardon. If it does not, then keep the paper until a hand can carry it."

Ephram took the parcel with the careful gravity of a man who knew how to move things across distance. He tucked a small coin and a scrap of cloth inside the fold, little things to grease a carrier's goodwill, and nodded. "I'll ask Joram at dawn," he promised. "He runs the caravan that goes south next week. He'll take it if I give him enough for the bread he needs." Photine watched him fold the parcel into his pack and felt the knot of hope loosen just a fraction.

A month passed and then another, the days folded into bread and barter and the small rhythm of children's feet. The road had swallowed the trader and spat him out again; news moved slower than gossip but truer for it. One afternoon, a man with sunburned cheeks and a pack that smelled of figs and iron came to the market and handed Ephram a small, tied bundle and a folded scrap of paper marked with Lois's careful hand. Ephram delivered the package with care and honor that same morning.

Photine sat with the children at the low table when she untied it. The house smelled of cooling barley; the light through the door leaned like a hand across the floor. She unfolded the note with fingers that had learned both steadiness and the tremor that comes when a longed-for thing finally arrives.

Lois's handwriting bent the lines gently; the letter read like someone speaking across a well. She wrote that the women's house in Akrabbim had found steadiness at last—marrow and bread, a patchwork roof mended, no fear in the night where there once had been much. She named the names of the women Photine had known by trade and by tending; she told Photine not to carry a burden not hers to bear and not to expect theatrical forgiveness where simple remembering would do. There was gratitude in the page— thankfulness that a girl who once felt lost in the world found home. There was no grand absolution, only this: "We are settled. We are safe. We remember you as aunt and as sister. When the road allows, I will come."

Tucked with the note was a gift: a narrow cloth band woven from the women's flax, sewn tight with a simple vine pattern and a single tiny bird stitched in blue thread. There was also a scrap of linen, embroidered in the corner with a seed motif, and between its folds a small bundle of seeds—lentil, barley, and one tiny mustard seed— pressed flat for planting. Nestled beside them, wrapped in oilcloth, lay the little shard of olive wood Photine had sent back as a token; the women had sanded and smoothed it and tied it with a thin strip of leather so it could sit safe beside a baby's head or be tucked into the hem of a swaddling cloth. A band, a seed, a splinter of home— promise and practical care in equal measure.

Photine read the letter aloud, each sentence a small bell in the room. Nessa leaned in, eyes bright; Tomer listened as if the words might rearrange what he knew. Donel stood with a slow smile and a touch around Photine's shoulder that said both apology and pride, and when she finished, she pressed the woven band to her breast.

"We will find a place for this," she said, voice thick with something that was not only relief. She smoothed the linen over the small cloth she folded, placed it in a chest, and placed the seeds in a tiny jar on the shelf where the sun would find them in the morning.

The gift was small and true: hands reaching back across two hard months to tuck hope into the world. Photine folded the letter and laid it beside the olive-wood shard, then slipped the band into the pocket of her tunic. Outside, the road hummed on; inside, the lamp burned a little brighter. The seeds would wait for planting and for the season, and the child—already a quiet presence in her belly—would one day be wrapped in a cloth tied by hands who had known what it meant to be kept and to keep.

Morning came with the ordinary ministrations of life: bread to be kneaded, ledgers to be checked, the slow carving of hours into useful pieces. They rose to it together. Donel and Tomer spent an entire bright week widening the doorway and raising a simple lean-to of poles and plaster on the north side of the room—more storage for grain, a place where the boys could work without tracking dust into the sleeping pallet. Their hands remembered muscle and measure; the house swallowed the new timber. In the evenings, they sat on the low step, plans still in the dust at their feet, and traded small jokes about whose hammer had bent what nail. The work was quiet proof that repair was possible.

Nessa grew out of a shy stiffness. She was almost thirteen, and the market no longer felt like a battlefield to be circled and avoided. Photine taught her how to fold a cloth so it would not untie in a basket, how to set a small price and hold it, and how to say "thank you" without giving away a bargain. On some afternoons, they stole away to plant the seeds from Lois's parcel — tiny, impatient things — and Nessa's laugh, clean and sudden, filled the yard like rain. For the first time in years, she let herself be a girl: stubborn, bossy, fond of a secret story. The house loosened its shoulders.

Inside, Photine kept the olive-wood shard and the folded letter where she could touch them without thinking. The woven band from Akrabbim lay by the child's small cloth, a promise sewn by hands she might never meet. She felt the child move sometimes like a hush against the world; each small stir was proof that a life was being held between past and promise. It was not a tidy joy — there were debts and rumors yet to settle, nights when worry made her fingers go cold — but it was a steady kind of peace, the kind that arrives from doing the work rather than from being cleared of consequence.

Jesus's words wandered like seed on the wind, and people who had once crossed to the other side of the street began to draw near. Men who had slept with grudges found themselves sharing a pot; women who had been strangers set a strip of cloth for one another's shade. The hillside teaching had not solved every wrong, nor had it promised an easy end. But the image of the lamp on a stand—*let your light do its work*—kept returning in small ways: a lamp not hidden, a debt returned, a cup handed across a boundary. Little by little, mouths and shoulders loosened; people put down the shame they had carried like a cloak and offered one another a thinner, lighter coat instead. The ministry grew not in thunder but in these quiet, repeated gestures, and word of it moved along roads and into ovens and through markets like a rumor of mercy.

www.ingramcontent.com/pod-product-compliance
Lightning Source LLC
Chambersburg PA
CBHW051227050726
47594CB00001B/62